# BEAR DAUGHTER

# BEAR
# DAUGHTER

## Judith Berman

ACE BOOKS, NEW YORK

**THE BERKLEY PUBLISHING GROUP**
**Published by the Penguin Group**
**Penguin Group (USA) Inc.**
**375 Hudson Street, New York, New York 10014, USA**
Penguin Group (Canada), 90 Eglinton Avenue East, Suite 700, Toronto, Ontario M4P 2Y3, Canada
(a division of Pearson Penguin Canada Inc.)
Penguin Books Ltd., 80 Strand, London WC2R 0RL, England
Penguin Group Ireland, 25 St. Stephen's Green, Dublin 2, Ireland (a division of Penguin Books Ltd.)
Penguin Group (Australia), 250 Camberwell Road, Camberwell, Victoria 3124, Australia
(a division of Pearson Australia Group Pty. Ltd.)
Penguin Books India Pvt. Ltd., 11 Community Centre, Panchsheel Park, New Delhi—110 017, India
Penguin Group (NZ), Cnr. Airborne and Rosedale Roads, Albany, Auckland 1310, New Zealand
(a division of Pearson New Zealand Ltd.)
Penguin Books (South Africa) (Pty.) Ltd., 24 Sturdee Avenue, Rosebank, Johannesburg 2196,
South Africa

Penguin Books Ltd., Registered Offices: 80 Strand, London WC2R 0RL, England

This is an original publication of The Berkley Publishing Group.

This is a work of fiction. Names, characters, places, and incidents either are the product of the author's imagination or are used fictitiously, and any resemblance to actual persons, living or dead, business establishments, events, or locales is entirely coincidental. The publisher does not have any control over and does not assume any responsibility for author or third-party websites or their content.

First edition: September 2005

Library of Congress Cataloging-in-Publication Data

Berman, Judith, 1958–
    Bear daughter / Judith Berman.— 1st ed.
        p. cm.
    ISBN 0-441-01322-8
    1. Girls—Fiction.   2. Bears—Fiction.   3. Metamorphosis—Fiction.   4. Human-animal relationships—Fiction.   I. Title.

PS3602.E7586B43 2005
813'.6—dc22

                                                                2005041199

PRINTED IN THE UNITED STATES OF AMERICA

10   9   8   7   6   5   4   3   2   1

*For*
*John and Sam*

# ACKNOWLEDGMENTS

Many people have aided in the extended gestation of this novel, with comments, critiques, encouragement, advice, and obscure bits of information. I am particularly in debt to the members of the Nameless Workshop of Philadelphia; my Clarion buddies Krista Dietrich, Chris East, and Susan Franzblau; my agent, Martha Millard; and my editors at Ace/Roc, Susan Alison and Liz Scheier. A special acknowledgment is due to Susan Franzblau and Victoria McManus for critiquing above and beyond the call of duty; to my mother, Katrina Berman, whose financial aid made writing this book possible; and to my husband, John Holland, for his unwavering support in all areas. And to the orcas who found my sister and me in our rowboat that day in Shellaligan Pass: thank you, swimmers, that we met.

This novel was inspired by the indigenous oral literature of the north Pacific coast. Nothing in it, however, is an attempt to depict any real peoples, communities, events, or individuals. It is not a "retelling" of indigenous stories. I have altered and jumbled elements taken from different traditions and time periods, and mixed these together with elements from Old World oral traditions and large doses of pure fantasy to construct, for better or worse, my own narrative. For the real thing, readers should look to the source.

Nevertheless, to those storytellers, the ones known and the ones whose names we now do not know, I must express my profound respect and gratitude.

gunalchéesh • háw'aa • t'ooyak̲siẏ n̓isim̓ • t'ooyax̲siẏ n̓isim̓ •
n t'oyaxsasm • analhzaqwnugwutla • ǧiáxsix̌a • ǧianakasi •
stutwinii • gelakas'la • tl'eekoo •
tl'ekoo tl'ekoo

PART ONE

# ONE

# Awakening

*When Cloud was twelve years old, she woke up one* morning to discover she had become a girl. She had been dozing the winter away, rising every now and then to root in the town middens and sniff forlornly after her mother. But this time she must have fallen asleep before returning to her den. She opened her eyes to see the steps leading into her mother's house. She lay beneath them, huddled against the bitterly sharp breeze of a winter dawn. A knot of men and women stared down at her in silence.

She tried to struggle onto four legs to growl at them, make them step back. But only a small gurgle emerged from her throat, and her limbs collapsed beneath her. She tried again to rise, more carefully, one foot at a time. That was when she noticed her right forelimb: delicate bones covered in smooth skin like humans wore. Five long fingers, slender little twigs that would break if someone stepped on them.

She could remember what had been in the place of that little human hand: shaggy fur, heavy claws—but it was a vague image, already fading. Her mind felt as peculiarly awkward as her legs. She knew she had just forgotten something important.

A woman turned and raced into the house. "Lady Thrush!" she shouted. "Master, master! Come quickly!"

A moment later Cloud's mother ducked through the low door, blinking sleep from her eyes. Thrush had wrapped a fur robe over her dress, and her black hair lay disordered on her shoulders. Cloud wanted to run to her mother, bury her face in her mother's hands and inhale the beloved fragrance, but then the king pushed out of the house behind her. When his gaze fell on Cloud, a ripple crawled up her back and her mouth pulled into a snarl.

The king also checked in his movements. "What!" he said. His eyes narrowed and his mouth drew down.

This man had always kept his distance, would circle her warily if they happened to meet. But now he jumped down the stairs toward her. He wore only a robe tied around his waist, and his necklace of teeth that rattled on his muscular chest.

Cloud backed away. But he caught her by the arm and yanked her onto her hind legs. Again a growl tried to push out of her belly, only to emerge as a ridiculous squeak.

"A girl now," he said.

"Rumble," said Cloud's mother.

King Rumble did not glance at his consort. Instead, he stared a long time at Cloud, mouth twisting as if he tasted something rotten, and then his gaze slid down from her face, past her chest and belly to her unsteady new legs, her awkward feet. Cloud tried to shield her exposed belly, but Rumble jerked her arm, forced her round again.

Thrush's hands went to her face. "Rumble," she said again.

"*How did this happen?*" Rumble demanded, in a voice that fell on Cloud like stones.

"Master," said one of the men nervously, "she was sleeping here last night, and this is how she looked this morning."

"Just like that?" he said, face darkening. "Nothing else?"

"Please don't hurt her, Rumble," Thrush begged, coming up behind him.

She took off her fur robe to wrap around Cloud. But Rumble ripped the robe from her and threw it on the ground. "You think you're going to take care of it now? You think you're going to take this creature into *my* house?"

"She's just a girl now."

"A girl!" he shouted. "You think I've forgotten where she came from?"

"It's all over," pleaded Thrush. "Oh, Rumble, that was all finished long ago."

Rumble slapped Thrush, and she stumbled back. "It's not finished!" he shouted. "Look at her! How can it ever be finished!" Cloud tried to wrench her arm away, and she clawed and swatted at him, but her new body had no more strength than a blade of grass. Rumble smashed his fist into her chin. Pain and darkness shot through her head as she crumpled to the ground. A noisy tumble of images surged after: children screaming, Rumble with a bloody spear, dogs baying. She ran, ran, ran . . .

"What's all this?" said another voice. An unfamiliar pair of arms circled Cloud. "Who is this girl?"

Trembling and whimpering, Cloud opened her eyes. An old woman crouched beside her, shielding her from Rumble, who held his fist ready to strike again.

Thrush shakily smoothed her hair with an arm crisscrossed by old scars. "It seems she's my four-legged child, Aunt Glory."

Glory pulled off her own robe to wrap it around Cloud. The robe was warm, but hardly enough to stop Cloud's convulsive shuddering. "And now she's turned into a girl?" said Glory. "It's a wonder!"

"A wonder!" Rumble spat. "The wizards will tell us what's really happened here."

Glory looked at him as if just noticing his presence. "Will you take care of your wife's daughter now that she's human?"

Rumble said, as if he could not get the rotten taste out of his mouth, "Let her own father take care of her."

Thrush closed her eyes. Cloud saw water beading her mother's lashes.

"Well, then," said Glory, and she stood, holding out her hand peremptorily toward Cloud. "The child had better come with me." Cloud tried once more to stand, but her feet still weren't working right, and she toppled, banging against the heavy planks of the stairway. This time Glory lifted Cloud onto her hind legs. "Come on now."

Glory tucked the robe more closely around Cloud and urged her to start walking. Cloud took a teetering step, glanced back at her mother. Neither Thrush nor Rumble had moved. Rumble was staring at them, eyes narrowed, but water now trickled down Thrush's cheeks.

"You can't stay here, child," Glory said in Cloud's ear.

She hurried Cloud along the beach path. Cloud still trembled uncontrollably, and she kept tripping and stumbling. "What's wrong with you, child?" Glory asked. "Can't you find your feet? Well, of course not; you're used to all fours." On the right, they were passing the long row of houses. Cloud knew their scents: wood smoke, fish, a vat of old urine, freshly cut cedar, human sweat. But the smells were faded today, hardly perceptible. Instead, everything looked so clear and sharp as to hurt her eyes. The weathered boards of the great houses shone silver in the dawn light. The still waters of the harbor rippled and shivered in a thousand colors, breaking apart reflections of houses, green forest, gray sky.

Men, women, and children stared as the two of them hurried along. A dog ran up to Cloud and sniffed. Before she could snarl and swat, Glory shooed it away.

Glory did not stop until they reached the far end of town, at the head of the long curving spit of sand that shielded the harbor. In front of them stood a house as large as King Rumble's, but cracks veined the wall planks, and grass and seedlings sprouted from the roof. Cloud looked back. She could see her mother's house, but it was tiny with distance, and the ground in front of it was empty now.

"Here we are," Glory said. She took a deep breath, as if she had expended great effort. "We will have to call you something. Do you know your four-legged name?"

Cloud glanced at her, unsure what Glory meant. She did remember walking on four legs. She could vaguely remember her old self—fur, claws—but she had no memory of a name at all.

"Well," Glory said. "I will have to give you one, then. Cloud, perhaps. You are a pretty girl. Very much like your mother was." Glory smoothed the hair from Cloud's forehead, and then stroked the spot Rumble had hit. Even so light a touch made it throb anew. "That's going to leave a nasty bruise. Yes, Cloud is a good name. Come on, child, you're filthy as a slave. Let's get you cleaned up."

Glory led Cloud into the house. The people at the hearth glanced at them. Cloud could smell the dried fish they were eating and wanted to stop. But Glory urged her on, rummaging for a moment in storage chests before sweeping her out the back.

A path led through the brush to the creek. Glory made Cloud stand in the swift, icy water while she rubbed her down with a gritty liquid, starting with her head. The liquid dripped into Cloud's eyes, stinging, and she jerked and whimpered. "You have to close your eyes, child!" Glory said, splashing clean water onto Cloud's face.

As Glory toweled her dry, she clucked over the white scars on Cloud's shoulder and side, tsk-ed over Cloud's flea bites. (Cloud remembered *fleas:* a torture of little thorn pricks that made you twitch and turn without rest. But the fleas had vanished along with her former self.) Then Glory struggled to pull a skin dress over Cloud's arms and head. Her arms felt like a pair of snakes, and they tangled with the dress, Glory, tree branches, each other, but at last Glory was tugging it down past her knees.

After combing Cloud's short hair, Glory wrapped the fur

robe around her once more and hugged her tightly. Not her mother's arms, not her mother's beloved smell and soft voice, but Cloud huddled into it anyway. Eventually the shivering lessened. Warmth—and comfort, of a sort. Cloud wondered when she would see her mother again.

"Now you look a proper young woman," said Glory. Cloud sniffed the dress: smoke, a faint old scent of deer. "How old are you now? Twelve? Can you speak, child? Can you say my name? I'm your Aunt Glory."

"Aunt," Cloud said, "Glory."

The words surprised her. They came out as if speaking was something she had always known how to do. Not like walking on two legs.

Aunt Glory let out a sigh. Then they walked back to the house, where Glory introduced her to the other residents. They were Thrush's relatives and in-laws, Glory explained. Everyone stared at Cloud, and she wished she were back in the forest.

But then Glory laid a piece of half-dried salmon upon a mat in front of her. Cloud's mouth began to water. She got down onto all fours, and with one hand holding the backbone in place, she tugged at the delicious orange flesh with her teeth. "Oh, no, child, no!" Aunt Glory grabbed Cloud by the shoulders and pulled her back. "Use your *hand*." Glory picked up the backbone, and pushed and twisted the fingers of Cloud's hand until they held on to the thing by themselves. "Lift it *up* to your mouth."

When Cloud tried to raise her arm, she lost control of her fingers, and the backbone dropped to the mat. Glory sighed and repeated the process. This time Cloud managed to move the fish to her mouth. "Small bites," Glory said. "You're a young lady now." But Cloud was hungry. She chewed all the flesh from the bones, then sucked the crumbs from her hand.

Aunt Glory pulled Cloud's fingers out of her mouth. "I see we have a long way to go."

\* \* \*

*Cloud's new home was called Halibut House.* She spent that day huddled beside its hearth at the center of the cavernous hall, trying to follow Glory's instructions: how to sit on her rump, upper limbs hanging loose; how to pick up things with her twiglike fingers. All the while Glory asked her questions: "Why did you change?" And "Can you change back?" And "Do you know why it happened now?"

"I don't know," was all Cloud could answer. Some things that day were familiar: the beach and houses, the smells of wood smoke and human skin, her ever-present hunger and her longing for Thrush. Many more things were strange: her shape, her weakness and confusion, the painful new vision that showed her a world whetted sharp as a knife.

Eventually Glory let her rest, and she just sat there as Glory had taught her, expecting that she would slip into a doze. But sitting like a girl was uncomfortable, and her wintertime sleepiness did not return. Other people came in and looked at her, and murmured nervously or with astonishment.

In the evening Aunt Glory gave her more dried fish, still not nearly enough to sate her hunger. Afterward, a few last visitors arrived at Halibut House.

The first to step through the door was an old man with tattoos crawling across his sunken chest and flabby arms. He wore a crown of animal claws and a skirt strung with puffin beaks, and the knot of gray hair atop his head was a greasy tangle. When he pushed through the doorway, everyone in the hall glanced first at him and then at Cloud, and fell silent.

Behind him, two boys maneuvered a box drum through the door and then pulled the door-plank shut behind them. The old man descended the stepped platforms in a rattle of puffin beaks. An icy draft wandered ahead of him, bringing Cloud the stink of rancid grease and mildew.

She tried to slink away, but Glory's hand gripped her shoulder. "Well, well," said the old man mildly when he reached the hearth, "so this is the four-legged child?"

"I don't believe anyone in this house hired your services," said Glory.

"No, indeed," he said. "The king sent me to see what I could see."

"The winter king," said Glory. "This is the summer side of town."

"Yes, yes," said the old man, "yes, indeed, but where is the summer king of Sandspit Town?" He sat beside Cloud. It felt as if someone had just set down a chunk of ice next to her; the cold draft rose from his flesh. "Where is the noble lord of Halibut House right now?"

Glory did not answer. The old man, or man-shaped chunk of ice, leaned forward. "You don't have any wizards left in your house," he said. "This is for your good as well as the king's. She's been skulking around town all these years, growing bigger, making everyone nervous, but no one dared do anything. A four-legs! The queen's daughter! And now she's taken off her fur robe. You think she isn't dangerous? This is for everyone's good. We have to know what it's about."

"It's plain what happened," said Glory. "She just grew old enough and shed the part she got from her father. Now she's human, like her mother."

"Nothing at all is plain," said the old man.

He put an icy hand on Cloud's arm and drew her closer to the light. His faded eyes, peering from their pouches of flesh, seemed to jab at Cloud like fingers.

"A pretty little thing," said the old man, "now that she's taken off her mask." He grinned at Cloud without kindness. "My name is Bone, little four-legs. Why don't you tell me where your animal skin is?" When she did not answer, he urged, "Speak, girl! Confess!"

Cloud shook her head. Bone's frigid hand was sucking the warmth from her body. "I don't know," she managed to whisper.

He leaned closer and the icy draft ruffled her hair. "You had better tell me. Or I might have to beat you."

"It's gone," Cloud said, beginning to shiver. "I don't know where it is!"

"We'll see," said Bone.

He made her lie down and beckoned to the two boys who still waited by the door. They staggered down to the hearth-side with the huge carved drum. Aunt Glory and the other residents withdrew to the shadows.

One boy held the drum on its corner while the other began to pound it with a stick. The drum's voice was deep, and it vibrated through the floor into Cloud's bones. The boys began to sing in high, clear voices. She could not understand the words.

Bone shook a rattle and opened his own mouth to sing. His voice was loud, nasal, and droning. The fire lit his wrinkled face from beneath and cast wild shadows against the roof. As he danced over her, bending slowly at knees and waist, his eyes rolled up into his head. The draft flared into a wind gusting out of him. Under its force, the oil lamps smoked, the hearth fire guttered, and clouds of ash sailed through the hall.

The relentless drumbeat and the constant chatter of beaks and claws and pebbles dizzied Cloud. The gloom of the hall deepened into impenetrable darkness. She felt as if she herself had become a flake of ash and flew through the wintery night.

All of a sudden a white-haired dog stood over her. "Where is her spirit mask?" said Bone's voice from nearby in the darkness.

The dog sniffed at Cloud. She wanted to push it away but could not move.

"I couldn't find it," said a deep, rough voice. The dog looked in Bone's direction, and Cloud realized that the voice must somehow belong to it. "It's beyond a maze of a hundred mountains. It must have gone back to her father's house."

"It must have," Bone mimicked. "But you don't know!"

"I can do no more," said the dog, and it bounded away.

"I didn't release you!" Bone shouted after it. But the dog was already gone.

The cold wind swirled, and Cloud spun with it. Maybe she slept. Then a touch startled her. Suckered tentacles streamed out of the darkness on an invisible current, curling, flicking against her. She tried to jerk away but still could not move.

"Why has her mask disappeared?" demanded Bone.

"She lost it," said a new voice, cold and sleek.

"I know she lost it!" shouted Bone. "I asked you *why*!"

But the octopus said, "I have no other answer," and it, too, shot away into the dark.

The drum pulsed on, like Cloud's heartbeat. Or maybe it *was* her heartbeat. The wind rose and fell, grew even colder. Snow flurried across the darkness.

"Why has this happened now?" Bone burst out, startling Cloud.

This time she could see only a swarm of ice-blue lights overhead. A high, ragged chorus answered, "The child becomes a woman."

"Yes, yes," Bone said angrily. "I see. But is that all? Will she regain her mask?" And when the flickering lights winked out, "I posed you questions! I sent you to do my bidding!" But the lights did not reappear.

Cloud sailed farther and farther into the dizzying night. After another long while footsteps approached her.

"Will she regain her spirit mask?" demanded Bone's voice.

The footsteps shuffled closer and a corpse came into view. Seaweed streamed from its long hair, and a tiny crab picked flesh from its cheek, and there was only darkness where its eyes should have been. But the corpse stooped over Cloud as tenderly as a mother with her child.

"Don't be angry, master," the drowned woman murmured, dribbling seawater from her mouth. "Something is sitting athwart our eyesight. The power of the First People is greater than ours. Even if we could find the trail to her father's house, none of our kind would be able to get through the door to glance inside. But look at her—she's naked as a real girl now. She could no more find her way to her father's house than she could open the door of the world and step outside. In that condition, how could she regain her four-legged shape? Leave it, master, just let her alone and she will never be a threat to anyone."

"Away with you, too," shouted Bone. "Useless, all of you!"

The wind surged and the drowned woman spun toward the zenith in a cloud of bubbles. Cloud was spinning after her when the drumbeat stopped suddenly. And Cloud tumbled down, fell and fell through darkness until she landed hard on the floor of Halibut House. Bone was crouching motionless above her. His eyes rolled forward. He lowered his rattle with a little slide of pebbles. Finally he straightened.

"Well?" asked Glory. "What did your servants tell you?"

"Hmph," was all he said. He slipped his rattle into its cover and hobbled stiffly up the stepped platforms to duck out the door. The boys, hauling the bulky drum, scrambled after.

The cold draft followed him out the door. The hearth fire and lamps flared up again. The residents of the house returned to the hearthside and their old conversations. Shivering violently, Cloud crawled up from the floor to sit beside Glory.

"What did they mean?" Cloud whispered.

Glory wrapped Cloud's robe around her. "What did *who* mean, child?"

"The ones who came and talked to him," said Cloud. "Who are the First People?"

"You *heard* his servants?" Glory's voice dropped to the same low whisper. She turned Cloud so they faced each other. "What did they say?"

"They think my, my mask has gone back to my—father's house." Cloud said the word *father's* very carefully. It felt dangerous in her mouth, as if sharp-edged. Who was this father that Rumble said should take care of her?

"Well," Glory said, "that's good, I suppose. Did they say you're going to stay a girl?"

Cloud nodded. "Is my—is my father one of the First People, Aunt Glory?"

Glory tightened her lips. "We don't talk about him, child."

She put Cloud to bed in her own room, which lay against the outer wall near the back of the house. She showed Cloud how to get into the bed, how to pull the furs over her. The furs were deliciously soft and thick, and warm; yes, much better than the muddy hollow in the forest where Cloud had been sleeping.

Glory climbed in after her and right away began to snore. Her breath stirred Cloud's hair. Cloud shut her eyes, looking at darkness. The events of the day had been too much to take in, and none of Aunt Glory's care made her feel less bewildered.

*What happened to her spirit mask?*

*She lost it.*

Cloud felt as if it was she, not her mask, that had been lost, as if she had been stranded in this new self a very long way from home. She touched the strange body through her clothes: a young woman's breasts, a narrow hairless belly.

*Do you know your four-legged name?* Glory had asked.

She could not remember any name before the one Glory had given her, and *Cloud* felt as unnatural as the fragile arms and legs she now wore. She did not know who or what she was, except Thrush's daughter, and Thrush was beyond her reach, in Rumble's house at the other end of town.

As Cloud lay there, drifting into sleep, the darkness faded to winter gray, and she was chasing after Thrush. She wanted to turn back, but Thrush kept running through the forest, and Cloud had to follow or lose her.

When Glory shook her awake in the morning, it was again to bewilderment. What was she doing here? Where had she found this body? It was only the smell of food that got her out of bed.

*That next day, after making her bathe again and* comb her hair, Aunt Glory started teaching her manners. Cloud tried hard to remember everything Aunt Glory told her, but there was a great deal of it. No licking or sniffing food before she ate it, no eager devouring of her meal no matter how hungry, no gorging until she was satiated. "Our stores have to last until the Bright Ones return," said Glory.

No scratching herself. No clawing at any human who came too close, though she was allowed to chase away dogs. She certainly must not relieve herself wherever or whenever she needed to.

She had to take care of the fish bones. "We don't let dogs get to them," Aunt Glory explained. Cloud nodded; she did not like dogs either. She was supposed to stack skin and bones upon a mat and place them in the fire afterward. Or when the tide was right, she and Aunt Glory would carry the bones down to the sandy mouth of the stream, wade into the channel to where fresh water mixed with salt, and with a prayer spill them into the outflowing current. "So the Bright Ones can be born again," Aunt Glory told her. "Treat them right and they will always return."

She had to learn all the names of her fellow residents in Halibut House, and how they were related to Thrush. The most important thing, Glory told her, was whether they belonged to the Halibut House mother-line. Cloud did, because what house you belonged to came through the mother, and Thrush was the highest-ranking princess of Halibut House. There were no Halibut House men, so the house sheltered only a few widows like Glory who had come back from their husbands' houses, a few men of other houses who lived there with Halibut House wives and children, and a handful of elderly slaves from the glory days of times past.

"What happened to the men?" Cloud asked.

"Misfortune," Glory said. "No, Cloud, sit with your knees together. You're a young lady now."

Cloud pressed her knees against each other. "What do you mean, misfortune? What happened?"

"They died," Glory said shortly.

Cloud could not help but ask, "But how do you die of misfortune?" *Misfortune* had no shape or smell; it didn't sound obviously threatening like Rumble's fist or a bloody spear.

"We don't like to talk about it, Cloud. It makes people grieve to remember." Glory looked sad herself, and tired.

"But," Cloud said, "I don't understand. All of them died? From misfortune?"

Glory sighed. "Your father killed them, child."

"My . . . father?" Cloud said. "Why did he do that?"

"They went searching for Thrush," said Glory.

"But how did Thrush get lost?"

"Your father abducted her," Glory said. "He forced her to be his wife. That's how you came about. Now leave it be, Cloud."

"But," Cloud said. She was not sure what it meant that her father had forced Thrush to be his wife. The way Glory said it, it had to have been dreadful. And all of the men killed. She understood *killed*: screams, blood everywhere—

Her father had killed them. No wonder Rumble hated her. But Thrush loved her anyway.

"How did Thrush get free?" Cloud whispered.

"Rumble rescued her," said Glory, "and killed your father. Listen to me, child. You must *always* be careful of other people's shame, and their pain. This was a thing that brought grief into every house in our town. So you must let it lie. And a girl shouldn't pester people with questions, no matter what the subject. Listen and observe to learn. All right? Now let me explain about the people you're related to through Thrush's father, who was the king in Storm House before Rumble."

Cloud tried to pay attention to Aunt Glory. But it was hard to put aside the subject of how her father, *her father,* had hurt Thrush and killed so many men, and how Rumble had then killed her father. No one seemed to know what Cloud was, but they all knew where she had come from. Everyone but her.

In the evening, as the residents gathered for their meal, Glory formally bestowed Cloud's new name. Glory gave a little speech to the assembly, telling them that although the name *Cloud* had not been used recently, it had been passed down for many generations in Halibut House, in the lineage of the summer kings of Sandspit Town, which was an old and proud mother-line even if they did not now have a king. The name, Glory explained, did not refer to the rain-heavy skies of winter, but to incandescent threads of cirrus on a splendid summer's day. The sun's younger sisters, they were called.

Then Glory gave each of the witnesses a trifle: a cedar-bark mat, a spoon, a berry cake. "Someone should hold a feast for you and do this properly," Glory muttered. "You are a highborn girl, the daughter of a queen."

That night, Cloud dreamed again: of sheer peaks lit by dawn, of a rude house under the trees, of small boys who splashed, laughing, through a swift creek. Though she did not see Thrush in those dreams, the air smelled of her, safe.

She woke again in the morning to her awkward new body, and the smell of humans.

She was sitting with Glory beside the hearth, trying not to gobble down her bit of fish, when quick, heavy footsteps sounded at the door. It was Rumble, dressed this morning in a fine deerskin tunic beneath his fur robe and gripping a jade battle-axe. As he came down toward the hearth, Glory rose to her feet. Cloud shrank into a corner, trying to be inconspicuous.

"You've made a mistake, old hag," Rumble said to Glory, his face purple with anger.

"A mistake?"

Rumble pointed his axe at Cloud. "You bestow *such* a name upon this, this bastard creature, as if it's a princess in this house—"

"Cloud?" Glory asked.

"—as if giving out mats and spoons to a few old slaves can buy such an honor! You've gone *too* far!"

"Cloud," said Glory, "was my grandmother's name. I have the right to give it to whom I choose. May I remind you that the name belongs to Halibut House, not to you."

"Thrush was going to give it to her daughter!"

Glory looked at him. "This *is* Thrush's daughter."

Rumble slammed his axe into the platform beside him and the old plank splintered. Cloud curled into a ball, trembling helplessly. But Glory didn't move.

"She was going to give it to Radiance!" Rumble shouted. "She was going to give it to the true princess of this house!"

"Thrush never told me so," Glory said. "And what does Thrush's other daughter need it for? Radiance already has a wonderful name, a royal name, and if she needs a second, or a third or fourth, Halibut House owns plenty of others. As for the mats and so on I gave away for Cloud, yes, I would have liked to do things properly. But we're not what we once were in this house. As you know. Anyway, it's done now."

A wild light leapt in Rumble's face. "You think it can't be undone?"

He smashed the axe into the wood right beside Cloud's head. She scrambled away, arms and legs weak with terror. Rumble leapt after her, seized her by the arm, and threw her hard against the platform. Noise rolled through Cloud's mind: dogs barking in a frenzy, children screaming, she ran—

"You leave this child alone!" Glory was shouting at Rumble. "She's nothing to you! She's Halibut House business!"

Glory had thrown herself in front of Cloud, clutching at Rumble's arm. "Old woman," he said wildly, "don't forget your place. Don't forget who my children are. They're Thrush's children; they are Halibut House children; they'll inherit everything in this house. Their business *is* my business."

"My brother was king in Halibut House," said Glory. "I know my place well enough. *You* would do better to show more respect under this roof."

For a moment Cloud was certain Rumble would strike Glory down. But he lowered his axe.

"Don't ever think," he ground out, "that this misbegotten animal will push aside my children in this house. This creature is less than a slave to me. If *you* feel sentimental because it looks human now, go ahead, feed it the scraps you save from the midden! But be careful. *It isn't human.*" Rumble aimed his axe at Cloud. "If I ever think it's a danger to anyone in this town, I'll strike it down where it stands."

And with that he ducked out the door. Glory sat down heavily beside Cloud. After a moment, she asked, "Are you all right, child?"

Cloud, still curled into a ball, was trembling so hard she couldn't speak. Something new was happening to her: water was leaking from her eyes, a terrible sharp lump had lodged in her chest that made it hard to breathe. Glory turned to look at Cloud, then gathered her into her arms. "Oh, you poor child," said Glory. "How can he not see that you're just an ordinary girl now? Don't cry, Cloud, it's over. It's over."

But Cloud knew it wasn't over.

# TWO

# Dreaming

*For a while after that, though, Cloud was allowed to* live in Halibut House and keep the name Glory had given her. Rumble did not come again.

Cloud ate regularly, though never enough, it seemed; she had a warm and comfortable place to sleep; and she had lost her fleas. All of that was an improvement.

But she grew restless in the eternally dim, smoky house. She wanted to stay outside for longer than it took to bathe or relieve herself. She loved the outdoor smells: salt and seaweed, balsam fir and old bracken, rain-soaked moss and rotten wood. She loved to listen to the minks quarreling on the beach at midnight, the ravens cawing hoarsely at dawn, and the plink-plink of raindrops hitting still water at dusk.

Worse than that was how she missed her mother. She remembered that before, when she had lived outside, she could smell Thrush at a distance, could approach when Thrush was alone. And Thrush would embrace her, scratch her back, ruffle her fur, kiss her, and murmur softly while Cloud sniffed at her mother's hair and skin. Those were the best moments of all.

Now Thrush was as inaccessible as if she lived across the ocean. Glory took care of her far more attentively than Thrush had ever done, hardly letting Cloud out of sight. But for all of Glory's hugs and caresses, Cloud couldn't get used to Glory's ashy smell, or the sharp edge so often in her voice.

And the others in the house acted as if they couldn't get used to Cloud's smell. No one was unkind to her, but wariness always lurked in their eyes. None of the girls or boys her age spoke to her, and little children avoided her outright. Only Glory seemed certain of her. Glory's conviction made Cloud uneasy, almost ashamed. What if she did change back to her old self and begin to hurt people, as Rumble had warned?

It was a great deal of work learning to be a girl. She had to learn how to dress and undress, how to wash herself, how to pick things up and put them down. Cloud tried to do everything Aunt Glory taught her. "Such a sweet, biddable child," Glory said. "It's so obvious you're no longer a four-legs. I'm even beginning to wonder if you're Thrush's daughter."

Cloud looked up, frightened by this suggestion. Glory smiled and patted Cloud's hair. "A joke, child." Then she looked away. "Though Thrush herself is not what she once was."

Cloud learned how to tend the hearth fire and serve food, though ordinarily the slaves undertook those chores. She learned how to open and close storage boxes, how to count dried fish or berry cakes on her fingers or with a tally-stick.

At night she dreamed. She ran after Thrush through deep woods, mile after mile, terrified and longing to turn back. Or she dreamed of small boys splashing in a cold mountain creek, of huge people who came and went from a house in the forest. She dreamed of sleeping in Thrush's arms, warm and safe.

She dreamed of dogs baying, of children screaming—

At first she didn't know what dreams were, couldn't remember having had them before. She asked Glory about the strange places she saw at night, and Glory explained: while the body slept, the soul flew through time and space like a wizard's servant. "What places do you see?" Glory asked her.

Cloud described them. Glory pressed her lips together. "Maybe it will pass," she said. But it did not.

Glory taught Cloud everything about being a girl, but she never talked about the past. Cloud told herself that she didn't want to know about her murderous father. But sometimes she burned to penetrate the fog that concealed the time before she had awakened, cold and naked, at her mother's doorstep. If she could learn where she came from, maybe she would be able to anchor herself there and no longer feel so lost.

One day, two grown cousins came visiting from Shark House on the winter side of town. Glory explained that they were the children of Thrush's brothers. That was the first time Cloud heard that Thrush had ever owned a single brother, much less two. Cloud knew enough by now about the Halibut House mother-line to understand Thrush's importance in it. The royal seats were passed down from the king to his sister's sons, and Thrush's mother had been the sister of the last summer king. If Thrush possessed a living brother, he would be lord of royal Halibut House, and king of the summer side of Sandspit Town. But Thrush's generation of the royal mother-line had no men.

When Cloud's cousins left, Cloud asked Glory, "Are my uncles dead, then?"

Glory glanced away. "The fathers of those boys are dead."

"So"—Cloud hesitated—"one of them would have been the summer king?"

"Yes," said Glory. Cloud knew that tone by now. *Don't ask questions.* But sometimes she couldn't stop herself, even when she could guess the answer.

"How did they die?" she asked.

Glory gazed at Cloud. "Your father killed them," Glory

said, "your uncles, and my sons, and every other Halibut House man who set out to rescue Thrush."

"*Your* children—?" At the expression on Aunt Glory's face, shame and guilt flooded Cloud. She looked at her feet. *You must always be careful of other people's pain,* Glory had said, but it had never occurred to her that Glory was talking about herself.

On another occasion, Glory was teaching her how to address various relatives, whether politely or familiarly or not at all. "Does . . ." Cloud hesitated. "Did my father have sisters? Do they know about me?"

"I haven't the slightest idea," Glory said. "I never asked."

"But what if I meet his relatives?" Cloud asked. "How should I address *them*?"

Glory's mouth tightened. "You don't want to meet them."

"What if I *do*?"

"You pray to them," Glory said angrily. "You say, 'Oh noble one, divine one, I am glad that we met today. Grant me good luck, remove all evil from my path, great warrior of the mountains.' And you cast your eyes down and you don't *move*, do you understand? If you're menstruating, they might tear you apart regardless."

Glory's words frightened Cloud. "But—"

"We *never* speak of them," Glory said. "The First People hear everything we say about them, and the four-legs will come looking if they think you've been disrespectful. Even the strongest hunter is afraid to face a four-legs and *you* are just a girl now. *You don't want to meet them.*"

Always that word, as though dogs, deer, and raccoons were not also four-legged! None of *those* could have slaughtered so many men of Sandspit Town. Cloud knew she shouldn't go on, but she couldn't stop herself. "What is a four-legs, Aunt Glory?"

"'Four-legs' is what we call your relatives," Glory said, "because we don't say their name. They hear it spoken no matter how far away, do you understand? And then they'll come. Your father's people are wild and murderous, with no respect for any law or living thing. They do what they want because no one can stop them."

And Thrush had been captive to such a monster for *years*.

But a part of Cloud could not help wondering if her father's kin might deign to recognize her, if they would take care of her instead of killing her, if they would do for her what Rumble would not.

*Because, Glory said, Cloud had arrived at that age,* she had to learn to take care of female blood, both the blood that flowed with the changing of the moon and, when the time might come, the blood of childbirth. The smell of it could enrage a four-legs; it made other creatures uneasy and could thus bring bad luck to a hunter, warrior, or wizard. On the other hand, if she had to travel by herself, a bit of menstrual napkin, wrapped up, would give dangerous spirits reason to avoid her.

Glory also insisted that Cloud learn the womanly arts of sewing, spinning, twining, and weaving. If etiquette and proper demeanor were difficult, these were sheer torture. Cloud would watch Aunt Glory's supple old fingers shred spruce roots into fibers narrow as a hair, or beat a hank of yellow cedar bark into a fluffy mound. She could see that it was possible, at least for those who had been born human. Her own hands looked far more delicate than Glory's, but they mauled whatever they touched. Her yarn was lumpy; her weaving was a misshapen tangle; she stabbed herself with the bone awl. Aunt Glory wove a spruce-root basket so tight that it could hold water, but Cloud's best attempts looked as if a dog had chewed on them.

Cloud tried to persevere, but she seemed to grow worse instead of better. Once, when she had been spinning for hours and her yarn broke for the hundredth time, she jumped up screaming and hurled her spindle into the fire.

Aunt Glory looked up in astonishment. "What are you doing? You bad girl!"

Glory fetched tongs and removed the spindle, but although the stone whorl was undamaged, flame had already charred the shaft. Glory lectured Cloud furiously about how a queen's daughter should behave. A spindle was valuable property, the product of many hours of a man's labor. "Why did you *do* that?"

But as soon as the spindle had flown out of her hand, Cloud's anger vanished. She could no longer comprehend what had made her do it. She fixed her eyes on Aunt Glory, trying to listen, but she felt so bewildered that tears spilled down her cheeks.

"Oh, child," said Aunt Glory, sighing in dismay. She plumped down beside Cloud and hugged her, smoothed her hair. "I know these things are difficult. But this is your life now. You have to try harder. A princess has to know these things."

So Cloud studied being hungry and never complaining, and sitting modestly, knees pressed together, and not pestering Glory even when her skin crawled with questions like a swarm of ants, and eating daintily, and looking aside when a man spoke to her, and using her new limbs for washing and combing, walking and spinning. Aunt Glory seemed to think that the more Cloud practiced these things, the more she would feel rooted in her human self. It wasn't so. Cloud learned to do a hundred human things, but she couldn't get the fit of her new skin.

Bone came again to visit her. "Have you had dreams, girl?"

"Dreams?" Cloud asked, shivering in the cold wind that blew from his flesh.

"When you sleep!" he said. "Have you seen anything while you sleep!"

"No," said Cloud, looking aside.

After Bone departed, Aunt Glory said, "You should have told him." But Glory had not mentioned Cloud's dreams, either.

As the endless cold rains of winter slowly gave way to fairer weather, Glory began to take Cloud out of doors now and then, though she still never let Cloud go anywhere alone. One day they made an expedition to gather red seaweed for eating.

The smells of the damp forest lifted Cloud's spirits. The path led to a beach on the far side of Maple Island. There they hiked up their skirts, pushed up their sleeves, and waded into the ebbing tide. This was work Cloud could manage. They splashed through shallow water, cutting seaweed with shell knives, while a breeze tossed the newly leafing maples behind them, and puffy clouds chased each other across the face of the sun.

When they had filled their baskets and the tide had begun to rise, they returned to dry land. Their labor had taken them down the beach a few hundred yards from where they had shed their outer wrappings. Cloud left Aunt Glory and trotted back along the beach. She was gathering up their robes when she noticed a couple standing at the forest verge. With a shock she saw the man was Rumble. He spoke to a cousin of Thrush's named Oriole. Rumble smiled at Oriole, making some joke Cloud couldn't hear. Oriole laughed and shook her head.

Cloud crept toward Aunt Glory as quietly as she could. But Rumble turned his head and fixed his eyes on her. Cloud's belly filled with ice. She backed along the beach, clutching the robes to her chest as if they could protect her.

"What are *you* doing here?" Rumble said angrily, striding toward Cloud. She kept backing up, never taking her eyes off him. "Are you spying on me?"

Cloud turned and sprinted until she reached Aunt Glory's side. Trembling from head to toe, she glanced back; Rumble had not followed, but he stared in their direction, hands on his hips.

**Shortly after Cloud came to stay in Halibut House,** the Bright Ones had started their yearly travels. First the oolachan swam in from the ocean, massing at the mouth of Egg Inlet in preparation for the long journey east into the Mountain Land. Many people left town to fish for them, though only a few from Halibut House.

A month later herring came into shore to spawn. Cloud had helped to lay hemlock branches in the water to collect the masses of roe, and in Halibut House they had feasted on fresh roe in oolachan oil.

Now, in late spring, it was sockeye season and the town was emptying again. Each clan and many of the houses owned a salmon stream, and every day another expedition set out over the ocean.

Glory had said they would not go. "There are more important matters for you to learn." But after the trip to gather seaweed, she changed her mind.

Cloud spent a day helping Glory and Oriole pack the canoe. The next morning they departed in a convoy that included most of the residents of Halibut House along with various in-laws, cousins, and hangers-on. She and Glory shared their canoe with Oriole, her husband, and the elderly slaves of Halibut House.

It was Cloud's first trip in a canoe. Glory did not allow her time to consider her misgivings. The slaves rushed the thing into the ocean and waited, knee-deep in water. Lifting her skirts, Aunt Glory splashed out and climbed in first, and Oriole and her husband followed. Cloud hesitated.

"Come on," said Aunt Glory, impatient.

The men, women, and children in the other canoes stared at Cloud. She waded deeper and put her hands on the tall gunwale, trying to imitate the way the others had swarmed aboard. She threw one leg over the side and pulled herself up. The canoe heeled alarmingly. The people in the canoe leaned the opposite direction and the slaves all pushed or pulled to keep the canoe steady.

"Careful!" said Glory. An old slave named Stick reached out to help Cloud. But her knee caught on the gunwale and she tumbled into the canoe headfirst, scraping her shin and splashing Glory, Stick, and herself with a great deal of water.

By the time Cloud had untwisted her dress and pulled her legs under her, the slaves had jumped in and pushed off. Everyone was paddling. Soon the canoe passed the tip of Sand Spit and a breeze sprang up.

Spray blew from the paddles onto Cloud. A light chop bumped against the prow and trickled noisily under the keel. A sky of blue and white arched overhead. Her spirits lifted.

A paddle lay nearby. "Should I help?" she asked Aunt Glory, who sat in front of her.

Aunt Glory rested her own paddle. "If you like."

Cloud picked up the paddle. It was big and solid, not like thread, or an awl. Her clumsy hands gripped the handle well. She looked at how Glory held her paddle, how they all dipped in rhythm, how the slave in the stern steered the canoe. Cloud ventured a stroke, then another. "Don't splash!" Glory chided. Cloud adjusted the angle of her blade and tried again.

Paddling was hard work. The water pushed back at her, and after every stroke came another. Cloud's muscles began to ache. No one said anything to her when she rested, but she could not sit still while others labored, and she soon took up her paddle again. And it did after all feel good to pull hard against the water, to stretch her arms and shoulders, to taste the salt and feel the wind on her face. Much, much better than embroidery.

That morning they traveled north from Sandspit Town up the long coast of Maple Island. Toward afternoon the island dwindled into a scatter of reefs. Beyond lay a strait, and beyond that, a string of smaller islands stretching westward.

Stick, the slave who sat behind Cloud, noticed her gazing in that direction. He was a lean old man, with gray hair and mustache and a few straggling chin hairs. "See the last island on the right?" he said, pointing. "There's a town there, Whale Town. That's where . . ." He broke off. "Look!"

Out in the strait, something crashed noisily. Cloud searched until she found it. About a half-mile distant, huge black-and-white shapes coursed through the water. Occasionally one would leap and splash down in sheets of spray.

"Orcas," said Stick. "They will help human beings in trouble who call on them."

At least a dozen orcas swam northward. How grand it would be, Cloud thought, to leap across the sea like that, following the green islands over the horizon, wind and sky above, the dark mysterious ocean below.

The closest she could get was in this canoe. But that wasn't so bad.

From the tip of Maple Island they headed east, away from the orcas and the place called Whale Town and into another tangle of islands. Now the glacier-capped peaks of the Mountain Land rose ahead of them. Stick explained that the great archipelago of the world—where sea and mountains met, sea flooding mountains, mountains marching into the sea—stretched north and south for many months' journey, no one knew how far.

That night they slept on a beach where Sandspit Town people often camped. In the morning Cloud's arms and shoulders were miserably sore. Still, when they set off, she picked up her paddle again. After her long confinement in Halibut House, it was splendid to be outdoors, nose to the wind.

The ramparts of the Mountain Land drew nearer until they blocked out half the sky. The sight held her eye, hour after hour. On the fourth day they entered a bay fringed with oyster-encrusted reefs. Weirs and platforms cluttered the river that emptied into the bay. Dozens of canoes were drawn up on the gravel beaches, and behind them rose a forest of drying racks, smokehouses, and camp houses. The smell of fish and seaweed mingled with the heavy pall of smoke.

People on shore hailed them. A large crowd had already gathered here. Cloud did not see many familiar faces, but Glory greeted everyone graciously.

As the slaves pulled up the canoes and began unloading boxes and bundles, Cloud asked Glory, "Who are all these people? I thought the river belonged to Halibut House."

"It does," said Aunt Glory. "It's the foundation of our wealth. But it's the richest salmon stream for a hundred miles, and we can't take all the fish, especially not these days. So we let our relatives fish here. No one comes here who doesn't have permission."

"Who gave them permission?" Cloud couldn't remember anyone coming to the house to ask.

"Rumble, child," said Glory. "He's taking care of our wealth for his children, who will rule Halibut House when they're grown."

A tendril of fear curled in Cloud's belly. "Is King Rumble here?"

Glory shook her head, a strange expression creasing her old face. "Rumble won't come *here,* child."

Cloud wanted to ask why not but for once managed to stop herself. She would be satisfied with Glory's answer, although Rumble's absence meant Thrush would stay away, too.

Fish camp was harder labor than the canoe. In early morning, the men brought the first accumulation from the fish traps, emptying their baskets in a glittering, flopping cascade. The women and girls—slaves, commoners, and aristocrats together—offered a prayer of thanks to the Bright Ones, and then they took up their slate knives. Every salmon had to be gutted, spread open, and strung up to dry. Some the women sliced thinly and hung on racks to desiccate in the sun; some they carried to the smokehouses, where fires burned night and day.

The work was slimy and exhausting, and it chapped and cramped her hands. Cloud lost count of how many times she cut herself or dropped the knife, or the fish skidded from her hands into the grass. Still, she didn't mind. She had never seen such a gorgeous sight as all that flesh the color of flame, the color of sunrise. Her appetite increased tenfold with the endless labor, but now she was surrounded by more salmon than she could eat, row after row, rack after rack. Their sweet smell comforted her while she worked, and at night, after she had finished, she gorged on heaps of juicy yellow salmonberries and on the delicate pink roasted flesh, small bites as Glory demanded, but as many as she wanted, until she was somnolent with content.

Day after day Bright Ones crowded into the river mouth, their skin glowing red with the heat of summer. The abalone disk of the sun burned in a cloudless sky, and incandescence leapt from every ripple in the bay. Cloud's contentment was marred only by longing for her mother and the wish that someone other than Glory or Stick would show her kindness. Just as at home, no one looked at her but with caution. Laughter and cheerful talk fell silent when Cloud approached, only to start again after she passed by.

In the evenings, they sat by their fire under the stars. While wolves sang from the mountainsides, Stick would make Cloud laugh out loud with his tales about the exploits of Wily One and others of the First People. Even Aunt Glory chuckled at the story of how Wily One had defeated the flatulent Master of Storm, forcing him to moderate the gales bursting out of his house.

But sometimes even Wily One's adventures turned serious. He married the mysterious immortal named Fog, who first invited the salmon from their home on the far side of the world. Wily One lost her, but their daughters eventually returned to live in the headwaters of the Mountain Land. "Every year the Bright Ones swim up the rivers to see them," Stick told Cloud.

Once Cloud asked him, "Who are the First People?"

Stick smiled. "The ones who came first in the world, of course." But he went on in his soft foreign accent. "The salmon—the Bright Ones—belong to the First People, and Wily One, and also the greater beings we sometimes call gods, like the Master of Storm and the Headwaters Women. It's said the First People used to live as we do now at the center of our world, between mountains and sea, sky and earth, wearing their masks or not as they chose. But Wily One changed the world forever. Now we almost never see the First People unmasked. You have to go to the edges of the world, or sneak up on them very stealthily."

*When the sockeye run dwindled, the women made* expeditions after berries. Most of the salmonberries had already ripened, but the lightning-burned hillsides above the river burgeoned with raspberries. One day Cloud overheard Aunt Glory talking with some of the women. "I think it's all right. No one's seen any."

And the next day they climbed up with the women to the burned-over slopes. In midafternoon, Cloud was following Glory and the others through a meadow of pink-blooming fireweed when she caught a glimpse of a broad shape lumbering away from them. Coldness stabbed the pit of her stomach. The other women stopped and began to sing loudly.

When the huge shaggy creature disappeared over the ridge top, everyone fell silent. "What kind of animal was that?" she asked. Glory did not answer. Cloud looked from one woman to another. The wariness sat on all their faces.

Her anger blossomed. "Tell me, tell me, tell me!" They just looked at her. Cloud threw down her basket and screamed, "Why won't you tell me?"

Glory seized her arm and slapped her hard. "What is there to tell you?" Glory shouted. "That was one of your father's people, who *condescended* to let us go on our way!"

Once again the anger poured away from Cloud almost as soon as it had come. The unsettling glimpse of that brown shape, and the shame of Glory striking her in front of all the women, overwhelmed her. She began to cry. "I'm sorry," she said.

This time Glory was not appeased. She gestured at the heap of spilled raspberries. "Pick them up!"

Cloud obeyed, tears dripping onto her hands. When she was finished, Glory marched her down the hillside. She did not speak to Cloud the whole way back to camp. Once there, Cloud crawled into their camp house and huddled there until darkness fell. Glory offered her dinner, but Cloud shook her head.

Soon Glory came to bed. Cloud lay beside her, listening to the sounds of the summer night: a host of crickets, a mink or otter splashing on the beach, wolves howling in the distance. When she fell asleep at last, she dreamed she stood in a salmonberry thicket. Their thorny canes arched above her head, and high above them, cedars and Douglas firs spired two hundred feet into a dim sky. A huge animal skull, toothless and stained green with moss, stared at her from the crotch of a maple. The skull had been tied into the tree with rope.

At first Cloud heard only a faint wind hushing in the firs. Then she realized she was not alone. Nearby, children wept quietly.

She looked around but saw no one. She wasn't sure what to do. She didn't know how to take care of children.

The children wept in the heartbroken way of the very young who have given up on anyone hearing them. Cloud thought that perhaps she could find their mother. "What is it?" she called, still casting around for them. "Are you lost?"

"Lost," one of them said, sniffling. "Lost," said another, and a third, "Lost."

"Where's your mother?"

"She left us." "Left us, left us," the others said.

Again Cloud looked all around but could see no sign of them in the gloom.

"I'm sure she didn't mean to leave you," Cloud said, trying to sound comforting. "She'll be back."

"No," said the children, "she left us, she's never coming back. *You* have to save us."

Their voices seemed to come from all directions, or from out of the air, or from inside her head. "Where are you?" she called. "Why can't I see you?"

They did not answer. Cloud pushed through the thicket.

Large bones lay scattered among the salmonberry bushes, and despite her care, she stepped on one. The bone rolled under her feet and she fell, sprawling, into the thorns. As she climbed to her feet again, she saw the children.

In another crotch of the spreading maple, to one side of the animal skull, someone had tied up a moldering basket holding the bones of three small children. A rain-beaded spiderweb stretched between the tree and one of the little skulls.

The children's voices wept in her ear, "Save us!"

In terror Cloud turned to run. But the bones under her feet tripped her, and the more she struggled to rise, the more they rolled and tangled in the grass. She woke with a sharp cry.

"What is it?" Glory mumbled. And then, more sharply, "What did you dream? It's best you tell me."

At last, sweating and shivering, Cloud managed to describe what she had seen. "Ghosts," said Glory when she had finished.

"What are ghosts?" Cloud asked.

"The dead who have not yet been reborn. It isn't good to be plagued by ghosts. You should talk to a wizard."

Cloud shook her head.

"It doesn't have to be Bone," Glory said, but without much conviction.

By now the sky outside their shelter glowed pink, and ravens cawed raucously from the beach. Cloud climbed out of bed without answering and began to comb her hair.

*Soon Cloud had cause to wonder if Bone's hearing* was as sharp as that of her father's people, and he knew the instant anyone spoke about him. A few days after her dream, a canoe came spidering over the bay to the beach. Its occupants proved to be Bone, his two young wives, and the two boys who assisted him. Cloud bent her head and tried to pretend she was just another of the girls crushing salal berries for cakes. She could hear Bone crunch up the gravel beach, could hear his giggling wives and solemn assistants haul up the canoe. He strolled through camp, greeting acquaintances and stopping now and then for murmured conversation. Cloud could tell that some of this talk concerned her because of the glances cast in her direction.

But Bone did not approach Cloud until that evening, when he and his entourage wandered by their campfire. Out of politeness Glory had to receive them. The icy breeze accompanying Bone raised gooseflesh on Cloud's fire-warmed skin.

"And how," said Bone to Glory, jovially, as he accepted a dish of fresh-picked currants, "is Thrush's four-legged child?"

"Well enough," said Glory.

Bone leaned toward Cloud. It was as though a large chunk of ice passed close to her skin—ice that smelled of stale grease. "Have you had any dreams, four-legged girl?"

One of his wives whispered in the other's ear, and both giggled behind their hands. The two boys squatted, silent.

"Fish," Cloud said. "I dreamed of fish."

"Only fish," Bone marveled. He grinned lewdly at Oriole, who glanced away. "Well, there are lots of fish here. I'd dream of fish, too." He picked a single currant from his dish, placed it between his wrinkled lips, and chewed. "Your spirit mask has never come back?"

Cloud looked at her lap. "She has been as you see her," said Glory sharply.

"A girl for good, maybe," Bone mused. "But then why start on four legs? Why be born with a mask only to lose it?"

"Perhaps only her father's people know," said Glory.

Bone peered at Cloud. As he leaned closer, the cold wind made the campfire shrink down and smoke. In the restless light his wrinkled face twisted fantastically. "But perhaps she knows, too," said Bone. "Perhaps, after all, she knows."

After Bone and his entourage departed, Aunt Glory told her, "You should have told him about the ghosts, child."

But again Glory herself had said nothing.

* * *

*Bone's presence spoiled everything. Cloud couldn't* escape his prying eyes in camp, and after their near-encounter with the four-legs, Glory wouldn't join the berrying expeditions.

Cloud could follow Bone's movements through camp by the cold breeze that carried his stale scent. He would stroll by the racks where Cloud helped Oriole pack away the dried salmon, or sometimes stop by their campfire in the evening. He rarely spoke to her directly, but his gaze was always upon her.

Nighttime brought dreams, now piled on each other like salmon in a trap. Sometimes she ran after Thrush. Sometimes dogs chased her down. Sometimes she was back at the house by the creek, where she played, laughing, with other children. Above them, the crags glowed in the red dawn as if all that soaring mass of rock were as weightless and translucent as a cloud.

But the new dream kept returning, of the glade of bones where ghost-children wept, "Take us away, save us."

Coho salmon arrived at Oyster Bay. Groups of women trekked after blueberries into the avalanche chutes. Cloud could tell when a four-legs had been spotted by the sidelong glances and the murmurs that would stop when she approached. When she thought of the brown shape she had seen in the meadow that day, a chill of unease crawled up her back. At the same time, Cloud could not help but wonder whether her father's people could explain the mysteries of her life: Why *had* she lost her mask? Why did she dream every night of ghosts?

Much more likely her kin would do to her as her father had done to Thrush's relatives: rip her flesh from the bones, feast on her blood. Still, a strange thought would visit her: she could sneak out of camp at night and climb into the mountains to search for them.

She never got farther than thinking about it. Once she woke in the night and ventured down to the beach to relieve herself. She stood for a few moments to watch the streaks of phosphorescence where tiny fish darted in the shallows.

A four-legged footstep startled her. She turned and saw, glimmering in the starlight, an immense white-haired dog.

It barked at her in a familiar rough voice. Cloud fled up the beach until she reached the camp house where she and Glory slept. She scrambled inside, pulled the blanket over her head, and huddled next to Glory.

In the morning, Bone stopped by the racks where she and Oriole worked. "Restless at night, aren't you, little four-legs?"

"Only sometimes," whispered Cloud, shivering.

# THREE

# Thrush

**When the humpback salmon had finished their run,** before the arrival of the dog salmon, Aunt Glory decided it was time to return to town. The Halibut House convoy arrived at Sand Spit late one autumn evening on a sea that was as smooth as oiled wood. Cloud found it strange to see the long row of houses again. It was all familiar, but it still did not feel like home.

Stick guided their canoe ashore in front of Halibut House. They went straight to bed. The next morning Cloud looked out to discover that a dense fog had swallowed the town, and only the nearest house was visible, a shapeless hulk swathed in mist.

That day, by lamplight, Cloud helped Glory and an elderly cousin named Mallard pack away their winter provisions. Mallard, a shriveled widow with a pearlshell bead in her lower lip, told them that the winter king would soon depart for southern lands.

"Raiding again?" Glory shook her head.

"Rumble wants slaves to sell up north," said Mallard.

"He's giving another feast for Radiance this winter, and he's got to buy presents for all the kings he's inviting."

"At least he's doing things properly for her," said Glory.

"Properly!" said Mallard. "I've never seen such lavish affairs. You could bury the town in the furs he gave away last time." She snorted. "Oh, he'll be one of the great ones, all right. People will talk about him for generations. Terrible in war, boundless in generosity—if raiding those poor southerners for slaves is the act of a great warrior."

"I wouldn't ever," said Glory, tying down the wooden lid on a storage box, "underestimate Rumble's strength or courage."

Mallard glanced sideways at Cloud. "No indeed," Mallard said, and the two women fell silent.

Cloud rose abruptly. She hated those looks, the sign that everyone in town knew more about her than she did. And she didn't like the reminder that since their return from Oyster Bay, Rumble was only a few hundred yards away.

She ducked outside. Old Stick was hauling up boxes from the canoes. Despite the raw fog, he wore no more than a breechcloth. She started down to help with some of the lighter bundles, but then halted, struck by what Mallard had said. Cloud was not supposed to ask prying questions. But Stick was just a slave.

"Stick," Cloud said.

He straightened stiffly. "Yes, miss?"

"Where did you come from?"

Stick blinked. "A place called Copper Town, miss."

"So—did Halibut House men capture you? Were they raiding for slaves?"

"No, miss. We had a war with another town up north, over a woman who died. A lot of people were killed, and then the other side captured me. I didn't have any kin left to pay the ransom, so they sold me to your great uncle."

"Have you ever thought about going back?" Cloud said.

A tremor passed across Stick's leathery face. "I couldn't do that."

"Who would stop you?" she asked. "There aren't any men left in this house."

"You don't understand, miss. I'd still be a slave. You can't go back after that."

"But why not?"

"I'm dead already, miss," Stick said. "I've been dead all these years. See? Those warriors seized my life and sold it to your people. I don't own it anymore. Sometimes your kin can ransom you back. But they have to be quick or you're dead forever." And he turned back to his work.

Cloud watched him for a moment longer, guiltily. *Be careful of other people's pain.* Maybe someday she would learn.

But she also thought: she was like a slave, too, whom her father's people had not ransomed. *Then you're dead forever.*

*Now there was fog nearly every morning—warrior's* weather, Aunt Glory called it. One murky dawn a few days after the return from Oyster Bay, the townsfolk gathered on the beach to see the raiders on their way. The Thunder Clan warriors launched their vessels and boarded them, except the men of the royal household, who waited, thigh-deep in water, beside the king's great war canoe. This was a vessel sixty feet in length, with a beaked figurehead and painted white wings sweeping along its sides.

At last Rumble descended from Storm House, looking both magnificent and terrifying. He wore red-painted slat armor and a visored helmet with a crown carved like a screaming thunderbird. He carried his jade battle-axe and an obsidian-tipped spear, and a sheathed dagger hung from his neck. He had tied a great shaggy robe over one shoulder. The hair on Cloud's nape bristled. That robe was peculiarly familiar, the very sight of it unsettling.

As the war party floated just offshore, Rumble shouted a speech which Cloud could not hear from where she stood at the edge of the crowd. Then the men yelled "Hai!" and all the warriors in Rumble's canoe, a dozen on each side, shoved their paddles into the ocean. The canoe began to gain way. The other canoes followed. Soon all had rounded Sand Spit and were speeding south down the straits, disappearing into fog.

The next morning, Glory told her they would make an expedition that day after cranberries and tea. Glory led her along a trail that ran behind town, past the funeral ground and up the ridge into a tall forest that lay above the fog. The cedars looming over the trail resembled those in Cloud's recurring nightmare, and she began to dread that they would soon reach a glade where a huge skull stared from a tree.

Instead, the cedars eventually petered into a sea of sword fern and alder that in turn opened onto a wide, grassy swamp. Autumn had touched the swamp with reds and browns.

Glory showed her the low-bush cranberries and the glossy swamp-tea leaves, but she seemed in no hurry to set to picking. Instead she put down her baskets and scanned the swamp.

Cloud swatted a mosquito. "Will there be any"—she hesitated over the word—"four-legs here?"

"No, child!" Glory said. "Not on our island."

Just then Cloud heard a footstep behind. A quiet voice said, *"There* you are."

The voice was achingly familiar, longed for through endless lonely days and nights. Cloud turned. Thrush stood at the edge of the swamp, uncertain. Cloud rushed to her mother and flung her arms around her. Thrush hugged her tightly in return. "Oh, my baby, my little girl," Thrush said over and over, weeping, and Cloud started to cry, too.

*They sat side by side on a log, while Glory and* Thrush's single attendant, an elderly slave woman, moved slowly through the swamp picking cranberries.

"How I've wanted to see you," Thrush said, hugging Cloud to her side, stroking Cloud's hair.

Cloud buried her face in Thrush's shoulder. She tried to absorb everything at once: the warmth of Thrush's embrace, the touch of her hand, the smell of sweetgrass and mock-orange in her hair, the old scars on her slender wrists—the only defect marring her mother's perfect beauty. Cloud felt sick to think of how her mother had gotten those scars—her father's claws ripping Thrush's skin.

"You are such a pretty girl," said Thrush, wiping away tears. "How do you like living with Aunt Glory? She's turned you into such a quiet young lady. Your hair is so lovely now that it's growing out! But you should have something prettier than this dress."

Cloud looked at her dress. She just put on what Aunt Glory told her to. She wore this particular dress often, though rarely for outdoor chores that promised to be messy. Glory always told her, "If there's a speck of dirt around, it will find you."

"And your hands," said Thrush, stroking Cloud's fingers. "So delicate. No one would know you had been a . . ." She faltered. "Such a miracle, how you've changed. Are you happy, darling?"

Cloud burrowed deeper into Thrush's arms, pressing her face against Thrush's neck. Cloud wanted to tell her mother how awful it was being a girl, how bewildered and out of place she felt all the time, as though she had lost her very substance and not just her mask, as the wizard called it, of fur and claws.

"You're so grown up already," said Thrush. "We'll have to get you married." She brushed a bit of spiderweb from Cloud's sleeve. "But—it will have to be in another town, far away . . ."

Thrush started to cry again. Cloud didn't want to get married. She didn't want to go to another town, not even to escape Rumble. She wanted to stay with her mother forever. She wanted it to be Thrush who combed her hair, who fussed over the dirt on her face, who told her what dress to wear. Maybe then she would feel solid again. She wouldn't even mind having to learn to spin, if it were Thrush who taught her.

She wanted to hug her mother forever. But looking at Thrush's scars started the questions crawling over her skin. Cloud knew she should ignore them, but the more she tried, the more they tickled like ants.

"Mama," she said. It was the first time Cloud had ever spoken the word. "Mama, was it bad when you were with my father? Did he hurt you all the time?"

A shudder ran through Thrush's body. "Sweetheart, let's not talk about that. Tell me what you do every day with Aunt Glory. Did you like going to the fish camp? Is she kind to you? She was always severe with me. But I wasn't well behaved like you. I was, I was—"

"No one will tell me anything," said Cloud. "Glory always tells me not to ask questions."

Thrush looked away. "He was a four-legs," she said. "He was their king."

Cloud waited for her mother to go on, waited so long she thought Thrush was never going to speak again.

Finally Thrush said, "Darling, you must always show respect. If you think only of yourself, you'll cause harm, terrible harm to the people you love. Better to suffer yourself than see anyone else get hurt."

Cloud didn't understand what this speech had to do with her questions. "But," she said, "Mama, what *happened*?"

Thrush took Cloud's face in her hands and kissed her. "I was taken away because I had no respect. I was selfish and spoiled and I made a terrible mistake. Your father took me away to punish me. But it's over now."

Tears streamed down Thrush's cheeks. But Cloud couldn't stop herself. She buried her face again in her mother's shoulder. "Mama, I keep having dreams. I never tell the wizard, even though he always asks me. I dream about playing with little boys outside a house in the forest. I dream that you're there, too. Is it my father's house? Everyone looks human. I don't remember my father hurting you. Wouldn't I dream about that? Those scars"—Cloud took her mother's hand— "he was so cruel to you."

"Oh, no," said Thrush, brushing at her tears, "you gave me these. You had *claws*. When you were small, you didn't know you were hurting me."

"*I* did it?" Horrified, Cloud lifted her head.

Thrush said with fierce intensity, "Cloud, that's not your life anymore. Don't look back. Things aren't perfect here. But it's what we've got. It's for the best. Do you understand?"

"No," said Cloud. "Mama, I dream all the time about little children begging me to free them, only they're dead and tied in a tree. Aunt Glory says they're ghosts."

For a moment Thrush sat so still that Cloud thought she had stopped breathing. Cloud grew frightened. Then huge sobs began to convulse Thrush's body, and she buried her face in her hands. "Oh, no, no, no," she sobbed.

"Mama, what is it? What's wrong?" But Thrush couldn't speak. "Mama, Aunt Glory says I should tell the wizards."

"No," Thrush choked, "don't tell Bone! Whatever you do!"

*Be careful of other people's pain,* Glory said, but Cloud couldn't keep the questions inside. "Who are the ghosts, Mama?"

After a very long time Thrush whispered, "They must be your brothers."

"I have *brothers*?" A chill swept along Cloud's spine.

"Had—they're dead these many years."

"But why do I dream about their ghosts?"

But Thrush was sobbing convulsively once more, hugging Cloud. "Please, darling, you mustn't listen to them. I don't want *you* hurt, too."

So many questions crawled over Cloud's skin. But she couldn't watch her mother in agony. She hugged Thrush back. "I'm sorry, Mama."

After a long, long while Thrush managed to stop crying. "It's all right, darling," she said, wiping her eyes, "but let's talk about something else. I want you to have something pretty to wear. You don't have any jewelry! Not even earrings. I don't blame Glory—Halibut House is so poor these days. But I want you to have this amulet. It will help keep you safe."

Thrush pulled one of her necklaces over her head and placed it around Cloud's neck. The amulet was an exquisite ivory carving, a raven, strung with beadlike whorls of copper wire.

Despite Aunt Glory's strictures against sniffing, Cloud could not help but lift the raven to her nose to inhale its faint perfume, the fragrance of Thrush's hair and skin. "Mama," she said, overwhelmed at the gift. "It's beautiful."

"And you are beautiful wearing it," said Thrush. She smoothed Cloud's hair. "Now we'd better pick some cranberries, hadn't we? Or people will wonder how we spent the day."

Cloud understood the warning: no one was to know that she and Thrush had met. They hiked up their skirts and headed into the swamp after Glory and Thrush's slave.

The four of them filled their baskets with cranberries all afternoon. Cloud was happy in her mother's company, happy to be doing something as simple as picking berries. She tried not to think of her dead brothers.

When the shadow of the forest stretched across the swamp, and sunlight touched only the topmost crowns, Thrush and her attendant left along the path they had come by. Cloud watched her mother disappear into the trees.

"What did you say to make your mother cry so?" Glory asked.

Cloud said, "I asked her about the ghosts."

"Oh, child!" Glory said. "What did I tell you! You should *not* have done that."

"She says they're my brothers." Cloud looked at her aunt. "Did you know I had brothers?"

Glory slung her basket across her shoulders and set out along their own path back to Sandspit Town. Cloud followed. They went up a hill and down again before her aunt spoke again. "You *should* talk to a wizard about the dreams."

"Oh, no," said Cloud. "I couldn't, not Bone—"

"Maybe you should go to Winter," Glory murmured, almost to herself.

"Who's Winter?" asked Cloud.

But Glory just said, "If you're going to wear the necklace, slip it inside your dress. You don't want people to talk."

*The alders had dropped their leaves before Rumble* and his men returned. During that time Thrush managed to slip away from Storm House a handful of times. After the first visit, Cloud and her mother never talked about anything but what was right in front of them: the nettle fibers they collected from the old town middens, or how to make Cloud's hair as smooth and glossy as her mother's. Sometimes, in passing, Thrush mentioned her other children, her daughter Radiance and the young prince named Great Mountain, who would someday be king in Halibut House. But she never spoke of Rumble. The necklace Cloud wore night and day until it no longer smelled of Thrush.

Before the waning moon shrank to darkness, storm clouds boiled up from the south. Rumble and his men arrived speeding ahead of the gale, with foam on their prows. In his war canoe the king brought the wealth he had seized: chests of glossy abalone, painted masks, bundles of elk hides. And he brought captives, weeping, bruised, and filthy.

The canoes also carried severed heads bearing the same short-cropped hair as the captives. The weather had been cold, but it was twenty days from the shores where the southerners lived in their many-doored longhouses, and the heads now reeked of old blood and rotting meat. The storm wind swept the stink all the way to Halibut House and set Cloud's nose twitching.

The heads sat in a heap on the foreshore, covered with mats, while the storm battered Sandspit Town. After a week of pouring rain and thundering waves, the clouds lifted and Rumble's men carried the heads out to the tip of Sand Spit. There they planted a forest of stakes, impaling the heads so they would stare down upon anyone entering the narrow mouth of the harbor. Ravens and gulls flocked to the feast.

Then the king set out again, this time to trade in the north. He took most of his captives with him, as well as the southern abalone and elk hides.

Now Storm House began to prepare for the feast in honor of Rumble's daughter, the princess Radiance. It seemed that Halibut House was obligated to contribute heavily. One morning, while cold rain dripped through Halibut House's dilapidated roof, Cloud helped Aunt Glory count out filets of dried salmon. "I thought these were our winter stores," Cloud said.

"We have plenty," said Glory, untying another chest.

Cloud, remembering how Glory had rationed food the previous spring, wondered if this could be true. "Storm House is wealthy," she said. "Why should we have to help?"

"Radiance is your *sister*, Cloud," said Glory sharply. "She and her mother belong to the mother-line of the Halibut House kings. As do you and I. Her brother, *your* brother, will be our king when he is grown. We must do what is proper for the future mother of our king's heirs."

The next day they began moving provisions across town to Storm House, with Stick and the other slaves carrying the heavy loads. Boxes of fur robes and copper bracelets followed the stores of salmon, deer meat, tallow, oil, and berry cakes.

Cloud's first sight of the interior of Storm House left her awestruck: magnificent painted screens and carved posts, cedar floors and apartment walls carpentered as masterfully as a treasure box. Even the vertical boards of the stepped platforms around the hearth bore carvings, fierce thunderbirds with outstretched wings. But despite Rumble's absence, the house seemed to smell of danger. While they were inside Storm House, Cloud stayed close to Aunt Glory and said nothing.

That day and on some of their visits thereafter, Cloud saw Thrush, who, surrounded by attendants and watched over by Rumble's fierce Aunt Snow, did not acknowledge her. Sometimes Cloud also saw Thrush's other two children. Great Mountain seemed like any other little boy, dirty and noisy.

But Radiance, who was perhaps nine or ten years old, already possessed her mother's grace. She wore five copper earrings in each ear, and a delicate raven-feather tattoo covered the backs of her hands. A feast for each time her ears had been pierced, Glory told her, and one for the tattoos as well. They often found Radiance seated decorously by the fire, spinning mountain-goat wool into yarn as fine as Aunt Glory's. Radiance greeted Aunt Glory with grave politeness, but like the other residents of Storm House, she acted as though Cloud did not exist.

Cloud's secret encounters with her mother grew less frequent as the feast approached. But one gray, chilly day she and Thrush met in the forest to cut alder bark for dyeing. Thrush prayed to the alder before they started and after they had finished. "Always show respect," Thrush said to Cloud. "The alders also belong to the First People."

As they cut sections of bark from the trees, Cloud heard noises in the brush, a squirrel or something larger but stealthier. Glory and Thrush didn't take any notice. Even though Cloud had found her smell and hearing to be keener than other people's, she could distinguish animals by scent only at close range. She reminded herself of Glory's assurance that no four-legs lived on the island, and then tried to ignore the noises.

When it was time to leave, Thrush kissed Cloud tearfully. "Darling," she said, "this is the last time we'll be able to meet for a while."

Cloud clung to her mother. She had known that the visits would cease when Rumble returned. But she wasn't ready for it.

"Come, now," said Aunt Glory at last, putting a hand on Cloud's shoulder. Thrush released her and stepped away. Cloud trudged back toward Halibut House with Glory, glancing over her shoulder until the trees hid her mother from view.

On the way to the house, Glory asked her to cut twigs for a new broom, so while Glory went ahead, Cloud stopped at a thicket of young spruces that grew behind the house. There she took out the jade adze Glory had given her.

As she began to chop, she again heard the rustling. This time Cloud gave in to her uneasy curiosity. She crept around the prickly spruce saplings. Neither a raccoon nor a stealthy four-legs lurked in the brush. There instead stood two children, a girl in an embroidered dress and a dirty little boy.

Her brother and sister. Radiance and Great Mountain, the princess and prince of Halibut House.

"Why are you watching me?" Cloud said.

She took another step toward them. For a moment she thought: maybe they want to make friends after all.

But then Radiance straightened her back and said, "You're going to be punished. You shouldn't be talking to my mother."

Cold gathered in Cloud's stomach. "She's my mother, too."

Radiance slapped Cloud across the cheek. "You don't have the right to talk about her. I'm going to tell my father what you've been doing."

"It's not your business," Cloud said, though she knew that if Radiance told Rumble, that wouldn't matter.

"It's not *your* business," said Radiance angrily. "My mother is farther above you than the roof of the sky. You're no better than a *slave*."

Cloud lifted her chin. "I'm not a slave. I belong to Halibut House as much as you do. It goes through the mother, and Thrush is my mother."

"No you don't!" yelled the little boy. "I'm going to be the lord of Halibut House, and I say you don't!"

"What is that?" Radiance demanded suddenly. She poked at a lump in the neckline of Cloud's dress, then pulled out the ivory pendant. "How *dare* you!" Radiance screeched. "That's mine! Mama was going to give it to *me!*"

Radiance tugged at the necklace, trying to jerk it over Cloud's head. Cloud grabbed the carving. Radiance slapped her and scratched at her, yanking at the necklace, but Cloud held tight, and then the strand broke, spilling little copper-wire whorls onto the forest floor.

Radiance screamed and struck Cloud across the face again. "You broke it! You filthy slave! My father will kill you the way he killed your brothers! Give me the raven!"

Great Mountain pummeled Cloud's arm and side with his fists. Radiance hit Cloud again and pried at Cloud's fingers. "Give it to me, give it to me, you slave!"

"I'm not a slave," Cloud said.

"No, you're an *animal*," Great Mountain flung at her. "You're a *bear*."

A cold icicle speared down Cloud's spine.

*Bear.*

A simple word. What did it mean? A brown shape in a sunny meadow, a vicious beast who had devoured countless men. Powerful claws, shaggy fur. The caution in people's eyes as they kept their distance from her.

A simple word, but it echoed over and over in her ears. A bright light dazzled her eyes, dawn welling over black crags.

"My father cut off your father's head," Great Mountain said. "He ate your father and brothers. Now he's going to eat *you*."

Radiance kept hitting Cloud, pulling at Cloud's fingers, screaming, "Give it to me!" Then she picked up the adze that Cloud had dropped in their struggle over the necklace, and she swung it into Cloud's shoulder. Cloud felt no pain. Instead, scalding rage poured into the cold space in her belly and she screamed so loudly that Radiance stumbled back in surprise. Cloud jumped on her sister, knocking her down, and smashed her fist into Radiance's face. Hot pleasure rushed through Cloud when blood spilled out, the sweet smell of it flooding her nostrils, and she hit her sister harder, pounding Radiance on the chest and stomach. The princess screamed in piercing gasps. The sound of Radiance's terror excited Cloud, exalted her. Rosy light half blinded her. She felt herself swell with strength—

Someone grabbed her arms and shouted. People came

running. Old Stick hauled Cloud to her feet. Radiance scrambled sobbing onto hands and knees, her face bloody and her dress torn.

"What have you *done!*" Aunt Glory shouted at Cloud.

"She hit her, she just started hitting her," said Great Mountain. "We weren't doing anything, she just started like that, she's crazy, she's an animal!"

And now here came august Aunt Snow, bearing down on Cloud with grim fury. "You wicked girl!" Snow slapped Cloud, hard. And then she dragged Cloud by the ear to a nearby stump and pushed her down.

*Thwack!*

The stick caught Cloud between the shoulder blades like a falling tree.

*Thwack!*

"Don't move!" Snow ordered.

*Thwack!*

Cloud's anger was slipping away, replaced by the familiar bewilderment. A part of her kept hoping that Thrush would appear and stop the beating. "Oh, darling," Thrush would cry, and rush to her, comforting Cloud in her arms while Cloud wept from the pain and humiliation.

But Thrush did not come. As the beating went on, Cloud realized that Thrush would never come. Cloud's few moments with Thrush had been stolen, and now that the theft had been discovered, there would be no more of them.

She did not know when the beating stopped. At some point she became aware of Glory shaking her. "Come, child. Let's get you inside."

Cloud slid backward onto her knees. Glory wanted her to stand, but she couldn't. Glory grabbed her by the armpits and lifted her, steadied Cloud when she nearly fell, guided her toward Halibut House. "What comes over you, child?" Glory was saying. "How can I protect you if you do things like that?"

Inside, Glory helped Cloud into their bedroom. "We'll have to have your dress off," said Glory.

Glory struggled to remove it. The hardest part was when Cloud had to raise her arms; the muscles didn't work. But at last Glory got the dress over her head and made Cloud lie facedown on her bed so she could swab medicine on the raw spots. Under her ministrations, Cloud's back began to throb.

"Oh, no. What happened, child?" Glory said, touching her shoulder. This time a sharp pain lanced straight to Cloud's belly. "The stick didn't make that. That's a cut. And it's bleeding."

Cloud didn't answer. She felt as if just lying there took all her endurance.

"You had better tell me," said Glory.

"Radiance hit me," said Cloud at last. Her voice didn't sound like her own; it was thick and clogged.

"With *what?*"

"The adze," said Cloud. Tears leaked from her eyes.

Aunt Glory let out her breath sharply. "Was that why you lost your temper?" She stroked Cloud's hair. "Cloud, you have to learn to control yourself no matter what happens. You're not a baby. You're a queen's daughter."

"But my father," whispered Cloud, "they said he was a bear."

"Don't *ever* say that word—" Glory began, furious.

"They said Rumble ate my brothers."

"No, child, no! Of course he did not!"

Cloud shut her eyes, more tears welling out. She could recall the strength coursing through her limbs, but it now felt as far away as the land beyond the ocean. "They said he's going to kill me."

"No, no, *no!*" Glory said. "That will *never* happen."

Glory covered Cloud with a blanket and departed. Cloud found she was clutching something tightly in her fist. Through her tears she saw that it was Thrush's ivory raven.

# FOUR

# Rumble

*While she lay in bed recovering from the beating,* Cloud had plenty of time to think. She thought about what Rumble would do to her when he returned. She could not blame him. He had been right: she was indeed her father's daughter. She had *wanted* to hurt Radiance, had felt joy at her sister's pain.

She thought about what Thrush must have felt to learn that her animal child had attacked her human one.

And she thought about Radiance, hoping she had not permanently disfigured her sister. No, a part of Cloud wished she *had*—and that part still wanted to hurt the princess. But Radiance scarred would make everything worse. It would remind Thrush every day of Cloud's true nature.

She dreamed nightly of dogs chasing her down. She would wake when jaws fastened upon her haunches, but not to the bedroom she shared with Aunt Glory. Instead she would open her eyes on the glade where ghost children wept eternally. She would try to run, but bones would trip her, and she would thrash among the salmonberry canes until at last she woke for real.

Cloud did not leave her bed until the dog salmon finished their run and the last families returned from fish camp. Even then she clung to Aunt Glory's side, waiting for Rumble to return and make good his promise.

Invitations had gone out long ago for Radiance's feast. Now the first guests began to arrive. Late one evening, as an icy drizzle fell on the town, the dogs began to bark in front of Halibut House. Cloud scrambled to her feet, heart pounding. But the voices that shouted at the door were unknown to her.

A dignified, elderly woman ducked into the hall, followed by men and women and a flock of wet and noisy children who surged toward the hearth shedding hats and cloaks. Glory greeted the elderly woman with cries of "Wren! Sister!" They embraced warmly. Glory directed the slaves to ready a welcoming meal, and then to haul the baggage to the empty rooms that lined the walls. Glory gave Cloud no instructions, so she listlessly resumed the task that had occupied her all evening, plucking the coarse guard hairs from a mountain-goat fleece.

Glory's sister Wren came down the stepped platforms, untied and shook out her rain cloak, and settled herself on the platform surrounding the hearth. Through her lashes Cloud watched Wren take in everything, the leaks, the cracked wallboards, the worn and splintered floor. Finally Wren's gaze reached Cloud herself.

When Glory returned to the hearthside, Wren asked, "Who is this lovely child? She looks just like Thrush."

"You haven't heard?" Glory said, surprised. "She's Thrush's four-legged daughter. She turned into a girl last winter. I have named her Cloud."

Wren gaped. After a moment she managed, "Human now! I had *not* heard. Is it—all the time?"

"It's been nearly a year," said Glory. "But for good? Rumble's wizard doesn't seem to be able to say. *I* think so. She is so human. You would hardly credit who her father is."

"Does she take after her mother in temperament, then, as well as looks?"

The two women looked at each other. "Not at all," said Glory. "She is for the most part quiet and very biddable. Nothing like her mother, or her father's people, for that matter, except that she has a bit of temper you have to watch out for. But of course Thrush has changed very much since you lived here. Everything has."

A bit of temper! Could Glory have convinced herself that Cloud's attack on Radiance was just *a bit of temper?* How hard Glory wanted to believe Cloud was a real girl!

"Ah, yes," said Wren, "our willful princess. You know, child"—she leaned toward Cloud—"your mother was the most famous beauty among the islands. Princes from every town in a month's journeying vied for her hand, but she wouldn't have any of them. How they were all in love with her! The gifts they'd bring, the stupid things they'd do to impress her—"

"I was in Round Bay Town with my husband then," said Glory. "I only returned after you remarried and went back north."

"That's right," Wren said. "Well, it was a merry band of jokers in those days, child, you have no idea. And to think it was Rumble who ended up with Thrush. Not much of a prospect for all his high birth, I would have said. Still hard to believe Rumble of all people rescued her. Not a forceful type, not a king's heart beating in his chest, as they say up north."

"Rumble has changed, too," said Glory. "You would hardly know *him*, either."

Her voice held a warning tone, but Wren gave no sign she had heard it. "Poor Thrush." Wren sighed. "She brought it on herself, but she suffered, how she suffered."

Cloud bent over her fleece, hoping Wren would continue. But Glory said, gesturing at the crowd now settled about the hearth, "I'd better attend to our guests. Sister, tell me how all these northerners are related to us."

Glory began to serve the meal that the slaves had prepared, while Wren launched into introductions of her numerous in-laws and grandchildren. Weary from the long voyage, the visitors soon retired to their rooms. Glory sent Cloud to bed as well, though she wanted to stay with her newfound aunt.

Cloud climbed up to their bedroom and crawled under the covers. But she found it hard to sleep with all the strangers in the house. Too many unfamiliar sounds leaked through the walls: thumps as guests settled into their beds, a child's complaint, a man's deep voice hushing him.

But as the house quieted, the murmurs of her aunts at the hearthside sharpened into soft words. At first Wren and Glory gossiped about cousins whose names Cloud barely knew. Then the sound of her own name caught her ear. Glory lowered her voice still further, and Cloud crawled to the door to listen.

"I want you to take Cloud away from here," Glory said. "Now, right away, before Rumble returns from the north."

The words shocked Cloud breathless. If Glory sent her away, she would never see Thrush again.

"Before the feast?" said Wren in disbelief.

"He's threatened to kill her."

"I don't believe it," said Wren. "Rumble wouldn't hurt a girl her age, his own kin. Thrush is his first cousin, for goodness' sake!"

"Sooner or later he'll try it."

"I've known Rumble since he was a baby. He hasn't got the—the—"

"He's not that Rumble," said Glory. "He's changed. What do you think drove Winter away?"

"But what could Rumble possibly gain from it?"

Glory was silent for a moment. Then she said, "Cloud is Thrush's eldest daughter. She's older than Radiance by several years. The summer kingship could descend to Cloud's sons—and bypass Rumble's children."

"Could!" said Wren. "All Rumble has to do is marry Cloud to a commoner. Her children would be low caste and could never inherit, and that would be the end of it! He doesn't need to *kill* her. Give me another reason, sister."

"Her father wasn't just any kidnapper," said Glory, lowering her voice still further. "He was an *immortal*. No one knows what Cloud got from him as her birthright, but there's bound to be something, no matter how human she's become."

"Rumble didn't hurt the girl all the years she was prowling around in her fur robe," said Wren. "Did he?"

"Her turning into a girl frightened him more than her being on four legs."

"But what does he think she'll do when she comes into her birthright? If he were kind to her, she might bring him power, fabulous gifts—the grace of the First People. It's happened that way in the past."

"It's too late for that," Glory said. "You don't know, sister. I'm afraid—" Her voice dropped to a whisper. "I'm afraid of what he's done to become what he is now."

Wren snorted. "It's never too late to step off a path and look for a different route."

"I don't think that's always true."

After a moment, Wren said, "I'll take her with me, if you ask it. But I can't tell my sons-in-law to turn right around and head back north. She'll be safe until after the feast. Rumble won't touch the girl with so many relatives in town who might be dragged into a fight."

Glory sighed. "I'll have to trust that you're right."

And that seemed to be the end of the conversation. The two elderly women gathered up their robes and climbed toward Glory's room. Cloud slipped back into bed and pulled her covers over her face, pretending to be asleep.

But just outside the door their footsteps halted again. "I think," Glory whispered, "when you leave, you should take her to Whale Town. Winter is a true seer, not like these wizards who keep servants to be their eyes and feet. But go there quietly! Or you might start—what we've been dreading since Winter left."

**Rumble arrived at Sandspit Town soon after Aunt** Wren. His heavy-laden canoes landed without fanfare, and

Cloud, sitting inside, did not even hear the news until Oriole brought it that evening. Cloud waited beside the hearth, cold, sweating, and shaky, for Rumble to descend upon Halibut House. But he did not come then, or thereafter. It seemed Aunt Wren was right: the guests in town made him cautious, or maybe he was too busy preparing for the feast.

Guests arrived now in convoys, and so many canoes had been drawn up on the beach that they looked like rows of drying fish. People and dogs and noise filled Halibut House to bursting. Many of the guests spoke strange languages, or spoke the tongue of Sandspit Town so badly that Cloud could hardly understand them.

Traffic flowed in and out of the house all day long. Glory and Wren also visited guests in other houses and took Cloud with them. With so many notables crowding the town, it seemed that a girl who last year had worn fur and claws hardly ranked as a topic of conversation. Some of the strange men did eye Cloud in a way that made her uncomfortable, but lacked the wariness she'd grown used to.

At night, the guests in Halibut House gathered at the hearth to gossip about politics or family matters in distant towns, or to reminisce over the great deeds of Glory's brother when he had reigned as the last king of the summer side of Sandspit Town.

Cloud felt lonelier than ever amid the commotion. Neither of her prospects were happy ones: either Rumble would kill her, or Glory would send her away. Glory had not yet informed her of the plan to take her to the mysterious Winter in Whale Town, and with all the comings and goings, and the work of hosting a house full of visitors, she didn't seem to notice Cloud's added burden of unhappiness. Cloud wanted to beg to see her mother one last time, but she didn't need Aunt Glory to tell her it was too dangerous now that Rumble was back.

And Glory always seemed to want Cloud ignorant of what really mattered. One day when Glory was busy elsewhere, Cloud asked shyly, "Aunt Wren?"

"Yes, child?"

"Aunt Wren, who's Winter?"

Wren started. "Glory hasn't told you?"

"She just mentioned the name."

Wren gazed at Cloud for a long moment. Around them children played a noisy game of tag. "Winter," Wren said, "is Rumble's—"

But the rest of her reply was lost when the children, shrieking with merriment, collided with an elderly lord and his retinue who had just begun to file through the door. Mothers yelled, a child who had been knocked over began to cry, and all was chaos for a few moments. By the time matters had settled, the visitors had reached the hearth and the greetings begun.

The next day was the feast in Radiance's honor. Cloud had assumed she would remain at home with the slaves, but Wren said, "Why are you dawdling, child? Hurry and get dressed."

Glory frowned. "I'm not sure she should go."

"What can Rumble do?" said Wren. "She'll be safer in a crowd of in-laws than sitting by herself."

Still dubious, Glory helped Cloud into her best dress, the one she had worn for her first meeting with Thrush. Wren raised her eyebrows when she saw the ivory raven that Cloud wore on a piece of string under her clothing. "How did she get *this*?"

"Thrush gave it to her, of course," said Glory. "No, leave it under her dress. I have some beads she can wear on top."

Glory also dug out threadbare sea-otter robes for Cloud and herself. "What happened to the feast robes?" Wren asked.

"Rumble has them in Storm House," Glory said. "He wanted them for his children."

Old Stick printed Halibut House crests on their cheeks with a bone stamp: raven's feet and a trapezoidal halibut abstracted into long thin lines. The other guests, the northern aristocrats, had already assembled in the hall, laughing and cheerful. Cloud had never seen such a glitter of abalone and polished copper. One of Wren's sons-in-law, heir to a northern kingship, wore a dazzling robe of black and yellow wool like the ones Rumble had claimed for his children.

The guests filed out of Halibut House. Stick finished Cloud's face and began to roll up his painting kit. "Let's go," said Glory, impatient.

At the top of the stairs leading from Halibut House, Cloud stopped. The northerners had formed a procession and marched up the beach, loudly singing an anthem in their own language. Rain pattered all around her, releasing the odor of cedar and decaying grass. She could see the whole curve of the town from where she stood. Storm House was easy to recognize, and not just from the crowds streaming toward its front door. It was the largest house on the winter side of town, and it stood behind a forest of monuments to the deceased winter kings. Smoke, belching from the roof vent, drifted in veils over the town.

Behind her Stick said, "You'll be all right, miss."

A strange note in his voice made her turn and look at him more carefully. His seamed face showed no expression, but a muscle twitched in one eyelid, and his dark eyes shone.

"Stick? Are *you* all right?" Cloud asked.

He just said, "Your aunts are waiting for you, miss."

Halibut House itself counted less than a dozen in its party, including Wren's daughters and their small children. They entered Storm House without song or ceremony and were guided to their seats by one of Thrush's dead brothers' sons. The place assigned to them was in the second row, near the back of the house. Wren glanced at their neighbors. "Well," she said, "it's not quite an insult."

"We're not what we once were," said Glory.

"He could honor his princess by honoring her kin," said Wren.

The room partitions and furnishings had been stripped from Storm House so that the floor was cleared to the outer

walls. All that remained were the carved thunderbirds supporting the roof beams, and the painted wall that divided
off the royal apartment at the rear. Cloud did not have to
worry about being conspicuous. Rumble's house was packed.
Wren might complain about their position in the hierarchy
of guests, but between their group and Rumble's carved seat
at the back of the hall, Cloud could see only visiting kings
and queens, a dizzying spectacle of painted crowns and dyed
wool. On the other side sat dozens of lesser aristocrats in
embroidered deerskin, while a sea of commoners in woven
cedar bark eddied by the door.

The house smelled of smoke and human skin. A huge
bonfire battered the guests with heat. The only clear space
in the house, outside of the sand-floored hearth well, was a
section of platform in front of the royal apartment, just above
and behind the carved throne. There Cloud finally spotted
Rumble. He stood with his back to the crowd, conferring
with a small group. A chill walked slowly up her back to
the nape of her neck.

Rumble turned and strode forward until he was scarcely
a dozen feet away. He carried a staff in his right hand. When
he thumped it on the planks at his feet, the crowd stilled
and heads swiveled toward him. "Welcome, my friends," he
began. And Rumble embarked upon a long oration.

What with its ornate rhetorical flourishes and Rumble's
terrifying nearness, Cloud soon lost the sense of it. Instead
she studied Rumble; she had never before had a quiet moment to do so. He was magnificent today in a long woolen
tunic and leggings, a fringed woolen robe, and a crown
shining with abalone and copper. He was of medium
height, but the tunic strained across his muscular chest and
powerful arms, and the hand that gripped his staff, pounding it against the floor every now and then for emphasis, was
large and strong. His broad face was not quite handsome:
his eyes were too wide-set, his smooth-plucked chin too
long and pointed. Compared to the other kings, he was so
young as to look almost boyish.

But even with words of welcome spilling gracefully from his lips, even with arms outstretched in peace, he seemed dangerous to Cloud. Turbulence seethed under his skin and coiled in his limbs, ready to burst into swift, bloody action. He looked more solid than everyone else in the house together, as if they all would have to strain together to budge him a hair's width.

At last Rumble finished, and the small group in the back corner parted. From behind them came Thrush.

Loss knotted into a hard, painful lump in Cloud's throat. The memory of Thrush's fragrance, the faint warm smell of her skin mixed with sweetgrass and mock-orange, washed over her. After today, she might never see her mother again.

Thrush walked slowly, an exquisite beauty. In her blue-dyed dress and her feather-trimmed mantle, she outshone every high-caste lady in the hall.

But she looked sad. She did not glance at Rumble as she passed him, did not gaze at the crowd or anywhere else. The fire was so bright that Cloud could see what looked like dirt or bruises shadowing her scarred, slender wrists.

Behind Thrush came her young son in a crown and outsize woolen robe, and behind him walked Aunt Snow, Rumble's aunt. The three of them sat down to one side of Rumble's throne. Radiance was not with them.

Now one of the visiting kings rose and replied to Rumble's speech. After him another rose, and then another. It seemed every one of the kings had to respond, and then all the clans had to perform their anthems, and then came a round of dances. While musicians sang and drummed, two men held up a robe in front of the round door to the royal apartment. The first figure to appear from behind the robe was a hook-nosed thunderbird beating its wings, followed by two sinuous, twirling young men imitating the two-headed lightning-snake. That dance belonged to Rumble, and the winter kings of Storm House.

Then came a long dance about Wily One's victory over the Master of Storm, which had brought the seasons of summer to the world. Cloud recognized the story from one Stick had told her at Oyster Bay, but this grand drama was a far cry from Stick's scatological and slapstick comedy.

The last time they lowered the robe, Radiance stood there.

A year or two short of womanhood, the summer princess of Sandspit Town was a miniature version of Thrush. The only trace of the beating Cloud had given her was a slightly swollen nose. When Rumble took Radiance by the hand and turned her around, the assembly could see the rayed sun that had been sewn across the back of her robe in squares of white shell. Cloud found it hard to believe this vision was her sister the way Glory and Wren were sisters. Of course she and Radiance were only half-sisters, and Radiance's father was a human king, while Cloud's was a vicious animal who had tortured Thrush.

Aunt Snow and another old woman of Storm House pierced Radiance's ears. Radiance gazed out at the assembly without a sign of discomfort; Glory and Wren murmured approvingly.

Then, while Radiance danced over four heraldic copper plaques, a chorus of men and women sang a beautiful antiphonal song about the first daylight to lance into the primeval storm.

After that came the feast: enormous heaps of roasted seal and mountain goat, of clover and cinquefoil roots, of cranberries and crabapples, and everywhere oil dishes for dipping. But today Cloud had no appetite. She would have slunk away if she could have reached the door without drawing Rumble's gaze, and if Thrush had not been sitting beside him. This might be her last sight of her mother. Thrush ate nothing, either.

At last it came time to distribute gifts thanking the guests who had come to witness Radiance's honor. Young men assisting Rumble handed out painted hats; bracelets of hammered copper and of twisted copper wire; earrings of sharks' teeth or abalone; necklaces of ivory, jade, and shell;

treasure boxes painted or inlaid; and more sea otter and marten robes than Cloud had thought could exist in the world.

Commoners received tanned deerskins, cedar-bark robes, mats and spoons. It went on and on, as if the presents came out of one of the magical boxes of legend that never emptied. People began to murmur in astonishment, and still the young men brought presents out of the back of the house. Eventually the murmurs faded, and people sat as if stunned.

Then, stepping carefully around and over the feasters, the young men brought in a painted canoe. They had to remove planks from the front wall of the house. Cloud first wondered if Rumble intended to give a canoe to each king or noble and, if so, how they all would fit in the house. But the young men set down the canoe beside the hearth and began to smash it to pieces with pile drivers, throwing the fragments onto the fire. Next they poured oil into the fire, box after box. Flames roared up, until smoke boiled out of the rooftop vent, and fire licked at the rafters. The house, stifling already, grew unbearably hot.

"Why is he destroying it?" whispered Cloud under cover of the roar of the fire. She remembered how angry Glory had been when she had thrown a mere spindle on the hearth.

"To show that no one will be able to match what he's done today," said Glory.

"But it's a waste—"

"It's not wasted on these kings sitting here, child, believe me."

The roof boards began to smolder. Little tongues of fire burst out. Cloud, pouring sweat, wondered how the kings by the hearth could stand it. But not one of them flinched. At last Rumble, who had impassively watched this display, gestured at the young men, and they climbed up to beat out the flames.

Last, Storm House men brought a line of men and women into the house, prodding them with the spears as they lagged. The crowd fell utterly silent. Some of the group, filthy and weeping, were the short-haired captives Rumble had taken in the south. But Cloud also recognized Stick and other Halibut House slaves, elderly men and women. Old Stick gazed straight ahead, but a tear trickled down each leathery cheek.

Fear cut into her belly like broken shells. Cloud clutched Glory's arm. "Be still!" Glory whispered.

The men lined up the slaves beside the still-roaring hearth. Rumble came down the steps. In the interval, he had changed into the shaggy robe that he had worn raiding, and over it he wore his necklace of huge animal teeth. He carried his battle-axe.

Cold swept across Cloud's skin. She *knew* that shaggy robe. She knew its musky smell, knew the texture of the long coarse brown hairs and the soft lighter underfur. She knew who should properly be wearing it, but she could not remember his face—

Rumble was speaking again. "It is not for myself that I do this. I do it for my daughter's honor, so people will remember her name forever."

And then—

It was as if he took off the calm mask he had been wearing and revealed the naked self beneath, forceful, violent, and heedless. His face changed and a wild light leaped into his eyes. Rumble swung his axe into the nearest slave's skull. The slave crumpled. The next in line tried to flee, but Rumble jumped upon him before he could take a step, smashing down with his axe. One of the southern women screamed—

Cloud tasted blood on her tongue, in her nose. Wild panic surged through her limbs and she wanted to run, run, run—

Hands seized her. "Be still!" Glory ordered. *"Be still!"* Cloud pressed her face against Glory, trembling and sick.

It seemed forever before the screaming ended, and an age after that before the bodies were carried out. The kings resumed their oratory as if nothing terrible had happened. Now the speeches were of praise and thanks. And Rumble, once more wearing woolen clothes and an impassive face, responded in kind.

*The night was late when Glory shook Cloud's shoul*der and said, "Time to go, child." Shakily—she had been dozing—Cloud rose and trailed after her aunts.

Crowds of people milled on the beach. Torchlight flickered over the dead slaves piled up like so many seals after a hunt. Cloud kept her eyes on her feet and tried to shut out the sweet smell of blood, the reek of voided bowels.

As they headed along the beach, the crowd thinned and the smell lessened. At Halibut House, Glory said, with quiet intensity, "It was a terrible thing to do. But he had the right to do it, Cloud. His children, your brother and sister, owned our slaves. Those others were his captives."

Cloud pretended that she had to relieve herself and crept into the woods, so that no one would see her crying over a dead slave, a poor old man who had told stories just to make her laugh.

*Later, when they were all in their beds and Cloud* thought Aunt Glory was about to blow out the lamp, Glory broke the news. "You will be leaving with Wren. The day after tomorrow."

"Leave?" said Cloud. Even though she had been expecting it, the news caught her unprepared. "I don't want to go."

"You have to. I can't protect you from Rumble forever."

"Please," Cloud whispered, "can I see my mother first?"

Glory said sadly, "Best not, child. I'll tell her you said goodbye."

"But," Cloud said, and then she couldn't speak. She turned her head away, trying to squeeze the emptiness into her belly. But it was no use. It was stronger than she was, and pushed up through her throat again, leaked out her eyes.

Glory reached out to stroke Cloud's hair. But her hand gave Cloud no more comfort than a twig. Glory had tried to help her become a girl, but without her mother, Cloud was nothing at all. Thrush was her one anchor in the world, the one thing that kept her from turning to mist and blowing away.

The two sisters murmured back and forth awhile longer, but Cloud heard none of it. Eventually Glory extinguished the lamp.

She lay awake all night in silent tears. In the morning she felt too weary to move, but when Glory told her to rise and dress herself, she obeyed.

Wren and her party were the only guests to leave so soon. They spent the day gathering their belongings. Cloud watched them miserably from the hearth. Glory was packing for her. She knew she ought to help but could not bring herself to do so.

Late in the afternoon, Glory made her stand up. "Come on, Cloud. No, don't argue. Just come with me."

Glory made her put on a cedar-bark cloak and hat; outside rain was falling hard. She and Wren led Cloud out the back door. They followed the path to the forest clearing where they had cut alder bark. Thrush now waited there alone.

At first Cloud couldn't move. Then she threw herself into Thrush's arms. "Mama," she wept, hugging Thrush as hard as she could, "Mama, Mama, Mama." Rain poured down on them.

Thrush squeezed her, sobbing into her hair. "You must be good for Aunt Wren. You must be happy. Promise me, darling?"

But before she could answer, heavy footsteps thudded on the grass and a powerful hand flung Cloud aside.

"How dare you!" Rumble shouted at Thrush. Thrush was reaching for Cloud, but Rumble slapped her so hard that she fell against a tree. "Haven't I told you that you are not to see this creature? Do you have any shame?"

He raised his hand again. Glory caught at his arm. Rumble turned toward her wild-eyed. "And you!" he shouted. "I know you helped my wife sneak around while I was gone.

I told you to keep this animal out of the way. I told you it was dangerous! And what did you do! You let it at *my daughter!* And now *this* treachery. It's time to finish this at last! At last!"

He fixed his gaze on Cloud. She now saw the axe in his other hand. She stepped back, trembling. Wren said, "I will take the girl away and you need never lay eyes on her again."

Rumble gave a short laugh. "Oh, of course. You think I don't know what you're plotting?"

"She is not yours to dispose of," said Wren. "She is not an animal or a slave. She is a daughter of Halibut House."

Rumble said contemptuously, "Don't worry, I'll pay the house for her death."

He moved toward Cloud. Thrush sobbed, hands to her bloodied nose. Glory stepped between Rumble and Cloud. "I will not let you have this girl," she said.

"No?" The murderous light leapt in Rumble's eyes. "I will have whatever I want."

He smashed his fist into Glory's face. She crumpled. Wren screamed at him. Rumble struck Wren, too, and threw her to the ground. Wailing, Thrush covered her face with her hands.

Rumble stepped once more toward Cloud. Her terror exploded into sheer, fiery panic. She fled down the trail. Rain fell in sheets, and the forest was as dark as twilight. She dodged away from the trail to crawl up a hillside through dense thickets of ocean-spray and salal, toward the muddy hollow beneath a stone that had once been her den.

Below her, footsteps thumped along the trail. She hunkered beneath the stone, listening intently and trying to still her noisy panting. Rain rattled on the salal leaves, making it hard to track Rumble's footsteps. They seemed to pass by onto the fork in the trail that ran up into the center of the island.

But then Cloud heard a noise in the thickets on the slope above her, a stealthy heavy crunching that only a large body could make. It came closer. She didn't know how Rumble could have circled around so fast. She crawled out of her den, wriggled on her belly through the salal as silently as she could, slid down a rock face and back onto the trail.

One direction led toward Halibut House, the other, deeper into the forest. She fled into the forest. Leafless gray alders stretched away into the gloom. Cold rain pelted her like gravel.

Footsteps trod heavily in front of her. She looked up to see Rumble. He still carried his axe.

They both stopped. After a moment, he said, "Try to run again, and I'll kill you right here."

He did not at first move toward her. He just stared, his mouth slowly twisting as if he tasted something rotten, as if he were in pain.

"You do," he said finally. "You do look just like her. The way she was."

He stepped closer and seized Cloud's arm, gazing into her face. Cloud could not move and she could not look away. She had not been so close to him since that long-ago morning when she had awakened beneath the steps of Storm House.

He was just the same: eyes set too wide; snubbed nose more like a boy's than a man's. With his beard plucked out, the skin of his face was smooth as a child's. For the briefest instant there was something different in Rumble's face: softness, regret. She would almost have said it was grief. In that moment he did not look like a man who could hurt anything.

"The way she was before," he said.

Rain splashed on his face, spilled down his cheeks like tears. But his grip on her arm only tightened. He dragged her through bristling spruces, over fallen alders, to a wet clearing that smelled sweetly of rotten wood. She tried to twist away, but he slapped her so hard her head spun, shoving her against an alder trunk. One hand gripped her face so that she could hardly breathe. The other twined in her hair. And then, breathing heavily, he began to kiss her. His mouth was cold from rainwater. It slid along her chin, her neck. His hands squeezed her breasts. The way he touched her terrified and repulsed her. The smell of his skin made her stomach churn.

Then, from the forest, Cloud heard that stealthy crunching again. Rumble must have heard it, too, because for a moment he stopped and cocked his head. Cloud took the opportunity to push against him, again trying to twist free. But he just clouted her on the head and threw her to the ground as if she were a dead seal, a slab of meat. And he knelt down and thrust his hand under her dress, yanking it to her waist. She pushed against him with all her strength, twisting and kicking, but it was like trying to move a cliff.

A stick snapped nearby. Rumble jumped to his feet, axe in hand, swiveling his head this way and that. Something brownish moved heavily, concealed by shivering hemlocks.

Had her father's people come to save her?

Cloud scrambled to her feet. A large buck erupted out of the foliage and leapt past Rumble, bounding over logs and through thickets. Cloud launched herself after it. Rumble crashed behind her, shouting.

She raced headlong, heedless of thorns and branches. When she stumbled onto a sandy path, she veered onto it. A glance behind showed her Rumble following with a powerful stride, gaining steadily.

Then she burst onto the beach that ran along the outside of Sand Spit. Directly in front of her, a pair of old women carried up the anchor stone of their small canoe. Cloud careened around them, barely clearing the rope, and sped toward the firm sand along the water's edge. But Rumble caught his foot on the rope and plowed straight into the women. Cloud's last glance behind her showed Rumble in the sand, his face purple with fury, tangled in rope and clucking old ladies.

But her feet would not stop running until the sand ended at a cliff. With the last of her strength she swarmed up the rain-slick stone and into a vicious tangle of wild rose high above the beach. There she could see in every direction. She crouched down, shaking like grass in the wind, and waited for Rumble.

But he did not appear. She grew colder and colder. After a while she noticed she was soaking wet and bleeding from dozens of scratches. She had also lost her rain hat. She pulled her cloak over her head. Again Cloud felt Rumble's mouth on her face, and shock gave way to a storm of rage. If only she *were* a four-legs. She would crush his bones to splinters for touching her that way. For hurting Thrush and Wren and Glory. *She would kill him.*

But she was not an animal. She was only a girl.

Light faded from the sky. Below her, the rain roughened a smooth groundswell that now rolled in from the southeast. Still Rumble did not come. At length exhaustion overtook her and she fell asleep. She dreamed she slammed Rumble to the ground with her paw and hunkered over him to feed. In her dream, his bloody flesh tasted just like deer meat.

Then she heard children weeping behind her. "Lost, lost." When she turned, she was human again, slender and small. She stood in the rain among bare salmonberry canes. The huge skull stared from the tree. "Don't leave us here," wept the voices in her ear. "Only you can save us."

She tried to flee, but huge bones rolled, tripping her, and she could not regain her feet . . .

When she woke, ice-cold, the rain had stopped and a three-quarters moon slid in and out of the clouds. The night was silent except for the waves breaking on Sand Spit, slowly and rhythmically, like a sleeper's breath.

She wondered if she could sneak back to town to find Wren, if Wren could still spirit her away. She wondered if Rumble had killed Wren and Glory.

The moon came out and spilled its light on the ocean. The whole world emerged from darkness: mountainous islands, glimmering waterways, and, tiny and remote, the glacier-capped peaks of the Mountain Land.

Cloud climbed down to the beach, feeling her way carefully among the rocks. When she reached the water's edge, she listened hard. Again she heard nothing but breaking waves.

She crept shivering along the moon-painted shore, past the small canoe that the old women had drawn up, to the short trail that led across the spit to the town. From this spot, the tall salal concealed Halibut House, except for the tip of a monument that rose from the foreshore. All seemed quiet. Not even a wisp of smoke hung against the curdled sky.

But as Cloud stepped onto the trail, a dog barked once.

A cold shock bristled the hair at the nape of her neck. The dog sounded many houses distant, on the winter side of Sandspit Town. But she knew its rough, deep voice.

She fled back to the canoe. The dog barked again. With trembling hands Cloud pulled off the mats with which the old women had covered the canoe, heaved the anchor stone aboard, then braced her feet and pushed with all her weight.

By the time she had the vessel afloat, the dog was barking without pause. Cloud glanced in the direction of the town. She imagined Rumble lying wakeful beside Thrush, hard eyes gazing into darkness, planning how he would hunt her down. And she thought of Bone listening to his dog servant. She jumped aboard her stolen canoe and dug one of the paddles into the water, heading out across the slowly rocking sea.

PART TWO

# FIVE

# Crossing

*She headed northward along the shore of Maple* Island. Her progress was excruciatingly slow. On the journey to and from Oyster Bay, she had shared a canoe with half a dozen other paddlers who had done most of the work. Now she had just herself to push her little canoe along, and steer it as well. The bruises Rumble had given her throbbed, and her arms soon burned with weariness. She longed to rest but didn't dare.

The sound of the barking dog echoed behind her. At first Cloud had paddled with no thought but to escape Rumble and Bone, and Bone's servants. But as she crept along the shore, she began to wonder where she could go that was out of their reach.

*Take her to Whale Town. To Winter,* Glory had begged Wren.

Winter: the name obviously belonged to a winter-side house. Wren had said, "Winter is Rumble's—" One of Rumble's Storm House relatives. That probably meant a woman, an aunt or cousin married out, for a man would be at home in Storm House in the service of mother-line and king. It was hard to believe such a woman would help Thrush's four-legged daughter.

As for Whale Town, all Cloud knew about it was the island it lay on, Stick's single gesture a lifetime ago on the trip to Oyster Bay. She had fled with only the clothes she was wearing, had no food or tools, not even a knife. How likely was it that she could reach Whale Town even if no one pursued her?

The cliffs of Maple Island slipped past. As the moon swam through the clouds, the ocean glittered like wet fish skin, then faded again to black. At some point the barking stopped and she became conscious of the stillness of the night. Only tiny noises broke it: the splash of her paddle, the trickle of water under her keel, the glug-glug of the groundswell pushing in and out of the rocks. Far away, a wolf sang from an invisible mountaintop.

When dawn lit the east, she had progressed no farther than the reefs at the tip of Maple Island. She could hardly lift her arms for another stroke, and she nearly let the current drag her to shore. But she thought again of Bone's dog and forced herself across a mile-wide passage to the next bit of land. With the last of her strength, she beached her canoe and hauled up the anchor stone. Wrapping herself in her cloak, she curled in the gravel and dropped into sleep.

When she woke, rain was falling. Cold, stiff, and aching with hunger, she climbed to her feet.

The islet she had reached was no more than a granite whale's-back of moss and wild rose amid a sea of slowly rolling gray. Curtains of mist now drifted over the water, and even the closest island in the direction Stick had pointed was no more than a shadow in the rain. It looked impossibly distant, on the far side of a strait ten miles wide.

The thought that she must cross so enormous a stretch of open water filled Cloud with despair. She found herself missing Glory fiercely. Brisk, efficient Glory would have found food and made sure she was warm and safe. Glory would have known how to reach Whale Town. Cloud wondered again how badly Rumble had hurt her, but she was too tired and frightened to grieve. What she wanted was comfort, and there was no comfort to be had.

No, what she wanted most of all was food. After stretching her knotted arms, and jumping up and down to warm herself, Cloud walked along the beach. The tide had withdrawn a long way. She found no edible seaweed, but as she crossed a patch of muddy gravel, a clam squirted on her toes.

Glory had always disdainfully referred to shellfish as poor man's food. Cloud had, however, seen other women digging clams. With an oyster shell and a great deal of effort she managed to excavate some littlenecks that she smashed open with stones. Her blistered hands could hardly grip either clam or rock, and in the end she got only a few tough mouthfuls filled with sand and bits of broken shell. Poor man's food indeed.

The rain kept falling, plastering Cloud's hair to her head. The food gave her a little courage. She'd come this far; maybe she could cross that strait after all. She would travel to Whale Town one island at a time.

She had just heaved her canoe the last few feet into the water when a dog began to bark. She spun around. Atop the highest rock on the island stood Bone's white-haired dog.

Still barking, it leapt a huge distance over the drift logs to the top of the beach, gathered its hindquarters to spring again. Cloud scrambled aboard her canoe and grabbed her paddle. She dug frantically, trying to turn the canoe outward through the surf, but her hands were so tender and her shoulders so knotted that she almost dropped it. She forced herself to push on the paddle again and again. Bone's servant stopped at the water's edge, snarling and growling. At last the canoe gained way, and the stretch of water separating her from it widened.

As she worked her way past the islet, the dog disappeared from view, and the wash of breakers drowned its noise. But she recalled how Bone's dog had supposedly searched the world for her lost mask. Why would it now cut short its pursuit?

The islet slowly fell away behind her. Her sharp panic settled into edgy trembling. Now the drifting mists revealed a chain of islets and exposed reefs that, at this low tide, extended far into the strait. From the tip of that chain, the stretch of open water she would have to cross was much narrower.

She paddled toward the reefs until she thought she had put enough distance between her and the dog to rest. But then movement along the reefs attracted her eye, a canoe a half-mile ahead of her. A single man wearing a rain hat paddled it. She could not identify him at this distance, but she did recognize the prick-eared silhouette in the bow: a dog sniffing the wind.

Panic rushed back. But the dog didn't notice her. Then Cloud *knew*—fleetingly she tasted the salt breeze in her nostrils as if it were as rich and solid as a mouthful of seaweed—that the dog sat upwind and couldn't smell her.

She still waited: who knew how a wizard's servant tracked its prey? But neither man nor dog glanced in her direction.

The man was a strong paddler; he swiftly rounded one of the larger reefs and disappeared. Ignoring her raw hands, Cloud took up her own paddle again and followed at a much slower pace.

She didn't see him again. At the tip of the reefs, the current strengthened, and she let it sweep her out into the strait. The reefs contained a hundred places where the man in the rain hat could be hiding. But no one emerged to pursue her.

Rain dribbled steadily down her nose and chin. Cloud wished *she* still had a hat. Less than five miles, she thought, now separated her from the nearest of the islands on the far side. She set her course toward it at a sharp angle to the swells. The sky had grown dark and murky; heavier rain approached, and perhaps nightfall as well.

Her canoe plunged through the swells. The raw patches on her hands spread and began to bleed. Every so often, when a hand's width of water had collected in the bottom of the canoe, she would ship her paddle to bail, glancing behind to make sure no one pursued her. But she always had to start paddling again.

Slowly the islets she had left behind turned bluer and vaguer, while the island she aimed for grew more solid. Out in the middle of the strait, steeper swells tipped her canoe alarmingly. She tried not to think about capsizing. Aunt Glory had never taught her to swim.

The sky grew darker still. Cold gusts kicked foam from the waves. Then lightning flashed overhead. Thunder rumbled, and a sudden avalanche of rain dropped on her. A gust grabbed her canoe and shoved it broadside.

She dug harder with her paddle to stay on course, but her arms already trembled with fatigue and her hands could hardly grip the paddle anymore. Soon the swells reared taller than her head. From the peak of the swells she could gaze in all directions. But the driving rain obscured the island ahead, and she could take her bearings only from the line of waves.

Lightning cracked again, this time right in front of the canoe. Rain turned to blizzarding snow, and the snow shimmered with blue lights that sparked in Cloud's eyes, stung like wasps. Faint voices chattered in her ear.

She had been so anxious about the dog that she had forgotten Bone's other servants. Whimpering from the pain of the stings, she fought to hold on to her paddle, to take one more stroke and then another, to keep her canoe on course. Another crack of lightning. Something moved in the corner of her eye, long and pale like a snake—

A suckered tentacle crawled over the gunwale. With terribly slow and clumsy movements, Cloud struck it with her paddle. The tentacle jerked but did not let go. She smashed the paddle down harder. Meanwhile a wave lifted her canoe and tipped it sideways. The blue lights were stinging her hands and arms to agony. More tentacles grabbed the gunwale. Another wave heaved and dropped again, and her canoe heeled further, swiveling into the trough.

Surely all Bone's dog had intended was to drive her onto the water to *this*. Cloud tried to push her canoe back on course, leaning to right it. But now a tentacle seized her paddle. She could not yank it free.

Somewhere in the blizzard, a dog barked. Another wave swelled up, higher and higher. As her canoe slid down sideways again, tentacles pulled it over. She tumbled into icy water.

Tentacles wrapped around her as she scrabbled at the overturned hull, She fought to rip them away, to keep her head above water. But cold jetted against her legs, and Bone's octopus surged downward, pulling her underwater. The light changed from green to black. Pain lanced through her ears, and still the creature dragged her down and down into blind, icy darkness, until her lungs were exploding and she knew she would have to open her mouth and breathe—

A hand grabbed her shoulder and yanked. She shot back to the surface, gasping and choking as tentacles thrashed around her in a welter of foam. A strange man in a rain hat and cape loomed over her, balancing in his canoe amid the huge cresting waves. Snow and flickering ice-blue lights swirled around him, and thunder rumbled continuously. He cast a—harpoon? A coppery shaft of light sank into the octopus. Its tentacles spasmed and released Cloud, and it reached for the canoe.

For a moment Cloud bobbed free, coughing. Then another hand gripped her arm. She looked. The last of Bone's servants, gazing at Cloud with empty eye sockets, embraced her tenderly as a mother with her child. And then the drowned woman pulled Cloud underwater again, down into the bitter cold. Darkness filled up Cloud's thoughts until nothing else was left.

**She woke lying beside a fire with a fur robe cocoon**ing her from head to toe. Rain drummed overhead. She hadn't drowned after all, unless this was the land beneath the ocean.

She wormed a hand free and pulled aside the robe for a better view. On the far side of the fire lay a dog, watching her with pricked ears. Cloud's stomach lurched and she fought her way to a sitting position. But the dog was not Bone's white-haired servant. This was a smallish animal with a mottled coat of gray and black. She relaxed a little. After a while the dog laid its chin on its paws.

She had been brought to a small lean-to of bark slabs. The dog lay across the entrance, blocking her escape. To one side of the fire lay leather bags and a heap of sea-hunting gear: a harpoon, a coil of rope, floats made from seal bladders. On the other side a stack of firewood steamed in the heat. The shelter smelled of wet dog and smoke.

The dog swiveled its head to stare outward into the rainy night. A moment later, a figure appeared: not a dead woman but a rather ordinary-looking man in a rain hat. He ducked into the shelter and dropped an armload of driftwood on the stack.

"How are you feeling?" he asked, sitting cross-legged next to the dog.

It was the wizard. He looked to be about Rumble's age, or maybe a little younger, with a fine-boned face and a slender, well-proportioned body. Beneath his rain cloak, he wore a commoner's tunic of woven cedar-bark, but a string of finely carved amulets hung around his neck, and on his left cheek he bore a small tattoo depicting what might have been a mink.

"Did you kill Bone's servants?" Cloud asked hoarsely. Her throat was raw with salt.

The wizard looked thoughtful. He scratched his dog behind the ears, and the dog put its head on his knee. "You knew it was Bone's spirits attacking you?"

He lacked Rumble's powerful build and he certainly did not possess Rumble's turbulent forcefulness. This wizard seemed rather unimpressive, in fact; hard to reconcile with the power that had hauled her out of the depths—twice.

"I'm afraid I didn't destroy them," he said, "but hopefully they won't bother us for a while. Are you hungry?"

Without waiting for an answer, he pulled a piece of dried salmon from his heap of gear and tossed it at her. She snatched it up and gnawed the hard, smoky flesh until she had sucked every scrap from the backbone.

Then she noticed him watching her curiously. Embarrassment flooded her. The way she had eaten would have appalled Aunt Glory. But the wizard just held out a dipper of water. "Where did you get that carving?" he asked.

Cloud's hand went to her throat. The little raven now hung outside her dress. It must have fallen out during her struggles in the water—lucky the cord had not broken. She clutched it tighter, not that she could prevent the wizard from stealing it if he chose.

"My mother gave it to me," she said.

"Your mother?"

Not wanting to explain more to this stranger, Cloud said nothing and slid the raven back under her dress. She wanted to ask why he had saved her and what he planned to do with her now, but for once she was too abashed to ask questions. She placed the salmon backbone and skin on the fire, wiped her abraded hands gingerly on her dress, and reached for the water dipper.

When she had drunk and handed back the little bowl, he said, "You should rest. I'll keep watch."

He picked up a shell knife and began whittling at a stick. His dog got up, shook itself, turned around twice, and lay down so that it faced into the night. For a while Cloud watched the wizard's long fingers gracefully wield his knife. The firelight made the little tattooed face on his cheek appear to blink. She wondered if she really dared sleep in his presence.

"Don't worry," the wizard said. "You're safe for now."

Outside she heard only rain and the rhythmic wash of the ocean. At last she lay down and fell into a deep slumber.

**When she next woke, it was morning and she was** alone. Clutching the furs around her, Cloud pushed out of the shelter.

She stood in the grass at the top of a gravel beach. Rain still poured down. Footsteps crunched along the beach, and soon wizard and dog tramped up the path toward the shelter. Cloud took a step back when the dog bounded ahead to sniff her. Then it sat on its haunches and joined its master in staring at her.

Cloud wondered what the wizard saw, if his sight was anywhere near as good as Bone's, who was himself not enough of a seer to divine what had caused Cloud's transformation from a four-legs into a girl. It was hard to think so. He looked too ordinary. There were even smile lines around his eyes, though he was not smiling now. His intent gaze made her uncomfortable.

After a moment, he crawled into the shelter and began tossing out gear. Cloud meanwhile kept a wary eye on the dog. When the wizard backed out, he hefted the coil of harpoon line over his shoulder. "Could you get those bags?" he asked.

Cloud looked down at them. He had made the request with casual familiarity, almost as if she were his wife or daughter—or slave. She wasn't used to men addressing her, and certainly not to strange men asking her to carry their possessions.

She grabbed a bag with each raw hand and trudged after him. The dog followed her, prancing and wagging its tail. When she reached the water's edge, the wizard took the bags from her and heaved them aboard. His dog jumped after them. It sat down in the bow where Cloud had yesterday mistaken it for Bone's servant.

"Are you coming?" the wizard asked Cloud.

She looked around: a forested bight amid rain and gray ocean, as forsaken as if there were not another bit of land in the world. Her canoe was nowhere in sight. She was afraid to embark with this mysterious wizard, but what choice did she have?

"Where are you going?" she asked.

"To my house."

That was not reassuring. "Where is that?"

"West and north," he said. "Less than a day's paddling."

"Do you live by yourself?" she asked, even more timidly.

"I live," he said, "with my wife and children at a place called Whale Town, and I'm not going to hurt you or make you my slave, if that's what you're worried about."

Cloud took a step forward. "You live in Whale Town?"

"That's right," he replied, with a flicker of impatience.

She crawled into the canoe. The wizard pushed off and leapt aboard. With a few quick strokes he had the canoe under way and was heading along the cliffs outside the bight.

Cloud looked for a paddle but saw none. She twisted around. "Do you know," she asked the wizard hesitantly, "a seer named Winter? In Whale Town?"

"Winter?" Again he favored her with that intent gaze. "What would you want with Winter?"

"My aunt thought—she thought she would consult Winter."

"And who's your aunt?"

"Her name is Glory."

"Glory, eh? Do you have a name?"

"It's Cloud."

"And who gave you that name?"

"My Aunt Glory."

He seemed to have no more questions. Cloud gathered up her nerve to ask him another of her own. "Who are you?"

"Otter," he said, without pausing in his stroke.

**They passed from island to island in silence, head**ing westward. Otter paddled with a strong, tireless rhythm. Cloud kept watch for Bone's servants but saw only waves and a few leaping porpoises. With Otter's furs under her cloak she stayed warm enough, although her clothes were still damp from her submersion, and rain drummed on her unprotected head. Otter did eventually open his mouth long enough to offer her more dried fish, so she could not claim to be mistreated. But she couldn't read his intentions toward her.

Around midday they rounded a point, and before them lay nothing but ocean all the way to the horizon. A wild fancy visited Cloud that Otter was really one of the First People, and he was bearing her across the sea to the Land of Wealth. But he turned north, and for the rest of the afternoon they traveled up the outer coast of that island. Atop its cliffs, swaying in a cold west wind, grew the mightiest cedars Cloud had ever seen.

At length they came to a long rocky arm sheltering a harbor. Inside the harbor, a row of moss-covered houses straggled along a gravel beach. Whale Town was smaller and considerably less impressive than Sandspit Town. It possessed no great royal halls like Storm House, no carved memorials to the dead. Some of the houses lacked gabled roofs and were hardly more than lean-tos of rough cedar slabs. At one end of the beach, a ribcage as tall as a man protruded from the gravel. Cloud decided it must be a whale skeleton. She hadn't believed Stick when he'd told her how big they could be.

Still without speaking, Otter beached the canoe, handed the satchels to Cloud, and lifted his harpoon line to his shoulder. She followed him and his dog up the beach, stiff from the long hours in the canoe. Few people in Whale Town were outdoors in the relentless rain. But Otter's dog bounded into one of the more prosperous-looking houses and emerged a moment later with a boy, a shrieking little girl, and last of all a woman wrapping a rain cloak around her shoulders.

The boy bounded up to Otter. "Weren't there any seals?"

"No seals," said Otter. Chasing the dog and giggling, the little girl darted around Otter's feet. "But I fished something else out of the sea."

The boy swiveled to stare at Cloud but quickly lost interest. He tugged at Otter's coil of rope. Dog and little girl looped this way and that.

"It's too heavy for you," said Otter.

"I can carry it!" the boy insisted. Otter let him pull it from his shoulder, and the boy staggered off toward one of the sheds on the foreshore.

Otter's wife reached them. "You found *her* in the sea?" she asked—coolly, Cloud thought. "She looks like Thrush."

Cloud started at the mention of her mother's name.

"Yes," said Otter, "she does, doesn't she?"

Although maybe it wasn't so surprising that these two knew Thrush. Otter's wife herself bore an unsettling resemblance to Rumble: the same strong build and broad cheekbones, the same snubbed nose and wide-set eyes.

Cloud felt pinned under the weight of their combined gaze. "I'm Thrush's daughter," she made herself say.

"You can't be," Otter's wife said. "You're too old to be Radiance."

"No," said Cloud, swallowing, "I'm Thrush's other daughter, her first daughter."

"But her first daughter was a b—" The woman stopped herself just in time.

"When I said I fished her out of the sea," Otter said, "that's exactly what happened. I spotted Bone's servants and followed them. They were trying to drown her. She says she was on her way here."

Otter's wife said sharply, "What about her companions?"

"She was alone," said Otter.

Otter's wife stepped closer. Cloud had to work hard not to squirm; that gaze felt like feathers tickling her skin. "She looks like an ordinary girl now," the woman said. "Except . . ." She blinked a few times. "Why were you coming here?"

"Rumble tried to kill me," Cloud said. A lump was swelling in her throat. These two knew Thrush, and yet they treated her like an unwelcome stranger.

"I meant," said the woman, "why *here*?"

Cloud managed, "Aunt Glory said I should consult a seer named Winter."

"I'm Winter," said the woman. "Did Glory really send you to Whale Town by yourself?"

Cloud shook her head, tears spilling down her cheeks.

Otter cleared his throat. "Why don't you take Cloud inside while I finish out here?"

For a moment Cloud thought Winter would refuse, would leave her standing on the beach in the rain. But at last Winter sighed and held out her hand. "All right then, niece, come inside."

"Niece?" Startled, Cloud glanced from Otter to Winter.

"Twice over," Winter said. "Otter is Thrush's brother, and Rumble is mine."

**The small house possessed a single door, a simple** plank floor with no hearth pit, and only two occupants: a middle-aged man setting the barb into a halibut hook, and an ancient woman twining a basket.

Winter crossed to the hearth, where she lifted out a piece of dried halibut that had been soaking in a cooking box. She started to break it into pieces. "But," Cloud said, following her, "all of Thrush's brothers were killed."

"Not Otter," said Winter.

"But Glory said they all died, hunting . . . my father."

Winter crumbled dried seaweed into the box, poured in more water, and with tongs added hot stones. Clouds of steam hissed up. She covered the box with a mat. "Otter was the youngest. He never tried to track your father to his den. That was how the others died. Otter tried to find Thrush by . . . spiritual means."

"But," Cloud said, "if Otter is Thrush's brother—shouldn't he be the head of Halibut House? Wouldn't he be the summer king of Sandspit Town?"

"*Should* is not always *is*," Winter said.

"But Glory didn't even *mention* Otter! Or you!"

"Glory did mention me. She told you to consult me."

"Not really," said Cloud uncomfortably. "I mean, she didn't say who you were—and my mother never, she didn't—"

Winter said, "Sometimes people think that if they don't talk about a thing, it can't hurt anyone."

"But," began Cloud.

Winter frowned. "I think we're the ones who should ask questions. You say you're Thrush's four-legged child. But you look ordinary to me. Why should I believe you?"

Cloud gaped at her.

"When do you say you became a girl?"

"L-last winter," Cloud stammered.

"Why did it happen?"

"No one knows. I'm just a girl now, all the time. Aunt Glory taught me how to act. I didn't know how to do anything."

"What sort of name is Cloud?"

"It's a Halibut House name," said Cloud. Was Winter testing her? "Aunt Glory gave it to me."

"It's not your four-legged name, then."

"I don't have a—one of those."

"Of course you do," said Winter.

"I don't!" said Cloud. "Well, no one knows what it is."

"*You* don't know?"

"I don't remember anything from . . . then." The lump grew again in Cloud's throat. Winter didn't even believe Cloud was Thrush's child. Cloud wondered if she should leave the house and go sit on the beach in the rain. She wasn't welcome here.

"So," said Winter, "why were you coming here by yourself?"

"Rumble . . ." Cloud stopped.

"Go on," said Winter. "Rumble what?"

"He hurt them. Aunt Glory and Aunt Wren." Cloud squeezed her eyes shut. Then she was crying and couldn't stop.

"Badly?" Winter asked, in a hard voice.

"I don't know!" Cloud said. "I couldn't go back to see, because Rumble, because he . . ."

"Because Rumble what?"

Cloud shook her head. She couldn't tell this hard, unsympathetic woman, Rumble's sister, about that chase through the woods and what Rumble had done at its end.

"Rumble gave you those bruises on your face?"

When Cloud managed to stifle her sobs, all she said was, "I ran away. I stole a canoe and left."

Winter went on staring at her for a moment longer. Finally she sighed. "You'd better take off your cloak. You're shedding water everywhere."

Cloud looked: she had indeed left a puddle on the floor. "I'm sorry." She reached for the tie of her cedar-bark cloak, but her hands were too sore to manage the water-swollen knot.

"What's wrong with your hands?" Winter asked.

Cloud held out her palms. Winter examined them but said nothing. Instead, she untied the knot, pulled off Cloud's cloak and the wet fur robe beneath, and threw them over the drying poles slung from the roof beams. Then she felt Cloud's dress and sighed again. "I'll have to find you something dry."

Cloud followed Winter into one of the bedrooms built against the side of the house. Inside, Cloud stripped off her damp, clinging clothing and put on the dress of woven cedar bark that Winter handed her.

"How did you get that?" Winter asked, pointing.

Cloud quickly covered the raven amulet with her hand. "Thrush gave it to me." And then, "You recognize it."

"Of course I do," Winter said. "Otter made it for his sister. Now, let's look at your hands."

Winter ducked out again and Cloud followed, relieved that her aunt didn't try to take the necklace. Back at the hearth, Winter cleaned Cloud's palms and spread seal fat over the raw spots with a touch gentler than either her voice or manner.

Otter, the children, and the dog entered, and commotion filled the house. Winter ladled out the halibut stew. As the warmth from stew and fire soaked into Cloud's bones, she began to feel better. Whether Winter liked her, whether she comforted her as Glory would have—as Thrush would have, if she could have—Cloud would rather be here, protected from weather and malevolent spirits, than alone on a deserted beach.

It was extraordinary, though, to discover these two close relatives whose existence no one had even hinted at before. Aristocrats of the highest rank, every bit the equal of Thrush and Rumble, and yet they lived like commoners. It was a mystery.

Night gathered while they ate. Then the ancient woman, who hadn't spoken since Cloud had entered the house, suddenly cleared her throat, opened her withered mouth, and said to no one in particular, "Thrush, that one, she was married to Carrying-Summer-on-His-Back, king of all the birds of earth."

It was a signal. Winter's little girl curled up on her mother's lap; the boy, who was leaning against Otter, looked up expectantly.

And the old woman, whose name Cloud still didn't know, began a story she had never heard before, about how the thunderbird king had fallen in love with the divine and beautiful Thrush, whose song brings springtime to the forest. The thunderbirds carried her away to their home in the highest mountains, or perhaps it was heaven itself, and Thrush's husband and his bird warriors dressed as salmon and swam upriver to rescue her. It was strange to hear a story of the First People so close in parts to what had happened to the mortal Thrush, stranger still because it lacked the hurt of the mortal version, the griefs that could neither be spoken nor forgotten. The immortals didn't seem to suffer more than transitory pain when they died, and through fire or water they always came back to life. Death for them was like grief, a short season of darkness that always flowered into summer again and was forgotten.

It was a long story, full of adventure and clever ruses. When it was over, the little girl squirmed upright, rubbing her eyes with two small fists. Winter and Otter carried their children to their beds, which lay on a platform atop their own bedroom. And then those two, sister of Rumble and brother of Thrush, descended the ladder and came to sit beside Cloud.

"Now," said Otter, "you'd better tell us everything from the beginning. I didn't blindfold Bone's servants for long. So we need to know all about you, and why you're here, before we fight another battle with Bone."

"*Another* battle?" For the first time it occurred to Cloud that her arrival might bring trouble on them. Now she remembered Glory's warning to Wren, *Take her to Whale Town quietly! Or you might start what we've been dreading since Winter left.*

"From the beginning," Winter said. "From the first thing you remember."

So Cloud started from the day a year ago when she had awakened beneath the stairs of Storm House. She told them how Glory had taken her in, how Bone's servants couldn't find her vanished spirit mask, how she had lost not just her four-legged form but seemingly her four-legged nature as well.

Otter asked Cloud, "You don't have memories from before your transformation, anything at all?"

"At first I remembered being on four legs, a little. But then I forgot that, too." It embarrassed her to talk about her lost self, as though she thereby exposed her naked skin to the world. "I do have dreams."

"What dreams?" Winter asked, leaning forward.

Reluctantly Cloud told them about the little boys playing by the house in the forest. A grim expression settled on Winter's face. Otter stared into the fire. Cloud thought she must have offended them. But because Glory had said she should, she went on to tell Winter the other dreams, the awful ones about the skull in the tree and the dead children. "The ghosts are always begging me to help them. Thrush says they're my brothers."

"Thrush!" Winter looked away—angry again, Cloud thought. Or maybe very sad. Cloud had a hard time reading her new aunt's face. "I don't know what *I* can do," Winter said.

"Glory said you were a true seer."

"It's not that, child," Winter said, suddenly fierce. "Oh, I could look for your lost mask. But what would it matter? You still have to find it yourself. I can't show you that road."

"I'm not looking for my *mask,*" said Cloud. "It's gone!"

Winter went on as if Cloud hadn't spoken. "And your dreams, Cloud. I can't send away *ghosts.* If your brothers are calling you, it's because you *are* the only one who can save them."

"But how can *I* do anything?" Cloud said, frightened, angry, and again close to tears. "I'm not a seer or a wizard. I'm just an ordinary—whatever it is that I am. How do you save ghosts? And how will that stop Rumble and Bone from wanting me dead?"

Winter sighed. "I'll see what I can see. But it's late. Tomorrow—we'll talk more tomorrow."

Winter laid out bedding for Cloud on the floor along the outside wall. Some part of Cloud had hoped that her newfound aunt and uncle would take her into their room as Glory had. But she lay down on the mats they gave her and pulled up the furs.

The other residents of the house retired to their beds. Winter and Otter remained by the hearth. Cloud watched from under her covers. Otter gazed into the fire, talking so quietly even she couldn't hear the words. Winter looked angry, or distraught. "It's my fault," she said. "I should have—"

Otter put his arms around his wife. She leaned her forehead against his shoulder. Cloud thought she might be crying.

At last, sleep engulfed Cloud, and she found herself in the glade in the forest. Children wept nearby. Cloud knew if she lifted her gaze, she would see a skull tied in a tree. She looked at her feet instead. Half-hidden in the grass lay a huge and moss-stained thighbone. She stepped carefully over it.

Even that small movement caught the ghosts' attention. "Don't leave us alone," the children begged.

She didn't answer, focusing on her next step. But this time a splintered rib stabbed her instep and she sprawled among the thorny canes. "Don't go," wailed her dead brothers. "Save us."

"Shut up!" she screamed with sudden rage. "Let me go!" She yanked at her clothing, but the thorns would not release her.

Then she found herself in her bed again. The hall was dark, the hearth fire banked for the night. Winter and Otter had disappeared into their bedroom, leaving Cloud with only the drumming of the rain for company.

# SIX

# Winter

*A stinking muzzle sniffed her face. Cloud scrambled* up in terror, then saw the dog was Otter's. "Get away!" she hissed, pushing it so violently that its claws skidded on the floor.

She sucked in deep breaths without being able to calm her racing heart. Then she grabbed her cloak and ducked out into the rain. The cold air, smelling of seaweed and salt, steadied her.

This morning Whale Town looked even more empty. Only the smoke that billowed out of two dozen roof vents, veiling the knoll behind the houses, showed that many people lived here.

Otter was one of the very few abroad. He approached now along the beachfront path, the raw wind pulling hair from the knot atop his head. Blood of her blood, summer king of Sandspit Town: that slight figure still didn't look impressive to her. Now that she knew he was Thrush's brother, she could see an echo in the line of cheekbone and jaw, the curve at the corners of his mouth—but it wasn't obvious. Not like the resemblance between Winter and Rumble.

"Good morning, niece," Otter said as he came up to her. The greeting was courteous but lacked warmth. He and Winter were so remote and careful and neutral with her, as if she were something too hot or cold to handle without a pair of tongs.

"Good morning," Cloud replied awkwardly. Trying to gather courage, she looked toward the harbor, where a family of tiny harlequin ducks bobbed along the rocks. "Uncle, what's the name of your house?"

"It's not my house," Otter said. "It belongs to our cousins, though only two of them live here now. They call it Snag House."

"Is that a summer or a winter name?"

He smiled faintly. "Winter. It's called after the monster snag that tried to eat Wily One; maybe you know the story."

Cloud shook her head. "Uncle," she said, diving in, "why are you here? Why is Rumble taking care of Halibut House's wealth as though you don't even exist? Why doesn't anyone in Sandspit Town even speak your name?"

Otter's smile faded. "Rumble had other plans for Winter. He wanted to marry her to some king up north. We had a big fight about it, and Winter and I came here."

"But—" Cloud said.

He shook his head. "It would take all day to tell you the whole story. Let's go inside and eat, and then we will talk, because we have to decide what to do with you, niece."

Winter served them berry cake and roast venison for breakfast. With her bandaged hands, Cloud ate slowly, one eye on Otter's dog. If she looked away for an instant, it would crawl forward, tail thumping, to lie at her feet.

"Why don't you like Seal?" Otter's little girl asked, the third or fourth time Cloud shoved the animal away.

"What seal?" Cloud said, caught off guard. Small children usually shied from her.

"Not *a* seal. Seal is the *dog*."

"I don't like dogs," said Cloud. Winter and Otter both glanced up.

"Why not?" asked the little girl.

"Blizzard," said Otter, "don't bother your cousin. And you, Seal, come here! Sit down and stay!"

The dog hunkered beside Otter. "I'm not *bothering* her," said Blizzard. The little girl sat down a few feet from Cloud, sucking her thumb, looking so serious and downcast that Cloud would have laughed if it hadn't seemed mean.

After the meal, Otter's son and the Snag House man departed to cut wood, and Winter, ignoring Blizzard's protests, sent the girl off with the ancient woman. Meanwhile Cloud changed back into her own dress, yanked a comb Winter had given her through her hair, and rinsed her face. Glory had always made certain she tidied herself every morning, but Winter clearly wasn't going to trouble herself any more with her niece than she had to.

When only the three of them were left in the hall, Winter and Otter joined Cloud at the hearth. Otter took out his knife and began to whittle. Winter stared into the fire. It was a long time before either of them spoke.

At last Winter sighed. "Who would have thought that Thrush's four-legged child would come to me for aid, looking for all the world like Thrush returned to haunt me?" She shook her head. "But I shouldn't make the mistake of thinking you're like Thrush, should I? Would Thrush have set off on her own at—what are you now, thirteen? Looking for a town she'd barely heard of?" Winter glanced at Cloud. "You really don't know what happened to your mask?"

Cloud couldn't argue with Winter's implied criticism: she *had* been reckless to set out for Whale Town alone, without knowing where it lay, in the stormy season of the year— not that she had had much choice. But she didn't know why Winter kept harping on the subject of her former animal shape.

She said impatiently, "Bone's servants searched for it. They said it was lost beyond a hundred mountains. That it might lie in my father's house, or entirely beyond the world. They said they couldn't find their way to my father's house to look."

"Bone told you that?"

"No," said Cloud. "But that's what his servants said to him."

Otter looked up, and Winter raised her eyebrows. "You heard them?" Cloud nodded. "And saw them, too?"

"Yes."

They kept staring at her. "That kind," Winter said, "never gives a straight answer."

"Their answers sounded plain enough."

Winter snorted. "That kind never tells the whole story, not even to their masters. I wouldn't be surprised if your four-legged mask is wandering around somewhere, and they know something about it."

"They said it's *gone,* and I'm just like a human being now! They said I could never find my way to wherever it is."

"Niece," Winter said, "the immortals don't have to *find* their masks. They *call* them. I can't give you advice on how to do so. Those masks are the birthright of the immortals, and I'm only human. But I have a hard time believing that one day you'd be wearing a fur robe, and the next you'd have lost it forever. Your nature couldn't change immutably between sunset and dawn."

"But it did."

"Cloud," Winter said, "look, I'll start at the beginning. You do know about your father? I hope Glory told you that much."

Cloud shifted. "She said he was a wild animal with a taste for human blood. That he abducted Thrush and forced her to live as his wife. And he slaughtered everyone who went to look for her until Rumble killed him and brought Thrush home."

"Yes, he was a wild animal," Winter said. "That's more or less what happened. But you have to understand your father better if you are to understand your own nature."

Her *own* nature! Her father had been a vicious monster and Rumble had killed him. Rescuing Thrush from her torment had been a good thing, a heroic thing, maybe the best deed Rumble had ever accomplished. If Cloud's nature was truly like her father's, Rumble would be right to exterminate her as well.

"I lost my spirit mask," Cloud said. "I'm just a girl now. I'm Thrush's daughter, too."

"You are the child of mortal and immortal," said Winter. "Listen to me. Your father was one of the Winter People, the people of darkness, hunger, and storm. The Winter People ruled our world first. Their nature is to *want,* just as the nature of the Summer People is to *give.* The Winter People are wild, but they aren't all evil. All of the First People, Winter and Summer, can be dangerous to humans—or generous to them. Both sides are necessary to sustain the world. That's why, even though human nature partakes of both sides, we humans imitate the immortals by having summer and winter halves to our towns, each with its own king. It's why each half uses crests and names that refer either to Summer or Winter People, and why they take turns as each other's hosts or guests, and marry spouses from the opposite side. These are marks not only of our awe of the First People, but of our recognition that giving and taking are as necessary in human concerns as for the world as a whole.

"Now, when they come to our country, the First People put on their masks, and we only see what they show us. In their own country, when they take off their masks—that's another story. Wizards say that it's hard for mortals, even wizards and seers, to see the true face of an immortal. To see beyond what we fear or desire. A mortal can only bring back from the spirit world what he is capable of understanding. What Thrush saw of your father might have been more her own thoughts than his true face. Are you listening, Cloud?"

"I'm listening," said Cloud, "but I don't understand it."

"It's a hard thing to understand," said Winter. "Thrush was there, in your father's house, and she only came up to the edge of it. And turned away again."

"She was a captive! What else did she need to understand?"

"Yes, a captive," said Winter, "but of what? In the end, she just walked away while your father was sleeping."

"Rumble rescued her."

"Rumble killed your father when he came after Thrush."

Cloud's smoldering anger flared. "Are you saying that all my mother's suffering, all the people who died, that was just because of what she was afraid of? That she just *imagined* being *mauled* by that monster? That she brought it on herself?"

"She did bring it on herself," Otter said, looking up. "She insulted a king of the Winter People. What he did to teach her a lesson wasn't very nice, but the first rule, the *first rule,* is to treat the First People with respect. Always."

Cloud jumped to her feet. "You're blaming her! I don't want to hear any more!"

"Sit down, niece," said Winter. "Of course Thrush's suffering was real. I can see why you don't want to be like the father you've been told about, but Glory was right: you can't escape having *some* of his nature. Don't look so stubborn. Men starve in the wilderness and purify themselves until they bleed to gain the smallest shred of divine power."

"I don't want it," said Cloud. "I don't want *anything* that came from my father."

"You can't escape it," said Winter again, "although your inheritance might be like the rest of the unmasked world— its true shape hard for mortals to discern. But let's leave that for now. We need to talk about your dreams."

Her expression grew bleak. "You think I blame Thrush, but I blame myself, Cloud, in all ways. I so wanted it to be over. The years when Thrush was gone were dreadful. I knew something had gone wrong with Rumble even then. He was always burning up inside about Thrush, and when she came back, she had changed, and he couldn't let alone what your father had done to her. I should have tried harder to keep Thrush from marrying him. But Thrush felt so strongly that she had to atone, and it seemed like the best sacrifice she could offer. She felt she owed it to Rumble for his devotion and bravery, and she wanted something steady to cling to. Rumble seemed to be that thing. She didn't know what Rumble had done. I didn't either, not all of it, not until now."

"What do you mean?" Cloud asked. She sat down again. "What did Rumble do?"

"Before the feast where they ate your father," Winter said, "Bone cut your father's heart into four pieces and fed it to Rumble. The king of the four-legs is wild and strong, you see, and has no respect for any living thing, and he is rich beyond dreams. When Bone fed Rumble your father's heart, Rumble swallowed as much of this power as would fit inside him."

A log in the hearth collapsed. Winter fell silent, watching the sparks fly up toward the smoke vent.

"But my father was an animal," said Cloud. "I know hunters don't bring back four-legs often, because they're so dangerous, but we eat animal flesh all the time. Maybe I've eaten four-legs meat myself."

"I hope not," said Otter. "It would be cruel to feed you the flesh of your own kind."

"They're not my kind!" Cloud said. And then, "You said that men try to gain the power of the First People all the time. What did Rumble do that was different?"

Otter leaned forward, flicking shavings into the fire. "Cloud, the meat and fish we eat, the hides we tan, the bark women strip from cedars, the berries and roots we use—all the world that we see is the flesh of the First People, which they create when they put on their spirit masks. They give us these things. But there are rules. There is a covenant. I've watched you put your fish in the fire. Where did you learn that?"

"Glory told me to do it," Cloud said. "The bones have to be returned to fire or water, or the Bright Ones won't come again."

"Yes," said Otter. "Those are the rules. And there are other rules for other First People, be they of summer or winter.

But no matter what, we have to show the immortals gratitude and respect. We have to take care so that they can be
reborn. That's the covenant that sustains our world. And
Rumble deliberately broke that covenant. Not by eating your
father's heart. You're right: hunters sometimes do that to gain
the power of their prey, though it will alter your nature. It's
the other thing Rumble seems to have done. After they finished eating your father and brothers, Rumble took their
bones—"

"Wait," Cloud said. "They ate my brothers?" An icy current stirred in the pit of her stomach. "Glory said it wasn't
true!"

"Your brothers, too," said Otter.

"But no," said Cloud, "how could, Thrush couldn't—"

Winter said, "She wasn't there. Otter and I were taking
care of her, and you. But what were your brothers? Animal
flesh, Cloud—you said it yourself."

"No," said Cloud, sickened. She saw the little boys of her
dreams, splashing through the mountain creek. "My brothers were *human* children. Like me, like your son and daughter. How could even Rumble do something like that?"

Winter and Otter gazed at her with pity, the first Cloud
had seen in their faces. "They were four-legged, just as you
were then," Winter said. "When Rumble killed them, I don't
think he knew the four of you were Thrush's children. Rumble just wanted to save Thrush from your father, and you
belonged to your father's people. Otter and I had to fight to
keep him from killing you, too."

Winter hugged herself. "But afterwards . . . he had to
have done that part in cold blood. I would have tried to stop
it if I'd known, but I didn't notice the bones were missing. I
didn't even think about them until now. I did ask the men
later where they'd gone with Rumble, and they told me.
Some place north and east of Oyster Bay. But no one mentioned the bones.

"Rumble and his men were gone a half-turn of the moon.
The men said Rumble traveled the last stage with only Bone

as his companion. That's all I know. I just wanted it to be over, so I—I suppose I didn't want to know what Rumble had done. But I should have suspected, I should have tried to—"

"No," Otter interrupted. "Or else we were *all* at fault."

"I knew something had gone wrong with Rumble—"

"We all knew," said Otter.                         .

"But *I* could have *looked*."

It was like the argument Cloud had watched last night. Or maybe it was the same one: Winter angry and distraught; Otter trying to steady her.

"But what did Rumble *do*?" asked Cloud. They looked at her.

"I think," Winter said, "he and Bone tied up their ghosts, Cloud. Your brothers and your father. So they can't be reborn."

"But why?"

"Perhaps to keep their power in the mortal world where Rumble can get at it. I've wondered—he seems to grow stronger and more violent as years go by, as if he keeps eating more."

"But . . ." Cloud tried to absorb this. "Why wouldn't the other four-legs come to free their king?"

"I don't know—"

"And why do *I* dream of my brothers all the time? I never hurt them. Why are they always calling to *me*?"

"What do they say?" asked Winter.

"That I'm to save them. That there's no one else. They say their mother—they say Thrush abandoned them."

"In a way," said Winter, "she did."

"You said she didn't know what Rumble did!"

"Not then," Winter said.

Cloud remembered Thrush's anguish that day at the cranberry swamp. "They're your brothers," she had wept. When Cloud told her about the dreams, Thrush, like Winter, must have realized the whole of Rumble's crime. Cloud was filled with a rush of pity for her mother, who had loved her four-

mainland in the space of a few breaths! A wide bay spun as she, or what carried her, swooped to the waves. Cloud recognized the empty smokehouses of Oyster Bay. The bird did not land there, however, but swept north over a wide headland. Mountains gave way to water and another scatter of islands.

Then, up ahead: a glimpse of squared planks—a little house? Before they could reach it, a fierce wind flung them back. The bird labored once more between the islands until Cloud again caught a flash of wooden eaves among evergreen boughs. But again the wind twisted under them.

Now the bird flew up into mist. When it plunged downward, this time it managed to pass over the little roof, and follow the shoreline as it bent around into an eastward-reaching bay. But when the bird tried to turn over the forest, the wind tossed them violently to the far side of the bay.

Next her bird-canoe spiraled up and up until the overcast dissolved to reveal the vast blue roof of heaven. Now an ocean of white cloud stretched below them, lapping at a coastline of craggy peaks. A blinding sun shone on snow and cloud-top.

The bird winged through the waves of mist that broke against the mountain wall. Cloud expected it to soar down and try once more to penetrate the forest behind the little house. Instead, it swung the opposite direction, into the mountains.

They sped just above the channels of white that flowed between peak and peak, or they portaged over high passes into new straits beyond. Panic welled inside her when it occurred to her where they must be heading: somewhere inside this vast archipelago of mountain and cloud lay her father's house.

The bird flew up a last inlet of cloud, and finally they came ashore for good. Snow lay heavy on this high forest. Frozen rivers wound through the valleys.

As they winged ever farther inland, Cloud could feel a change. It was as if something warm as sunlight fell aslant the mountain air. Something scented the wind like balsam fir, touched her skin and filled the pit of her stomach with a wild tingling. Way off to the left—what were those snowy crags? Hadn't she dreamed of them a hundred times? Only hadn't they glowed then with the rosy blush of dawn, rather than the cold yellow of a winter's evening?

Terror and a strange exhilaration built in Cloud. But the bird winged onward, and soon another flank of mountain blocked her view. Slowly the eastern wall of the world drew closer until she thought she might reach out and touch it. On this ice-clear evening, the wall was like the glossy inner surface of a clamshell, an achingly rich purple bleeding into the dark blue zenith.

The bird rose in an arc, higher and higher, until they flew level with the highest mountain peaks. For a moment Cloud saw something immense but insubstantial rearing up against the sky, like shadow or smoke—a pillar?

Then the bird completed its turn, and they raced westward toward the sinking sun.

*Cloud came back to herself slowly, hard floor be-*neath her, the fire's warmth on her side. She sat up.

Nearby, Winter huddled on her mat. She looked exhausted. "That was hard work, niece—carrying you on my back."

"I . . ." said Cloud. Her mouth was scummy, as if she had slept a long time. "I didn't, I don't know how—"

"You've never traveled like that before?" Cloud shook her head. "I have to say I've never carried anyone before, either, on purpose or by accident. How did you do it?"

"I don't know. It just happened."

"What did you see?" Otter asked softly.

"Why don't *you* tell him?" Winter said to Cloud, with what sounded like a note of accusation.

"Well," Cloud said. She glanced from one to the other. "I—we went east to Oyster Bay and then north, to a little, well, it was like a tiny house. But we couldn't get into the forest behind it. And then we went east again for a long time, through the mountains, until we turned and came back."

"The mountains?" Otter glanced at Winter.

"I thought I'd try her father's house. But I couldn't find my way this time." Winter took a few unsteady steps to the water bucket, where she drank from the dipper. Then she sat again. "Carrying you on my back—I don't know what to say about that. And you go to that forest time after time in your dreams, while I couldn't enter it at all. Maybe it's part of your four-legged birthright. I'd say you're destined to be a wizard regardless."

Cloud said nothing. The thought of becoming like Bone made her skin crawl. Though Otter was a wizard, of course, and Winter a seer. They didn't seem unpleasant, just not very warmhearted.

"Did you see any place you recognized?" Otter asked. "Besides Oyster Bay, that is."

"No," Cloud lied, remembering the tingling in her belly, the shape of those distant crags.

Winter said wearily, "There was a little house, as Cloud said, on a point, and just north of there a wide bay. That's where something kept pushing me back. I've never been to that place in the flesh."

"I think I might know it," Otter said. "I stopped at a place like that once, a long time ago, when I was searching for the power to find Thrush. It was supposed to be the grave house of a famous wizard named Raven Tongue, a northerner."

"You could find it again?"

"I'm sure of it," said Otter.

"What's a grave house?" Cloud asked.

They looked at her. "The northerners lay out their dead wizards in little houses," said Winter. "Though I didn't know there were any wizards' tombs that far south."

"But," said Cloud, "doesn't that mean the wizards wouldn't be reborn? Their ghosts would stay with their bones?"

Winter shrugged. "The northerners say you can't burn a wizard's body, but we do it all the time. I think those wizards don't want to be reborn. Immortals, see, they come back to life as themselves. But humans have to pass through the womb again, and there we forget who we were. We're always reborn as someone new. If you were a wizard who didn't want to lose all your knowledge and power, you could have your relatives build you a cedar tomb so your bones wouldn't decay."

"Was it the dead wizard who kept us out of the forest?"

"I don't think so," said Otter. "I walked in that forest when I was trying to get the wizard's servants. There was nothing strange about it then. But it would be a good place to hide something. Most people would be afraid of the tomb, and even a wizard might not survive an encounter with those spirits."

*The entire short winter's day had passed while Win-*ter had flown into the mountains and back, and now the other residents of Snag House began returning. Otter climbed to his feet to prepare dinner. Cloud had never seen a man busy at the hearth other than a slave, but Winter wasn't recovering quickly from her flight. She looked drained and ill.

It embarrassed Cloud to see her uncle, the summer king of Sandspit Town, hauling water like a slave. Squatting unsteadily by the fire, she started breaking up soaked dried halibut with her scabbed hands. No one thanked her or seemed to take notice, as if this was just what they expected from her. When the stew was finished, Cloud ladled it out. Otter carried a bowl to his wife while Cloud served the other people.

She was still hungry after emptying her bowl. She supposed she could serve herself a second helping, but she didn't think Glory would have approved of such forwardness—or greed.

Blizzard came over to her. "You eat fast," she said.

Cloud blushed. "You're right."

Blizzard kept looking at her. Cloud had no idea how to talk to a child. "Why do you call your dog Seal?" she said finally.

Blizzard flashed a smile. "Because the Master of the Undersea keeps seals as his dogs. Don't you know that?"

"I never heard that story," said Cloud. Then curiosity overcame her distaste for the subject. "Doesn't it bother you that I used to be a four-legs?"

Blizzard started to giggle. "Are you going to eat me?"

"Of course not!" said Cloud, disturbed. "I eat salmon, just like you."

Still giggling, Blizzard ran to whisper in Winter's ear. Amused, Winter said, "She thinks you're funny, Cloud."

"She doesn't believe I used to be a four-legs."

"Oh, she believes it," said Winter. "She thinks you're a funny four-legs. You're not very fierce."

Blizzard clambered down again and, still giggling, returned to Cloud. "I'm *not* fierce," Cloud said. "Except . . ." She thought ashamedly of Radiance. "Except when I lose my temper."

**After dinner, the children listened to the old woman** tell stories. Cloud listened, too, trying not to think about her dreams or the day's long, strange flight. She imagined instead that she could stay here safe from Rumble and Bone. Winter and Otter would say, "Live with us as long as you want."

But she knew they weren't going to extend the invitation. They might not say so directly, but it was clear they wanted Cloud to leave. They expected her to go take care of her dead brothers' ghosts.

It wasn't fair. She *was* an ordinary girl, whatever they said. Her aunt and uncle should protect her from the misfortunes of her life, not send her out to right them by herself.

She watched them covertly. Blizzard now dozed in Winter's arms. Otter whittled at his stick of wood. Sometimes one would speak to the other so softly that Cloud, on the other side of the hearth, heard only an unintelligible murmur. It occurred to her that she had never seen Thrush and Rumble even looking at each other. Rumble shouted or threatened; Thrush pleaded. Or they stood apart and silent. It was strange that her aunt and uncle's quiet comfort with each other excluded Cloud more thoroughly than all the distance between Thrush and her husband.

The king of Halibut House and his queen scraping together a living like commoners, while Rumble sucked dry the wealth of the mother-line: Cloud suddenly hated her aunt and uncle for their foolishness. So she *had* brought trouble on them. Had they really thought, before her arrival, that Rumble would leave them alone forever? A king's heirs were his sister's children, and so far as she knew, Winter was Rumble's only sister. Someday Rumble would bear her children back to Storm House. Then Rumble would have the heirs of both royal mother-lines, and control over the wealth of both halves of Sandspit Town.

Winter and Otter already knew they weren't strong enough to stand against Rumble. Did they have any plan at all, or were they just trying to hoard time for themselves? Like a little crow that's stolen a piece of fish and is trying to gobble down as much as possible before a bigger bird grabs it away? Winter, Cloud thought, might not really care about Cloud's dreams or her brothers' fate. But she would want Cloud out of her house to protect her family, and her life with Otter.

The stories came to an end, and the residents of Snag House sought their beds. Cloud found her place of exile by the wall. Otter's dog wouldn't leave her alone until Otter came out of his bedroom and tied it by the door. The dog stared at Cloud, mournful, long after she had crawled under her furs.

In the night, she woke to the sound of barking and sat up in a panic, wildly disoriented: a rude house with no covering on the door, dim red coals in the hearth.

Then she heard the crash of waves: Whale Town. The barking dog, tied up near the door, belonged to her uncle Otter.

Otter came out to hush the dog. The two of them, wizard and dog, peered out into the rainy darkness for a long time before Otter returned to his bedroom.

**Then, all of a sudden, daylight showed beyond the** smoke vent and Winter was making a clatter. When Cloud sat up, Winter said to her, "Bone knows you're here."

"Did his servants come last night?"

Winter ignored the question. She was transferring sheets of berry cake from one box to another. "What chance is there," she asked, "that Rumble knows about your dreams? That he knows where you might go next?"

Cloud shook her head. "I only told Glory and Thrush. I never told Bone, no matter how many times he asked."

"That doesn't mean he hasn't found out." Winter sighed. "You'll have to leave today."

All the breath rushed out of Cloud's body. "Today?"

Winter was exiling her from their house already? How could she survive Bone's servants, much less the oncoming winter, by herself? Her aunt was sending her away to die!

Winter put the lid back on the chest, opened another, and began emptying it of bundled strips of dried venison. "Otter's readying the canoe now."

"He's going with . . ." Cloud inhaled shakily. "But—so soon?"

"Bone and Rumble are close on your heels. If Rumble's grown afraid of you, he'd do anything, I imagine, to keep you from reaching the place where they tied up your father's bones. You need to get there before they figure out what you're up to."

"Then why go there now? Why not go someplace safe instead, someplace far away?"

"The ghosts are calling you, Cloud. And you can't run forever. Your best chance against Rumble and Bone is to free your father's ghost. It would take away much of Rumble's power."

"I won't free my *father*!" said Cloud, horrified. "He's a monster!"

"Maybe."

"You don't even know if my father's there. He's never spoken to me!"

"His ghost must be there," said Winter. "His bones are."

Cloud wished Winter had not said that. It would mean that her father watched her silently, every dream. "I won't do it!"

"Glory told you to consult me," Winter said, "and I've given you my advice. You should release *all* the ghosts, and seek your four-legged mask—"

"Glory wanted me to be an ordinary girl!"

"You can't be what you aren't," said Winter. "Of course we'll help, but you must hurry. Bone will be here soon."

Cloud jumped to her feet and stalked away to wash. Winter wouldn't admit that she and Otter were simply too weak to protect her from Rumble, and too selfish to want to do so.

Cloud wondered if, once they were under way, she could appeal to Otter to take her to another destination, maybe to Aunt Wren. Maybe in the north they had wizards who, unlike her aunt and uncle, were strong enough to fight Bone and win.

When Cloud returned to the hearth, Winter, without saying anything further, handed Cloud fish with which to prepare the household's morning meal. Slaves' work. But who else in her uncle's house was going to do it?

Soon the other residents of Snag House joined Cloud at the hearth. Blizzard sat beside Cloud again, this time leaning her sleep-tousled head against Cloud's arm and flashing a brilliant smile. "Hello," Cloud said shyly. Blizzard's head reached only to her shoulder, and the child's hand, toying with Cloud's fingers, was half the size of her own. Cloud suddenly imagined Rumble carrying Blizzard away to Storm

House and the discipline of stern Aunt Snow. Fierce anger
flared in her—

—followed by a return of helplessness. She couldn't take
care of herself. How could she save anyone else?

After they had finished eating, Winter asked Cloud to
carry out the boxes she had been packing. One by one Cloud
hoisted them with her sore hands and bore them down to
the beach, where Otter loaded them into a large journeying
canoe.

Cloud had just brought him the last box when shouts
rang out from the knoll behind Whale Town. She didn't
catch the words, but beside her, Otter straightened. "Go inside, Cloud. Hurry."

"What is it?" Cloud asked. Otter took her arm and hus-
tled her up the path to Snag House. "What's happened?"

Winter met them at the door, grim-faced. "Rumble is
fast."

The two of them urged Cloud into the house, where
they made her crouch down in a narrow space between the
wall and a row of storage chests. "Stay here," Winter said.
"You mustn't move, do you understand? Or we can't protect you."

Cloud nodded, squeezing herself smaller as they hurriedly restacked boxes around and above her. Otter murmured something she could not hear. A weight settled on
the box over her head, a child or perhaps the dog. Her aunt
and uncle's footsteps crossed to the door, then crunched
along the shell-strewn path outside.

The only light in her hiding place came from a gap in the
outside wall of Snag House where the vertical planks did
not quite meet. By twisting her head, she could see a small
piece of foreshore and harbor through the gap.

Rain curtained the horizon, and this morning's tide had
risen so high it seemed as if it would flood the town. A few
houses down, Winter and Otter conferred with a handful of
Whale Town men who carried clubs and spears. The Whale
Town men gestured forcefully.

Cloud wriggled but could not ease the crick in her neck. More and more armed Whale Town men spilled into view, two dozen, fifty, a hundred. Winter and Otter headed back toward Snag House, Otter's dog trotting in their wake.

Now Cloud could hear a rhythmic splash and knock. A canoe appeared beyond the harbor entrance. It approached end-on, making it hard to measure how big the craft was. It kept coming, paddles lifting and dipping, for what seemed forever. The splash and knock grew steadily louder, blades biting the water in unison, striking the gunwales.

At last the canoe passed through the harbor entrance and aimed at the beach of Whale Town, foam curling in its wake. Now its size was revealed: over twenty armspans long, with at least that many men paddling. Painted thunderbird wings reached along the sides, and in the center of the canoe stood a motionless figure wearing a rain hat and cloak.

In a few strokes, the paddlers stopped the great canoe at the beach. Battle-axe in hand, the erect figure leapt to shore and strode up the path to where Winter and Otter waited in front of Snag House, not ten feet from Cloud's hiding place.

Rumble did not look at his sister. Without preamble he said to Otter, "Where is she?"

Otter said mildly, "Good day to you, brother-in-law."

At the sight of Rumble, Cloud was back in the forest behind Sandspit Town, suffocating as Rumble crushed his mouth against hers. Her first wild impulse was to burst free and run. Instead, she pushed the panic down into her belly and clapped hands over her mouth, exerting every bit of will to remain quiet.

Rumble's warriors followed him out of the canoe, but Whale Town men had already spread along the tide-narrowed beach and now crowded the visitors on both sides. Neither Otter nor Rumble appeared to notice these maneuvers, however. Rumble stood with his feet apart, the necklace of huge teeth slowly rising and falling on his chest. Rain dripped from the brim of his hat.

"Where is she?" Rumble demanded again.

"Whom do you mean?" said Otter.

Rumble's axe twitched. "You know who I mean. The little four-legs. I know she was here!"

Down on the beach two last figures had climbed out of Rumble's canoe, an old man with ropy gray hair and a woman's seaweed-draped corpse, and now they climbed the beach. The Whale Town men let Bone through and closed ranks behind him. Otter's dog began to bark, and whatever sat above Cloud's head shifted its weight.

"If you mean my sister's oldest child," Otter said, "yes, she was here."

Rumble pointed his axe at Otter. "I want her back."

"What would you want with my niece?" Otter asked. "She's a Halibut House girl, brother-in-law."

"A girl?" Rumble said. "An animal! You'd better tell me where she's gone."

"No, no," Bone said, hobbling up to Rumble. "The girl is here. He's just hidden her from me—for the moment."

Otter glanced at Bone, and their eyes locked. "Concealing her," said Otter, "is my prerogative." He held out his palm. Upon it sat something Cloud could not see well, a knot of twine, perhaps. Bone's gaze flicked toward it; he grabbed—

But Otter tossed it at the drowned woman. The little knot vanished, and Bone's servant dissolved like snow in seawater.

Rumble took a step toward Otter, raising his axe. "This beast is *my* quarry, little boy, and you had better not get in the way when I am hunting!"

The anger that always seemed to coil inside Rumble pushed outward. Rumble looked half again Otter's weight; now he seemed to grow a hundred times as solid. He might as well have been a rockslide roaring down a mountain, and Otter a blade of grass.

But Otter ignored Rumble. He was still watching Bone.

Trembling, hands over her mouth, Cloud knew what was going to happen. Rumble would slam his axe into her uncle's head, and Otter would crumple to the ground. The Whale Town men would leap on Rumble's warriors, thinking their far greater numbers made them invincible. But Rumble would explode in his killing frenzy. It would be like the·slaves ten times over: screams, the crack of shattering bone, and when it was over, men strewn like dead seals along the foreshore, blood mixing with the rain.

Maybe Rumble would kill Winter, too, and Cloud would have no one to protect her.

But instead Rumble lowered his axe and said, in an entirely different tone, "Who's this boy?"

Cloud twisted her neck a final painful inch to see what Rumble pointed at. It was Otter's son. Winter gripped the boy's shoulder as if she had caught him in the act of dashing forward. Winter's knuckles were white, her face hard as stone.

"Your son?" Rumble bent to look at the boy. "What name did my sister give him?"

"Thunder Follows Him," Otter said, watching Bone. The boy stood wide-eyed and wordless.

"A thunderbird name," Rumble said with satisfaction. "A good name for the future king of Storm House. And look how well grown he is already. Soon it will be time for him to come home for his education. You don't want people to say he's soft like a man brought up by his father."

"No, indeed," said Otter.

Then Winter spoke in a hard, flat voice: "He will come back to Storm House only when you are gone from it."

Cloud knew that a grown brother and sister spoke to each other only with greatest courtesy, so there was something particularly awful about the searing gaze Rumble cast upon his sister. Then, without another word, he spun on his heel and stalked down through the jittery circles of men, Whale Town and his own, to his great canoe. The Whale Town men drew aside; the Sandspit Town men followed him. Bone held back. He smiled gently at Winter and Otter, lines creasing his wrinkled old face. "You youngsters should not forget there are a dozen ways to twine a net. The fish meets the same fate regardless."

Then he, too, turned and hobbled down to the water, and soon Rumble's canoe was forging rapidly across the harbor.

Otter and Winter stood in silence in the pouring rain. The Whale Town men muttered among themselves. A sturdy man near Otter said, "He'll be back with more men."

"I'm taking the girl away," said Otter wearily. "Bone will know we've left and they'll follow us. They'll leave Whale Town in peace—at least for the moment."

"Let them come!" said the Whale Town man.

Otter and Winter turned toward Snag House. Cloud heard their footsteps and then Otter's muffled voice. The box above her creaked as whatever sat on it scrabbled from its perch. It was too light, she realized, for either a child or a dog.

Otter shoved the boxes aside to release Cloud into the now spacious-seeming gloom of Snag House. She crawled out, trembling, to sit upon one of the boxes. Winter was shoving objects into a large leather bag: awls, a comb, coils of twine, shredded cedar bark, and more. "Go on, get ready," she said sharply to Cloud. "Where's your rain cloak?"

Cloud pushed herself to her feet, tottered across the hall, and swung her cloak to her shoulders. Winter closed up the bag and brought it to Cloud, along with a rain hat and a carrying strap. Then she hurried Cloud out the door. Otter already waited outside with his own pack. Cloud barely had time to arrange the strap across her shoulders and settle the bag on her back before Otter set off. She glanced behind her. Winter stood at the door without a gesture or word of farewell.

Cloud hurried after Otter. He did not head for the canoe they had loaded but turned the other direction, onto a path that wound up the side of the granite knoll behind Whale Town. The path smelled of wet stone and sphagnum moss. Otter strode up easily; Cloud stumbled and slid after him. The dog ran beside Cloud, nosing at her, until she smacked it away.

At the top of the knoll stood the watchmen who had warned the town of Rumble's approach. As Cloud trotted past them, conscious of their gaze upon her, she searched the ocean for Rumble's canoe. It had already disappeared into the rain.

Not until the trail had descended the inland side of the knoll did she finally catch up with Otter. "Where are we going? Why are we walking?"

"We're crossing the island," he said. "Winter will bring our canoe around by sea and return this way. That will send Bone's servants in circles for a while—I hope."

For the rest of the short day they hiked through a gloomy, dripping forest. Cloud's feet soon grew sore from stumbling over roots, and despite the hat Winter had given her, every swagging branch spilled more rainwater down her neck. But the exertion kept her warm, and in the open air, her trembling faded at last.

As the daylight waned, she smelled seaweed and heard the rush of breaking waves. Otter led her to a shelter above a small gravel beach. They camped there that night without a fire. Otter's smelly dog kept snuffling near her head, though Cloud would have been too cold and anxious to sleep well regardless. At least the dog did not bark, which meant, she hoped, that Bone's servants had not yet found her.

Voices woke her before dawn. Cloud climbed down to the beach to find that Otter's journeying canoe had arrived. Its crew waited on board. Winter and Otter stood on the beach with their children: the boy was quiet under Otter's hand, but little Blizzard clung to her father, face pressed into his side.

Cloud slowly crossed the beach, aching to be with them, knowing she didn't belong.

"You should come with us," Otter was saying to Winter. "I'll drop you at Round Bay Town, or—"

"*They* won't protect us." Winter sounded very tired. "At least Whale Town has old scores to settle with Rumble. Anyway, it's the girl he wants at the moment."

"I don't like leaving you unprotected."

"I'm not unprotected," said Winter. "And you can't stay with me. The girl can't go alone."

Cloud stopped, again remembering the hushed conversation between Glory and Wren, only a few days past but belonging to a distant age. Cloud *had* begun the thing they dreaded: a fight between Rumble and Otter, perhaps war between the two towns.

It might have been inevitable that Rumble would come to Whale Town, but Cloud had caused *this* moment. She didn't have to partake of her father's nature to drag bloodshed in her wake.

Cloud thought then that she ought to run away into the forest to face Bone's servants alone. Or she ought to return to Sandspit Town to meet the fate Rumble planned for her. Anything else would cost too much.

But as she hesitated, Winter and Otter turned toward her.

"It's time to go," Winter said to her children. "We have to start back to town."

The boy hugged his father and released him. But Blizzard sobbed wildly, clinging to Otter. "Don't go, don't go."

Otter gently pried her loose and kissed the top of her head. "I'll be back very soon," he said.

"No!" screamed Blizzard, tears streaming down her face. "No! No! No!"

# SEVEN

# Otter

*Otter's crew paddled a day and night and another* whole day before they finally stopped to sleep. They crossed many miles of ocean in that time but passed only a scatter of islands and no sign of human habitation, not even another canoe. Cloud guessed Otter had chosen their route for that very reason.

Their course led them far north of the flight she had taken with Winter, and she no longer had a bird's view of the world, so she became lost soon after their departure. She sat behind her uncle and his dog, huddled into her rain cloak, staring at the swells. Rain pattered ceaselessly on her hat. Three crewmen paddled in front of Otter; three others, including the steersman, labored behind Cloud. No one spoke much. The canoe smelled of brine and wet dog, of wet cedar-bark rain cloaks and tunics, of smoky boxes packed with dried salmon.

Otter alone of the men rested his paddle from time to time. Sometimes he would cock his head, and Cloud would hear a mysterious birdlike piping. At other moments he would mutter so softly that his words were drowned by the splash of paddles, or he would touch one of the amulets at his neck and close his eyes, appearing to sleep. Watching him made the hair on her neck prickle. She supposed he was engaged in wizardry to keep Bone's servants from their trail.

She spent much of the first day hungry. Otter, anxious to start as quickly as possible, had set out without eating and did not call a halt until afternoon. Glory had taught her not to complain, so Cloud said nothing, even though the boxes carrying food sat just in front of Otter. She had to wonder if he was simply impervious to hunger, or if his stomach now hurt like hers, if the hollow inside him was also growing larger and more achy with every moment, until his soul seemed to consist of one giant pang. That was hard to believe. No one would choose to endure such deprivation if they didn't have to.

So many things she did not want to dwell on and she had nothing to distract her from her thoughts; they had not given her a paddle, and anyway her hands were too sore to use one. After a while Cloud followed the example of Otter's dog and curled against a storage box to sleep.

But she was soon roused by that high-pitched piping. This time it resolved into words: "What you asked for is done, master. I have coiled your trail like a rope around a tree, I have tied a knot at every pass, I have made the bark of the tree grow over it. The wolves sniff in vain for the spoor of the mice."

Cloud lifted her eyelids. On the gunwale beside Otter perched a small creature with brown, rain-misted fur. Otter, paddle poised in midair, murmured a reply too soft to hear.

She jerked upright, blinking. But the gunwale was empty. Otter paddled as though nothing had happened.

She recalled the weight on the boxes over her head in Snag House, the sound of claws on wood. Otter must possess a wizard's servant of his own. Winter hadn't mentioned it when disparaging such spirits, and neither had Otter. But then he didn't speak much regardless. Cloud curled up again, now too unsettled for sleep.

When they finally came ashore to eat, Cloud had to use all her self-control not to bolt her share of the meal. The men took extra filets of dried fish to keep with them, and no one looked askance at her when she did likewise.

She slept fitfully in the canoe that night, trying to keep her hands and feet tucked under her furs, and the furs dry under her cloak. By the next morning, rain had soaked the furs anyway.

The second day was even colder and more uncomfortable. At last, long after nightfall, they landed at a campsite on a sandy beach. Cloud climbed out stiffly, wiping her runny nose with cold hands. The first words Otter spoke to her since their departure were to direct her to one of the camp shelters. The crewmen moved toward the others.

Her shelter smelled of rotting bark. While Otter lit a fire, she spread sleeping mats on the ground. Cloud wanted to talk, but all the subjects burning in her thoughts seemed too terrible to broach, and he did not open his mouth. And Glory always told her not to bother people with questions. Cloud might not be able to become a proper girl, but she could act as much like one as possible.

So they ate and drank in silence. The dog chewed its own piece of deer meat. Then Otter stretched out beside his dog and closed his eyes. Cloud lay down as well, wrinkling her nose at the wet dog's smell. She could not sleep; uncomfortable as the canoe had been, she would rather be hurrying forward. Bone's spirits would not stop to rest, would they?

On the other side of the shelter, Otter murmured, "What have you seen and done?"

At first she thought he was talking in his sleep. But that birdlike voice answered:

"I have traveled far and wide, master. Two brothers hunting for deer became lost; two who hunted for seals found their game. The west wind shifts to the southeast."

Cloud turned her head as quietly as she could. A small shape sat atop Otter's chest. Firelight glowed on its fur. Its face reminded her of a mink's, though it had a blunter nose, and it did not smell of shellfish and musk as a mink did.

"So," Otter murmured. He looked bone-tired even in the dim firelight. "Two of Bone's servants are still searching, but two are looking for other game, have gone on another errand—southeastward? Why would they do that?"

Said the little servant, its gaze fixed on Otter: "The sea hunter fashions his harpoon. The black canoe is coming—"

"All right!" said Otter. "Leave those two servants for now. You must watch the two who are still looking for us, and help me hide our trail from them."

The spirit took a step, then glanced back toward Otter. "What is it?" Otter asked.

"The black canoe is coming."

"Yes, yes," said Otter. "Now go and guard our trail."

The servant swiveled its head to stare at Cloud. Her heart pounded wildly as she gazed right into its dark and shiny eyes. Its face, she realized, was the one tattooed on Otter's cheek.

The spirit hopped down and slipped into the night.

*For the next two days the expedition set out at first* light and paddled until long after dark, stopping to sleep for only a few hours each night. They wound through islands big and small. Every so often Otter would have them paddle the canoe backward, or circle an islet first sunwise and then in reverse. Cloud did not see Otter's servant again.

By listening to the sporadic talk of the weary crew, she began to learn their names. Listener, the bowman, was the oldest, a humorous, gray-haired man. The lean steersman they called Invincible. The mustached warrior with shark heads tattooed on his forearms bore the incongruous nickname Squeaky. Invincible's two cousins, the brothers Harrowing and Fortitude, sat between Cloud and the steersman. The youngest crewman, Brant, came from a Whale Town house with the memorable name of Wily One's Bottom.

The men, Cloud learned, had made other journeys with
Otter. Despite Otter's less than commanding demeanor,
they deferred to him—perhaps, she thought, because he was
a wizard, or perhaps because he would have been a king in
Sandspit Town.

On the fourth day, a huge black-and-white shape erupted
from the ocean not ten yards away and fell back with a thun-
derous crash. Cloud started in terror. Then a seeming multitude swarmed past: sleek giants leaping and crashing, or
streaming along at the surface, tall black fins cutting the
sea. The men stopped, paddles checking in midair. The canoe rocked in the turbulence. Otter prayed softly: "Welcome, great hunters, it is good that we meet today; protect
us so that no evil may befall us, great spirit powers, divine
ones."

Otter twisted in his seat to watch the creatures swim away.
When Cloud caught her breath, she asked, "What are they?"

He looked at her as if he had forgotten she was there.
"Orcas."

Orcas—of course. She had never seen them so close. She
wondered if they could be the ones Stick had pointed out to
her last summer on the way to Oyster Bay. That trip, with
its warm sun and sparkling vistas of ocean, was so different
from this cold journey full of dread.

In the afternoon, the clouds lifted and the Mountain
Land appeared for the first time. The mountains were star-
tlingly close now, their snowy flanks rearing halfway to the
zenith before disappearing into the overcast. Cloud began to
think that they would after all reach her brothers' ghosts before Rumble and Bone found them.

But as the afternoon wore on, the sea began to slap rest-
lessly, and dark, curdled clouds streamed out of the southeast. A rising wind beat the water to a heavy chop. Even
Cloud could see that the approaching storm had caught
them in a bad place: the ocean to the southeast lay open for
many miles, while the shore off the port bow was all reefs
and steep rock.

From the bow, Listener yelled over the noise of the wind, "Did Bone call this storm?"

"I don't think so," Otter yelled. "But we'd better make for Willow Beach as fast as we can."

Listener began to shout, "Hai! Hai! Hai!" and the men paddled double time to his chant.

They gained speed. Invincible steered the canoe farther from shore. But the wind kept building, and the chop grew quickly into charcoal-dark, foam-capped swells. Rain whipped in gusts. The dog huddled miserably at Otter's feet.

Cloud found a bailer and, moving aside the bottom boards, began tossing water over the side. She told herself that this wind was ordinary, that Otter's big journeying craft would be much harder to capsize than her little canoe had been, that with a wizard and six other crewmen paddling she would surely reach protected waters in safety. Her uncle, who had saved her before, would not let her drown this time, either.

Otter offered no such reassurance. Like the other men, he paddled with grim concentration. Soon the canoe was climbing swells taller than the side of a house, dropping on the far side as if sliding down a hill. Rain and spray blasted horizontally. Water poured into the canoe faster than she could bail it out.

But at last an island loomed out of the rain on the starboard bow. Invincible guided them past a reef and into a deeply indented cove where the canoe coasted over flat water. Cloud slumped, weak with relief.

Otter slumped, too, rubbing his face. "We almost made it."

*Almost?* They had reached safe waters, hadn't they?

Then Cloud realized Otter meant their ultimate destination. "Can't we hide from Bone until the storm is over?"

"I'll do my best," said Otter. He was already exhausted, though. His arms hung limply, and dark skin sagged beneath his bloodshot eyes. He did not look capable of any defense at all.

Willow Beach was no more than a stretch of tumbled boulders where a stream emptied into the cove. Behind the willows that had given the place its name, someone had taken the trouble to build a frame on a platform of logs and dirt, a sign of how much people valued this otherwise poor landing.

Despite their weariness, the men set up camp swiftly, removing mats and bottom boards from the canoe to lash against the frame. Then they spread mats inside and started a fire from the slow match they carried with them. By now rain fell in a noisy deluge and the trees surrounding the cove moaned and thrashed in the wind. Cloud crawled into the smoky shelter gratefully, followed by her uncle, the wet dog, and the six Whale Town men hauling supplies. The dog promptly shook itself.

They lived in that shelter for three days. They ate meals cheek by jowl; they slept practically in each other's arms. Cloud's place lay between Otter and the side of the shelter. This was the wettest, dirtiest, most drafty spot, but the alternative was to be crammed against one of the men, and it was strange enough to lie down so close to her uncle, who was a relative. At night she just turned her back and covered her head with her blanket. The dog slept on her feet. She would have kicked it away, but there was absolutely no other place for it.

The shelter smelled of wet dog, of smoke, and stronger day by day, of unwashed men. Otter's crew slept a great deal, recovering from the grueling journey. At other times they talked in fits and starts. The big handsome man they called Squeaky explained his plan to harvest tooth shells and trade them in the south for obsidian. Listener kept joking about an affair he claimed Invincible was having with an apparently notorious widow. Fortitude sang a beautiful melody about mountain goats. Listener and Fortitude traded bawdy stories: Wily One marrying a frog. Wily One plotting to seduce his stepdaughter. Wily One and the daughter of the river.

Meanwhile rain poured down on their shelter as if from a bucket, the gale roared in the treetops, and waves thundered outside the cove. In contrast to his men, Otter looked more tired every day. He spent hour after hour lying down, eyes closed, hands folded over his amulets. At other times, he whittled. His little carving now sported eyes on each side of its beak, and a hint of gracefully folded wings.

Every night Cloud dreamed of her brothers. The dreams had not changed. Her brothers' ghosts pleaded with her. She tried to flee the glade, but every time her father's bones tripped her. She dreamed of other things, too: of running behind Thrush, desperate to catch up; of dogs with bloody mouths.

During the day she sat quietly as she had since leaving Whale Town, mindful of Glory's strictures on talking in front of strange men. She was at first too shy to speak regardless, even though she could not stand her own thoughts, and she came to hate the chatter of the men. Otter, while he seemed more or less well disposed toward her, said little to anyone. She felt as if she, too, had become a ghost, and at the same time as exposed as an animal trapped by a deadfall, waiting for the hunter's arrival. She felt horribly responsible for bringing them all here, perhaps to die with her.

Cloud had brought the bag Winter packed for her into the shelter, and on the first morning she emptied it: comb, sewing kit, slate knife, pestle, bark-beater, adze, twine, several flattened baskets, coils of spruce and cedar root, soft shredded cedar bark for menstrual napkins and a dozen other uses, a digging stick of yew. Cloud cut a length of twine, put away everything but twine and comb, and dressed her tangled hair.

On the third day Listener and Squeaky fell into an argument about the best route to take from here. Squeaky thought they should head north around the island, while Listener felt that would take them too far into the territory of the Gull Islanders, a people with whom Whale Town did not seem to be on the best of terms.

Otter flicked away a shaving. "The southern route, I think, and then straight across the bay." That stopped the argument.

One of the mats jerked free and began to flap noisily, spraying rain into the shelter. Invincible crawled outside to tie it down. Cloud couldn't stand her silence any longer.

"Uncle," she said. Otter, startled by her voice, turned around. "Uncle, who are the Gull Islanders?"

He blinked. "The Gull Islanders are the residents of the Gull Islands, an archipelago that lies north and west—" He pointed. "You could just see them from here on a sunny day. The Islanders claim hunting territory in these parts and drive out all others, so we'd like not to attract their attention."

Cloud searched for another question that wasn't too frightening to ask. "Uncle, you said the tomb we're headed for belonged to a famous wizard. How was he famous? Winter hadn't heard of him."

"Raven Tongue?" Otter looked down at his carving. Cloud knew he would rather think his own thoughts. She knew it was wrong to pester him with questions. But it made her angry that he would only talk to her, his niece, with great reluctance.

"Well, not many know about him nowadays," Otter said, "because his people moved away. But he was powerful and lived to a great age, and he performed many impressive deeds in a war his people fought with the Gull Islanders."

Invincible stirred. "Raven Tongue belonged to my great-grandfather's people. Grandfather used to tell us about him. He was so powerful that eight spirits served him. Once he forced Islanders out of their fort and to their deaths by persuading a frog to drain the water from their spring. Another time, he drowned an enemy wizard by dropping a hot coal into a basket of water."

Cloud, shivering, wondered if Bone would attempt to kill Otter with a trick like that. She decided that she loathed wizardry. "Did he do anything besides kill people?"

"He was protecting his *own* people," Invincible said. "In the end they had to flee, and Raven Tongue died in the north. His nephews brought his body back to the point where he used to watch for his foot servants returning. The Islanders didn't interfere—they were still too afraid of him, and his servants."

Otter had resumed carving. Cloud's anger grew: at Invincible for silencing him, at Otter for allowing it.

"Why are they called foot servants?" she asked. The question sounded abrupt and impatient even to her ears.

Invincible said, "That's a subject for a wizard."

An uncomfortable silence ensued. Otter scraped away another flake. The other men began talking about the exploits of a northern warrior named Giant Face. Cloud had just decided that her uncle intended to speak to her as little as possible when he said, in a low voice, "They are called foot servants because they do a wizard's traveling for him."

It was clear he meant his answer only for her ears. These were not public matters. "But," Cloud said in the same low tone, "Winter doesn't use a servant to travel."

"Winter can fly on her own better than any wizard I know, including myself," said Otter. "And as she told you, wizards' servants aren't reliable. They love riddles and talking in circles, or they give you only half the story and never say so. Some people say they take pleasure in confusing mortals, but I think it's their nature. They can't be any other way."

"But then why do wizards use them?"

"Some servants are very strong," said Otter, "and some wizards have very little power otherwise."

Cloud hated wizardry, but this topic was better than not talking at all. "Uncle, when your servant told you, 'The west wind shifts to the southeast,' why did you think it was talking about Bone's servants traveling southeast? Didn't your servant say *exactly* what happened? The weather was from the west when we left Whale Town, and now it's shifted to the southeast."

He lifted his head. "What do you know about my servant?"

Cloud wondered if she had broken another rule of wizardry. "It comes and talks to you."

"Oh, that's right. You can see them, can't you?" He settled back. "If only I could be certain of what my servant tells me. He helps in many things, but he's a worse riddler even than most others of his kind. And all divinations can have more than one true meaning as well as many false ones. But in this case I had set him to watch Bone's four servants, and he riddled me first about the four brothers hunting."

Cloud digested this. "But what about the black canoe? Rumble's canoe is painted."

"You're right," Otter said. "I don't know yet. It could be a real canoe, or something that travels like a canoe—a whale or orca, for example."

Right then one of the men, who had started the evening meal, interrupted with a question for Otter about their supplies. Cloud had no further opportunity to speak to him.

Otter woke her in the middle of the night, when the fire had burned to red embers and his tattoo was only a shadow on his cheek. Cloud sat up. Outside, the wind and rain had fallen silent. Even the waves no longer crashed so thunderously. "We're lucky," Otter said. "A storm this time of year could have lasted for weeks."

By the first light of dawn they threaded the still-turbulent reefs outside the cove, and then they followed the shore south to a wide bay. Snowy mountains walled in that bay. The overcast had lifted high enough to reveal, through one sheer pass, the eastern clouds aflame with orange and red.

Invincible set their course due east, at an angle to the swells that still rolled across the bay. Today Otter's canoe rode the waves as sleekly as a porpoise. Cloud was relieved to be free of the confining shelter, but fresh and almost intolerable dread settled on her as they approached the source of her nightmares.

Halfway across the bay, a pair of large canoes slipped out of a break in the cliffs and sped toward them. Cloud experienced a moment of panic. The strangers, fierce-looking men in armor, outnumbered Otter's men three to one, and Otter's crew had no weapons at hand. But Otter's men waited calmly while the strangers swept up to them. A warrior in the lead canoe shouted. Listener stood up and the two called back and forth in words Cloud did not understand. At length the strangers' canoes returned the way they had come.

Otter's crew followed them into the gap in the cliffs. At closer range it proved to be a steep-sided inlet perhaps a half-mile across. On one side, a cascade poured down a terraced cliff. High on the cliff, beside the waterfall, a large palisade clung to rock like a sea anemone. Smoke trailed from housetops barely visible beyond it.

**They followed the strangers' canoes to the base of** the waterfall. The town kept most of its canoes afloat there, secured to wooden piles driven into the cliff. Armed men guarded the canoes and the icy stone shelf that served as a landing. There was more talk between Listener, the guards, and the warriors in the canoes that had preceded them. "Gull Islanders have killed four people this season," Listener translated. "That's why they're so watchful."

Guards held their canoe while Otter, the dog, and the crew disembarked. Then it was Cloud's turn. Two feet of dark green, icy water separated the canoe from the landing. She climbed onto the gunwale, teetering as she hiked up her dress.

"Here, Cloud." Otter extended his hand. She took it gratefully and jumped to the landing.

When the crew had secured the canoe, the guards led them up a log stair to a well-worn trail. This zigzagged up the snow-covered terraces to a heavy plank wall angled out over the cliffs. The waterfall poured from under the palisade.

"A good fort," Squeaky shouted over the thunder of the

cascade. "If they have a trail into the interior for hunting, it would be hard to starve them out."

Cloud made the mistake of peering over the edge of the cliff. The canoes at the landing looked very small.

A narrow door in the palisade opened, and she followed Otter into a very odd sort of town. A double handful of houses were jammed behind the palisade along both banks of the stream. People spilled out of the houses to crowd what little open space remained. Slaves hauled water or packed firewood; women flensed hides while children batted at a shuttlecock. Warriors stood sentry on the palisade. A breeze eddied among the houses, mixing the smells of fir needles, wood smoke, human skin, curing meat, and cold wet stone. The people dressed like those of Sandspit Town with one exception: men, women, and children wore moccasins or hip-high boots like leggings. Stepping along the snowy path with bare feet, Cloud could understand why.

The people watched them pass. Cloud started when one boy yawned to reveal a brilliant red cod peering from his mouth. Then she noticed other spirits: an armored woman with a dorsal fin between her shoulders; a sticklike man squatting atop the palisade.

"Cloud," Otter said. "Stay close."

She hurried toward him. He put his hand on her shoulder and drew her to his side. Encouraged by the gesture, Cloud asked, "What is this place, Uncle? Why are we stopping here?"

"This is Waterfall," Otter said, "and these people abandoned their old town and built this fort because of endless raids by the Gull Islanders, which seem to be a hazard of living in this region. Since we don't want to risk *their* warriors mistaking us for Islanders, we are stopping to ask permission to travel the last stage of our journey."

They crossed the stream on a large plank. Beyond, a higher terrace with more houses overlooked the palisade and the dark ocean beyond. The turbulent clouds had lifted further,

dark and light rolling together and tumbling past the
newly revealed shoulders of the mountains.

The height offered a view back to the island where they
had weathered the storm. With a jolt, Cloud realized where
they were. She had seen this bay from Winter's back. To the
south, still half-veiled with rising shreds of cloud, lay
the point Winter had not been able to cross, the tomb of the
famous wizard Raven Tongue. There waited the bones of her
father and brothers.

*Outside the largest house stood a tall old man*
dressed in plain buckskins. Listener introduced him as
Shining Down, the summer king of Waterfall. The king's
face was lined and his hair and beard had turned white, but
he had such a resonant voice and imposing posture that next
to him Otter seemed a mere boy. The king, however, greeted
Otter as an old friend, and through Listener offered hospitality as courteously as if Otter had in fact come straight from a
royal seat in Sandspit Town.

"I must tell you," Otter said, "that my brother-in-law is
pursuing us. His wizard has been trying to follow our trail."

When Listener translated this speech, the king raised his
eyebrows. But he said, "Should I turn away my friend because of that? The servants of every wizard in Waterfall keep
watch day and night, and they will spot Bone's emissaries as
easily as spirits from the Gull Islands. We'll chase away your
enemies long before they reach Waterfall."

Otter looked relieved. "I thank you, my friend, for your
generous welcome."

Otter tied up his dog, and the king ushered them into
his dwelling, which Listener told them was called Celestial
House. Cloud followed Otter through running children,
stacks of firewood, storage boxes, looms, dogs chewing bones,
racks of drying deer meat, gossiping old men, and old
women weaving baskets. The king seated Otter in the place
of honor at the rear of the hall. "Here, Cloud," Otter said,
gesturing at the neighboring spot. She sat self-consciously,

unused to the privileges of rank. Otter's crew took places along one side of the hearth.

An elderly man, his eyes closed, lay on the platform nearby. A boy whispered into his ear. Without opening his eyes, the old man said, "We will indeed keep guard for you, friend Otter." Unlike the king, he spoke in the tongue of Sandspit Town.

Otter smiled and bowed his head. "I thank you, friend Mouse."

Cloud at first thought old Mouse must be blind, and the boy was his helper. Then, as Mouse sat up, the boy straightened, staring at Cloud. His pale eyes weren't eyes at all, but openings into fog . . .

He shrank to the size of a fly and swooped up through the smoke vent as if the sky sucked him out of the house. Cloud shuddered, hugging herself.

The king asked Otter a question and Listener translated it. "I know your men, but who's this pretty girl? She looks just like your sister."

"She is Thrush's daughter," Otter told the king, through Listener.

"I thought that girl was living in Sandspit Town with her mother."

Cloud steeled herself for the revelation: this is the four-legged child; she lost her fur robe. But Otter just said, "She's staying with me now."

The old king nodded. Cloud let out her breath, half-grateful, half-uneasy that Otter was allowing the king to think she was Thrush's *other* daughter.

A pair of girls Cloud's age served out dishes of steaming, fatty mountain-goat ribs. Despite her fierce appetite, Cloud forced herself to nibble delicately at them.

The hearth fire thawed her snow-numbed feet. Otter relaxed into his seat, stretching his legs in front of him. A steady incomprehensible babble filled the king's hall. Dozens of men, women, and children watched her and Otter, but without those sideways, nervous glances Cloud hated so much. It was strange to be where people did not know she was a bear. They must think her a very dirty and disheveled princess, though.

She finished the ribs, wishing fervently for a second helping. But Otter had not taken the one that was offered him, and Cloud was sure a well-brought-up princess did not eat more than her uncle. The girls brought shredded cedar bark so she could wipe the fat from her hands and face. Cloud wondered if she would be able to wash properly later on.

Then the king turned to Otter, who straightened, stifling a yawn. "Now, my friend," the king said, "you may tell me what brings you to this troubled shore in winter, with King Rumble and his wizard dogging your heels. I do not suppose you came to sell us whale oil."

Otter said, "I came to ask permission to visit the peninsula on the south side of your bay. On its point stands the old grave house of a wizard named Raven Tongue. Do you know the place I mean?"

As Listener translated this speech, the old king's brows drew down. He said, "It is not a peninsula, although that is an easy mistake to make; the channel that divides the island from the mainland is very narrow. Why do you want to go there?"

"Because of a dream," said Otter.

Most of the residents of Celestial House had already been attending to the conversation. Now, however, silence spread throughout the hall.

The king shook his head. "None of my people have stopped on that shore for years. No one who hunts there ever returns."

Otter's fingers curled and uncurled on his knees. Cloud wondered if he missed his carving knife. He looked as if he would rather be anywhere than in the seat of honor beside the king, all ears in the hall straining for his next soft words.

"Fifteen years back," he said, "I camped there for at least a week. I didn't meet anything dangerous."

"A great power has taken up residence since then," said the king. "A power hidden from us, but one with a taste for human flesh."

Otter frowned. "Human flesh?"

The king said, "The last of our people to travel to that island went to search for the others. This was ten years ago. The only man to return said that his party had discovered a heap of corpses in the forest. Their brains had all been eaten—the skulls cracked open and gouged by huge claws. As his party argued whether to press onward, this man spotted a robe that had belonged to his father and strayed to one side. When he heard the screams of his comrades, he fled. He saw nothing clearly—only a large dark shape moving through the brush.

"No seers have been able to travel into that forest to discover what the man encountered. Even our wizards' servants cannot see it clearly. They can make out only a divine shadow squatting in a hole into the underworld; they cannot pass through that hole. We in Waterfall think this is an immortal who has hunted our people before. Something happened to bring this god back to the human realm. We don't know what."

As Listener echoed the king's words in the language of Sandspit Town, a grim expression settled on Otter's face. "Nevertheless," he said, "we have to go there."

The king's story had turned the meal in Cloud's belly to rocks. Of course the terrible creature with a taste for human flesh was her father's ghost, in her dreams always somewhere out of sight. *An immortal who hunted our people long ago.* Cloud remembered the slaughter her father had inflicted on the men who had tried to rescue Thrush, and she wondered how many people of Waterfall he had murdered in a previous age.

She hugged herself. Rumble and Bone and his servants hunted behind her; her father's terrible ghost waited ahead of her; she was surrounded by uncanny spirits and staring strangers. The smells of human skin, of meat and smoke and dogs, seemed to press on her until she could hardly breathe.

The king spoke again to Otter. "It must be a very urgent dream. You are sure it requires a visit to *this* island?"

"It can be no other place," said Otter, Listener echoing the words.

"I don't like your going," said the king. "You are under my protection, and I will share responsibility for your deaths."

"We will not be your guests *there,*" Otter said slowly. "We will be only relatives who have asked for and received permission to hunt in your territory."

"Pah!" said the king. "Is *this* how you intend to resolve your quarrel with your brother-in-law? With your own death? And why drag your pretty young niece with you?"

"I can't see any other way," said Otter.

The king glanced at Mouse as if asking his wizard to intervene. But that old man just said, "Perhaps they must go."

He spoke now in the language of Waterfall, so Listener began to translate for him. "Perhaps the divinations my servants have made to me about that island refer to our friends here: 'The four-legs comes to the meadow because of the berry bushes'; 'The Bright Ones only sojourn in the fish trap.'"

"Why this should refer to our guests," the king said, "is not clear to me."

"The first divination," said Mouse, "surely means that the immortal—the four-legs mentioned—haunts the island because of something particular—the berry bushes. Both mean that whatever has happened will not persist forever. Berries have their season; the Bright Ones die and are reborn again. Whatever keeps the god on the island will change or be changed.

"Now here comes our friend Otter, by no means an ordinary man, who is sent to the island by a dream. He is not telling us the contents of the dream, which is his right. But the dream is sending him there with a purpose. Who are the Bright Ones of the prophecy? Might they not be those who have died on the island, whom our friend will bring back from the land of the ghosts?"

Listener could not begin his translation until the wizard had finished, and then he had to do the whole long speech from memory. He abridged it and left out altogether the part about Otter himself. Cloud supposed that didn't matter.

But she didn't know how Mouse could be so sure what his servants meant. *That kind never gives a straight answer,* Winter had said. Cloud thought that *she* was just as likely to be the four-legs, drawn to the island because of her brothers' ghosts. The Bright Ones of the prophecy would then also be her brothers, who had died and might now be reborn through her agency. But the spirits could have meant something else entirely! Otter had said, *They only tell half the story.*

The residents kept staring at her and Otter. A horrible thought occurred to Cloud: they all knew it was *her* dream sending them to the island. Because why else would Otter bring a girl her age on such a dangerous journey?

The unbearable tension in her condensed into a flood of anger. She wanted to jump up and scream to the house at large, *Stop staring!* She wanted to flee deep into the mountains. She wanted to sink her teeth into Mouse's flesh. Stupid old man!

She wanted to beg Otter: can't we turn aside, isn't there another way? Cloud twisted in her seat, although she knew a girl was supposed to sit quietly while grown men talked. But she had already swallowed more dread than her flesh could bear.

"I still don't like it," said the king. "Dreams and prophecies—a person has to follow them, but it's a voyage through unknown waters. Only spiritual grace will guide you through. I know you're a man of power, friend Otter, but I don't like sending you to what would be certain death for anyone else. This is one of the great immortals we are talking about."

Listener echoed what the king had said. And then Cloud's spine bristled. Listener echoing—*When had she started to understand the king?* She forced herself to sit still and *listen*: the incomprehensible language of Waterfall was now as clear to her as the tongue of her own people. She could hear two distinct languages. *But she understood them both.*

Cloud did not need to ask Otter to know that this was not how most people learned a stranger's language.

The First People, Glory had said, understood all languages.

If only Otter could take her to some place where she was not a bear's daughter and had no impossible supernatural task, where everything was absolutely human and ordinary!

**A slave threaded her way through the hall to set** down a bucket of water beside the hearth. Then she turned aside to examine the contents of a cooking box, no doubt in preparation for the evening meal.

"We have to go to the island," Otter said. "But I thank you for your generosity, hospitality, and tolerance."

"*I* am sorry." The king gave Otter a sharp look. "You still have not told me why King Rumble is hunting on your trail."

Otter rubbed his tattooed cheek. "He has reason to be afraid of this dream—if he finds out what it is."

As Otter spoke these words, the wizard Mouse leaned forward to stare into the bucket. Cloud could not help wondering what had snagged his attention. From her position, she could see only bits of charred wood floating in the water. Or was he inspecting the bucket itself? It seemed entirely ordinary, a square box made of a single board kerfed, bent, and sewn to a wooden bottom, the whole darkened by years of smoke and use.

Those bits of floating wood were odd, though. If she looked at them straight on, they wavered gently, as if anchored in a flowing stream. Out of the corner of her eye, they seemed bigger than they could possibly be, branches hidden in dark water.

And the bucket smelled of brine, not fresh water. Surely the slave would not have brought seawater into the house.

Frowning, the old wizard rose from his seat and stooped over the bucket. One of the branches seemed to flex as if alive. Cloud exclaimed involuntarily and jumped to her feet.

Everyone stared at her. Otter blinked, as if finding it hard to focus. She felt exceedingly foolish.

Then a clawed, white-furred hand reached out of the box to seize the old wizard's throat. He clutched at the hand and staggered back. At the same time seawater gushed out of the box, flooding the hearth, and the fire exploded into agitated billows of steam, smoke, and ash. A mass of octopus tentacles and white-furred dog limbs boiled out of the box along with the water.

Cloud stumbled backward. The king and others near him also rushed back from the hearth. But Otter rose too sluggishly, and a tentacle snaked around his leg.

He managed to step out of the rising flood, onto the next platform, dragging the tentacle with him. But more tentacles wrapped his arms and legs, and the octopus jetted into the air.

Screaming "Uncle! Uncle!" Cloud grabbed after Otter's hand but missed. Despite its bulk, the octopus slipped through the smoke vent. Otter caught hold of the frame, and for a moment he hung in the billowing smoke, gripping with all his strength.

Cloud ran along the edge of the hearth well, looking for a ladder into the rafters. The whole house was in an uproar, men yelling, dogs barking, children shrieking. A huge fly or bat swooped upon Bone's dog, which was still choking the old wizard. With a final hiss, the gushing seawater quenched the last bit of flame, plunging the house into near-darkness. Otter lost his hold on the timbers of the smoke vent and was pulled through.

"Uncle!" Cloud wailed. She shoved through the chaos, ducked out the door into the cold evening. Otter's dog was barking wildly. Otter and the octopus sailed over the ocean at a great height. Cloud ran down the slope toward her uncle, but the palisade blocked her way, so she ran upward again trying to keep him in sight. The octopus zigzagged as if struggling with its prey.

A well-traveled path led her out of the fort and up into sparse, snowy forest. The octopus was now jetting parallel to the mountainside, trending back toward land. She abandoned the trail and tried to follow it, climbing over the rocks until sheer cliffs blocked her way.

She turned in a circle, gasping for breath. Up ahead, she heard Otter's faint voice. "Uncle!" she shouted.

A glittery object like an opalescent jellyfish dropped onto a nearby rock. As she backed away, the thing sprang at her, and red-hot fire pierced the roof of her mouth. A hard obstruction choked off her scream, and the pain jerked her, mouth first, into the air.

She flailed as the world swung wildly: clouds, steep forest, the long drop to the night-dark sea. For a heartbeat she glimpsed Bone's dog standing on hind legs, gripping something in its hands. Then she plummeted hard to the snow and tumbled down the slope, a length of translucent rope tangling her arms and legs. The rope snagged in a bush, pulling her up short.

"Cloud!" Otter shouted, leaping down through the trees. He clutched another length of the rope. "Cloud! Where are you?"

She tried to answer, but the obstruction clogged her mouth, and her reply emerged only as a muffled grunt. She struggled to her feet. At the sight of her, Otter slumped against an outcrop, chest heaving. Otter's small servant hopped to the rock beside him and bared its fangs, piping. Otter held out the length of rope; it seized the end in its front paws and began to eat.

"Cloud, are you all right?" said Otter.

She wanted to fling her arms around him and weep into his shoulder. But she couldn't hug this quiet man still nearly a stranger. So, trembling from cold and the aftermath of terror, she just shook her head. Otter peered at her, hauled himself upright, thrust his hand inside her half-open mouth, and yanked. Searing pain blazed in the roof of her mouth. He held up a hook as big as a halibut hook, but translucent and rainbow-colored like a jellyfish. Hot blood spilled from her mouth.

The huge fish hook glowed in the twilight. "Uncle," she began. It hurt to speak. "Are *you* all right?"

"You should not have tried to follow me," Otter said sternly. "It's you I am trying to protect! And *you*—"He turned to his servant. "You should have been watching! Why didn't you warn me?"

"Master, I watched and I saw," the spirit piped. "But the gate was barred, the walls garrisoned. The ant does not talk to the wasp's children."

"Bone's servants found their way in," said Otter.

His servant swallowed the last of the rope, and now Otter offered the fish hook. "Master, the black canoe is coming," it said, as it took the hook.

"You told me that already," said Otter.

**As they climbed down the mountain, Otter had** Cloud suck ice to reduce the swelling in her mouth. It just made her colder. But then they met men with torches whom the king had sent out to search for them, and soon Cloud was sitting by the hearth of Celestial House. The flood had mostly drained through the sand-floored hearth well, and the slaves had managed to rebuild the fire atop a rack of logs. The old wizard Mouse rested nearby, massaging his bruised throat. Above his head, a boy with bat wings walked upside down upon a roof beam.

"It is shameful to have guests dragged out of my house," said the king to Otter. "I beg your forgiveness. I see we are not so well guarded after all."

Otter shook his head. "I didn't see through their disguise myself."

She and Otter slept that night in one of the apartments in the back of Celestial House. At another time, Cloud would have kept the lamp burning long enough to examine the painted chests, the carved spears, the woolen robe lined with green-feathered mallard skin. But exhaustion dragged her straight toward sleep.

She half expected that she would dream all night of her weeping brothers, since their bones were just across the bay. But instead sleep brought images of a rosy dawn welling behind the mountains, of little boys running through the pines, of Thrush, in rags, laughing as she tossed Cloud high into the air.

# EIGHT

# The Glade of Bones

*Invincible woke Cloud and Otter when it was still* deep night. Cloud was shocked to see how haggard her uncle looked, how he shuffled like an old man. He spoke a few words to the king, who had arisen to see them depart. Then, by torchlight, Cloud and Otter followed Invincible down to the seaside and the waiting crew. After Invincible helped them into their seats, the crewmen extinguished their torches and set out.

They paddled silently down the black inlet, entering the wide reaches of the bay just as sunrise touched the east with fire. The dawn revealed that Otter did not paddle. Instead he lay motionless, wrapped in furs, eyes closed, head propped against a box. Except for the dog slumbering beside him, he might have been laid out for his funeral.

The sunrise faded behind the overcast. Out on the windless bay the canoe cut through a sea that was flat and full of light as polished marble. The wake spread out behind them, rippling a perfect inverted image of the mountains.

Slowly the blue smudge on the southern horizon grew

darker and greener. By midday Cloud could make out individual trees on the island. She began to recognize landmarks from her flight with Winter: an islet, the mouth of a creek.

They came ashore at a long beach near the island's western tip. As keel crunched against gravel, Otter, to Cloud's immense relief, opened his eyes and raised his head. "So," he said. "We're here." His dog jumped from the canoe and trotted up the beach, but he called it back sharply.

Otter and his crew broke their fast before unloading the canoe. With her injured mouth, Cloud could only suck one tiny fragment of fish at a time. She did not have much appetite anyway. All morning she had been trying to hold her thoughts still, like a frightened hare hoping to disappear in front of the dog that hunts it down. The knots in her gut had tightened relentlessly even so. When she had stepped on land, distant voices had begun to clamor inside her ears—the ghosts, she thought, calling to her. They had to know she was near.

While the men made camp, Otter called Cloud over to him. He stood on a drift log that jutted into the water and now floated on the rising tide. When she had climbed the roots anchoring the log to the beach, and walked down the broad trunk to his side, she discovered that this lookout offered a view up and down the shore. To the left, the island stepped back in sections, each higher and bluer and more snow-covered, until it seemed to merge with the mountains of the mainland. To the right, the beach ended two hundred yards away, at a knob of granite thrusting out of the sea. Beyond that knob, she knew, lay the point with the wizard's tomb. Invincible had brought them ashore at the very spot where Winter had tried in vain to enter the forest.

Cloud wondered how far away her father's ghost was at this moment, how fast it could travel.

"Do you recognize anything?" Otter asked her.

She wanted to lie outright. Instead she pointed at the

brush that grew along the beach. Directly in front of them, a tall, decaying pole rose from a thicket.

"It's carved," she said. Speaking hurt.

"A memorial to a lord who used the wolf as his crest," Otter said. Extra sleep had done him good, but his face was still drawn, his eyes sunk in dark hollows. "If you walk through the brush, you can see charred beams and the pits where they dug their hearths. And look at all the broken shell on the beach. This was a large town before the Gull Islanders burned it."

"Was this," Cloud said, "where the people of Waterfall used to live?"

"No. A much older place. This was Raven Tongue's town."

Cloud could not help but glance west toward that wizard's tomb, although it was not visible from their present vantage.

"Let's walk," Otter said. They retraced their steps along the trunk. He helped her down, and without talking, they crunched along the gravel in the direction of the point. His dog, which he had tied up earlier, barked after them, then subsided.

On their left, the brushy ruins gave way to overhanging forest. Cloud's scalp prickled. There was something very strange about this forest now that she saw it with her waking eyes. Everything looked exactly like itself—beach grass, currant bush, towering cedar—and at the same time, out of the corner of her eye, like something much bigger, the way Bone's servants had appeared when disguised as bits of wood.

But surely Bone's servants could not have disguised themselves as an entire island. "Uncle," she asked, "is there wizardry here?"

Otter nodded. "Wizardry, and the echoes of a divine presence, and maybe more as well. Do you remember what King Shining Down said about this island? A great deal has happened here since I last camped on this beach.

Rumble and Bone are responsible for some of it, but not all, I think."

They reached the granite knob. Otter climbed up rapidly toward its grassy, treeless summit. Cloud did not want to follow. Wouldn't they be in terrible danger if they strayed from the beach? But she was afraid to let Otter out of her sight. With her stomach twisting ever tighter, she hurried to catch up.

The rich smells that rose from the forest on either side, rotten wood, moldering fir needles, failed to seduce her now. She felt as if millipedes scurried up and down her back. At the edge of her vision, eyes seemed to stare out of tree bark, immense bodies twisted and crawled. She wanted to clutch her uncle's hand but was afraid to presume.

At the top of the knoll, she was surprised to discover that the ocean on the far side was closer than the beach they had just left. The low islands she and Winter had flown through lay scattered like shells all the way to the horizon. Below and to her left stood the forest that Winter had not been able to enter, the forest of the ghosts. Cloud's heart began to race.

But now, at last, her terror of that forest paradoxically gave her courage to speak. "Uncle," she said. Wrapped in his own thoughts, Otter was slow to turn toward her. "Uncle, how do I dare go near my father's ghost? He killed all those Waterfall men."

Otter placed a firm hand on her shoulder. "He is wild. But you're his *daughter,* Cloud."

"But," she said, forging on despite the pain in her mouth, "why should that make a difference? And what about you? He hates everyone from Sandspit Town."

"I've never done him any harm," Otter said, "so I'll just hope for the best. But how to go about your task—from here on, you will have to lead the way."

*She* lead? She had no idea what to do and didn't want to do it anyway. It was *Otter's* job to take care of *her.* A lump swelled in her throat. "But how do I dare bring him back to life? What's to stop him from finding some way of crossing the water and returning for Thrush, and slaughtering the rest of Sandspit Town? If Rumble killed Thrush, or Glory or Wren, maybe he deserves to die, but I don't want anyone else to get hurt."

"Cloud," Otter said, "Winter didn't tell you to bring your *father* back to life."

"You weren't there. She *did*. She said it would destroy Rumble's strength. And isn't that the only way you and Winter and your children and I can all go free? Or is there someplace Rumble and Bone can't reach us? Is there somebody strong enough to fight them?"

She had to stop because her injured mouth hurt too much. But she also felt ashamed. She had really asked her uncle, *Is there somebody stronger than you?*

Otter regarded her steadily. "We don't know yet how you will bring *any* of the dead back to life. King Shining Down said there was now a hole into the underworld in this forest, which may also affect your task. But . . ." He released her shoulder. "It might be that your father will spare us because of what we are trying to do. The First People acknowledge their debts."

Abruptly Otter headed downhill and pushed through a salal thicket toward the beach on the far side. Trying to ignore the shapes coiling at the edge of her vision, Cloud hurried in his wake. They walked in the direction of the point atop the driftwood, more copious on this windward shore than on the beach where they had landed. All at once Otter stopped short. "Look."

Cloud knew they were not far enough along the point to have reached the wizard's tomb. Nevertheless, it was with extreme reluctance that she stepped up to see what Otter had found.

A swath of beach grass formed a clearing at the margin of the shore. Rain and frost had flattened the grass to reveal, ten feet above the storm-tide line, a tumble of half-rotten driftwood logs. Otter tramped across the grass and kicked over the logs. They were well charred. "This wasn't here when I came last," he said. "I'd guess it's Rumble's old camp. Waterfall men would stop on the north shore, where it's sheltered, but Rumble would have tried to conceal his presence."

He swung around. "There. You can just see it."

Twenty yards farther west, the corner of a little building protruded through low cedar boughs. Otter returned to the beach to walk closer, Cloud dogging his footsteps.

Her uncle did not stop until he reached the grave house. It really did look like a miniature house, with square posts, plank walls, and a shingled roof. "The northerners leave a wizard's tools in his tomb," Otter said, "his masks and amulets and so on. Because he used those things to summon and direct his servants, they're attracted to the spot and stay close by. That's why I came here." He sighed. "Some wizards have to search long and hard for servants, but spirits buzz like wasps around others no matter what they do. Raven Tongue must have been one of those, to acquire eight."

Cloud did not like being so near the dead wizard's remains or his former servants. Moreover, the daylight had begun to wane, making the shapes at the edges of her vision more definite. "Isn't it dangerous?"

She meant that it was dangerous now; they should turn back, but he misunderstood her. "I was ready to take the risk. My brothers were great hunters and warriors. I was hardly more than a boy. After they died, I knew I couldn't hunt your father better than they had. But I was the only brother Thrush had left. I thought it was up to me to save her. This was only one of the places I came, searching for spiritual power. As it happened, these spirits would have nothing to do with me."

The guilty discomfort seized Cloud. She hated hearing about the days when everyone was looking for Thrush, about the terrible havoc her father had wreaked. Rumble had killed her brothers, but her father had killed Otter's.

But then she realized that her reticent uncle, preoccupied since she had met him with his own thoughts, was finally telling her what those thoughts were. She might have felt honored if she wasn't so frightened of what he was going to say.

Otter turned from the grave house to stare out at the ocean. "I did eventually find power, but I never found Thrush. Winter had more luck—she once flew all the way to your father's house. But in the end Thrush made her own way home."

For a moment he fell silent again. Then he said, "Before you showed up, I hadn't thought about those days in a long time. As Winter said, after Rumble brought Thrush home, we thought it was over. I hadn't saved Thrush, but she had survived. I had done all I could for her. I thought I could marry Winter and live my life.

"But here you are with your dreams, Rumble and Bone on your trail . . . It hasn't ended. I was prepared to die as my brothers had, if it would save my sister. But the only thing I ever accomplished for Thrush was to help save one of her children. Now it's time for me to follow through, and do what I can to save her child again, for good. And then maybe everything that happened all those years ago can finally be put to rest. The sacrifice my brothers made can be turned to something good: your future, my children's future."

Cloud had been right to be frightened of what he would say. Otter sounded as if he was again preparing to die, for *her,* right here on this island. That wasn't the way it was supposed to be. He was supposed to stay around to keep her safe forever.

Looking at her uncle's reserved face, haunted by too much guilt and too much grief, Cloud's heart swelled into her throat until it hurt more than she could bear. She didn't know how to bargain with her father's ghost, but she knew that her father, if he chose to, could protect Otter from Bone and Rumble.

Cloud wondered bitterly if Thrush ever thought about

her one surviving brother, whose name no one in Sandspit Town ever mentioned. If the thought of Otter gnawed a hole in Thrush the way Otter's guilt still ate at him.

And then she remembered the ivory raven. Of course Thrush still thought about Otter. The necklace had been a message: a message for Cloud, and perhaps for Otter, too.

Cloud touched the lump where the raven hung beneath her dress. She wanted to speak to Otter as he had spoken to her, opening her heart to him. She wanted to thank him for the times he had saved her life. She wanted to say she was sorry that her father had caused so much trouble, and sorry that she was causing so much more. But she did not even know how to begin. It was as if her heart, like a ghost's, had too little substance to speak into the waking world.

Instead, wiping tears from her cheek, she said, "Uncle, after Rumble first tried to kill me, why did he let me live so long as a"—she caught herself in time—"as a four-legs?"

Otter turned from the ocean. "Well . . . I think for a long time he still hoped to win Thrush's love. After killing your brothers he didn't want to make matters worse between them. Then—I don't know. Maybe he didn't think of you as a threat because you grew at a human child's pace. Maybe he thought that a baby like you, so far from the country of the First People, would never discover the divine half of your nature. You were the only four-legs on Maple Island! Who would ever show you?"

A shadow stooped to land beside them, making Cloud jump. But it was only Otter's little servant.

"You've been away a long time," Otter chided it. "Where are Bone's servants now?"

"Master," it said, "I have kept watch as you told me to. The black canoe is coming."

"Where are Bone's servants?" Otter repeated.

"Even the mouse knows to scurry from the path of the falling tree."

"Where," said Otter sternly, "are Bone's servants?"

The servant gazed at him without blinking. "If the fisherman does not see him, the salmon who swims past the trap will also escape the spear. But it will enter the house of the Headwaters Women regardless."

Otter seemed to understand this last riddle, because he sagged. "Just give me as much warning as you can." The servant leapt into the air and was gone.

*Out on the ocean, fog crept nearer. A large blue is-*land had vanished completely, and a nearer, smaller one had grown misty and vague. As Cloud watched, that island disappeared as well. In weather like this, she thought, it would have been easy for Gull Islanders to sneak up on the old town.

A frog croaked once from atop the grave house. Otter glanced at it and turned back the way they had come. Cloud followed. At Rumble's old camp, he stopped and looked up and down the beach. "Which way would Rumble have gone from here, do you think?"

The knoll they had descended was, on this shore, a steep tangle of brush. Between the knoll and the tip of the point stood a dense grove of young cedars. Eastward, however—toward the mainland—lay a beach of flat, wave-smoothed stones, easy passage even for a man with a heavy burden.

But she knew where Rumble had taken the bones anyway.

"You can feel it?" Otter asked her.

"I can hear them," Cloud said.

Otter put his hand on her shoulder again. "We'll get you through this," he said.

Tears stung her eyes again. She had been wrong about everything. Otter *was* doing this for her, and for Thrush. If he believed he might have to die to set things right, it was no wonder Winter had not been able to summon any warmth for Cloud. But Winter had not stopped her husband from coming.

Otter released her shoulder. "We'll go tomorrow, and you will guide us."

They returned over the knoll the way they had come, as shadows moved ponderously at the edge of her vision and the skin on her back twitched with the feeling that something watched her. Cloud again wondered how they could be safe walking so close to the forest. She could only trust Otter's judgment.

At last they reached the other beach and were heading toward their camp. Otter's men had lit a fire, but it was only a tiny speck of light in the vast darkness of the world.

A hoof clicked on gravel. In the first dislocating moment, Cloud knew it by smell: deer, female, alive. Then she saw it. It stood scarcely ten feet away, nose twitching, ears flicking, seemingly unafraid.

Then it bolted along the beach toward the canoe. One of the men jumped up from the fire to hurl a spear into its shoulder with terrific force. The deer plowed to its knees, then pitched to the gravel. The crewman began to pray softly.

She and Otter approached. The crewman was Listener, and the deer sprawled at his feet, one dark eye staring at Cloud. She could still smell its warm skin and hair, but the new scent of hot blood made her belly hurt. She had to fight the urge to jump down and lap at the deer's slowly dripping wound.

Then a huge shape rose up beside or behind the deer, a shadow, a knot of light, or was it a slender, long-legged woman? Cloud fell toward her, dropping off the world into a spinning abyss. For a moment she could not breathe.

Then the world came right again. She stood beside an ordinary lifeless deer—although, out of the corner of her eye, it still looked much larger than it really was.

The men chopped off one haunch and cached the rest in a tree. The smell of the bloody flesh, and then of the juices that dripped from roasting meat, nearly blinded Cloud with desire. But when it came time to eat, a wave of horror coursed through her just as if it were a piece of Thrush's leg they offered her. She could not shake her vision of the dead woman, as beautiful as Thrush. She sucked instead on a berry cake.

Fog drifted along the beach. Otter's dog, still leashed, gnawed upon a deer bone. The men spoke only a little, not enough to drown the distant voices in her ears.

Then a wolf howl soared over the forest. The dog scrambled to its feet, ears pricked. As the howl wailed down into silence, a second call answered the first. The pure high sound made Cloud shiver. The wolves were closer than she had ever heard them.

"Are they on the island?" she asked.

"They must be. They can't be more than a mile away."

She hugged her knees to her chest. "Are they here because of the dead Waterfall men?"

Otter shook his head. "They're interested in food, not old bones," he said.

The winter darkness sucked away what little warmth and light the fire produced. Despite her injured mouth, Cloud wanted to talk, and she wanted even more to keep Otter talking.

"Do the wolves belong to the Winter People?" she asked. "Wolf is a winter-side crest in Sandspit Town."

"Wolves are Winter People, yes," Otter said. "They're hunters." He seemed to sense her mood, because he went on. "Wolves are special among the Winter People, though. They were the first wizards in the world, long before humans came to be."

And Otter began a story about how Wily One turned himself into the first human being after stealing wizardry from the king of the wolves. The story was very much like one Stick had related to her at Oyster Bay beneath the starry summer sky. She remembered that Stick had lived most of his long life in Halibut House, and must have told stories to Otter and Thrush, and to their brothers who were now dead, back when all of them were children. Otter was now recounting one of Stick's stories.

The wolves howled again, but farther away. She wished Otter had chosen another story, or something else to talk about, because this one made her too sad. It was hard not to

imagine Stick in Halibut House still, hauling wood, starting up the fire in the morning. Hard not to think about
Aunt Glory, and Thrush—

She rested her face on her arms so Otter would not see
her wiping her eyes. When he finished the story, he said,
"Tired?"

She nodded. The wolves howled in the distance now. Otter's crew were bedding down around the campfire. She
joined them, wrapping herself in layers of fur blankets. Otter himself sat awake, watchful, his dog dozing lightly at his
feet.

*Otter shook her awake at first light. Fog still*
wrapped the world. Her mouth felt better, but as soon as
she remembered where she was, her stomach knotted up so
tightly that she could not eat. The faint voices still clamored inside her head.

Otter fed the last of his deer meat to his dog. "Let's go,"
he said. He looked as if he had not slept at all.

He untied the dog and, holding its leash, walked with it
along the top of the beach until they reached a gap where deer
had worn an opening in a row of spruce saplings. Pulling a
branch aside, Otter stepped through it.

Cloud's heart pounded wildly, but she hurried after him.
Otter's crew tramped behind her. The deer track wound
through the old town site, past the charred beams Otter
had mentioned, through young trees and brush the deer
had heavily browsed. Grass stalks, brittle with frost, broke
under her feet.

At the back of the town, the trail branched, one fork
leading south toward the beach Cloud and Otter had visited
the night before. The dog sniffed in that direction, but Otter shook its leash. They headed along the other branch.

Slowly the ground began to rise. Smaller trees gave way
to ancient Douglas firs and hemlocks, and the foggy morning dimmed to twilight. At the edge of Cloud's vision, the
soaring trunks looked big as cliffs, as mountains.

When a breeze stirred the forest canopy, causing a branch to creak overhead, she started violently. The breeze brought smells from the trail ahead: moist peat, fresh deer pellets. It also carried a whiff of other things that set Cloud's nose twitching: fresh blood and also rotten offal, the latter scent so faint and attenuated she thought she might be imagining it.

They came over a hill and the trail forked a second time. One branch again bent south, where foggy ocean showed between the trees. The other aimed to the left, northward. There the island widened out, and Cloud could see only forest spiring above dim slopes of moss and stone.

"Do you know which way?" a voice asked her.

Again Cloud jumped. Of course, it was just Otter who had spoken. She shook her head in reply, but she was not being honest. From the voices, she knew it was the left-hand fork. And something about the way the forest opened out along that trail, giving way again to winter-killed grass and gray light, reminded her of her dreams. The scents of blood and rotten offal were stronger in that direction, too, and another out-of-place smell, like fresh human waste, floated on the air.

Otter watched her; the men shifted. Otter's dog stared back the way they had come, ears flicking. Cloud wanted nothing more than to flee the forest and this island while they were all still safe. But Otter, having apparently marked where she had gazed the longest, pulled at the dog's leash and took the left-hand fork. She followed on wobbly legs.

As they marched along, the resemblance to the forest of her dreams became even more pronounced, and the smell of blood grew stronger. A meadow opened up before them. With an exclamation Otter stopped in his tracks.

Terrified, Cloud peered from behind the shelter of his body. It was not what she had expected. Men lay scattered across the meadow. The smell of blood and ordure originated from this spot.

"Stay back, Cloud!" Otter said, and then, "Invincible, what do you think?"

Invincible came forward. "They have short hair," he said, a slight tremor in his voice. "It's hard to tell—their heads are all—cracked open and emptied—but chin length, I think. Short rain capes, braided headbands—they look like Longhouse People."

"I think so, too," said Otter. "And those towns lie at least twenty days south."

"Eight men dead," said Invincible, taking another step. "The blood is still dripping. They were killed within the hour. What would bring eight southerners to this island today?"

Cloud wanted to scream at Otter, *Why are you wasting time?* Her father's ghost would kill them as quickly as it had these stray southerners. She glanced around at the forest, hugging herself. Nothing moved.

" 'Two brothers went hunting seals,' " Otter said tiredly, rubbing the tattoo on his cheek. " ' The sea hunter fashions his harpoon.' "

Cloud recognized his foot-servant's prophecies. The two seal-hunting brothers, Otter had said, were the two servants of Bone's who had traveled south on other business.

Was he saying *Bone's servants* had sent these men here?

Otter turned to Cloud. "Are we getting close?"

"Maybe," she said. She could barely force out the word.

Otter put his arm around her shoulders to guide her past the dead men. They walked on. The grassy stretch of forest continued ahead for several hundred yards, interspersed with denser stands of young hemlocks and huckleberries.

She jumped again when a frog croaked from a stump beside the trail. Then Otter's dog began to bark. Otter's servant streaked through the air, piping. Heavy snow blizzarded out of the treetops, and shapes ghosted through it: a shadow that flung tentacles around Otter; a white-haired dog that leaped on him with bared fangs. Among the snowflakes glittered blue lights that flowered into young girls made of translucent ice, each no bigger than a sparrow, and they swarmed

over Otter, stabbing him with tiny hands turned to knives.
He gasped, staggered, and began to sing.

A tentacle scattered the crewmen like leaves. Terrified of
the spirits, Cloud nevertheless stepped toward her uncle.
But at that moment cold water dripped on her neck. She
turned. A hand reached for her that was part bones and part
bloodless flesh.

"Get away, Cloud!" Otter yelled. "Run!" With enormous
effort he ripped an arm free of tentacles to cast a harpoon of
light at the drowned woman. She spun away in a torrent of
bubbles. "Run!" he yelled again. But he had fallen to his
knees.

Then footsteps drummed through the forest. Dozens of
strange men poured up the trail, waving clubs and shouting. The warriors wore short rain capes and braided headbands over cropped hair, and they swarmed over Otter's
crewmen. At first Cloud thought they might also be spirits,
some additional conjuring of Bone's. But they smelled of
human flesh, and their clubs thudded against Invincible's
head and shoulders as they beat him to the ground.

One of the strange men turned toward Cloud. *"Run!"*
Otter screamed at her.

She fled.


**Branches whipped at her face and stones bruised**
her feet. Cloud careened into trees, tripped over roots, crashed
through thickets, found her balance, and raced headlong
over the grass. A stick rolled under her and sent her sprawling. As she tried to rise, gasping for air, she saw that what
had tripped her was not a stick but a massive, moss-stained
thighbone.

Cloud climbed unsteadily to her feet. She stood alone in
a glade among bare salmonberry bushes. Except for her own
labored panting, the forest around her had fallen profoundly
silent. She could hear no shouts or screams or barking even
in the distance, nothing but the voices clamoring inside her
head, and they sounded nearly as faint and far off as they had

on the beach. A hundred feet over her head, dark fir branches swayed in the breeze.

Slowly she caught her breath. Heart pounding, she turned her gaze to the spreading maple that stood on the right-hand side of the glade. A huge animal skull stared from the crotch where the trunklike limbs divided, and she knew that just around the side, rope tied a rotting basket full of little bones into another fold of that crotch.

She took a careful step away from the maple, fitting her foot between the bones that lay scattered under the dead grass. And then another. The bones did not move. She inched through the salmonberries, pushing canes gingerly aside so the thorns did not catch her hair and clothes.

There were no ghost-children weeping. But the glade was otherwise the familiar scenery of her dreams. Viewed straight on, it was far more ordinary than she had expected, almost harmless-seeming. She had seen old deer bones just as gray and mossy as that skull. The leafless canes arching over her head were mundane salmonberries, not some terrible thorn bush of the underworld.

But out of the corner of her eyes, another place much vaster and solider loomed behind this glade, all half-seen shapes and slow-moving shadows. She was beginning to think that after all something far more sinister than her brothers' ghosts lay in wait here when a child cried out, "Don't go!"

On the far side of the maple, where she had never gone in her dreams, stood a little boy, shadowed and misty like an island seen through rain. All of a sudden she *remembered* his voice: laughing as she bowled him onto the pine needles; sighing with pleasure as Thrush lifted him to her breast to nurse; weeping for Thrush while they all struggled after her, running down through the endless forest.

Between one heartbeat and the next, two other boys joined the first. She remembered their smells now, too: sweet, milky, with sun-warmed dirt on their hands and pine sap in their tangled hair. They were as much a part of her as

Thrush's soft voice and beloved scent, had just been buried out of sight all this time, deep in her heart. Now she could remember curling up to sleep with them countless times, nose to cheek, arm flung across belly. She could almost remember their names.

She edged past salmonberry bushes toward her brothers, who stopped weeping as she approached. Huge shapes teetered under her feet.

Then other smells hit her: butchered meat, putrefying offal. Her foot touched warm stickiness where cold grass should have been. She jerked it back.

Then she saw the man's body. Claws had ripped him shoulder to thigh. The top of his skull had been cracked off and the brains scooped out, and his scalp lay like a scrap of hide in the grass. But she could see that he had worn his hair chin-length and bound by a braided headband.

Other dead southerners, more than a dozen, lay heaped like broken dolls beyond him. Faces stared at the sky, at a splayed hand or a fallen branch. The inside of every skull top had been scraped out. Blood dripped from their wounds. These men, too, had been dead only a few moments.

Her brothers had vanished. In their place, beside the dead men, a doorway gaped into the earth. Dizziness swam over her. A passage led down between the fresh corpses, through soil and water-logged clay and then stone, each layer darker and denser and more airless, more filled with desperation and sadness, until the blackness within the earth seemed to reach up and clamp down over her nose and mouth, over her heart, as inexorably as Rumble's suffocating hand. In the sooty darkness at the bottom, bones eddied slowly, rotten hands and half-glimpsed cadaver faces rolled over and sank down. The faint voices in her head were calling *down there,* and it was from this hole that the smell of putrefaction had come. She took a step back, and another, not daring to look away.

Then a shrill croak yanked her gaze around. A little brown frog squatted atop one of the dead southerners. "The salmon have entered the fisherwoman's trap," it said in a man's deep voice. "Do you want to follow?"

The air grew colder and darker, as if a thunderstorm approached and rain was about to pour down. Something rattled in the forest on the far side of the glade. A vast, indistinct shape moved in the shadows there.

Blind panic beat her heart like a drum. Cloud launched herself back the way she had come, fighting her way through the salmonberries and across her father's bones, sprinting over the grass and up the animal track beyond with no thought but to escape this glade of death.

Then a half-dozen of the southern men jogged over a rise. A shout went up at the sight of her. She veered from the trail into the brush, so that they had to stop and change directions. One of the southerners jumped over a tangle of fallen alders to snatch at her, but she pulled free before his fist closed on her arm, and she ran, ran, ran . . .

She collided with another warrior so hard it knocked the wind out of her. He hauled her to her feet. He held a bloody club in his other hand, and he smelled sweaty and excited. As she struggled to draw breath, he smacked the side of her head so hard her ear rang. Then he dragged her farther up the trail, across a body that lay in a pool of blood—she could barely make out Invincible's battered features—and past another body, facedown, that Cloud recognized as Listener's by the fur-trimmed rain cloak. Beyond him, sprawled in the brush, Squeaky and Brant, Harrowing and Fortitude, all of Otter's crew, all bloody and motionless. Their skulls, at least, were more or less intact. Killed by human beings.

A scream arrowed through the forest. Cloud's captor whipped around to stare in the direction she had come. A second shriek followed the first. She writhed against his grip so fiercely that her cloak ripped at the neck, but she could not break free.

And then she saw another man sprawled across a fallen log. It was Otter. Blood spilled down his cheek. His lips were parted, his eyes wide. His dog crouched beside him licking his face. Cloud thought her uncle was dead, too, until his eyes tracked to her. "Cloud," he whispered. "Cloud, you must . . ."

Otter stopped to draw a labored, wheezing breath. With all her strength Cloud yanked free of her captor to fall on her knees by Otter's side.

"You must," he began again.

More shrieks echoed through the forest. The southerner smashed his club down on Otter's skull. Otter's body jerked and slid from the log, nearly toppling the dog.

"Uncle," she wailed, reaching for him.

The warrior tossed Cloud onto the trail, slapping her again. Wild, scalding hate poured into her belly. She leapt on him screaming and sank her teeth into his shoulder, tasting blood. Light dazzled her eyes, as brilliant as the sun welling over the mountains. She swelled with strength—

Her captor's fist smashed against her jaw, and blackness fell on her like a stone.

PART THREE

# nine

# The Box

*Cloud woke in a canoe, lying against a heap of* boxes. A coppery taste filled her mouth. At first she wondered why her skull pounded so sickeningly, and why the boxes had been thrown aboard Otter's canoe in such haste. Then her gaze fell on the men who sat aft of her, paddling. They were not Otter's crewmen, and this was not Otter's canoe.

Alarmed, she struggled upright, trying to push through the fog that wrapped her thoughts. The men wore rain capes over sleeveless tunics, and headbands bound their cropped hair. Rumble's captives from the south, the ones who had died with Stick; yes, they had looked like that.

Behind this canoe, six other vessels spread out in a bird-wing pattern. All were about the same length as Otter's journeying canoe, but narrower and with lower prows. Cloud lifted her gaze and saw, across miles of ocean, the Mountain Land rearing into the clouds like the wall of the world. At its foot, the island of the bones was only a faint smudge.

The sight cleared her thoughts like a cold wind: Otter dead, his crew dead, southerners overrunning the island.

Her father's ghost, a dark shape in the thickets . . . That powerful, mustached warrior who sat near her, his shoulder wrapped in blood-soaked moss, was the one who had killed Otter. Who had seized Cloud and borne her away with him.

The effort of sitting caught up with her and she leaned over the side to vomit. Then she sagged against the boxes. Her head throbbed as if someone had sunk an adze in it. At least the men ignored her.

She closed her eyes, wanting to weep, finding no tears. She tried instead not to think or feel anything. She listened to paddles splash. The warriors reeked of sweat, fear, spilled blood, and butchered meat. But she could also smell cold sea air, the resinous breath of the canoe's pitchwood caulking, and fainter odors rising from the boxes: smoke, fish, tallow, a tinge somewhere of mold and decay. If she sat still, her headache receded ever so slightly.

She slipped into an uncomfortable doze. Sometime later, the scrape of the hull on gravel roused her. She barely had time to open her eyes before her captor dragged her out of the canoe, shouting and slapping her so hard the world turned black. The renewed blast of headache and the reek of his body made her gag. When she started to vomit again, he threw her from him in disgust.

At last there was not even bile left in her stomach. He yanked her onto her battered feet and propelled her up the beach to the tide line, where he thrust driftwood into her hands. She could not understand the words he shouted, but the meaning was clear. She took off her cloak and slowly loaded it with firewood. Without her cloak, the evening was very cold.

The southerners were lighting campfires at the top of the beach. Cloud gathered up her cloak by the corners, as she had sometimes seen Stick do, and hauled the wood to the fire, where her captor now sat gnawing on a strip of dried fish. He shoved her away for more. She collected another bundle, and another.

But when she brought her fourth bundle, it was to discover that he had departed from the fire. She was afraid that if she stopped gathering wood, he would beat her again. But she was also weary beyond bearing, and almost blind from the pain in her skull. She sat down outside the circle of firelight. An older southerner at her captor's fire cast disapproving glances in her direction. Otherwise the men acted as if she didn't exist. No one offered her food. It didn't matter: the smell of fish nauseated her.

Shouts from the direction of the campfire made her glance up in alarm. But it proved to have nothing to do with her. Her captor had brought a large box to the fire and was sawing at the cords that bound it shut while the older man berated him angrily. After a moment her captor sheathed his dagger, frowning, and the two argued.

Then the older man began to sing, dancing in place. It reminded Cloud of the song Bone had droned over her. She felt herself rise and fall with the music, though she did not grow light enough to fly. Snowflakes sifted down, followed by lights that resolved into tiny blue girls. They fluttered over the wizard's head while he questioned them. He did not seem to be able to see the ice girls; he addressed the falling snow instead.

They drifted to the box, then burst upward in an agitated flock. Most vanished, but one of the remaining girls swooped down and stuck out her blue tongue, which grew longer and longer until it slid like a snake into the wizard's ear. The wizard cocked his head. Faint chatter echoed inside Cloud's own ear.

The ice girl sucked in her tongue. Wiping melted snowflakes from his face, the wizard spoke at length to Cloud's captor, whose frown deepened. Then the wizard hoisted the box to his shoulder and bore it down to the canoe. The handful of remaining ice girls flickered above it like blue sparks.

The southerners arranged themselves for sleep. Her master stared in the direction of the box for a long time before he, too, lay down.

Cloud huddled with her adze-headache, trying *not* to look at those blue lights. Here, obviously, was the means by which Bone had used the southerners to kill Otter: having the ice girls come to their wizard as if they were his own true servants. But that didn't matter now. Nothing about Bone's spirits mattered anymore, not their interest in the southerners' box or in any other thing. Otter was dead and she was a slave, a captive like Stick, dead even if she lived on. Bone had won.

Cold seeped from the gravel into her bones. She wrapped her torn cloak more tightly around her and, as she started to shiver, draped a mass of dried eelgrass over her legs.

Blue sparks swarmed out of the sky, the larger portion of the ice girls returning from wherever they had gone. This time they circled Cloud before swooping away to join their sisters.

Eventually sleep overcame her. She saw Otter jerking as the club slammed down on his head, Otter as he lay bleeding, his gaze fastened on her. "Cloud, you must—"

Then she stood in the clearing among the salmonberries. The child-voices cried out, "Don't leave us! Save us!" Her father's skull gazed down at her in silence.

**In the morning her head still throbbed brutally.** When she recalled where she was and why, despair pinned her like a boulder, squeezing breath from her lungs. With that weight crushing her, even the simplest actions seemed impossible: standing up, taking a step.

If she did not move, her master would beat her.

She rose and trudged past the just-stirring southerners toward the sound of running water. Dawn light showed her the red and white figures that decorated most of the southern canoes. The canoe of her captor, though—of Otter's murderer—was an unrelieved soot-black.

*The black canoe is coming.* Not a riddle after all but plain speech.

The stream she could hear was, on the beach, no more than

a line of algae-scummed gravel. Cloud pushed wearily into
the trees, then halted at the sound of a man singing. It was
only meaningless syllables chanted on a single note, but the
hair on her nape lifted.

She peered around the roots of a large fallen spruce. A
rivulet trickled into the cavity the roots had left behind,
and in that pool her captor, intoning his song, scoured his
naked flesh with hemlock twigs.

She could not drink where Otter's murderer was bathing.
Cloud retreated to the beach and plodded farther until she
found an outcrop that had trapped puddles of rain. She
drank and then, hands in her armpits to warm them, gazed
up at the forest.

Its smells beckoned: cold earth, wet cedars. But running
away would take a mountain more strength than she possessed right now. And what would be the point? Without
food and shelter, she would perish in the next winter storm.

Likely her master would catch her anyway. He would just
beat her harder than ever.

Voices rose in argument down at the canoes. Cloud turned.
"You shouldn't even touch it!" the wizard was yelling. "The
spirit said, 'Keep it from those who are not pure!'"

Her master had returned to the beach and now squatted inside the black canoe. Above his head hung the agitated flock of ice girls. "You always need to be pure to
approach a spirit treasure," he said. "Why is *this* box so
dangerous?"

"I already told you," said the wizard. "My spirits say
you'll die if you open it. The creature who attacked us in the
forest is one of the bloodthirsty gods."

"If the god is going to punish me for taking his box,"
said her master, "or pursue me to fetch it back, he would
have done so already. I think your spirits have made another
mistake."

"They have made no mistakes!"

"They promised us a camp full of the enemy, not to mention their king. All we found were a few hunters and a pretty

slave-girl, and we lost a third of our men to that monster. Why should I believe what they say about this box?"

"My spirits warned of the god," said the wizard. "They said we shouldn't venture from the beach. Now they've warned about the box, in plain speech as well as prophecy. Pay attention this time. We'll be destroyed if the wrong person opens it."

Her master jumped down from the canoe and stalked away up the beach. Just then, behind Cloud, a warm, deep voice said, "Of course what the spirit told him is true."

She spun around. Upon the outcrop sat a little brown frog. "Our kind can *only* tell the truth," it said.

"Go away," she whispered, stepping back in terror.

The frog crawled after her. "The power that attacked those warriors was indeed one of the bloodthirsty gods. But which one? The loon dives deep, but she is not a fish. And those men will truly meet disaster if the wrong person opens the box. But the bear"—its voice turned sly—"the bear need not fear the eagle."

"Go away!" Cloud kept backing up.

"Here is even more wisdom, bear girl. The cougar painted itself in fawn's spots and bit off a mouthful of leaves."

Then feet crunched in the gravel behind her, and Cloud's master seized her arm with a grip as unbreakable as Rumble's. "Walk, slave," he said, shoving her ahead of him. "Go on, hurry up!" When she glanced back, the frog had vanished.

At the water's edge, her master tossed her aboard his canoe. She landed in a sprawl beside the heap of boxes.

"She'll bring us bad luck even if she doesn't start her bleeding," the southern wizard complained from his seat. "My spirits particularly warned to keep the box away from women."

"So you have said," said Cloud's master as he leapt aboard, But he hauled up Cloud and shoved her farther to stern, and he seated himself at the thwart closest to the boxes.

Only at that moment did Cloud realize she could now understand the southerners' speech. Just as had happened at

Waterfall. Mocking spirits, useless powers: she wished the spirit world would leave her to her misery.

*Even without the swarm of ice girls, she would have* been able to identify the box that had caused the argument. Many in the heap, smoke-blackened utilitarian containers, Cloud recognized as having come in Otter's canoe from Whale Town. This box was larger and cleaner, and bore a faded, once-fine painting. Before the wizard had stopped him, her master had severed most of the brittle-looking cords wrapping the box. But its lid was still closed tight.

Now Cloud could trace to it the scent of decayed flesh she had noticed yesterday. She was trying not to think or feel anything, but surely the box could not belong, as the southerners believed, to the island's *bloodthirsty god.* She already knew the location of her father's bones. Old remains in a well-crafted chest: it must come from Raven Tongue's tomb, and the talking frog-thing must have traveled with it. Perhaps these men from the far south did not know about the grave houses of northern wizards. But didn't the *smell* tell them what the box contained?

*The warriors paddled northwest along the island* they had camped on. When they reached its last rocky tip, the wizard directed them to continue, even though no land was visible ahead. The spirits, he told them, had promised an archipelago over the horizon.

Aching with grief, Cloud remembered that Otter had indeed pointed in that direction to the Gull Islands. But the southerners started arguing. One asked, "You want us to venture onto the open ocean in winter?"

The wizard gestured. "Have you ever seen the ocean as calm as this in winter? My spirits have quieted the winds for us."

Indeed, only a light northwesterly breeze roughened the low swells. The overcast rode high enough to reveal the white shoulders of the mainland.

"This can't be the way," another man said. "My uncle once visited the enemy. He said their town lay in sight of the mainland, in a harbor protected by a long sand spit."

"Trust my spirits that there is land ahead," said the wizard, "and that we'll be reunited with our captured kinsfolk."

The men looked at Cloud's master. He said, "Perhaps this time they'll be right."

The warriors paddled onward. The island they had camped on shrank to a small blue lump, and the horizon ahead grew mistier. Cloud began to feel the first stirrings of hunger. And although she did not want to think, thoughts came to her anyway. She thought: these men were searching for *a town protected by a long sand spit.* They must come from the southern towns Rumble had raided last fall. Her captor had protested, *The spirits promised us their king,* but Otter *was* a king of Sandspit Town, just not the one they were looking for.

She thought: maybe wizards' servants did always speak the truth. But truths told in certain ways were as good as lies.

Land appeared near midday. It proved, however, to be only a string of barren islets: granite whitened by gull droppings, waves breaking in roars of foam.

Another argument broke out as they drifted off the last islet, rocking in the waves. This time, Cloud's captor was more doubtful, but once again he directed the men to continue.

He was right to be skeptical, Cloud thought. Because now that Bone was done using these men to destroy Otter, he had to make sure they never reached Sandspit Town.

*We will be reunited with our captured kinsfolk,* the spirits had promised. But Rumble's captives were already dead.

Now she noticed an indistinct woman's shape swimming in the wake of her canoe. It never once broke the surface to breathe.

**Cloud heard the deep roar of breakers long before** she saw them. At last a headland loomed out of the mist.

The wizard directed them up its leeward shore. No one argued this time.

The forest atop the unbroken cliffs reminded Cloud of Whale Town: cedars, great mounds of moss. Orcas breached in the distance. As evening approached, they found a sliver of beach to camp on. Again Cloud's master dragged her roughly from the canoe. But this time he was uninterested in the wood she gathered. Now that the southerners had reached what they presumed to be enemy territory, they were lighting no fires.

Her master disappeared into the trees, and soon faint song drifted out from there. Cloud stepped down the beach, wondering how far she could stray before he would haul her back and beat her. A little stream crossed her path. She drank, then climbed into a narrow space sheltered by two logs, pulling tangles of dried seaweed after her. Hunger gnawed at her belly.

"Let us serve you, bear girl," said the frog's deep voice out of the darkness.

The horrors, large and small, wouldn't leave her alone. "Go away," Cloud whispered, stuffing her cloak into her mouth to stifle her sobs.

"You will not get better advice," it said. "We can tell you how to free your brothers: fire that isn't fire, water that isn't water. Your shortest journey will be longest and hardest."

"Go away!" How she hated these spirits! Their deceiving ways had caused Otter's death. They had brought her to *this* place. How could that frog imagine she would listen?

Then an ocean of hopelessness drowned her anger. Free her brothers? That task would lie unfinished forever. They would haunt her dreams, a slave's dreams, until she died.

Which, Bone surely intended, would be soon.

"Go away," she whispered again.

The frog fell silent. Perhaps it did go away. The voices at the campfires died down. Cloud's master emerged from the forest and walked down to the box, causing the ice girls to mill in sparking turbulence. But he turned away without touching it, and Bone's servants settled back to their vigil. And Cloud tumbled into that glade where the ghosts endlessly beseeched her.

*Her first sensation the next morning was of empti-*ness burning in her stomach like a wound.

Her second sensation was the aroma of smoke-dried salmon. It pulled her to her feet as inexorably as the dog-servant's fish hook. But the warriors were already packing up their provision boxes, the source of the intoxicating smell.

Surely, she thought, her master would feed her when he grew tired of humiliating her. You might kill a slave to show how great you were, but who would starve one to death?

Although—her hunger was trivial in the face of Otter's death. She did not deserve the comfort of food.

She returned to the stream where she had drunk the night before. Filling her stomach with water did not extinguish the red-hot coal of hunger. She looked at the forest, thinking once again that she could try to run away. Dying there would be a better fate than any Bone planned for her.

But before she could act on the thought, her master, hair dripping, strode out of the forest again. "Hurry up, slave."

Soon the convoy was under way again, with an ice girl chittering in the wizard's ear, and the drowned woman swimming in their wake. Hunger bored a hole in Cloud's stomach all morning. From time to time her master glanced up and down the high cliffs that guarded this shore, frowning. They had hardly passed a possible landing, much less any sign of habitation, and banks of heavy fog were beginning to drift across the water.

In early afternoon they reached a wide strait. On its far shore, snow-capped mountains rose into the clouds; on this side lay other, lower islands wrapped in fog. A narrow channel wound away between them.

"Which way now?" Cloud's master demanded.

The ice girl chattered in the wizard's ear. He said, "The spirits tell me, game for our arrows waits inside this channel."

The new channel led through canyons of forest, along dark, obsidian-smooth waters. Fog poured over them, chill and blank, then poured away. As the afternoon waned, the channel branched and branched again. Now Cloud saw Bone's octopus swimming beside the drowned woman.

Suddenly Cloud's master slammed his paddle on the gunwale in a violent *crack!* "We're being led in circles!" he shouted. "Your spirits are weak and confused! Do you see that ridge? We spied it only a little while ago from the other side!"

"The spirits haven't led us astray yet," said the wizard. "Perhaps this is the fastest route to the town."

"Or perhaps an enemy wizard sent his own spirits to confound them," said Cloud's master. "We need more spiritual aid than you can command. We need what's in my box."

The wizard closed his eyes. "For all our sakes, don't open the box. We'd be better off throwing it overboard."

But just then a watchman in another canoe called out. Farther up the channel, blue-gray smoke wound through the trees. It was a small plume, no more than the smoke of a few campfires.

"The enemy," said the wizard.

Edgy and excited, the southerners proceeded in silence now. And around the next point lay a cove where a half-dozen canoes had been drawn out of the water. Campfires burned on the beach; beside them families ate and talked. Children ran helter-skelter through a scatter of baskets and open boxes.

Cloud's master stood up in the canoe. "Don't shrink back," he shouted. "Don't forget how they butchered our wives, our children, how they enslaved our brothers and sisters!" He held a spear aloft. "I am going to catch some salmon today!"

The southerners answered with a storm of eagles' cries as they drove toward the beach. Only then did the Islanders

look up. They scrambled for weapons, but the first southerners were already upon them. Shrieking like a great bird
of prey, Cloud's master hurled a spear deep into the chest of
the nearest Islander, who vomited a stream of blood. Then
he jumped ashore, laying about him with his club. More
southerners followed, stabbing, swinging. Dogs barked hys-
terically. Battle cries mixed with the Islanders' screams, a
noise like a thousand shrieking seagulls echoing between
the narrow stone walls of the cove.

The rocks grew slick with blood, and blood even spat-
tered Cloud where she crouched in the canoe. She didn't
know why she couldn't turn her head away, when just a few
weeks ago she had been unable to watch Stick's death. The
stinks set her nose twitching and stirred the pit of her stomach: vomit, acrid sweat, ordure, meat, and the coppery smell
of blood. Her skin crawled as if ants scurried on it.

But worst was the change, slow but impossible to ignore,
of the warm blood-smell into the scent of food: rich, salty,
sweet, so sweet. Hunger roared in her belly.

When there was no one left to kill, the southerners
returned to their canoes carrying fur and woolen robes,
bracelets, earrings, hats, boxes of food.

Then Cloud spied a spirit perched upon the rocks, an armored man with the head of a gull. As the southerners set
out again, the spirit unfurled wings and launched itself into
the darkening sky.

**Night had arrived. The southerners came ashore to**
camp not far from the scene of the slaughter, setting a watch
and again lighting no fires. Tonight Cloud's master showed
no interest in humiliating her but disappeared right away
into the woods.

For a long time Cloud crouched in the canoe, unable to
contain her sick trembling. At last she crawled out in search
of water. One of the southerners had dropped a fur robe on
the gravel, and she stooped to pick it up. She could smell no

blood on it, only the scents of wood smoke and tanned hide. On closer inspection the garment proved moth-eaten, no doubt why he had thrown it away. She wrapped herself in the robe. Its warmth made her feel worse: emptier, more unfit to live.

She climbed along the beach until she found a brackish puddle to drink from. Then she curled up in the gravel, cold, aching, and sick to her bones. She kept seeing the Gull Islander vomit blood, a child's head crushed, and then Otter again, the horrible way his body had flopped like a salmon when her master had clubbed him that last time.

Her master emerged from the forest. More purification, she thought, more washing off the smell of blood. But only so he could shed more. A tidal wave of hatred surged through Cloud. She wanted to rip at his guts, claw the flesh from his throat. How could he think any amount of bathing could cleanse him? If she were a man, she would snatch up that branch and split his skull as if opening a clam.

But she was only a girl, weak from hunger, despair, and a blow to her own skull.

Blood was all they wanted, the southerners, Bone, Rumble, her father. They wanted only to bring suffering to the world. Otter had been different, but how far had that taken him?

*One of the bloodthirsty gods.* Her father had killed so many southerners with such awful swiftness. But he hadn't saved Otter, who had only been trying to free him. Was he still bent on vengeance because of Thrush? Or was it just his nature, and his pleasure, to destroy?

As for her: back on the island of the bones, she had not been able to eat a fresh-killed deer, and today she had ached for human flesh. Her empty stomach still hurt fiercely.

"Let us serve you, bear girl," pleaded the frog, out of the darkness.

"Go *away!*" she said.

The night deepened. After a while she became conscious of a change in its sounds. A wind stirred in the treetops, and the ocean began to mutter up and down the shore.

*She stood once more in the haunted glade. But as* she began to step through her father's bones, she saw that this time, in this dream, an old painted box blocked her way.

On top of the box perched a frog. Cloud jerked back, then halted as she realized she was trapped between the box and the skull in the tree. "I told you to go away!" she hissed.

"We did," said the frog. "We came here."

"Why do you keep bothering me?"

The frog blinked. "You smell good to us."

Smelled good—that's how she felt, as if she were a drop of tree sap and the frog an ant who'd sniffed her out.

"We want to help you," it said, in its deep, warm voice. "We can tell you so many true and wonderful things."

Of course it could. And no doubt every true thing the frog told her would also be a despicable lie. Rage boiled in her gut. "If you really want to help me," she said, "kill these murderers, bind Bone's servants, and set me free!"

"Oh yes, we will, Lady!" said the frog.

A noise like a thousand croaking frogs shook the box, then stopped as suddenly as it had started. The last sinew lashings of the box snapped and fell to the ground.

Then, to Cloud's horror, whitish liquid dripped out of the crack between box and lid, solidifying into a dwarf wearing an outsized rain hat. Other monsters squeezed after it: an owl with a woman's face, a fiery, zigzagging figure like a lightning bolt, an obese woman with a huge clamshell on her back, a woodworm the size of a raccoon, a gaunt man in a tattered robe, a woman with a shark's toothy jaw, a yellow butterfly with a tiny man's body. The butterfly flapped up to perch on the owl woman's shoulder.

Last, a pair of featureless black hands slid through the crack, gripped the rim, and pulled a head and the rest of a body through. A black man-shape stood up on the grass.

"Let us also," said the man-shape, in the deep, smooth voice the frog had spoken with, "help you find your bear mask. I know how hungry you are."

"I'm not—I'm not hungry that way," Cloud whispered.

"Don't fight your hunger," said the man-shape. "The whaler did not cut off his right arm and cast it out of the canoe."

"I'm not a bear!" she said. "Bone's servants said so!"

"They couldn't have said *that*," said the man-shape. "Our kind always speaks the truth."

The spirits pushed toward Cloud. The woodworm was already crawling on her feet, a sensation like a trickle of cold water. She backed around salmonberry bushes, danced over her father's thigh bones. A shadow loomed above her head and she glanced up. They had cornered her beneath the skull. Cold touched the nape of her neck; this close, she could see brown stains where tendons and flesh had once been.

Cloud yelled, "I'm not a bear!"

The spirits stopped several armspans away, as if unwilling to approach the skull. "Then why do you haunt this place?" the man-shape asked. "What did you lose that you think you'll find here?"

"*I'm* not haunting *them* . . ." Cloud began in a fury, but she stopped. It was true that *she* came *here,* every time, and that the ghosts did not visit her.

But the ghosts begged her, they begged her to free them. They wanted something from *her,* not the other way around.

"I'm not a bear!" she screamed.

She bolted toward the far side of the glade. Stones bruised her feet, thorns slashed her face and legs—

The dizzying hole into the earth yawned before her and she just barely pulled up at its brink. "Are you sure you are ready to take this trail?" the man-shape said beside her.

The air grew dark and cold as if a line of thunderheads had rolled in and rain was about to pour down. Branches rattled. The man-shape glanced toward the sound and vanished. A dark shape swept toward her. Cloud turned and ran, ran, ran—

*Heart pounding, she sat bolt upright. With relief she* saw no spirits nearby except for the ice girls at the box.

The clouds were too dark for Cloud to tell whether morning had arrived yet. A gale now stalked through the treetops in rushing, roaring squalls and had whipped up a heavy chop even on the narrow channel. The southerners were launching their canoes anyway.

They soon set out with Cloud in her usual place. The drowned woman and Bone's octopus trailed the black canoe, the ice girls guarded the box, and on the shore—a white dog sat, watching.

But they had hardly begun to paddle when a watchman called out. A mile down the channel, a high-prowed vessel had just rounded a headland. The craft was as large as Rumble's war canoe, and it cut through the water just as swiftly.

Then more of the great canoes slid around the point, three, five, six. Cloud's master shouted, "To shore! To shore!"

As the southern canoes landed again and their crews poured onto the beach, Cloud's master lifted out the box.

"What are you doing?" the wizard shouted, aghast.

"We need its power. Those canoes must carry a hundred men!"

"*No!*" the wizard shouted. "You'll bring disaster on us!"

"You said the pure could touch it. Haven't I been scouring myself morning and night since I found it?"

"And handling that slave girl in between. Spirits dislike the smell of young women."

"Then open the box yourself." Cloud's master set it down.

"With the smell of blood all around? My spirits have promised that we'll prevail. If you're afraid, run away."

"If your spirits did not foretell our enemy's arrival, they can no longer see!"

Cloud's master pulled out his whalebone dagger. The

wizard wrestled with him, trying to shove him away from the box. Then, shockingly, Cloud's master plunged the dagger into the wizard's chest, and he sagged to the ground.

The other men were gaping. "We have to risk this!" Cloud's master shouted. "If I survive, we'll share the power."

With his bloody dagger he severed the last cords wrapping the box. As he did so, ice girls swarmed downward, the drowned woman and octopus thrust out of the water, the dog leapt snarling down the beach. In an instant Bone's spirits had crushed her master onto the rocks, and he lay motionless.

But whitish liquid was dripping through the crack between the box and its lid. It coagulated into the dwarf with the oversized hat. The ice girls rushed at him, but the dwarf doffed his hat and swept them up as easily as scooping herring into a net. As Bone's other servants attacked, he swept them up as well.

Then the dwarf set the hat back on his head. His fellow spirits squeezed out of the box: the owl woman and the butterfly, the woodworm and the gaunt man, the obese woman with the clamshell, the lightning figure, the shark woman.

They watched as Cloud's master shuddered, gasped, and raised his head. His neck was bruised, burst capillaries stained his skin, dog bites and tiny stab wounds dripped blood. But he struggled to his feet and with trembling hands worked his dagger under the box's tight-fitting lid. He levered up first one side, then another. With a final push the lid popped free.

Up rose the smell of mold and decay. Cloud's master set down the lid and reached inside.

First he pulled out a puffin-beak rattle and a necklace of amulets, which he laid atop the box lid. Then he lifted out a worn mask depicting a face half-concealed by a large hat. He put that on the lid as well and brought out a second mask, this of a woman with feather designs on her cheeks. A third followed, and a fourth. With each, more of his strength seemed to return.

Cloud's master pulled out eight masks in all. Then he began tossing out rotted pieces of matting. Something small flew wide, clattering; he glanced after it, then bent down to grasp another object inside the box. A terrible spasm convulsed his body.

When the spasm passed, he lifted out a blocky mass decorated with rolls of gray hair. The smell of decomposition grew stronger. He turned the object around. Beneath the hair was a skull covered in stretched, brown skin, its lips drawn back in a hideous grimace. Cloud shuddered.

Her master addressed the mummified head solemnly. "Welcome, Grandfather. Will you not aid us today? Grant us the power to vanquish our enemies."

There was no answer. But her master's short hair lifted into the air, each lock sliding from side to side like a snake's head.

He handed the mummified head to his steersman, who stood beside him. As that southerner touched the head, a spasm coursed through his body as well.

Cloud's master stepped to the water's edge. The Islanders, a hundred warriors armored in elk hide and painted wood, were an awesome sight. As they neared shore, they shipped paddles to take up weapons. In their lead canoe stood a helmeted lord who must, Cloud thought, be their king. With him was the gull-headed spirit she had seen watching yesterday's slaughter.

She still sat in the black canoe, between the two parties of warriors about to collide. She knew she ought to get out of the way. But she did not seem to be able to move.

Now her master flung out a hand. The lead Islander canoe burst into flame. Again he gestured, and another canoe blazed up. He shouted to the air, "Thank you, Grandfather!"

"Back! Back!" the Islander king yelled, and his men furiously backed water. The king began to sing loudly and the flames went out, but Cloud's master had already ignited more canoes, and now the steersman, his hair a seething black halo, stepped up beside him and pointed. An Islander slumped with a hole in his forehead.

The southerners were passing the head from one to another. Soon a third southerner was casting boulders; a fourth
hurled driftwood logs. All the Islander canoes were aflame,
and two had shattered into pieces. Corpses bobbed in the
choppy sea. The Islanders were still back-paddling, but
the storm wind kept driving them shoreward.

The spirits from the box looked on dispassionately. Then
her master clutched his belly and opened his mouth as if to
scream. A chorus of shrill croaks emerged instead. He fell to
the ground in agonized convulsions, belly swelling with
each spasm. His tunic pulled tighter and tighter until the
seams ripped from hem to armpit. Cloud briefly glimpsed
skin blown up tight as a fishing float, and then skin, too,
ruptured.

Blood and tatters of flesh and small brown missiles foun-
tained into the air, pelted down. A stink of blood, shit, bile,
and the incongruous smell of swamp mud filled her nose.
One of the missiles bounced up to hit Cloud, and she jerked
to her feet. It was a frog.

With that, it was as if the ropes that had bound her
since her capture snapped. She crawled over the side of the
canoe and scrambled up the beach. No one tried to stop
her; the southerner's were falling to the ground one after
the other, bellies exploding like beads of water on a red-
hot stone. An ear-splitting cacophony of frogs shrilled all
along the shore.

She climbed toward the wind-tossed forest, tasting its
clean, wet scent. She was going to run until this horror lay
far behind, and rain washed away the last trace of her spoor,
and no human or spirit could find her. She would be free—

Cold fell on her like a shadow. A black, featureless man-
shape stood over her, holding the mummified head in its
hands.

Terror spiked in Cloud's chest. But instead of forcing the
head on her, the man-shape placed it upon its own shoulders, sliding it into the dimensionless spirit head. Smoky
spirit-stuff flowed over dried skin and old bone, encasing

them. Dried eyelids creased open. The corpse's grimace widened into a smile.

Cloud scuttled backward, flinched when she saw the other spirits from the box blocking her retreat.

"We have done what you wanted, bear girl," said the man-shape, in that sunlit, mellifluous voice.

"No," Cloud whispered, hardly able to speak.

But she *had* asked for this. She had begged the spirits to kill the southerners and set her free.

"My name is Raven Tongue," said the spirit. The shrunken skin of his face was growing malleable, and every moment he looked more like an eyeless old man staring at her through black water. "You can have all my former servants, and myself, too. I have made myself into a spirit stronger than any of them and await only a master to command my actions. Your enemy's servants are powerful, but if you accept my service, I will bind them for you forever."

The owl woman screeched so loudly that Cloud's ears rang. Then she said, "A strong crew makes the sea journey short."

A riddle even Cloud could understand. Accept these servants—the strong crew—and with such paddlers, with such power, she could finish any task swiftly.

Wizard's servants always tell the truth. But they never tell the whole story, not even to those they serve.

There were many ways to shorten a journey besides reaching its destination quickly. By her death, for instance.

Raven Tongue gazed at her with those empty eye sockets, awaiting her answer. Cloud could no longer detect an odor of decay from the head, or any smell at all. In fact, none of these spirits had a scent. It was one of the things, she realized, that made her so uneasy around them. The *living* world smelled.

She looked toward the carnage Raven Tongue had caused. So many blood-covered frogs hopped on the beach that it seethed with red and brown. From the slaughter arose the sweet, salty smell of blood, of bloody intestines, of meat.

*Acknowledge your hunger,* Raven Tongue had said. *Use it.* He might as well tell her to take joy in butchery. She would rather die than become such a creature.

Oh, but she already was one. She had been born one. Black hatred like broken shells stabbed her gut: for all lying spirits, for Bone and Rumble, for the southern warriors and the Gull Islanders, but most of all for herself, the ravenous bear's daughter. She had not deserved Otter's sacrifice, and she did not deserve life or freedom now.

"I don't want anything to do with you or your servants," she snarled at the dead wizard. *"Leave me alone!"*

Raven Tongue smiled a slow, cruel smile. "If you say so."

His servants fluttered into the air like a startled flock of birds, then vanished. The cacophony of frogs ceased, leaving only the roar of the wind and the rush of waves.

Cloud crawled under the forest eaves. When she looked back, Raven Tongue was stooped over his former grave box, lifting out bones, tossing away matting. The bones, some with dried flesh still clinging to them, he inserted into his black spirit-body, giving it dimension and substance.

But he didn't seem to be able to find all he wanted. He tipped the box and bent to look inside, then searched through the scraps of matting on the gravel.

Out on the water, the Gull Islanders had regrouped, and the king's canoe approached the shore once again. With a glance in that direction, Raven Tongue abandoned his search, hastily placed the masks, rattle, and amulets inside the box, then crawled in after them and pulled the lid over his head.

Thinking herself safely hidden in the trees, Cloud climbed to her feet to run. But just as Raven Tongue had stopped her earlier, now the Islander king's gull-headed servant blocked her way.

The spirit bent to grab her. Cloud scooted backward. The spirit stepped after her, reaching. There was only one direction to flee in; she scrambled back down to the beach. The spirit kept following, driving her—

—Into the king's arms. She could not evade his heavy grip. "What have we here?" he asked. Only his eyes showed between the rim of his helmet and its neck guard.

She struggled in vain as he dragged her through the mutilated southerners, prodding them with his spear. "All dead," he marveled. "That is strong wizardry." It was impossible not to look: contorted faces, filth and severed loops of intestine tossed everywhere. The stink made her dizzy with nausea.

But at the same time, there was so much red bleeding meat. She was so cavernously, monstrously hungry.

They reached Raven Tongue's box. The king examined it carefully, and then, without relaxing his grip on Cloud, pried up the lid with a dagger tip. Cloud did not know what the king saw; to her the contents looked like a jumble of bones, but they no longer smelled like anything at all.

The king replaced the lid. "Find some twine," he called to his men, who had all remained by the canoe.

He marched Cloud toward the water. On the way he bent to pick up a small, yellow-brown object. This he stowed in a pouch that hung from his neck.

He handed Cloud to a warrior who, twisting her arms painfully, heaved her into the canoe. The king took the skein of twine offered him, returned to the box, and tightly lashed down its lid. He carried the box aboard himself.

Then he addressed his men, shouting above the wind. "A storm is coming, and we must return home. But when we discover where these men are from, we will finish what we started here today. We will give our murdered kin justice!"

Thrusting their paddles aloft, the men roared in unison.

**In a moment the four remaining Islander canoes** were under way. With only a few twists and turns they reached the broad strait where the southerners had first entered the tangle of channels. Foam-crested swells now drove up the strait, and rain whipped over the charcoal water.

The Islanders spread out and set a course down the wind, the men paddling with swift, powerful strokes. The king's great canoe shuddered as each following wave broke over the stern. Heavier rain curtained the land on all sides, and then hid the other canoes as well.

Cloud pulled her tattered cloak around her. Off the port bow, an orca breached in a cloud of spray. She thought again of Stick, who had first told her about the orcas, and how he had come to live so far from his own people, ending his days as a token of Rumble's pride, thrown on the midden like a dead dog. And she thought of Otter, her kind uncle, who had watched the orcas swim west with her on the journey to Waterfall.

Despair crushed her beneath its intolerable weight. She sat straight in her seat, hoping that the orca would breach again, but it had vanished into the wilderness of swells. "Welcome, great one," she whispered, remembering Otter's prayer to the orcas, "it is good that we meet today. Protect me so that no evil befalls me, divine one."

But what good had Otter's prayer done him?

Thunder rumbled like a landslide over their heads. A crosswind blasted suddenly out of the northeast. The king's men strained at the paddles, but the crosswind hammered the canoe, swinging it broadside so that swells cascaded over the gunwale. Ice girls drove down like knives, like wind-whipped hail, and the men cried out and dropped their paddles. Huge tentacles snaked over the side. The canoe lost way and heeled.

When the next wave poured into the canoe, tipping it farther, Cloud did not try to check her slide into the ocean. Yet the icy shock of the water made her arms flail. When a tentacle caressed her legs, she kicked in wild panic.

A giant swell lifted her high, and the stretch of ocean separating her from the canoe widened. Cloud glimpsed the king shouting a song while his servant stabbed at the octopus. As she thrashed to keep her head above water, her hand struck something solid. It was a painted box of buoyant cedar, the lid lashed down tight enough to seal out the water.

She jerked her hand back. Then she and the box slid down the far side of the swell.

The drowned woman waited there, floating just under the surface. She reached toward Cloud with a half-eaten hand.

Cloud grabbed at the box, managed to hook her fingers under the cords. The drowned woman turned away. And Cloud hugged the box, alone among the swells.

# TEN

# The Fishermen

*The box heaved and twisted and rolled as Bone's* crosswind drove it westward. Cloud clung to the box as long as she could. The cold water leached the strength from her limbs, and the waves almost tore the box from her grasp countless times. She was sure Raven Tongue expected her to plead for help, and in fact once or twice she almost called out to him. But she did not. Perhaps it was because the cold made her lethargic. She was so cold it was hard to open her mouth, much less think what to say. And keeping her head above water, grabbing hand over hand at the cords on the spinning, rocking box, demanded all her attention.

At last the crosswind died away. Once it no longer slammed her forward at an angle to the swells, the box grew easier to ride, heaving and sinking rhythmically, and she managed to drag herself onto its top. The wind was colder than the ocean had been, but it was easier to lie still than struggle in the waves. For a while she shivered violently, but she became too cold even for that. The lethargy crept farther into her bones.

A pulsing roar grew louder by degrees until it overwhelmed even the din of the storm. The swells turned chaotic. The box rolled, tipping her back into the water, and a strong undertow yanked at Cloud's legs. At first her fingers remained wedged beneath the cords while the box still dragged her forward. Then the current ripped away the box and sucked her under.

Rocks all around; another wave thrust her into the air. She saw the box crash against a boulder and topple into a lagoon of boiling foam beyond. The next swell hurled her after the box. Black stones rushed at her head. But the breaker swept her past them. It smashed her instead against a steep gravel slope and then, retreating, rolled her down in an avalanche of foam, gravel, and uprooted seaweed.

She had been only half-conscious, but the shock of that impact roused her. When the next wave threw her higher onto the gravel, she began to move her arms and legs, sluggishly at first. As she was pulled down again, she succeeded in bracing a foot against a half-buried boulder. In the momentary respite before the following breaker, she crawled up the beach, gravel crumbling under her hands and knees. The next wave, less vigorous, caught her at the waist, but she kept climbing, kept struggling.

She wasn't thinking; something deep in her belly, blind panic or desperation, or just a desire to escape pain, drove her to fight her way out of the surf.

At last she found purchase on another of the half-buried boulders. Hauling herself above it, she reached a height where the surf could only splash her. And there she lay, gasping, bruised, too weak even to cough the water from her lungs.

The waves thundered ashore. Icy rain battered her. She was drifting out of the cold toward comfortable darkness, but an irregular resonant thumping, almost like the voice of a wooden drum, held her back.

The thumping grew louder. Slowly the waves pushed the source of the sound to where she could see it. It was Raven Tongue's box. A larger wave heaved it over a shoal and rushed it toward her on a hill of foam. The box caught first upon a protruding boulder, and then, as the sea returned, tumbled higher onto the beach. The next breaker wedged it in the roots of a waterlogged stump.

Successive waves rocked it but failed to dislodge it. Cloud stared at the box, her cheek pressed against gravel. She so badly wanted to pull the darkness over her like a blanket and sleep. Now she was afraid to close her eyes.

Then a frog slipped out of the crack between box and lid and hopped toward her. Cloud had been sure she couldn't move so much as a finger, but something—revulsion, rage—woke inside her. She pushed into a sitting position and scooted backward. When a stone outcrop blocked her retreat, she crawled up it, and at the top, gazed around to see where she might go next.

She had washed ashore at the western tip of a low, barren island, with no other land in sight. The ocean had ground the softer veins of stone into gravel, but for the most part the shore had eroded into jagged reefs and fields of boulders. She had survived so far because, at this tide, an outer reef bore the brunt of the storm. Each swell shattered there and churned across the rocky lagoon. By the time it slammed against the inner beach, it retained only a tiny part of its original power.

Nothing higher than her knee grew on the island, but about a quarter-mile inland, the stony ground rose to a ridge. Its leeward side, she thought, would be more sheltered than this beach. Stiff and sore from her battering by the waves, she stumbled toward the ridge. The wind and rain blasting her were brutally cold. That was when she realized she had lost her cloak; she no longer had even that protection against the storm.

When she reached the top of the ridge, she jerked back so quickly she nearly fell. At her feet, cliffs plunged straight to the sea. She had found not just the highest point on the island but its opposite shore. This vantage revealed that, except for the exposed southern side where the waves had deposited her, the island had no beaches at all. There was no respite from the weather to be had.

Blowing mist took shape as a dead old man. "The harpooneer who had never seen a whale," Raven Tongue said, "thought it a sea monster and fled. Let us serve you, bear girl!"

Paralysis gripped Cloud from the shock of another riddle that pierced straight to her understanding. Then she limped away along the cliff edge.

"Why do you keep rejecting us?" he called.

She rejected him because she loathed and feared him, because she hated his smug mystification, because the spirits' half-truths were more dangerous than lies. Because she resented the way he pursued her so ruthlessly. Because even if the spirits of the box were the whale of that riddle—even if they were an awesome mass of power she could obtain if she were only a fearless harpooneer—they were malignant beings. They would do her bidding, but only by working evil.

Still, she could not put out of her mind the other suggestion of the riddle: that through ignorance she *mistook* the spirits for something malignant.

As she moved along the ridge top, a fold in the cliffs came into view where the rock was more tumbled and broken. She wormed down the rain-slicked stone in search of a sheltered crevice. Her muscles were nearly ungovernable from cold.

"Do you *want* to die?" asked Raven Tongue, once more misting into solidity beside her.

Did she? Apparently not, given the trouble she was going to. But she was not very certain she wanted to live, either.

She kept crawling downward. Then, from one outflung terrace, she caught a glimpse of what lay inside that fold in the shoreline: green water barely rippled.

She glanced up. Raven Tongue had not moved.

She did not want to live, did not deserve to. And yet . . .

If she could reach that sheltered cove, perhaps she *could*

survive the storm without his aid. If there was even a yard of foreshore, she could build a shelter and cocoon herself in dead grass and seaweed. There would be mussels and oysters, crabs and limpets. She might even find a fisherman's cached supplies.

Right below her, at the foot of the cliffs, lay an apron of oyster-encrusted rocks. Cloud slid down a last granite face to land atop them, and then hobbled over the oysters. The air here was almost warm compared to the heights. Now that she was out of the worst of the wind, other scents rose up: the oyster beds, seaweed, scat from a mink's recent crab dinner.

Rock turned to gravel, and gravel in turn led her around another arm of the cliffs, into the protected cove she had glimpsed. Then she stopped in utter dismay.

She was not alone.

Numerous soot-black canoes littered the beach. Among them stood men who turned toward her, one after the other, mouths agape.

*The black canoe is coming.* Only one?

Even if Cloud had possessed the strength to flee, it would have been pointless to try. She had nearly tripped over one of the canoes, and the crewman frozen in the act of climbing out of it would seize her before she ran two steps. So she just stood there, waiting for him to speak to her or kill her, or worse.

He kept staring at her. Finally he set down what he was holding—a fish hook?—and stepped all the way out of his canoe. He splashed through shallow water toward her.

Although her heart banged against her ribs, Cloud didn't back away. She was too exhausted and frozen even to flinch in anticipation of the grip that would crush her arm, the blows that would batter her face.

The man halted before coming within arm's reach. He still did not speak, but his sharp gaze, so alert as to be almost predatory, never wavered from Cloud's face. Others came up behind him, men and boys, and women, too.

Cloud had forgotten to breathe. Now she inhaled deeply. A second glance showed her that the fisherman was not so much a man as a tall slim boy. Despite the harsh weather, he wore only a breechcloth of fish skin. A fish scale glittered on his wrist.

The boy slicked back his shoulder-length hair with both hands, squeezing water from it. She caught the smell of his skin: warm, damp, briny from a swim in saltwater.

Another scent, a much-loved one, led her eye from the boy back to his canoe. On the rain-flooded bottom boards lay four large chinook salmon. As if the smell of food had caused it, her teeth began to chatter again.

The boy opened his mouth to speak. But through the gathering crowd came an older woman, who put a hand on his shoulder to silence him.

"Well, girl," she said, "you have caught us out. Now you can ask from us whatever you want. What will it be?"

Her tone was ironic but not unfriendly. She wore only a short, ragged skirt of fish skin, but from the way she carried herself, and the way the others moved aside for her, Cloud was sure she must be their queen. Her gaze was even keener and more uncomfortable than the boy's.

Cloud did not know what to reply. What had she caught them at, other than beaching their canoes?

Without turning away from Cloud, the foreign queen gestured. Several of the strangers hurried to bring her small bundles. "Here," said the queen to Cloud, "you can have a harpoon that never lets go of its target."

Cloud understood the queen's words—she was obviously growing faster at this trick of understanding foreign tongues—but not their meaning. The bone harpoon point the queen held out to her was well crafted but ordinary enough. Was the offer some kind of joke? These strangers couldn't expect a harpoon to be useful: Cloud had no canoe to harpoon from and could barely paddle one in fine weather, much less in a raging winter storm. And she, a girl, was no sea hunter at all.

A woman next to the queen said, "She thinks it's of no use to her."

At another time Cloud would have been embarrassed to have her face so easily read, but right now she was too worn out to care. Raising an eyebrow, the queen handed the harpoon to the man who had brought it. She put her hand into another bag. "Then perhaps you would like my amulet? Or"—she gestured and another man stepped forward—"a chest filled with my wealth?"

With one hand the queen proffered an ivory carving; with the other hand she pointed toward her feet. Cloud blinked rain from her eyes. Her sight must have deceived her, because the box sitting on the gravel could not have fit inside the pouch from which she thought she had seen the man remove it.

The man lifted the box lid. Cloud was astonished to see hammered figures of salmon and sea urchins, cockles and porpoises, whales and sea otters, all exuding the warm glow of polished copper. This queen in her ragged skirt scarcely looked as if she could afford a roof over her head, much less riches surpassing any king's treasure Cloud had ever heard of.

Still, what help was such wealth to her at this moment?

The woman beside the queen said, "She thinks these things aren't any help to her."

Cloud's heart lurched. It was impossible that the queen's attendant could hear her thoughts.

"No help?" said the queen. "Then perhaps you'd like my canoe?" She held out a canoe only a handspan long. It was made of copper and exquisitely detailed, down to the riveted prow and miniature thwarts.

Anger stirred in Cloud. She was close to perishing from exposure. Surely they could see how hard she shivered. She was so cold, so tired, so unutterably hungry, and these strangers were playing some obscure game at her expense, offering her—what? Tools she couldn't use, carvings that couldn't keep her warm, fabulous riches she couldn't eat! Oh, a canoe *would* be wonderful, if only she possessed the strength and the

skill, and was granted the fortunate weather, to leave this island and find her way to a friendly town.

What she *really* wanted right now, more than any treasure on earth—what she would not have been able to tear
her gaze from if it weren't for the foreign queen's spate of
peculiar offers—were the salmon in the boy's canoe. The
smell tormented her.

"She likes the canoe," said the woman beside the queen.
"But what she really wants is a fire, shelter from the storm,
and a good meal."

Through her convulsive shuddering, a fresh shiver crawled
up Cloud's spine: that attendant *really could hear her thoughts.*

The queen's eyebrows drew down and she subjected Cloud
to an even sharper scrutiny. Then a corner of her mouth curved
into a mocking half-smile. She handed the miniature canoe to
one of her people. "Food, then," she said. "For our guest."

She had laid the slightest stress on the last word. The
strangers glanced at each other, glanced at their queen. Then
they got busy. Some stowed away the gifts the queen had offered Cloud. Others gathered driftwood and, despite the
downpour, quickly kindled fires. Still others lashed bottom
boards upon a pair of tumbledown frames at the head of the
cove. The strangers were all as scantily clad as the queen:
not one of them, man or woman, wore a scrap of clothing
above the waist.

The boy did not join the others. Instead, with a private
smile both like and unlike the queen's, he set a foot back in
his canoe and, one by one, heaved his four chinooks onto the
gravel. Then he took up a knife and with deft motions began to gut them.

"Come sit at the fire, girl," said the queen. "I don't want
you to die of cold."

Cloud became aware that the vision of salmon flesh had
rooted her to the spot. As she turned to follow the queen, she
stumbled and had to steady herself on the prow of the boy's
canoe. His head flew up. Cloud snatched her hand away, wondering if she ought to apologize for touching his property.

But she was too abashed to speak to him, and her teeth were chattering too hard anyway.

He didn't seem angry. He returned to his task, the enigmatic smile still on his face. And Cloud continued up the beach. A few moments passed before she absorbed what had happened: in the instant before she pulled away her hand, the adzed cedar of his canoe prow had *twitched*.

**The queen seated Cloud on mats spread beside one** of the campfires. Other women wrapped her in robes of sea otter and fur seal, and over those a cloak and odd shapeless hat sewn from waterproof gut. Cloud thanked them as best she could through her chattering teeth.

Tortured by the smell of barbecuing salmon, she nevertheless tried to make sense of the situation. The queen was extraordinary. Cloud had always thought Thrush the most beautiful woman she had ever seen, but this half-naked foreigner was something else again: white-skinned and black-haired, sleek and hard-muscled, as graceful as a fish in water. She was so beautiful it almost hurt to look at her, and at the same time dangerous-looking as a knife. Her navel, and the nipples of her small breasts, were nearly as black as her hair.

So, now that Cloud noticed, were everyone else's.

The boy was a young male version of her, almost certainly a son or much younger brother. These people were real; Cloud had felt their hands on her. She could smell their skin and their breath. Yet they were the oddest humans Cloud had met.

And where was Raven Tongue? Why had he stopped harassing her?

She uneasily recalled a story Stick had told her, about a woman kidnapped by the king of the drowned men. At the beginning he, like these strangers, had seemed like a living human being. The story did not say whether he possessed a scent.

But when Cloud's hosts laid food before her, hunger conquered all doubts. The fish was fresh and sweet, and oily enough to drip down her chin, not like salmon caught in the rivers that had begun to throw off their fat. The flesh was so hot that it burned her fingers and the still-healing roof of her mouth, but it glowed in her belly like summertime.

They kept bringing food to her, bowl after bowl of perfumed flesh that was rose-orange like a hearth fire, like sunrise. The strangers, including the boy, gathered at the fires to eat as well. There was plenty for everyone—each of those chinooks could have fed thirty men—but as the first desperate edge of hunger wore off, Cloud began to feel ashamed of what Aunt Glory would have said to see her consume such a huge amount of food, five helpings already. Although she hadn't asked for it, the strangers unblinkingly offered her more and still more.

Eventually she grew warm and sleepy, and her eating slowed to a standstill. The queen, observing this, gestured and one of the women brought a dipper of fresh water. When Cloud had drunk, the queen spoke:

"Now, young friend, you'll want to rest. We'll talk more tomorrow. But first I'll introduce myself. I'm Foam-at-Sunset, and these others are my brothers and sisters, and our children and grandchildren."

The queen paused as if waiting for a reply. Pale, rain-wet faces stared at Cloud from all sides. She did not know how to speak in front of such an audience.

But there was no one else to talk for her—no Otter, no Glory. She cleared her throat. Recalling Glory's lectures on politeness, she said, "Thank you for the food—for your hospitality." The words came out in hardly more than a whisper. "My name is Cloud. I come from Sandspit Town, originally."

"Yes, child," said Queen Foam, that half-smile once more lifting the corner of her mouth. "We know who *you* are."

**They led Cloud into one of the shelters, where they** bedded her down in furs. She slept hard. She was aware at times of people coming and going, of darkness, of the warmth in her belly and the discomfort of her damp clothing. But the rain, dropping on the shelter like an endless stream of gravel, always lulled her back to sleep. It was her first dreamless rest in months.

When she finally woke, day had come again and she was alone. She sat up. Her bruises throbbed, stiff muscles screamed, and her tumbling in the surf had abraded large patches of skin. In spite of all that, she felt better than she had—

—since Otter's death. Darkness moved inside her at the memory.

Outside, wind and rain still raged. Cloud reached for the cloak and hat they had given her. Just then the walls of the shelter wavered, opening into a dim, impossibly wide space. She fell off the world, spinning into an abyss with no bottom.

She scrambled out of the shelter. On the beach, the world came right again, and her vertigo subsided. But that terrifying moment had been too much like her visions on the island of the bones. Heart still pounding, she tied on her cloak and hat.

The strangers were now repairing their canoes, men and women alike sewing wooden patches to damaged sections of gunwales, caulking joins, or repainting the black hulls. (Cloud could smell the fish oil they used as a base, and despite yesterday's huge meal, her stomach grumbled.) Though the strangers worked intently, they also talked and joked back and forth.

It was in some ways a reassuringly ordinary scene. But there were too many strange things about it—for example, how scantily all the people were clad despite the icy downpour. And what kept splashing at the mouth of the cove, as if some of the foreigners *swam* in the icy water? Why were there no babies or children—no one younger than Cloud, in fact—when there were so many women?

And how, using hook and line, had that boy caught four chinooks on the open ocean in winter?

The wind plastered a lock of Cloud's hair across her face and she pushed it aside. Her hands were sticky with fish grease.

A voice spoke behind her. "What can we do for our friend?"

Queen Foam sat by a campfire, plaiting her black, shiny, rain-soaked hair. An ivory comb lay in her lap. Out of the corner of Cloud's eye, the comb moved crabwise.

Beside the queen sat the attendant who could hear thoughts. "She'd like to wash herself and comb her hair," said the attendant, "but she's a little nervous about your comb."

Queen and attendant laughed in their high, clear voices. Cloud flushed at the mockery, but at the same time shivered to have her thoughts *overheard;* an uncomfortable combination in her belly, hot and cold.

"I can offer you nothing but the sweet saltwater to wash in," said Queen Foam, "unless rain is more to your liking. But my comb is yours to use, child. Don't worry, it won't hurt you."

She held out the ivory comb. Cloud wanted to shove the thing away, but she was also aware that, while the queen's ultimate intentions might be unclear, she owed Foam her life. Recalling Glory once again on the subject of manners, Cloud took the comb. At least it didn't squirm as the boy's canoe had done.

"Thank you, Lady," she said.

"Sit down, Cloud," said Foam, indicating a spot on the driftwood log beside her.

Cloud sat gingerly. Here was yet another strange thing: a queen performing her toilet on the beach in a downpour. Still, she herself was not uncomfortable compared to the privations of the last few days. The queen kept her fire large enough to withstand the deluge, so Cloud was warm inside her bundle of furs and gut skin. And the huge meal she had eaten the day before had just begun to wear off; she was only a little hungry, just a few complaints coming from the direction of her stomach.

Cloud scrubbed her fishy hands with a sodden hank of dead grass and scooped handfuls of rain out of the air to rinse salt from her face and eyes. Then she picked up the comb again.

It *was* carved with the figure of a crab, front and back. Inlaid pearlshell eyes stared at her, but it did not move in her hand. She took off her hat and yanked at her matted hair.

"How did you catch us here, friend Cloud?" asked Foam. "It was an amazing piece of fortune. We just stopped for a day or two to mend our canoes."

The queen spoke as if Cloud and not she were the curiosity. "I fell overboard, Lady," she said. "And washed up here."

"Really?" asked Foam. "Have you been purifying yourself lately? To attract fortune?"

Like Cloud's dead master? The question was grotesque. "No! I've been very unlucky, not fortunate at all!"

Foam said, "Fortune and misfortune often go hand in hand."

Cloud did not reply, but she thought, anger stabbing her belly, how could you call it fortune, then?

But it was all so hard to take in. Here she sat on a remote beach in a blinding winter rainstorm, beside the strange and beautiful Foam-at-Sunset. Aunt Glory had never mentioned any queen who ruled like a king. Hatless, cold water streaming from breasts as white as the sea foam of her name, Cloud's host carried herself more proudly than any noblewoman in modest doeskin and dyed wool. Cloud imagined that even Rumble would hesitate to cross Queen Foam. Dangerous as a knife.

Why had Foam offered those gifts? Perhaps the strangers were just mocking her with the pretense that she was not to be their slave. Beatings or worse would start at any moment.

Foam's attendant spoke from the far side of the queen. "She thinks, Lady, that you might plan to keep her for a slave."

The queen shook her head. "You're our guest, friend Cloud. You caught us out. You trapped us in your condition, and we could only return to our former state by bringing you with us."

A chill touched Cloud's spine. "Bring me to where, Lady?"

That half-smile crooked Foam's mouth. "To our world."

*Our world.* Cloud guessed, suddenly, what Foam meant: that abyss she had glimpsed inside the shelter. The same sort of place, perhaps, that she had seen on the island haunted by her father's ghost. It was not a world she wanted to be in.

At that moment a pang wracked her stomach. "She's hungry again," said the attendant. Both women laughed.

Humiliation twisted in Cloud's gut. It was true that she was hungry, that she was hungry nearly all the time. But she hadn't complained. Were they going to ridicule her for every thought that crossed her mind?

"Don't worry, child," said the queen. "We don't starve our guests. Look"—she pointed with her chin, still smiling—"my son Black Fin has been fishing for you."

Cloud had not heard them arrive, but down on the beach, fishermen were pulling ashore their slim black canoes. Only one person dragged each vessel—impossible that *any* canoe had ventured onto the mountainous storm seas, much less one paddled by a single person! And each as long as Otter's journeying canoe—

Something was *profoundly* wrong. These people were deceiving her with spirit power, and laughing at her confusion and unease.

One of the fishermen was the boy who had yesterday supplied the chinooks. Cloud took him to be the son Foam mentioned. Graceful and confident, Black Fin climbed the beach toward Cloud, fingers of each hand hooked into the gills of a large sockeye. His wide mouth and high-bridged nose, his foam-pale skin and soot-black hair, were all like his mother's. He was as sleek as she was, tall and slender, beautiful as a diving hawk. But the smile now on his face showed an emotion very different from Foam's ironic amusement.

Cloud did not know how to name that emotion, but the smile sent heat sweeping over her skin. Surely she was imagining that he smiled *at her,* that his eyes were fixed on her alone . . .

She was not.

Rage swallowed up her humiliation and anxiety, and her mouth drew back into an involuntary snarl. The boy stopped in his tracks as if he had been struck, his smile vanishing. He dropped his catch beside the fire and stalked away without speaking.

Something tightened like a fist in her chest. Cloud did not understand what had just happened—with him, to her—but she felt as if a bucket holding her guts had been upended.

Foam raised an eyebrow but said nothing. One of the women began gutting the fish. After a while Cloud dared to glance in the direction Black Fin had gone. He squatted at another campfire, arms dangling over his knees, rain dripping from his hatless head. He poked with a stick as if adjusting the fire, but he was watching her, mouth tight, brows drawn down.

To escape that stare she stood and limped down the beach. The aroma of stewing salmon wove through the other smells of the strangers' camp, fish oil, wood smoke, seaweed, decaying beach grass. The canoe-menders glanced at her but continued their work. The newly returned canoes, she saw, contained salmon, most merely stunned and with gills beating. Of course none of the fish showed the red flush of spawning season. Cloud didn't know much about trolling, but she thought it no more possible to hook so many salmon in winter than to paddle a canoe in this storm alone.

Then, out of the corners of her eyes, the canoes *squirmed.* The salmon wavered, too, skin glittering like incandescent abalone, like the ocean under a naked summer sun.

Blinking, Cloud retreated to Queen Foam's campfire. But her vision would not settle now, and the people at the campfire looked as huge as trees. Cloud remembered, suddenly, more about the woman kidnapped by the king of the drowned men. Another captive, who helped the heroine escape, was herself unable to leave because she had eaten the king's food. It had looked and tasted exactly like salmon, but was really offal of the dead.

Hadn't everything here appeared ordinary until she had eaten their food?

Fear coiled like a snake in Cloud's belly. The icy fear, the sickening twist of humiliation, the warmth of the boy's smile, the heat of anger, her vertigo as the world changed shape, the dark knife-edge of grief lodged inside her . . . it all churned together, an unnavigable flood-tide of emotion that for a moment threatened to drown her.

Then the woman ladled out a bowl of stew from the cooking box. Cloud's mouth flooded with saliva. She edged closer. The stew smelled so good. Even if it wasn't real salmon, how could it be worse to eat more than she already had? At last she took the bowl offered her and looked for a place to sit.

And then she dropped the bowl. Hot liquid splashed her feet, but she barely felt it.

"What's wrong?" asked the queen.

Black Fin stood up. "Isn't that your box?"

It seemed she was fated never to leave it behind. The tumbling in the lagoon had cracked one side and scraped away its remaining paint, but the cords still bound it tightly.

Black Fin stepped toward her. "They said they brought you here." His voice had a dangerous edge.

"No," Cloud said, backing away from both him and the box. "It isn't mine. I don't want it."

"Those spirits could be a help to you, Cloud," said Foam.

Foam, too, was going to press them on her? Cloud said, angrily, "They don't give straight answers."

"And what about the human heart is straight?" asked Foam.

"They're *liars*," said Cloud. "They're evil, *horrible*!"

"You do have to learn their ways," said the queen.

"I don't want this box," said Cloud. "It isn't mine; I tried to leave it behind; the only thing I want is to *burn it up.*"

"Well, then," Black Fin said in that dangerous voice, "that's what we'll do."

In a single swift movement he set the box on Foam's magnificent bonfire. Foam reached out as if to prevent him but then dropped her arm. The wet cedar smoked, tentatively at first, then in gray choking billows.

Doubt tugged at Cloud. Raven Tongue and his servants could have been hers to command. Without the box, she was at the mercy of these unsettling strangers.

But she didn't pull the box off the fire. No, she could never accept the service of its evil spirits. Bad enough that *she* was—what she was.

The bottom of the box ignited, and then the sides. Fire licked upward along the cords. The cords burned to ash. As the box itself dried out and shrank, the bottom split open. Masks tumbled onto the coals and caught fire.

The dwarf was the first spirit to depart, a spruce-root rain hat sailing into the sky. As more fire forced its way through the cracks, the lid collapsed as well. Flames roared even higher, and owl feathers danced away in the updrafts. A cascade of shrilling frogs nearly extinguished the fire, then hopped away unscathed.

"This won't rid you of them," Foam said. "Destroying the masks just makes those servants freer to move where they like. They can't follow you to our home, but they'll find you later, and keep after you until you accept them, or another master captures their allegiance."

*To our home?* Cloud certainly did not want to be abandoned on this island, but she was very much afraid of where *home* might be for Foam and her people.

# ELEVEN

# The End of the Ocean

*They offered Cloud another bowl of stew. She* accepted it, but only after the last spirit had fled, yellow butterfly wings vanishing into the sky, did she sit down to eat.

"Now, Cloud," the queen said, "I know who your father was, and what it is you have to do."

Cloud choked, hot broth scalding the back of her nose. She hadn't been thinking at all about her father or her brothers. The queen's attendant *couldn't* have overheard her.

Foam went on as if she didn't notice Cloud's consternation. "Those spirits can't solve all your problems even if you do accept their service. We are on our way home for the winter. We will take you with us—as our guest, of course. Once there we can obtain more help for you."

Cloud wanted to beg Foam, *I don't want to go to your home. I don't want the favors you're offering me. Thank you for the food and the furs; please take me back to—*

But she didn't know where she could go. Not Whale Town. She couldn't face Winter, or Otter's children. Not Sandspit Town.

The attendant told Foam, "The bear child wants to refuse your gifts altogether. She doesn't even want to be a bear."

This time Foam did not smile. She said in a voice sharp as a knife, "You may have been living in your mother's world, naked, but you are still Lord Stink's daughter. Do you think you can escape your obligations by pretending you're human?"

Cloud hated these strangers for talking about her bear inheritance, for telling her her father's name. She hated Foam's cold disapproval. But just then the queen *wavered*.

Cloud's heart stumbled and an icy spear stabbed from the pit of her stomach straight through the top of her head. She was not sure what Foam had become in that tiny moment, but it was predatory, sleek, and far too large. It froze her guts. She knew she could no more argue with a being like Foam-at-Sunset than tell a mountain not to fall on her. *She had no choice.*

Foam waited for an answer. "I—I haven't forgotten the dead," Cloud whispered. "I just don't know what to do."

"Am I to believe those little servants told you nothing?"

"They told me all kinds of things. Water that isn't water, fire that isn't fire. It didn't make sense."

"No?" said Foam. "Well, finish your meal. We'll leave soon."

Cloud's appetite had vanished, but she obediently spooned up the stew. Meanwhile Foam's people packed their belongings. When Foam asked, "Are you ready?" Cloud did not want to turn toward her again—did not want Foam's other self to swell in the edge of her vision, immense and terrifying—but she thought it would be rude not to look at the queen, and where Foam was concerned, *she did not want to be rude.*

Cloud turned, and as she did so, that other shape did indeed flicker into being for a heartbeat. "Yes, Lady," she whispered.

"We will speak more when we reach our home," Foam said. Her mocking smile returned. "My son is ready to take you."

Cloud followed the queen's gaze. Black Fin did not look ready to take her. He had stalked down to his canoe and was pitching stones into the water without so much as a glance in Cloud's direction. He was angry, she thought, about the box, and his fish. But why should he expect her to welcome his favors?

Perhaps his mother was reason enough. Who would have courage to refuse the son?

Just being with these people frightened her, and Foam wanted her to go *home* with them. On top of that, Cloud had to face Black Fin's moods and caprices. She had no experience receiving attention from young men, and she didn't want to start now.

She forced herself to walk down to him. He fixed her with a smoldering gaze. "You don't," he said, "need to come with me."

Cloud took a deep breath. "Lady Foam said I should."

"Do you think I can manage it without offending you?"

"It was your fault about the box!" said Cloud before she could stop herself. She groped against her will for courtesy toward Foam's son. "You could have asked whether I wanted it."

But that sounded surly as well. Cloud took a deep breath. "Thank you for the fish. I'm sorry if—if I was rude."

He did not indicate that he had heard her. Instead he turned away to push his canoe into the water.

Cloud's stomach flip-flopped at the thought of riding in that canoe, which had twitched under her hand. She told herself that Foam wanted her to go with Black Fin, and Foam hadn't harmed her—so far. And the other canoes would be no better. She'd seen them twitching, too.

Cloud took a few steps forward. Black Fin guided his canoe deeper, wading in until the water reached his chest.

"Where *is* your home?" she asked.

His frown gave way to an expression she could not read. "Don't worry. I won't let any harm come to you."

He spoke without inflection, but heat once more rushed

into her face. She felt ashamed that he thought her afraid, and grateful for the promise to keep her safe, and both were like swallowing rocks. Before her resolve could slip away, she splashed into the ice-cold ocean after him.

"Stay where you are," Black Fin said. "I have to dress—"

While *in* the water? She averted her gaze and set her hand on the gunwale, hoping it wouldn't squirm this time. She wasn't sure how she would climb in from such deep water. Oddly, the canoe had no paddles. In fact, now that she thought about it, she could not recall seeing any paddles in the strangers' camp. It was an extraordinary deficiency.

"Wait!" said Black Fin, prying her fingers from the canoe. "Just *stay there*." She snatched her hand out of his and jammed it under her arm.

He vaulted into his canoe—

—which wavered and twitched, and she was no longer looking at a boy in a journeying canoe but a black fish as big as a canoe. But what was that *black fin* knifing over Cloud's head, pushing straight up from the fish's back, and look at those tail flukes idly curling out of the water: they were wrong, side-to-side, not like any fish tail in the world—

The tail slapped lightly. She took a step back, then two. The fish blew out a shower of fine spray. "Climb on," said Black Fin, peering at her from the giant fish's mouth. He had lifted the top half of the jaw as if it were a hat—

—the fish wasn't all black: white covered the lower jaw and neck, a patch of white gleamed behind the eye—

Beyond, a convoy of black fins cut smoothly across the cove. No men and women or canoes anywhere. One of the huge creatures breached. Its sleek black-and-white shape arced toward the entrance of the cove.

*Orcas!*

"Cloud," said Black Fin, "climb on! It's time to go!"

His orca-canoe was enormous. Teeth like halibut-hook barbs. Jaws that could crush her arm like a stalk of grass. "I can't," she whispered. All the breath had fled her lungs.

*First People.* She had stumbled upon immortals without their masks. No wonder Foam awed her.

The other orcas were departing through the outlet of the cove. Beside Black Fin's toothy jaws, Cloud felt as small as the fish he had caught. Orcas were not kindly, generous Summer People like the salmon; they were Winter People, whose nature, Winter had said, was to *want.* They were merciless hunters, warriors of the sea. Black Fin could savage her as easily as he would a seal, though she would provide him with a lot less meat.

Orcas help those in trouble who call to them, Stick had told her.

But Otter had prayed to them. And they hadn't answered. *They hadn't helped him.*

Black rage steadied her. The choice before her was simple. Either she stayed on this island alone, with no canoe and what scraps of food and shelter the orcas might have left behind. Or she went where they took her.

Even as her feet kept stepping away from Black Fin, her rage broadened to take in herself: cringing, pathetic Cloud. So the orcas hadn't helped Otter. All *she* had done for him, for her uncle who had died for her, was run away. All she had ever done was run, and hide, and cower. It was too late to help Otter, but she could, for once in her life, *stand her ground.*

"How," she said through clenched teeth, trying to stop her shaking, "do I climb on?"

"Grab the fin," said Black Fin, that prince of the immortals. His spirit mask blew spray again.

She half swam to the tall dorsal fin. It was firm and rubbery. Behind the fin lay a grayish patch that looked as if an earlier human rider had sat there with wet paint on her dress. The patch felt no different from the rest of his skin. Cloud swung her leg across and hauled herself onto his back.

Before she settled into place, he moved, a gentle wriggle into deeper water. Then, without warning, power rolled through him like a wave, nose to tail. He shot forward, lifting and plunging her back into icy water, lifting and plunging. She slid wildly, clutched the dorsal fin, tried to grip with her legs.

They emerged through the outlet of the cove into howling wind and rain. Charcoal-gray walls reared up in their path, shattered into tree-high columns of spray. Water foamed around and over Cloud as if she were a boulder in a river. She clung to his dorsal fin as she slipped and slid, rose and fell.

The surf disappeared behind them. The orcas coursed through mountains of water, past wind-whipped cornices and avalanches of foam, as if the storm meant nothing to them. She didn't know how she stayed on. Black Fin moved constantly beneath her. The dorsal fin, reaching over her head, was too wide and sharp and slippery to hug comfortably. Her legs already ached with the impossible effort of gripping his back, and she skidded on her precarious seat no matter how hard she squeezed. His back was like the edge of a precipice and the wild ocean around them a gulf of air; if she slid off, she would be lost.

But she didn't slide off.

After a while Cloud realized Black Fin swam so smoothly and carefully that—except for lashing rain and spray, and frequent boiling surges of foam—the water never reached higher than her chest. By increments her blind terror dissipated. She grew used to the idea that he would not let her fall off; whatever the orcas planned for her, it was not drowning. She began to think Black Fin might be extending other powers for her benefit: while the water flowing over her was cold, *she* did not grow cold from it. The water-laden furs under her rain cloak did not drag her from his back, although they ought to have.

Foam had said Bone's servants could not follow Cloud to the orcas' home, and indeed she saw no sign of them. Except for a lone petrel sweeping across the wave tops, the orcas forged through the wilderness alone.

She began to notice other things. From time to time, when his head was underwater, Black Fin ticked like an insect in the summer grass. Sometimes air bubbled from his head, or blew out in a plume of mist that smelled of him, fishy, warmer than the salt spray. It hadn't occurred to Cloud that with his spirit mask he would have to breathe air as she did. That orcas had no gills.

They kept gathering speed. Cloud felt more and more secure on Black Fin's back as she learned to relax into the driving rhythm of the tail flukes, the constant undulation of his body beneath her. On the face of the vast ocean, she began to find his size and strength reassuring.

And the wonder of it increased, as if she had passed into a story: a lost girl who by chance or virtue had become the guest of the First People and now traveled with them to the end of the world. As the orcas swam ever faster, the Cloud she had known seemed to fall away, and her past shrank into the distance behind her. It was as if she had left all her fear and pain and grief on that little island, the last outpost of the human realm. She was flying with the orcas over the wide, mysterious, terrible ocean, and it was pure exhilaration.

Night fell. The rain stopped, and sometime later the orcas emerged from under the clouds. The orcas swam so fast now that the sky seemed to unreel out of the sea, stars spreading from the west until the glittering seam of heaven stitched the sky from horizon to horizon. A part of her wished it would never end. Another part of her was plain uncomfortable: thirsty, hungry, weary, chafed, wind-chapped, pickled with salt, and wet, wet, wet.

As the sky lightened, the ocean grew calmer until their wake rippled a surface as smooth as polished quartz. Then an archipelago wavered into solidity on the horizon. Cloud's heart rose into her throat. She knew what islands they must be: the realm of the immortals across the sea, the Land of Wealth.

But as they drew closer, she spied a dark current flowing through the archipelago. At first she thought it must be a line of gigantic kelp beds—and they did indeed begin to pass great mats of uprooted seaweed, red and green and brown, lacy or stringy. With it, though, drifted other flotsam: hundreds upon hundreds of trees, some freshly uprooted and others gray and worm-eaten; bird down, sand, ash, and old shells floating on the topmost skin of the water; rotting fish; burned house posts and storage boxes, half-sunk canoes bearing human skeletons green with algae. The current smelled of rot cleansed by sun, rain, salt, and wind.

Dawn kindled behind them. The orcas slowed until they nosed almost lazily through the debris. To the north, she saw a massive and nearly invisible pillar soaring into clouds. The pillar was the color of the cloud-mottled sky before sunrise, of the rainbows that glimmer in the depths of pearl-shell. Cloud shivered. *That* had to be one of the posts holding up the sky.

As they swam on, the colors grew more intense. The sea turned greener, the charcoal blacker, bird down whiter. Old driftwood shone like polished shell. A breath of west wind carried to her a rich, unnameable perfume, and the air itself seemed to change, as if up ahead a brightness rippled through the world like sunlight across a sea bottom.

The first rays of the rising sun outlined a doorway tall as a mountain, and through it Cloud glimpsed a strange bright ocean with no horizon. Then the orcas turned north. The sun climbed higher, and the place where the doorway had been became a cloud-flecked blue like any fairweather sky in human lands. At last the orcas entered a sea largely free of wrack. Ahead lay one of the low islands of the archipelago, and on it a bright row of houses shimmering in the morning sun.

**As Black Fin drifted to a stop, he looked back toward** Cloud: a tiny-looking eye on that great head, but a very alert and intelligent gaze. She became conscious of how she straddled his back with bare legs and, embarrassed, dropped quickly into the cool water, tugging down her dress.

After so long astride, she could only wobble to shore. Black Fin splashed out of the ocean behind her, a boy pulling a canoe.

How did you act among immortals? Otter had told her, *The first rule is respect.* She had not shown much respect, not to Black Fin at any rate.

She took a deep breath. "Thank you for—the ride."

"You're welcome," he said, and smiled unexpectedly.

That smile again sent heat rushing over her skin, and something thrashed uncomfortably in her chest, as if she had inhaled a panicked bird. The sense of unreality that had kept Cloud's old self at a distance abruptly departed, and a dark, sharp anger replaced it. She hobbled away from him.

The other orcas had already drawn up their canoes, and Foam waited with her attendants at the top of the beach. "We're due as guests in another town," Foam told Cloud, "but we'll rest before we leave."

The attendants led Cloud into the forest behind the house. There sat a washing box carved from orange-pink shell or stone, big enough to sit in. "We know you like fresh water," one of the attendants said to her, but they did not explain how they had filled the box in the absence of a nearby creek, or heated the water until it steamed. The trees looked like madrones but grew straight and tall as firs. Their leaves rustled overhead as she washed the salt from her skin and hair. The bath made her angrier; she did not, she thought, deserve such luxury.

They oiled her peeling skin and combed her hair, and gave her back her own dress, now inexplicably clean and dry. Then they tied a sea-otter robe around her shoulders and led her inside. It was only when they sat her in the place of honor, beside Foam's ivory throne, that Cloud realized what she had missed during her bath. The amulet Thrush had given her no longer hung around her neck.

The shock of the discovery was like a blow from Rumble's fist. She tried to sit straight, to pull her clutching hand from her neck and place it in her lap, but her effort at composure did not deceive Foam. "What's wrong, Cloud?" the queen demanded. "Have you lost something?"

Cloud didn't want to talk about it, but how could she refuse to answer an immortal? "A necklace." It was hard to speak around the hard lump in her throat. "The cord must have broken in the surf. I didn't know I'd lost it until now."

Foam watched her with narrowed eyes. Cloud tried to focus on the meal the orcas had laid in front of her. It might as well have been rocks, but she was sure it would be disrespectful not to eat what an immortal served you. She nibbled at a chunk of food. An orca man rose and left; it was Black Fin. Had she insulted the orcas by not thanking Foam before she ate? *The first rule is respect.* Cloud's mother had brought disaster on herself and Sandspit Town through disrespect of an immortal. The only thing that could be worse than what had already happened to Cloud would be to follow in Thrush's footsteps.

She attempted to thank Foam, though she wasn't sure what she said. She ate something, but not very much. Sometime later Foam led her to a bedroom. "Rest here," she said, smiling. "Just be up in time for dinner." At that moment, the mockery of Cloud's usual appetite seemed cruel beyond bearing.

Cloud lay down on the rich furs. She expected to fall asleep immediately, but now that she was alone, any barrier she had against her grief vanished, and crushing blackness roared up inside her. She tried to swallow it as she had always swallowed her unhappiness, tried to pack that suffocating, obsidian-sharp emptiness into a box and bury it deep in her belly again. But this time she could not. That necklace had been her last link to Thrush and Otter, who were lost to her forever.

She wanted to weep, but she could only stare at the wall with dry, burning eyes. From the boxes lining the walls, carved and painted eyes stared back at her.

Slow currents seemed to rock her, but the room was too bright for comfort. Sunlight glowed inside walls made of translucent shell. Paintings of fish and eels had been traced across those walls. She could hear water lapping and gurgling—on the beach outside, she supposed—and also a strange, distant music: sliding squeals that rose or fell; a counterpoint of deep grunts and hooting whistles. But nothing nearby and nothing human: no footsteps or voices, no clatter of wooden dishes.

No wood smoke in the house. Had she smelled it earlier? Hadn't she just eaten cooked salmon?

Every time she blinked, the room seemed larger. Ripples of light swam across the floor. At the edges of her vision, the paintings moved, the eyes on the boxes proliferated. Was she staring up at a ceiling of abalone, was she outdoors under a glossy blue-green sky, or was she undersea, gazing up at the mirrored surface of the ocean?

One set of eyes blinked at her. Then another. Noises started up inside the boxes, tentative scrapings and scuttlings. The room wavered and for a heartbeat became a light-filled void.

Finally Cloud could stand it no longer and left the room, passing through the nearly empty hall to the beach. Orca people glanced at her, some pointedly, but no one spoke.

A worn path led her along the houses. When one of the house-front carvings snapped its jaws at her, she fled into the forest of almost-madrones. From this vantage, if she ignored the way the houses gleamed and shifted, and the way the trees, in the corner of her eye, looked each as big as a cliff, and the way the canoes on the beach more and more resembled orca bodies, the town almost looked like a human one. She curled up in the sand at the top of the beach and dropped into sleep.

**Light rain woke her. She opened her eyes to see** Black Fin squatting nearby.

As she shot upright in alarm, every muscle in her body protested. "You should be more careful where you sleep," he said, frowning. "In our house we only eat fish, but not all our kind are as choosy."

"I couldn't sleep indoors."

His frown deepened. "My mother's house isn't nice enough?"

"Too nice," said Cloud, and then added, the words sounding more surly than she had intended, "There are things moving around in those boxes."

To her mortification he burst out laughing. "Terrible things."

What about her did the orcas find so amusing? Or did they laugh just because they were cruel Winter People, and the urge to ridicule was part of their nature? Couldn't Black Fin understand that a mortal might find his world unnerving, even terrifying? Or did he understand but not care?

And why was he crossing his legs and settling himself like that, as if by invitation? He was not close enough to touch her, but he still crowded her, eyeing her like a hunter watching his prey. In some ways he made her less uneasy in his orca shape.

Black Fin yawned prodigiously, showing a mouthful of white teeth. He looked even more tired than when they arrived; surely he had not been resting while she slept. "If you can stand before my mother without fear," he said, still amused, "you don't need to worry about what's in those boxes."

Cloud was not, of course, able to stand before Foam without fear. She looked away to where the setting sun now burnished the ocean with yellow light.

"It is a beautiful thing," said Black Fin. "I can see why you missed it."

She glanced back at him, not sure what he meant. Then her heart seemed to stop beating.

He held up Otter's little raven. "Where did you find that?" she whispered. She could barely manage the words.

"I went back to the island. It must have come off in the surf as you said. Here—I put a new cord on it."

He moved to her side. As he slipped it over her head, his fingers brushed her hair and throat. Cloud turned rigid with anger. She wanted to sink her teeth into his hand, but she wanted the carving even more.

His hand slid to the raven itself. "Who made it?" he asked. "A master carver—"

Cloud yanked it away. "Why bother with this—this trifle? Don't you have a house full of treasure?"

Anger leapt in his face and subsided. His hands dropped to his lap. "You grieved for it," he said.

The knife-edged blackness roared up inside her like a storm sea. She hated him for knowing that the carving was the one gift she could not refuse. But what cut even sharper was the way he spoke about her loss as if he cared. If he was lying, she despised him. If he was telling the truth—he had no more right to comment on her grief than touch her hair.

"Who gave it to you?" Black Fin asked.

"Don't you already know everything about me?" Cloud snarled, and she jumped up and stalked down the beach.

A tangle of flotsam blocked her way: a great knot of rope-like bull kelp nearly buried in the sand, and in its coils a splintered grave box, a long one unlike Raven Tongue's. The skull within gleamed like the slick interior of a clam shell. The sight stopped her cold. She savagely wiped tears from her face. How could the orcas leave it on their beach as if those bones were no more than a dead crab cast up by the tide?

Because that's what human remains were to them.

*The first rule is respect.* You had to show courtesy even to those immortals you did not like. Look what Thrush had set in motion when she broke that rule.

She looked back. Black Fin stood at the edge of the trees. He hesitated, then walked toward her, frowning fiercely.

"My uncle made it for my mother," she said when he caught up to her, "and my mother gave it to me. It's the only thing I have of either of them. My uncle's dead and I'll never see my mother again. Are you happy now?" She hadn't meant to fling her words in his face—it wasn't *respectful*—but the ocean of emptiness roared all around her now, trying to drown her in its depths. Her anger was all she had to cling to.

"No," he said.

"My uncle prayed to you. He prayed for protection, for good fortune. Did you even hear his prayer?"

"No," said Black Fin. "It wasn't me he prayed to. But we're sea people. Did he die at sea?"

"No," Cloud said. The knot in her throat tightened until she could not speak. There was no safe place to look: not at the skull; not at the shining, shifting houses or trees striding like giants along the shore; not at the sea where, in the near distance, the dark river of everything ever carried from mortal shores, everything dead and discarded and rotten, flowed away to the end of the world.

Black Fin sighed. "You are a mouthful of bones, aren't you?"

His hand touched her shoulder. Not skin to skin, as in that moment when he had slipped the carving around her neck. But still: pale fingers sunk into the rain-beaded fur of her robe, gripping her tightly. She wanted to bury her teeth in that hand and rip it bloodily from his arm, and she wanted to hold it against her cheek. She already knew his skin was warm.

Had this stranger swum across the world and back in a day because he truly cared about her unhappiness? Why should the mere thought of that sharpen the pain inside her unendurably?

She knew she should thank him for finding the raven, but she could not speak. At last Black Fin released her shoulder and Cloud moved away, rounding the grave box to continue along the beach. He followed.

As they neared Foam's house, Cloud saw yet another strange thing, this a sight that would have been commonplace in Sandspit Town: a woman suckling a baby. The woman was Foam. She sat on a bench in front of her house in the rays of the declining sun, having untied the dress she now wore to expose one white breast.

Cloud stopped. "Is that your mother's child?" she asked Black Fin.

"Who else's?"

"But she didn't have a baby—there weren't any babies on that island."

"The little ones can't leave water. You have to grow up to learn how to take off your mask." He grinned. "As in your case."

She did not expect the attack, and fury exploded inside her. "I," she said, "*did not take off my mask! It disappeared!*"

Then she tried to calm herself. Respect, respect, respect. But the very thought of treating Black Fin with careful politeness made her want to bite him.

What had happened to her old self? The *sweet, biddable child* who always tried to do what was wanted of her? Glory would be ashamed of her bad temper. *Otter* would have been ashamed.

"If they can't take off their masks," she said through gritted teeth, "why does that baby look human?"

"Not *human*," said Black Fin. A smile still lurked around his eyes. "*Naked.* Humans are people who've lost their clothes."

She exhaled slowly, trying to control her temper. "If they are masked in spite of what I see, how can they be on land?"

Then, uneasily, Cloud recalled her earlier doubts that this town was on land.

Black Fin did not at first reply. Then he said, "My mother could give you a better answer. But . . . you're in our country now, in the unmasked world. Your eyes are used to the mortal world, so even in our country you will see . . . as you are used to seeing, whether things really are that way or not."

Cloud did not know what to make of this explanation. In memory and dream her brothers always appeared to be human boys, while to Thrush they had looked four-legged. Which of them had seen more clearly, Thrush or the half-bear Cloud, who had been born in spirit lands? The subject was confusing and disquieting, and she did not want to linger on it.

**As they ate the evening meal, the walls of Foam's** house blazed with the salmon-colored sunset, then faded to gray. The house became ever more shifting, watery, and insubstantial. *The world unmasked.* The orca people, too, grew more changeable in her vision: huge or human-sized; dressed in elegant black and white, or wearing only their black hair and pale flesh.

What did not change was how out of place Cloud felt, a granite pebble among polished jade beads. How beautiful and alert the orcas were, how sly their laughter. How little reassurance they gave her. The only thing to put her at ease was that they ate more than she did.

They dined on lingcod, greenling, flounder, and sole. For Cloud they also brought crisp sweet eelgrass roots, and fresh water to drink. Her mouth where Bone's dog had hooked it no longer hurt. In fact, all her bruises, scrapes, and sore muscles were healing much faster than they would have in mortal lands.

She thanked Foam as best she could. Her words seemed as awkward as ever. Black Fin did not try to talk to her from his place on Foam's other side, but the weight of his gaze kept the anger roiling in her gut. Still, if she had not had that to anchor her, the whole unsettling dinner would have been worse.

After dinner some of the orcas sang. It was the same uncomfortable music she had heard earlier, all hoots, grunts, and squeals. She found herself drifting despite having slept much of the day. When she woke, Foam was regaling the assembly with a comic story about a girl beset by spirits. Despite everything *she* did, they would not leave her alone; despite everything *they* did, she would not accept their service.

It was enough like Cloud's experience that, even though she did not find the story as amusing as the orcas did, she pricked up her ears to hear how the problem would resolve.

The heroine of the story went on to surprise orcas who had stopped to mend their canoes, and she was appalled to realize the story was her own. Smiling wickedly, Foam ended the tale with the love-smitten orca prince bearing away the beautiful girl to his home.

Until his appearance in the story, Black Fin had laughed with the rest, but now he ducked his head. Cloud would have been more dismayed by Foam's mockery of her son if she had not had to struggle with her own public humiliation. No matter how she might want to shout at the orcas to quit ridiculing her, she had to endure it without complaint.

*Beautiful,* she wanted to scream in their faces, *that word says nothing about me. My mother is beautiful, but I'm a* bear's *daughter.* She might wear Thrush's face—everyone said so—but inside she was as unlike Thrush as it was possible to be: rough, awkward, clumsy, messy, timid, foul-tempered. To make her the princess of a story, the kind of beauty an immortal like Black Fin would fall in love with, was just cruel orca mockery. Such a prince might love the mask of Thrush's skin, but to him, and to that story, the bear child inside could not exist.

Then another, crueler thought occurred to Cloud: what Foam laughed at was *precisely* the comedy of the bear's daughter dressed in Thrush's skin, and *her own son* unable to see it. Cold rage pierced Cloud so sharply that it hurt to breathe.

When the orcas' laughter stilled, Foam spoke again. "You've heard our young guest's story. Now, only water or fire from beyond the world are strong enough to break the knots binding Lord Stink. Tomorrow we'll take our friend with us to Swimming's house, and he will provide what is needed."

After that, the orcas dispersed to their beds. With a backward glance at Cloud, Black Fin left, too. But Foam waited upon her ivory seat, watching Cloud curiously.

In the stories Stick had told, mortals never questioned the First People. Perhaps it was *disrespectful.* But Cloud could not stop herself, even though anger made her face so stiff that she could hardly move her lips.

"Why are you helping me, Lady?"

"You prayed to me, did you not, the day we met?" said Foam. "And then you were fortunate enough to catch us undressed in your world, so that we were forced to bring you into our world to keep the balance. But in the end this is simply what I choose to do. Not many humans find their way to us, and when they do, they want—oh, hunting prowess, spiritual power, retribution against enemies . . . you amuse me, girl. All you really did want was food and shelter, and you aren't without courage, when you choose to use it. Be true to your nature and the task before you, and I will be pleased."

"But . . ." Cloud said, groping for words through the tumbling chaos of her emotions. Foam was wrong to attribute to her any special humility. She just hadn't known during their first encounter that she spoke to immortals. If she *had* known, she would have asked for aid—for herself, for everyone who had been hurt because of her. Foam could surely help defeat Rumble and Bone without Cloud having to release her father's ghost.

"I don't want—thank you for your offer of help, Lady, but—why do you want me to free my father? He hurt many people when he was alive, and if I release him—my mother—Sandspit Town—"

Foam regarded her coldly. "Those mortals are of no concern to me."

Another, almost intolerable surge of anger churned through Cloud. That gaze told her that *Foam did not care what happened to her.* Foam did not care if Cloud was hurt or afraid, if everything she loved was burnt to ash.

*Beautiful girl.* A princess taken into the spirit lands by an immortal who wanted her: that was Thrush's story, and it contained only blood and heartbreak that still had not come to an end. Now Foam would send the bear girl to blunder along the path her beautiful mother had followed, the story told this time, like one of Stick's tales, for laughter instead of tears—though perhaps to no different end.

The orcas were Winter People. They did what they *wanted*. Foam's apparent generosity was only for—as Foam said—amusement, and not from kindness or pity. Cloud held Foam's interest just so long as she stayed amusing. What recourse did a mortal have, when an immortal interfered in her life on such terms? Despair and anger wound tighter and tighter inside Cloud until she thought she would break.

"I can only do my own kind of favors, child," said Foam softly. "But here is one reason to free your father. It's why our host tomorrow will help you, too—this once. Your father's power and his soul belong with the unmasked world, where they help to sustain both realms, masked and unmasked. Bound as they have been in the mortal world, they have ripped a hole in it, and that hole is wounding the unmasked world as well, blocking the currents we all swim in. Now, go sleep, child. We have another journey tomorrow, and a big feast."

Cloud crept away to her bedroom, tears mantling her face. She fell asleep clutching the little raven while whatever lived in Foam's treasure boxes gnawed and gurgled and skittered. She dreamed that night. She was flying over the ocean as if on a bird's back, searching for land, but no matter how far she flew, the horizon brought her only more gray, stormy swells.

# TWELVE

# The Doorway Beyond

*Foam's attendants woke Cloud early, when the walls* glowed the color of storm clouds and the denizens of the boxes had quieted but for an occasional thump. The attendants clothed her for the feast in an impossibly fine white dress, they braided dangles of sharks' teeth and pearlshell into her hair, they draped a sea-otter robe around her shoulders. Otter's raven they placed outside her dress. "How kind of young Black Fin to fetch this for you," one of the women said, smiling.

A part of Cloud wanted to be a girl who belonged in such clothes. But she was not; this was just more of Foam's mockery. Dark anger stirred in the hollow of her belly.

The attendants handed her the bundle of her old clothes and led her out of the gray-lit watery vastness of the house. On the beach, under a light rain, the rest of the orcas were gathering. Today they wore black and white feast clothes like hers.

Cloud's anger sharpened when Foam, arching an eyebrow, told her she was to ride again with Black Fin. How it amused Foam to watch her son with Cloud! Cloud wondered why Black Fin did not hate his mother; *she* was ready to do so.

And she hated the way Black Fin eyed her as if she were something he wanted to *taste*.

They descended together to the water's edge. When she halted suddenly, he asked, "What's wrong?"

"My clothes will get soaked."

"Of course they will," he said, amused. "But it's warm where we're going."

Which was not the point, but an orca would not see wetness as a problem, would he? Although why try to preserve the false image Foam had tried to create? Still, she could not help but mourn the handful of moments when the bear's daughter had looked like an entirely different girl.

Then, as she did plunge into the water in her lovely clothes, Black Fin reached out a hand to stop her. "Cloud," he said, "we are going to visit the Summer People. I warned you that some of our kind could be a danger to you. Our hosts today are far more dangerous, in their way, than we could ever be. Don't . . ." He looked away at his canoe. "Don't be rude."

Cloud could feel herself starting to snarl. *Of course* she knew not to be rude to her hosts, especially when they were powerful immortals.

But his solemnity also pricked her in an unfamiliar place, and the words that came out of her mouth were, "I'm *never* rude." The absurdity of that made her burst out laughing, a noise in turn so strange that she clapped a hand over her mouth to stifle it. Black Fin looked up, and despite Cloud's best intentions, their eyes met. He turned away to his canoe, but she had already seen that he was smiling, too.

So she was relieved when he vaulted into his canoe, boy becoming orca. She climbed on and they joined the others heading southwest from the beach. Soon they reached the great river of debris. The orcas traversed it slowly, slipping between uprooted trees, dead birds, and wrecked canoes.

Cloud was startled when an island rose from the depths, lifting the cluttered surface of the ocean. Then it rolled, and she realized that—of course—it was no island at all: a gigantic pectoral fin waved, clifflike gills opened and closed, and the monster sank once more.

As they progressed, the rain dried up and blue sky approached from the south. Across the debris wafted hints of that sweet scent Cloud had smelled yesterday. Today she could not see the great doorway in the sky, but there was a gap on the horizon where the ocean curved upward like the side of a bowl, or perhaps downward—vertigo forced her to turn away.

She pondered Black Fin's warning. She had always been told that Summer People wanted mortals to be warm, well fed, and content. Their essential nature, Winter had said, was *to give.* Cloud did not see how such beings could be *much more dangerous* than the orcas, but she did resolve to try her hardest for courtesy.

And upon consideration, she was grateful for the warning. Advice, which implied concern for her well-being, was better than Foam's mocking detachment—even if Black Fin's advice was directed toward the princess he imagined her to be, rather than to Cloud herself, soaked and disheveled bear girl.

After a while, she thought: *any* girl who took up with an orca, princess or not, would be wet and smell like fish all the time. Surely Black Fin knew that.

On the south side of the current, sky and water were blue and as warm as human skin. When they emerged from the debris, the orcas altered their course to swim due west, along the edge of it. The sea grew even brighter and more intensely colored until its depths seemed to glow. Water dripped from Black Fin's back like beads of coruscating oil; spray shot up in fountains of fire.

Soon a long, low, treeless island lifted over the horizon. It was nearly covered by a vast town. As they approached, Cloud saw a crowd waiting in front of one of the largest houses. There the orcas stopped at last. Cloud slid off Black Fin's back and waded ashore onto warm sand. While Black Fin pulled up his canoe, she shed her robe and basked with closed eyes, perfumed by sunlight.

A fat man descended toward the orcas, a king crowned with copper and clothed in a robe that dazzled like sun on water. He beamed as he greeted Foam. "My friend the fisherwoman, you are always welcome in our town! And today you've brought the little bear girl. My name is Swimming-at-the-Head-of-the-Multitude, little one. Welcome! Welcome to our town! Welcome to our feast! I know why you've brought the bear girl, my friends. We've been expecting her. Come into my house."

Cloud was surprised to recognize the clan of immortals to which her hosts belonged. The king's name and his magnificent clothing were clues, as was the splendor of the immense house behind him, fashioned entirely of polished copper. The size of the crowd also helped, and the bright rainbowed shapes her hosts cast at the edges of her vision. Taken together, it was obvious the orcas had brought her to the home of the Bright Swimmers, the Lords of Summer, the immortals humans prayed to most.

That puzzled her, though. How could Black Fin think the Bright Ones posed a threat to Cloud—the salmon who, every summer, joyously offered their flesh to humans?

Of course Cloud would show *them* respect. Look at the consequences when Wily One had insulted his divine wife: the salmon had shunned mortal lands for generations, until the daughters of the union had taken pity on a starving world.

Cloud followed the orcas through a doorway so tall that even Black Fin did not have to duck. Inside—

By now she should be growing used to the opulence of the Land of Wealth. But King Swimming's house was almost beyond comprehension: an extravagance of platforms and stairs and level after level of rooms, an entire town somehow fitted into one dwelling as tall as a forest, and the whole wrought as exquisitely as a treasure box. There was no fire on the sandy rectangle in the center of the hall, but sunlight flooded through vents in the roof and bounced between the polished walls so that the hall glittered as brightly as the beach outside.

The house was beyond beautiful, although all that copper did make it smell uncomfortably like blood.

The Summer People seated the orcas on the right-hand side of the king, with Foam next to the king and the other orcas beside her. Cloud was placed next to Black Fin, who sat well down in the order of rank. She was at first self-conscious about dripping on the floor—but of course the orcas were as wet as she, and why should salmon mind wet-ness any more than orcas? After a moment she followed Black Fin's example by squeezing water out of her hair. Her white dress was almost dry already, and soaking it in brine had not affected its softness.

Other guests took their places, while crowds of Bright Ones pressed in from the beach to sit near the door. Then Foam, King Swimming, and other nobles stood forth by turns and elegantly thanked and welcomed and praised each other. It reminded Cloud of Rumble's feast, and she was grateful that among the Summer People there would be no bloodshed, only happy feasting.

Not having breakfasted, Cloud was eager for the speeches to end. Her curiosity was nevertheless piqued when she no-ticed that all the immortals spoke a tongue unlike those she had so far encountered. When at last their hosts began to lay out mats, bowls, and spoons, Cloud touched Black Fin's arm to get his attention. "Do you—when a human being talks to you, do you always understand? No matter what language they speak?"

Her question amused him. "Yes—not that I've needed the talent with you." When he saw her puzzlement, his smile broadened. "You've been speaking the immortals' tongue almost since we first met. Don't snarl at me, bear girl. Your father was a king of the First People. What do you expect?"

Cloud reminded herself: in this house she had to be polite no matter *what* she felt like.

Young men carried in large feast dishes filled with
berries in sweet oil: black caps and red huckleberries, blueberries and fat yellow salmonberries. The guests on the far
side of the king began to eat. But when she reached toward
the nearest dish to fill her own bowl, Black Fin grabbed her
arm. A part of her worried that she had violated some bit of
protocol; another part was fiercely annoyed that he had
come between her and her meal.

Foam said in a loud, clear voice, "Our friend can't eat this
kind of food."

The servers milled in consternation. Salmon, orcas, and
other guests stared. What was Foam doing? After Black
Fin's lecture to *her* on rudeness!

But the king, flustered, signaled his attendants to remove
the dishes. "I'm so sorry! I forgot she was partly human!"

Black Fin bent toward Cloud's ear and hissed, "Look
again!"

She did not want to. She wanted to eat. She knew how
those fresh summer berries would taste: tart and splendid in
her mouth, so sweet she could eat them forever.

And what would the benevolent Bright Ones offer their
guests that could possibly harm her?

Black Fin's grip on her wrist tightened. She lifted her
nose in the direction of the berries. They smelled . . . briny,
meaty, sweetly rotten. Blinking, rubbing her eyes, she unwillingly looked at the dishes sidewise. Not berries at all—

—but eyeballs, mounds and mounds of human eyes.

A whimper tried to push out of her mouth even as she
clamped her lips shut. Don't insult your host's food.

"Drowned men," Black Fin whispered in her ear.

Cloud thought of that dark current sweeping every dead
thing to the end of the world . . . and wondered if Black Fin
would have eaten the berries if she had not been there.

King Swimming spoke in a low voice to an attendant,
then addressed the house once more. "My friends, we are

poor hosts if we cannot offer our guest food she can eat." He gestured; the attendant led out a group of plump and beautiful children, boys and girls. Cloud at first thought the children were bringing other dishes to feed to her. But the king picked up a club and smashed it deep into the skull of the nearest child. The girl crumpled to the sand of the king's hearth well.

Cloud could not stifle her outcry this time, despite Black Fin's crushing grip on her arm. The king did not, however, show any sign of having heard her. One after the other he clubbed the solemn, waiting children to the ground.

She clapped her free hand over her mouth, trembling. The small hands and feet jerked and quivered. Attendants lifted the children onto clean mats and began to gut and dismember them. Their hearts still pulsed, spurting blood.

A conviction settled on her that their hosts were not the Bright Ones after all but a tribe of monsters. What *bloodthirsty gods* would serve the eyeballs of drowned men as a delicacy and murder their own children to feed a guest?

But doubts immediately began to erode that conviction. She could see the children's rainbowed fish-shapes at the edges of her vision. The meat beneath their human-looking skin was orange and translucent. It smelled like salmon: fresh, sweet, and oily.

She had to suppose that despite how the children looked to her, Black Fin was right and they were wearing masks. Within the shifting multiplicity of the unmasked world, even a masked child had more than one aspect.

Other attendants built a fire, although Cloud did not take in how they accomplished it. The fire was as yellow as summer sunlight. As the happy smell of cooking salmon lifted into the air, she changed her mind. She might not be able to trust her eyes in spirit lands, but her nose had never deceived her.

The Lords of Summer set before their guests the barbecued orange flesh of their own children. The sight overwhelmed Cloud with grief and terror, but she was also extremely hungry.

Cloud became aware that the entire assembly gazed at her. Waiting. Terrified, she glanced first at Black Fin, then at Foam, who nodded. She tried to recall the elegant phrases Foam had used, but they sifted like sand from her grasp. She stood up, knees trembling, to face the king. "Your generosity to me and—and—is . . . it can't be matched." Her voice cracked and she stopped to clear her throat; she had already run out of words.

Then, like a drowning fisherman who at last catches hold of his canoe, she remembered a prayer Glory had taught her. "Thank you, grandfathers," she said, "for keeping me alive, thank you, Swimmers, for keeping me from hunger, thank you, Summer Women, for banishing my sickness and misfortune, thank you, Bright Ones; I will always treat you well so that we may meet again."

She sat down, sick with apprehension. Could her mistakes here doom the entire human world to starvation?

"Eat something!" Black Fin whispered. Cloud made herself reach for a chunk of meat. It was almost too hot to touch. The aroma, the way the dark-orange, partly charred crust split to reveal the moist pink flesh inside, nearly made her drool.

How she loathed her hunger. But she couldn't *not* eat this terrible gift. She had to show respect in proportion to the sacrifice. *The first rule.* She took a small bite. The taste, as with everything in the Land of Wealth, was more intense than what she was used to; the oil richer, the sweetness more bursting, the flesh more tenderly melting. Her mouth seemed to glow inside with light.

She was eating children, as Rumble had eaten her brothers.

Her brothers were just animals, Winter had said.

Beside her, Black Fin chewed with every indication of pleasure. All the guests partook of the new dish, talking and laughing. The salmon people spooned up berries. Evidently her speech had been good enough.

She discovered she had finished the chunk in her hand

and picked up another. She was ashamed, but she couldn't stop from biting into that one, too, and then a third. It was the most delicious food she had ever tasted. The orcas ate until their hands glistened with oil.

When the meal was over, the women gathered up the small eating mats, carried them to the covered heap of bones and offal left over from butchering the children, and carefully swept the smaller mats clean. Cloud had remembered to stack all her bones and charred skin in a neat pile on one side of her own mat, as Glory had taught her.

The women rolled up all the refuse inside larger mats. At this juncture, Foam approached. "Come with me, Cloud."

Cloud obeyed uneasily. Foam led her in the wake of the salmon women, through the crowded house and onto the summer-hot beach. There, as Cloud had seen hundreds of times in human lands, the women waded into the water to shake out the mats. But the sight of the small, bloody, human-looking heads tumbling into the sea was not like anything Cloud had seen before, and again she clapped hands over her mouth to stifle her cry.

"Watch," commanded Foam. And Cloud watched. Here in the Land of Wealth the remains did not drift gently in the tide but coalesced toward each other. Blood and intestines seethed in the bright water, skin flipped around bones—

—young chinook jumped, flashing in the sun.

The women returned to shore and waited, ignoring Foam and Cloud. Cloud wondered if they were the mothers of the children. "Doesn't it hurt?" Cloud whispered to Foam. "To be killed?"

"Of course it hurts!" Foam said. "It hurts every time they give themselves to the fisherman's spear or hook. Did you think good things came to you without sacrifice? But what else would you eat? Do you suppose eel grass and clover roots aren't also part of the unmasked world?"

What else would you expect an orca to say? A *hunter.*

The children climbed out of the water, whole and healthy.

Their faces were somber as they walked toward the salmon women. Cloud wanted to weep, to beg forgiveness that she had caused them such pain just to fill her belly. But the children started pushing each other, and one laughed, and the next moment they were chasing each other down the beach. The women gazed after them, shading their eyes and smiling, too.

She and Foam returned into the house, Cloud puzzling over why Foam had made her see this; surely Foam had no pity in her.

Inside, the dancing was about to start. The salmon people went first. As they wove in and out, leaping forward, falling back, their arms undulating above their heads and their torsos swaying, Cloud began to feel as if she truly were watching fish at the entrance to a stream. A group of salmon men sang for the dancers: rippling music like water over stone.

Next came the orcas. She disliked their music, but she could have watched them dance forever. Black Fin was one of the performers. Cloud could not take her eyes off his slim body as he leaped and squatted, arched and spun, making it all look effortless—and joyous. If his recent journeys had tired him, he did not show it. He was breathing hard when he returned to his seat, and sweat trickled down his skin, but he grinned at her.

Other guests danced. As none wore masks, Cloud had to guess from their dances, and the shapes flickering in the corners of her eyes, to which species of First People they belonged: cormorant, loon, seals, more orcas? When she could not decide and asked Black Fin, he just laughed.

The sun set. The sky overhead turned purple and then a starry black. Another meal was brought out, this time smelts (which, Black Fin assured her, were exactly what they appeared). A few salmon people staged a noisy argument over the smelts in which one group pretended to be eagles and the other, seagulls. The orcas laughed as loudly as the other salmon.

How could the Bright Ones so cheerfully host the orcas, who hunted them from the Mountain Land to the end of the ocean? How could they kill their own children to feed a castaway human of no importance? In the stories when Bright Ones died, it sounded no more painful than trimming your nails. In reality, the deaths of those children had not differed much from Rumble's slaughter of his slaves, except that the children had come willingly, had stood quietly—had perhaps even looked proud. Proud to be the gift.

Every bite Cloud had eaten had been founded in blood. Feeding the world was not easy even for the Bright Ones. It meant facing pain and death with utmost courage, and no guarantee of rebirth if the beneficiary of your sacrifice lacked respect for it.

Cloud had thought suffering was a thundercloud hanging over her life, bad weather she could escape if only the world would let her. But in fact pain was twisted into the very yarn the world had been woven of—part of its very nature, part of its *divine* nature. Pain dwelt even here among the Summer People. You could be a hunter or the hunted, but even the hunted lived off death, and their food might be you.

Cloud saw, suddenly, beneath the generosity and good cheer, the utter implacability of the Bright Ones. Treat them right or the world will starve. Yes, they *were* more dangerous than the orcas. How could you blame them?

And yet they were happy. Even those children still found joy after suffering. Amid the dancing and singing, the fire and starlight, the brilliant clothes and the magnificent house, Cloud felt more insubstantial than ever. As the orcas beside her laughed and joked, giddy with food and good cheer, as they shouted back and forth to each other and to the salmon and the other guests, she felt the knife-sharp emptiness grow again in her belly. Even here, in the land of joy, nothing could contain that hollow, nothing could fill it up.

The singing and dancing went on deep into the night. Cloud nodded, then dozed. A hand shook her awake. When she opened her eyes, she was falling through a spinning, swelling, light-spangled gulf the size of the world. "Cloud!" a voice called.

She struggled to seize hold of her understanding. The rainbowed gulf steadied into firelit copper floors and walls, into salmon people dressed in shimmering clothes. The shape of the huge creature beside her shrank in on itself, collapsing, and all the shining, turbulent attributes she had seen and not understood took a form her thoughts could compass: the sleek blackness of Black Fin's hair, the exquisite hard line of his cheek, the warmth of his fingers felt through her dress, the smell of his skin.

"Cloud," he said, shaking her, "wake up, time for bed."

He was amused, that boy, laughing at her sleepiness and the difficulty of waking her. She hated him for it. The hungry look in his eye, orca chasing a fish—that frightened her.

"Careful," he said, laughing, when she stood too fast and vertigo returned. She growled, but she let him hold her until the hall stopped spinning.

The feast had ended. Some people still sat talking, but many had retired, the hosts into their rooms, the guests onto mats spread upon the floor.

"The king is waiting outside," Black Fin told her.

"Waiting?" she said stupidly.

"To get what you came for."

She did not know what that was, but she followed him outside. There, at least, the vertigo affected her less. Huge, brilliant stars blazed overhead; a luminous sea lapped at the sand. The light in the sea was a deep pearly blue like the inside of a mussel shell. In the distance a cascade roared.

"Let's go," said the king, who was standing by the water's edge. He and Black Fin set off. Cloud stumbled after them, past tall houses that reflected the blue sea-light. No one else was abroad. The town went on and on, for miles perhaps. The noise of rushing water grew louder.

Eventually the houses petered out. Flotsam crowded the water now, drifting along the shore faster than they could walk. Wrack littered the beach: canoe prows, human skulls, tangles of kelp. The shore bent westward. When they came around a last lobe of sand, the wall of the world thrust up before them.

Sand and debris led up to the base of the wall. It was black here but hung with stars high above their heads. A gap pierced it as tall as mountains and so wide that, despite the radiant night sea, Cloud could not make out the far side. The scent she had smelled before was strong now. It was impossible to name: at once sweet, coppery, and rich like the forest floor after rain.

As the current of flotsam approached the gap, it quickened, thumping and jostling like beach drift in a storm tide. It roared through the gap into another, brighter ocean, dissolving until blue seawater and flotsam alike vanished into light.

Black Fin and the king walked to the very threshold of the doorway. When Cloud came up to them, Black Fin put a hand on her arm. "Stay on this side," he said.

But King Swimming continued through the door and along a sandbar extending beyond, on one side of the jostling outflow. There he waded into the water and, with a little splash, disappeared.

She wanted to shrug off Black Fin's grip on her arm but did not. By now the eerie significance of this doorway had sunk in. She, a human girl, did not belong here at the very end of the world. She could not help but be grateful for his company.

They waited for the king to return. The sky beyond the gap was dark and featureless, but the ocean was glossy, thick, rainbowed in its depths, and shimmering on the surface as if with the reflections of an unseen sun. That ocean curved away in a dimension Cloud's mind could not take in: neither up nor down, but both together.

After a while she noticed shapes moving upriver made of the same glossy, rainbow-bright stuff as the ocean. As the shapes threaded the debris into bluer, less iridescent water,

at times leaping to climb the current, she saw that they resembled fish. Glowing and glittering, they raced away into
the world.

"What are those?" she asked Black Fin, pointing.

"Salmon," he said. "Returning from the Headwaters
Women."

The Headwaters Women, Cloud had been told, were the
daughters of Wily One whom the salmon visited every year.
"But they live way in the east, high up in the mountains."

"Yes," said Black Fin. "This is how the salmon people
who die there return into our world."

"But . . ." Cloud began, about to object that those who
had gone east could not *return* into the world from the west.
But just then a very large chinook approached the doorway.
And a heartbeat later, King Swimming climbed from the
water, pushing his dripping, fish-bright robe from his
shoulders.

The king carried a stoppered container about two
handspans long, with the bulb-and-stem shape of a kelp
bottle but looking as if it had been carved from a solid form
of the otherworldly water. As he handed the bottle to Cloud,
a rainbowed drop clinging to it broke loose and spilled
across her fingers. Her skin tingled in its wake.

"What is it?" she asked.

"The water of life," said the king with a smile. "It re-
stores life and heals all hurts."

The bottle was as slick and hard as marble. Cloud bit
down on the questions pushing out of her mouth. "Thank
you, Lord," she whispered.

They returned the way they had come, Cloud terrified
that she would drop the bottle and spill the contents. By
the time they reached King Swimming's house again, day-
break colored the eastern horizon. Foam was waiting for
them on the beach. She favored Cloud with her uncomfortable half-smile.

"I have my own gifts for you, Cloud," she said, "whether
you think they're of any use or not." She hung a large fish-skin

pouch around Cloud's neck. "Now go fetch your things. And eat something. You have a long journey today."

With those words, ice squeezed Cloud's chest so tightly that she could not breathe. She knew where Foam was sending her.

But if Foam told her to go, she had no choice.

"Thank you," Cloud managed, once again swallowing what she really wanted to say. "Thank you for saving my life and taking care of me. And . . ." She turned to Swimming. "Thank you, Lord, for your hospitality and generosity, for your gift . . ." She had to stop there, because an idea was taking root in her with regard to that gift, and it aroused so much terror and longing that it choked off words altogether.

**Once again Black Fin climbed into his orca canoe,** and once again she pulled herself onto his back. He headed northeast from the town. By the time they emerged from the northern edge of the flotsam, the ocean had grown cold, clouds darkened the sky, and the islands of the Land of Wealth had disappeared behind them. They were returning to winter, and to mortal lands.

He coursed through white-capped waves, seemingly tireless. The big winter storm had broken up, but spatters of rain still gusted over the water. By midday the first blue shadow lifted over the horizon. It grew solider, turned green, passed by. Then they were flying past islands with dreamlike speed. Cloud spotted smoke in the distance, and canoes like water insects. Rain fell harder.

How could anyone expect her to return to that island where Otter's corpse rotted among scores of the dead, to the bloodthirsty god who was her father? She had a wild urge to slip off Black Fin's back. But he wouldn't let her drown, and he would carry her to his intended destination regardless.

*I can only do you my own kind of favors:* more of Foam's mockery to call this a *favor.* And foisting those gifts on her—

This was all for Foam's *amusement.*

But she had to carry out her task. Now it was not just Winter but *immortals* who had charged her with it. She was not going to show them disrespect; she was *not* going to follow in Thrush's footsteps. She certainly was not going to let herself dwell on the notion, seductive and terrible, that kept tickling her thoughts. So many stories warned of the consequences of misusing the First People's gifts.

Black Fin had already entered the wide bay beneath the mountains. All too soon he was drifting to a stop at the beach where she had camped with Otter and his men. Cloud could not at first dismount. She could not even look at the shore. Despair and dread clawed at her guts.

Beneath her, Black Fin twitched with impatience. The orcas had no pity. They were Winter People, indifferent to her terror.

At last she forced herself to slide off and splash to the beach. She glanced behind her—

Black Fin had disappeared.

The shock jolted her to her bones. But, she thought, her anger sharp as obsidian, she should not be surprised that he had left without a goodbye, without offering to help her survive on this dreadful island. *The Winter People were not her friends.*

The ghost-voices were already calling to her. She climbed the beach through a steady rain. The storm had hit this bay hard. The huge beached snag had traveled east a hundred yards, and the waves had battered Otter's canoe against drift logs until the hull had split. Cloud made herself approach it. Bits of gear poked through the gravel: rope, a broken bailer. Beneath the overturned hull was a dry space big enough to sleep in.

Movement at the edge of the beach made her spin around, heart thumping. But it was only a small brown creature, a raccoon or mink, that retreated when it spied her.

But—there, in the brush where the animal had crouched—wasn't that the bag Winter had packed for her? The southerners must have thrown it aside while looking for something more valuable than a woman's sewing kit. Evening shadows were already gathering under the trees, and Cloud approached the forest verge with great reluctance. The bag was much the worse for its time in the rain. Since she had been gone (was it seven days now? eight?), the strap had become tangled in dead grass and blackberry vines, and the bag itself now sheltered beneath it mold, bare dirt, and a host of sowbugs. Cloud worked it free and brushed off the sowbugs.

When she turned back to the canoe, Black Fin stood in her path. She started violently.

She wanted to berate him for frightening her, for making her think he had abandoned her, for forcing her to return to this place. But what she said was, savagely, "I'm here, aren't I? What else do you want?"

His jaw tightened. He stalked away to Otter's ruined canoe and began yanking out dry sticks. Soon, without slow match or firedrill, he had flames leaping: a First People trick. When the fire was burning properly, he stomped down to his canoe. This time, she thought, he really would leave her. Instead, he lifted out several large rockfish and set to gutting them.

Cloud watched, anger churning in her gut. Those fish were nothing less than what he owed her. Why should *she* offer to clean them? His knife would be sharper than anything in Winter's bag. So what if in his movements she could see the first signs of weariness from his long journeys of the past few days?

The cold darkness reached out from the forest to swallow the beach. She sat down by the fire he had lit. The white dress she wore was almost dry. She shook the water from her robe and untied her wet bundle of clothes to get at her rain cloak and hat.

Black Fin cut up the fish, brought the spitted sections to the fire, and planted them in a lean-to, all without a glance in her direction. Then he squatted down, staring into the flames. The last light faded from the sky.

"Why are you always angry with me?" he asked finally. "I haven't hurt you. I've tried to help, to please you—"

How could he ask such a question in *this* place? "Please *me*!" she said. "How could one of the Winter People care what would please *me*? You're hunters. You do what you want. What am I to you but—something to amuse you?"

"And you're never amusing?" He turned toward her now, his brows lowering ominously. "You think Summer People would have more concern for your fate than I do? I told you—"

"At least it's in their nature to *give*—"

"—to *beware the Summer People!* As far as *what are you to me* . . ." The dangerous edge slipped into his voice. "Yes, I hunt what I want. I want you. I want you to desire me the way I desire you. I want your happiness so I can be happy with you. What do you want me to *give* you? I *want* you to have it!"

This speech caused her heart to hammer wildly. Black Fin had spoken the thought that had waited in his gaze since their first meeting. A declaration of—what? Well, his word: desire.

All of a sudden, unable to breathe, Cloud was back in the forest behind Sandspit Town. Rumble squeezed her against a tree while he pushed his lips along her face. Rumble threw her on the ground, yanking up her dress—

Desire? Rage boiled through Cloud like scalding oil. Orca or no, if Black Fin touched her that way, she would rip him with her claws, she would tear out mouthfuls of flesh, she would gulp down his gushing blood.

But he did not move. He just watched her, an awful tightness around his mouth.

Desire. Look at the evil that Thrush's two husbands, Stink and Rumble, had caused; look at how cruelly they had treated her, because of *desire*. They had crushed her with *wanting*.

"You don't want my happiness," Cloud said. If he did, he would offer kindness and reassurance. He would not threaten her with *desire*. "You don't even want *me*. You want some, some beautiful princess—"

"You think so?" he asked. "What do *you* want?"

"I want . . ." Cloud began, and then she was crying. She gestured toward the darkness behind them. "I want this to be taken from me."

Black Fin looked that direction. "That's beyond my power."

"You could at least come with me," said Cloud, hating how pitiful she sounded; she already knew he would not.

"I can't help you in that forest."

Her rage mounted even higher: the immortal prince was supposed to *save* the girl he courted, not send her into danger.

"Then there's nothing you can do for me," she said.

"Then," he said, "I'll remove myself from your presence." And he rose and walked down the beach toward his canoe. Cloud watched him go, rage cutting through her belly like knives. She was supposed to beg him not to abandon her. No, she was supposed to act like the daughter of a queen. She was supposed to thank him quietly for the fire and the fish he had caught for her, for the long journeys he had carried her on without complaint, for his care of her in the spirit lands. She was supposed to have the courage to embrace her fate.

But she hated him so much for leaving that she could hardly breathe.

At the water's edge he glanced back. She almost called after him, but not knowing what to say, she waited too long. In another heartbeat he had floated his canoe and was gone.

## THIRTEEN

## The House in the Forest

*Cloud crawled under the edge of the canoe and* pulled her wet fur robe over her rain cloak. With Black Fin gone, even her shelter felt unsafe. Firelight could not penetrate the darkness in the corners of the overturned hull. And beyond the canoe—

She had seen the signs on this island before, but now she knew what they meant. Here, in human lands, something was tugging loose the masks. Even on the beach, every shadow loomed larger than it should. But the forest was where the heart of it lay. She could feel it behind her: a terrible immensity of whispering, dripping blackness as big as the world.

A wolf's howl lifted over the forest, and then a second wolf answered. Prickles stabbed up her spine. Otter had said the wolves were interested in food, not the old dead, but with all the corpses up in the forest, they had plenty to eat now.

Cloud disentangled Foam's pouch from her clothing and fingered the contents through the delicate fish skin. The salmon king's bottle, which she had added to the pouch, was easy to identify. She counted four other objects: a harpoon point, a cylindrical carving, a tiny box, a toy canoe. Surely these were the very gifts Foam had offered at their first encounter? Cloud still could not guess how they would be useful against wolves, ghosts, or wizard's servants.

She slipped the pouch back inside her cloak. When the fish was cooked, she pulled the skewers into her shelter. Out loud she said, "Thank you, Black Fin." But she was still so angry with him that the words were like nettles in her mouth.

She ate sparingly; this was all the food she had. When another wolf howled, she piled more wood on the fire and propped herself upright, hoping it would keep her awake.

But she had missed still more sleep last night and today made the long, wearying journey from the west. Rain drummed monotonously on the canoe hull. In spite of all the dangers on this island, her eyelids drooped and she sank toward a glade in the forest—

A thought pierced her drowsiness: *that mink would steal her fish.*

She fought to wake up. When she finally unstuck her eyelids, she thought she was still trapped in a dream. On the far side of the fire, a pack of dogs stared at her. Their eyes glowed like red coals. These dogs were rangier than the ones she knew, with gray-white heads and white-furred legs. Rain plastered down their rank fur—

*Wolves.* They had cornered her under the canoe. Cloud jumped up, cracking her head on the canoe hull and in the same moment tripping on her robe. They didn't move. Her hand was shaking so hard she couldn't pull her robe out of the way.

Perhaps she should pray to them. They were First People, too, like the orcas.

But orcas were fishermen. Wolves weren't just hunters; they were scavengers, carrion eaters. These wolves had been up in the forest. They might have been eating Otter—

She plucked a blazing stick from the fire and stabbed at the wolves. They drew back. She thrust it at them again. The largest wolf blinked, then trotted away. The rest followed.

She leaned out of the shelter and held up her stick like a torch, watching them go.

But here came more wolves and still more loping past her camp. She had always imagined a wolf pack as something like the mobs of dogs that would form up in Sandspit Town to snarl over bones, maybe a dozen animals at a time. But wolves kept coming along the beach; dozens, no, hundreds splashing in the water, clambering over driftwood, some sniffing in her direction before trotting after their fellows. Their feet in the gravel made a susurration like swift-flowing water, louder than the rain.

But no more of them approached her, and eventually the flood slowed to a trickle. A last few wolves hurried by, and the beach was empty again. Rain washed their rank doggy odor from the air.

She sat down. After a while, despite her best efforts, she slept again, dreaming of her brothers.

She woke to daylight and the ashes of her fire. An unfamiliar weight rested on her lap. She struggled upward to see that it was a *wolf head*—

—the head lifted, gray and black, blinking at her. In a panic she shoved the creature away. It landed hard against the far side of the canoe hull—

It wasn't a wolf. This was a dog after all: a skinny, scarred, cowering creature, tail curled between its legs.

It was Otter's dog.

It smelled of wet fur and barbecued fish. She cast around for the skewers she had piled inside her shelter. They were scattered, and only one still bore much flesh on it. The dog had gorged on what little food she had.

"Out!" she yelled, shoving it. "Get out!" But it lay flat, tail beating against the ground. She picked it up bodily and threw it out of her shelter. It landed half in the fire pit and yelped, hopped a few steps on three legs, sat down in the rain to lick its burned foot. When Cloud tried to chase it farther, it put its chin on the gravel and again thumped its tail. For a moment she thought she would drive it away with fire as she had done with the wolves, but then, somehow, she lost her anger.

It was Otter's dog.

Wouldn't he want her to take care of it? The animal's flanks were gaunt and its ribs protruded. She was surprised the wolves hadn't killed it.

She crawled into her shelter and wrapped up all the unchewed pieces of rockfish in a mildewed pouch from Winter's bag. The remaining scraps she dropped in front of the dog, who left off nosing its foot to gobble them down.

**On the beach waited evidence that her encounter** last night had not been a dream. Thousands of wolf prints pocked the gravel, extending under the water and into green depths.

The forest hung upside down in the rain-dimpled ocean, huge, dark, wavering. She turned unwillingly to face it straight on. Let Foam tell her what Cloud owed her father, that the binding of his ghost had hurt the world itself. Foam and Black Fin, who had such power at their disposal, were not the ones who had to venture into that forest alone.

Foam and her *amusements.* Cloud stripped off the orca dress and put on her old deerskin dress. She yanked out the pearlshell hair ornaments and fiercely combed her hair. However much she might long to become someone else and escape the pain of her life, to *be* the princess of the story, she was not going to give Foam any more to laugh at than she had to.

And no matter what the consequences, she was not going to abandon her most important obligation. The immortals cared only about her bloodthirsty father, but Otter had given his *life* for her.

She tried to guess how far the day had progressed. But today's was a half-moon tide, one that would move little over the course of the morning, and the low overcast hid all trace of the sun.

Cloud banked her fire, drank from the stream that had once supplied the old town with water, and settled Winter's bag across her shoulders. Then she reluctantly climbed the beach. Otter's dog had been sitting beneath the canoe out of the rain. Now it trotted after her, limping only a bit. This time she did not chase it away.

At the top of the beach she stopped and took a deep breath. Her legs were shaky, her hands and feet cold as ice, her stomach like a nest of coiling snakes. At last she pushed through the barrier of young spruces.

The deer trail led her through the grassy ruins of the old town. Her breath fogged the winter air. She could smell no hint of death yet.

Behind the ruins the trail grew steeper and muddier. Older trees stalked up the slope beside her, slow-moving giants with arms uplifted into the mists. Panic struggled to erupt through her thoughts and she clamped down hard on it. Otter, she told herself, had been sure her father wouldn't harm her.

Raven Tongue had even said, *It wasn't your father who killed those warriors in the forest*—but he must have meant it was Bone who had done so, by luring them to this island.

At least there was no sign of Bone's servants today.

When the trail branched at the top of the slope, she halted. The dog thrust its nose into her hand, making her jump.

She did not need to stop. The ghost-voices guided her, and she remembered the route with perfect clarity: that leaning alder, that outcrop of mossy stone.

Cloud tried in vain to recall the dog's name. She was actually glad to have it with her.

She walked on, trying to ignore the slow movement at the edge of her vision. The forest was a convocation of shadows, an overhanging world-roof of wet evergreen darkness. Her clothes rustled louder than the drip-drip of rain.

Here was the branch of the trail that led to the south shore, where the southerners must have landed that morning. She dreaded the first whiff of the corpses waiting at the meadow.

But she found no trace of them there, only more grass trampled by deer. Otter's dog poked its nose into deer droppings, indifferent to anything else.

Soon afterward, the trail brought her to the spot where Bone's servants and then the southerners had attacked Otter. Still no smell and no corpses. Cloud forced herself to search the brush on either side. Invincible had lain right there, and this was the very log where Otter had gasped his last words. But she saw no bodies anywhere.

She moved farther from the trail, stepping around the log, pulling back mats of dead grass and ferns. Otter's dog pawed under a fallen branch. Feeling as if she had swallowed a heavy stone, Cloud walked toward it.

The dog's name, she remembered suddenly, was Seal. The Master of the Undersea keeps seals as dogs—so Otter's little girl had said. She could have asked Black Fin if the story was true.

She heaved up the branch and tossed it aside. Only an empty leather sheath lay beneath. The neck strap was broken. It had been Squeaky's, or maybe Brant's—she couldn't recall now.

She worked the sheath loose from grass that had grown through the slits in the leather. Beneath it were sowbugs, mold, bare dirt, and a spiderweb of white rootlets.

Just what she had found under Winter's bag.

Cloud stared at the moldy leather in her hand. As far as she knew, she had been gone from this island less than a half-turn of the moon. But the sheath and bag—and now that she thought about it, that wretched dog—looked as if they had been abandoned far longer.

At least a year, for grass to die and sprout again.

"Seal," she said. She felt foolish talking to a dog. "How long have I been gone?" The dog just wagged its tail.

Surely the sheath would not have survived for as long as it took whole corpses to rot into the soil?

The constant stirring at the edge of her vision made her neck twitch. She glanced behind but saw only the dark wet trees.

Cloud lifted fallen sticks and scuffed through dead grass. She poked and prodded up and down the stretch of trail where Otter's men had died, and found only a broken spear shaft, a rotting cloak, and (carefully setting this on the log) a bit of leathery scalp with human hair attached.

The dead had been removed. But who could have done so? What *human* person?

She had been prepared to find Otter's remains scattered across the forest floor. She had been determined to collect every last gruesome scrap. She had readied herself to defy Foam, who did not care about the suffering of mortals.

An ache gripped her chest that was sharper than she could bear. She had trekked into this awful forest with water from beyond the world that would *restore life* and *heal all hurts,* and she could not find Otter's corpse.

Again, Cloud felt cold on the back of her neck; something—*small*—moved in the corner of her eye. She whirled.

A brownish creature slipped from the log where Otter had died. This time Cloud saw it clearly. *"You!"* she said.

It stopped. "You," she said to Otter's servant, "what happened to my uncle's body?"

The spirit stared at her without blinking. She had just decided she was foolish to expect an answer when it flitted along the trail in the direction of the glade of bones. Just as suddenly, it stopped and glanced back at her.

Heart racing, neck prickling, Cloud walked toward it. When she drew near, the servant skittered farther along the trail.

She followed, ducking under the boles of fallen giants, climbing around roots of trees whose trunks would have filled half the central hall of Halibut House. Meanwhile the rain dripped and the forest kept darkening as if a lid were shutting over the world. The ghosts called, faint and far away.

The trail topped a mossy granite knoll. Otter's servant had vanished, but below, no more than fifty yards away, a huge old maple spread its naked branches above grass and salmonberries. Shadows were congealing down there, swimming like fish through the thickets. Cloud waited for a darker shape to stir, but the forest dripped on as it had been, immense as mountains, gloomy as twilight.

Why had Otter's servant led her *here*?

With a jolt she realized that it *was* twilight. The darkness was simply darkness. She had awakened that morning later than she thought, and the short winter day had already ended.

She began stepping away from the glade as if through the bones in her dream. She was too stupid to take care of herself. She needed others to help her survive—Aunt Glory, Otter, Foam, Black Fin. Now nightfall had caught her in a forest where a bloodthirsty god prowled, and she hadn't even brought a torch.

Whether or not her father's ghost would harm her, she couldn't face it in the dark. Her camp was hours away now, but she couldn't be far from the southern shore of the island.

Cloud stopped to listen. She heard only the faint cries of the ghosts, and a breeze like an exhalation in the trees. She sniffed at the air. A cold perfume of fir needles drifted down with the rain; a scent of freezing dirt and damp dog rose up from the ground; and from her person wafted the smells of skin, wood smoke, and fish. The dusk bore only the most elusive whiff of rotten meat. She could not smell the sea at all.

Lastly, she looked—not straight on, but out of the corners of her eyes. There was nothing she had not been seeing the whole day: slow-moving giants, faces in bark and stone that seemed to surface and dive deep again.

*"Hello!" she called softly. "Hello!" And then, to the* dog, "Do you know where that spirit is?"

As if in response, Otter's dog, who had been pressing

against her legs, growled in a low, penetrating whine. Cloud glanced wildly around her.

But instead of her father's ghost, wolves bounded out of the shadows. When Seal burst into a frenzy of barking, they stopped, tongues lolling, breath emerging in puffs of steam.

Seal began to lunge toward them and pull back as he barked. Cloud thought: if this scrawny, starving dog attacked, he would be killed in a heartbeat. She grabbed his scruff and hauled him away from the wolves, away from the haunted glade, in the direction she thought was south, while Seal snarled and snapped at the air. Then she let go of him and began striking his rump, driving him forward. The wolves gathered atop the knoll, staring in their direction. "Go!" she yelled at Seal.

Now that she had left the open flanks of the knoll and plunged under the trees again, it was too dark to see. For a while she was able to grope along a muddy and well-trodden trail. Then they came to a hollow beneath densely branched cedars, and in that sooty blackness she lost the way completely.

Daylight had vanished. The forest leaned over her, huge and black. She had barely managed to fend off terror all day, but now it clogged her throat like stone. "Where's the trail?" she asked Seal. Her voice emerged as a hoarse whisper.

Seal whined. She could smell him but couldn't see him.

She stumbled outward in what she hoped was a circular path, colliding with saplings and fallen branches and stones. When her feet found an indentation where sticks and needles had been crushed into the loam, she edged along it.

The forest opened up ahead; she could glimpse trees like cliffs sailing through seas of darkness. A faint scent of old bones and rotting offal drifted on the breeze.

"Seal, come here!" she whispered. "Come on, dog!"

This time she heard no response, not even the sound of his footsteps. She crept forward, flinching from branches and spiderwebs. Disorientation rolled over her in waves. Southward, she thought. To the beach. She could get there.

The ground fell away and Cloud toppled through air, crashed to earth. For a few moments she was too shaken by the impact to move. Then she climbed to her feet.

She had reached the opening in the trees. Overhead, black branches hung against a sky that was only a little less dark.

Then she saw a light. It had to be a camp on the shore. She cautioned herself that it could belong to anybody—sea hunters from Waterfall, Gull Islanders, more southerners, perhaps even travelers from Sandspit Town—even while she hurried toward it. And then her feet once more touched a path, thorny but well trodden. Wood smoke blew over her—

It was not an open campfire but a house. Light and smoke alike squeezed out through gaps in what must be rather ill-seasoned boards. Cloud followed the path to a door covered with a hide curtain. As she approached, she wrinkled her nose against a stink of rotting offal that must rise from a nearby midden. A hunter's smokehouse, she thought. She had no idea who would be able to hunt in this forest, but the hunter must at least be *alive,* since what ghost would raise beams and split planks?

**She stepped up to the door. "Hello," she called** tremulously.

She could hear movement inside, but no footsteps approached the doorway. "Hello," she called, louder.

Still no answer. Cloud ducked past the curtain.

Inside, on a mess of frames, hung numerous splayed and gutted deer carcasses. In their midst burned a fire of wet, green wood. It smoked so thickly that her eyes blurred with tears. The fire was dimmer than it had appeared from outside, and it gave off very little heat; the house was as cold as the forest.

The only visible occupant of the house was a woman tending the fire. She glanced up as Cloud entered. Either the hunter—probably her husband—was still in the forest, or he was napping in the back, behind the shadowy chaos of storage boxes, bales of hides, and stacks of firewood that must conceal where the occupants kept their bedding. Cloud thought she heard snores from that direction, but it was hard to be sure with all the sap crackling in the fire.

She coughed and wiped away tears. "Hello," she said, wishing she had Foam's knack for pretty speeches. "I'm lost and wolves were chasing me. I saw your house—"

"Wolves!" said the woman. She shoved past Cloud to poke her head out the door. At that very moment a wolf howled nearby. The woman pulled her head in, heaved a wooden door across the opening, and barred it shut. The door was a single squared plank a hand's-width thick and both wider and taller than Cloud; she was amazed the woman could move it.

The hunter's wife turned to Cloud. "Well, then," she said grudgingly, "come and sit down."

Cloud squeezed after her through the clutter and, setting down her bag, perched on the edge of a box beside the smoking fire. The deer carcasses loomed over her. Her hostess was a gaunt woman with a large nose, straggling hair, and an unpleasantly swollen throat. She wore a string or two of beads but no other ornamentation. Like everything in this house, her dress was crudely made: the hide was stiff and the sewing uneven. When the woman had pushed by her a moment ago, Cloud had been grateful for the smoke: her hostess had not washed herself or her clothes in a long time, and her breath had a powerful sour-rancid stink.

The hunter's wife peered at Cloud. "Are you hungry?"

Smoke turned Cloud's answer into a coughing fit. Her hostess evidently took this as a "yes," because she turned to a box and ladled out a bowlful of what Cloud at first mistook for herring roe. After holding the lopsided bowl closer to the fire, however, and sniffing discreetly, she concluded the stuff was not anything from the sea. Cloud thought it might be deer brains, which Sandspit Town women used to tan hides. These brains did not smell fresh. Some old people in Halibut House would eat the brains out of boiled seal heads,

but Cloud had never done so. She would have greatly preferred some of the drying meat, but she was not going to be
so rude as to ask.

"Thank you very much," she coughed, wiping away tears.

She told herself that she could eat brains, even spoiled
brains. Smoke would mask the taste. She lifted a spoonful
to her mouth, but the wolves howled again, so close by
that Cloud started and nearly overset the bowl. Her hostess just scowled, apparently confident that the rickety walls
would protect her. Cloud wondered why the woman kept
her midden so near when it guaranteed scavengers on her
doorstep.

She couldn't hear any noise outside indicating that the
wolves had fallen on Otter's dog. Seal had, she told herself,
survived many months in the forest without her help. Still,
she would rather have brought him into the house.

Cloud tilted her bowl to reclaim the brains that had
nearly slopped out. Another coughing fit seized her. "Could
I please have a drink of water?" she asked her hostess.

Staring at her with an odd intensity, the woman handed
over a dipper from a bucket. Cloud drank and rubbed her
tearing eyes. Her hostess had not yet introduced herself
or asked Cloud's name, which seemed strange. This frigid,
smoky, crowded house was an odd place in and of itself, and
now some trick of the half-light made it look as if the deer
carcasses were falling upward. No, not a trick of the light:
walls and roof *were* pulling away, the room was growing
larger. In the corners of her eyes, the whole building wavered. The masks were tearing loose—

There was no respite in this house from the ailment that
afflicted the forest. Cloud was tired and frightened; she just
wanted to rest here in safety until daylight. Dutifully,
though—remembering the berries in the salmon house—
she looked sideways at her bowl. Gray, lumpy, threaded with
blood; that didn't change, nor did the smell. But beneath
the pungent smoke, the smell tugged at her memory—

Something bumped in the rear of the house. Cloud's heart

stuttered. Her hostess darted a glance in that direction, too. Someone was definitely back there.

And as if the unseen movement had caused it, the flames began to burn with more air. A tongue of flame found a splinter of dry wood and flared up brightly, casting wild shadows that flew through the house like bird wings. The surging fire lit the carcasses overhead. Those were *human* corpses, the torsos gutted and skinned, the flesh peeled away from the bones and spread wide with sticks, meat and bone alike darkened with smoke, the lidless skulls emptied of brains.

Cloud sprang to her feet, crying out. But her nameless hostess jumped up faster. At last, from Rumble's feast, from her time with the southerners, Cloud recognized the smells that the smoke had nearly obscured: *human* flesh, human guts, human bones, old human blood. And in her bowl—

Dizziness poured over her. She and the woman fell through a black gulf of desiccating corpses and harsh, billowing smoke. Sickened and terrified, Cloud was also furious with herself all over again: she ought to have guessed that anyone living on this island must be an immortal.

Another coughing fit seized her. "Thank you for the meal," she choked out through chattering teeth. "But I can't eat this sort of food."

"No?" hissed the woman. "And what do you eat?" She took a step toward Cloud, swelling in size—

"Salmon," Cloud stammered, "or deer or mountain goat, or berries, or, or clover roots, anything like that."

Her hostess kept growing larger. Now her head reached into the shadowed rafters. Cloud wanted to back away, but the corpses crowded around her, the house was spinning, and they all toppled together through the smoke. The huge woman took another step, peering down through the racks of corpses to examine Cloud more closely. The fire lit up her necklace, revealing it to be the string of Otter's amulets. Cloud dropped the bowl to clap both hands over her mouth.

At that same moment the woman shrieked, *"Don't lie to me!"*

"I didn't," gasped Cloud. "I don't eat human flesh!"

The woman screeched, "Try to deceive me! I see who you are now! You're Stink's child. Don't lie to *me*!" The noise was like knives slicing through Cloud's ears.

A long yellow beak, sharp as a spear, protruded where the woman's nose had been; sooty feathers sprouted on her body; her feet became scaly yellow claws. As the bird-woman stepped past the fire, the flames shrank down once more and smoke vomited upward, whirling into blackness. "I know why you're here!" she screeched. "Do you think you can steal from *me*?"

The bird-woman lowered her head through the ranks of corpses until her beak hovered right above Cloud.

Then she stabbed downward. Cloud threw herself to the side, scrambled toward the doorway, and tossed away the bar, heaving at the door-plank with all her strength, but she couldn't budge it. The bird-woman stepped deliberately through the smoke, planting one three-toed foot after the other, poking her head through the smoke-cured corpses. Cloud twisted away from the door just as the monster stabbed again. This time, she tripped on a box and the beak gouged her shoulder.

Nearly fainting from pain, Cloud pulled herself to her feet. She slid along the wall for a few steps, hitting at the boards to see if any were loose enough to knock aside, but it was like swimming through clay. Warm blood coursed down her arm. The bird-woman stepped after her. When she stabbed again, Cloud could not dodge in time. The beak pierced her chest, a spear-thrust of ice. She fell—

She toppled past split-open corpses, past mountains of bones and rotten offal. The whirling, congealing smoke grew ever darker and denser and more airless as she fell, until at last she crashed down into cold, putrid mud. The mud clogged her mouth and nose, choking her. Above her reared an unending forest of the drying corpses, and next to her head, in the lowest spot between the middens, sat her father's huge and toothless skull.

A loud clamor rose out of bones and rotting flesh and the smoky blackness they all drowned in. Her brothers' child-voices cried, "Save us, save us!" Otter's voice was calling to her, too, from the forest of corpses. "Cloud," he said, "you must go on. Leave me, you must go on."

But with every shallow, agonizing breath, she sucked more mud into her lungs. She could not go on. She knew this place, these splintered bones, this suffocating pit of despair. She had carried it inside her since Otter's death, maybe her whole life. She could not go on.

"Wait," called a distant, sleepy voice. "Aunt, wait!"

The voice was a mote of light farther away than a star. Footsteps approached, and the speck grew larger.

"She's beautiful," said the voice. "Aunt, you can't have her."

The house changed again. The new brightness showed Cloud that she slumped against the wall in a dark, spreading pool. The wound in her chest kept her from drawing breath.

Above her, corpses spun in lazy circles. The bird-woman spun, too, as she bent over, peering at Cloud. "She came here to steal from me!" she hissed.

"I'll take her away," said the voice. "*Please* let me have her, Aunt."

The monster hissed in reply. Now a second head joined the bird-woman's. The light shone from it. A hand also appeared, holding a bottle over Cloud. The bottle was as slick as iridescent marble, as bright as salmon in the sunlight.

A rainbowed drop shimmered out to fall endlessly through smoke. When it landed, warmth rippled through Cloud's chest, driving away the pain. A second drop landed, and air burst back into her lungs. A third drop, a fourth; now the liquid was falling in a thick stream.

The stream stopped. Hand and bottle withdrew. Her benefactor lifted her to a sitting position. Cloud's pain had vanished completely, and the pool of blood beneath her was melting away like ice in the sun. She put her hand to her chest and then her shoulder. The wounds were gone. Even the rips in her clothing had mended.

Foam's pouch was as lumpy as it had been; that familiar-looking bottle was not hers.

The new arrival was a young, handsome man. He wore a red tunic and a robe of spotless white feathers. "Why don't you come back to the hearth?" he said in a warm and gentle voice.

He lifted her to her feet. She let him guide her back to her seat. As he sat down beside her, smiling in reassurance, the fire quit smoking and burned yellow.

The giant bird had resumed the shape of a gaunt woman. Cloud glanced away from her. It was a relief to look at the young man instead. His skin was as smooth as polished maple; his eyes were an astonishing deep blue, the color of the zenith on a cloudless day. His heavy black hair was braided at his neck. What she had mistaken as a bright halo surrounding him was a pair of abalone disks that he wore as earrings. When he moved his head, spangles of light from the earrings glanced through the house.

He took her hand. From that touch, a summertime warmth spread up her arm and down into her belly.

"You've had a terrible shock," he said. "You'll feel better if you eat." He held out to Cloud not the crude dish of brains she had dropped, but another bowl, beautifully carved and filled with something bright. "Perhaps this is more to your taste."

Cloud took the new bowl. Just holding it warmed her cold hands. When she looked at the bowl sideways, bright-ness dazzled her eyes, but the contents did not change. Its faint perfume seemed to drive away the smoked-meat stench of the house.

The young man mistook the nature of her hesitation. "Don't be afraid of my aunt. She won't eat you while I'm here."

He was so kind. He cared how frightened she was; he

understood that the horrors of this place were more than she could endure.

"I am Looks-Down-From-the-Center-of-Heaven," he said in that warm voice, "and my aunt is called Huntress."

He offered her a spoonful of the bright stuff. Cautiously, Cloud tested the smallest bit from the tip of the spoon. Whether it was meat or fish, or roots slow-roasted until they were sweeter than sun-ripened berries, she could not tell, but at that moment it seemed like the most delicious thing she had ever tasted. She took another taste, then swallowed the whole spoonful. He fed her another.

Smoke and shadows fled from him; his earrings dappled the house with light; a glow radiated from his very skin. But the brightness he shed did not illuminate everything. It did not shine into the spot where Huntress stood, or the rough shadows swaying over her head. Someone was whispering in the rafters. "You must go on," the voice said. "Cloud, you must go on."

She averted her gaze from those shadows and looked at Center-of-Heaven instead. He offered her another spoonful, and she ate it. Warmth and pleasure budded in her stomach. A welcome haziness drifted over her thoughts.

He leaned so close that the perfumed white feathers of his robe tickled her face. "My aunt's temper is never certain," he said in her ear. "Let's go now."

As he urged her to her feet, she picked up her bag. He steered her past the dour Huntress. With one hand he shoved aside the enormous door-plank and with the other he guided her into the pitch-black forest beyond.

"Hold on to me," Center-of-Heaven said, and she shyly put her arms around his neck. He lifted her into his arms.

# FOURTEEN

# Pearlshell-of-the-Sky

*Pearlshell-of-the-Sky was a most beloved princess.* Her husband adored her, and his father, that magnificent king, indulged her like a favorite daughter. Her attendants were her husband's younger sisters. They bathed her and dressed her and sang for her pleasure; they embroidered her clothing and tidied her bed. They combed her hair in the morning and brought her perfume in the evening, before she lay down with her husband. They would not let her do anything for herself.

For Pearlshell, the king opened his treasure boxes. Her attendants dressed her in cloth dyed all the colors of sunrise, so soft it slipped over her skin like a lover's kisses. They adorned her with pearls, with beads of red and yellow crystal, with the sunny yellow copper, heavy and incorruptible, that bedecked her husband's house and everyone in it. They presented her with trinket boxes and embroidered pouches, mirrors and painted hats. She had no robe, but days were so warm in her husband's country that no one wore an outer garment, and at night—she never went out at night.

The name of the king's house was Where People Cannot
See From One Side to the Other. The house was indeed very
large; a person had to shout to be heard on the opposite side
of the hall. Not that Pearlshell ever shouted. If she needed
anything, an attendant ran to get it for her.

The wood the house was built of (Pearlshell never learned
its name) was a wonderful thing: it never cracked or rotted,
and when burnished it glowed with a sunny light even in
the depths of night. Carvings adorned every post and beam
of the house, and treasure boxes, stacked floor to ceiling,
lined the walls.

The food in the king's house (she never learned its name,
either) was as delightful as everything else: sweet, fatty,
smooth on her tongue. They always encouraged her to eat
as much as she liked. Only the queen consumed more than
she did.

House Where People Cannot See From One Side to the
Other stood atop a white sand beach, overlooking a sea of
transparent blue. Behind the house rose a forest of the
yellow-copper trees from which, they told her, the house
had been built. Its leaves chimed in the breeze that blew
from the sea. Clad in bark, the trees did not shine as the
house did, so the forest—unlike house or beach—was a
place of shifting, light-spangled shadow.

The house was beautiful; the people were beautiful; her
food and clothes were beautiful. What gave Pearlshell true
joy, however, was how much her husband's family loved her.
In the morning they greeted her as if she brought happiness
the way the dawn brings light. In the evening they said good
night as if parting from her grieved them. In between, they
invited her into every pastime; they made her feel as if nothing could happen properly without her. Even the queen,
whom Pearlshell suspected of disapproving of her son's bride,
never did worse than offer a greeting in place of a kiss, or a single word in contrast with her daughters' affectionate chatter.

And nights, when Pearlshell retired with her handsome,
ardent, adoring husband—the nights, when she was the sole

object of his attention—those were the most glorious of all. He would call himself a slave and Pearlshell his master; he would murmur the delights of each swell and hollow of her body. His caresses were like summer all over her skin. He would heat her up until he burned her blind and unknowing, and then he would hold her in his arms until they cooled enough to begin again.

On the night they had married, after he kissed her the very first time, he had whispered promises in her ear, "I know what you want," he told her. "I will give it all to you."

And he had.

That was how she lived for a long time.

### Then the dreams began.

Later she thought they must have lived inside her all along, drifting on currents that flowed far beneath thought and memory. Slowly the dreams swam upward.

In one dream that returned over and over, she struggled through blue water, desperate for air. In another she pushed at the stars, trying to break through to the darkness beyond. She was searching in every dream, but she never knew in the dream or upon waking what she searched for.

After one of those dreams, she always woke to doubt. She was so different from these people. She did not know how to be merry and bright, how to laugh and chatter or joke, how to hug or kiss her sisters-in-law with half the warmth they so spontaneously radiated upon her. Her husband whispered the most rapturous words in her ear, but she could not speak that way to him in return. She did not know why. They called her sweet-tempered and loving, but during those wakeful nights she could discover no love inside her, only a blank mist.

At times Pearlshell felt she resembled her mother-in-law. The queen, like her, had come from another place. The queen, like her, lacked the luminous skin and blue eyes of her husband's family. The queen, like her, was hungry and reticent.

On the other hand, Stoops-From-Above was clearly not a

person with doubts. The rare embrace or few quiet words she would give her children, the looks she cast in the king's direction, made Pearlshell certain that wherever the unsmiling queen kept her emotions, they were neither insubstantial nor hidden from her.

And the queen knew where she came from. The king hosted the queen's relatives from time to time, and they looked like her: dark, sharp-nosed, with hooded eyes and enormous appetites. Even after feasting from sundown to sunup, they would eye Pearlshell in a predatory way she found unsettling.

No one ever mentioned Pearlshell's relatives and they never came to visit. At night she would wonder why she could not remember her life before her marriage, but it was not a thing she was able to ask about in daylight.

Other dreams came to her as time went on, of running endlessly, of people lying broken and red-stained. She began to feel that her dreams were monsters lurking beneath the bright surface of her life, hungry to wrench her down into darkness. After such a dream she would cling to her husband until he awoke and chased away all glimpses of the monsters with his love.

Once she tried to tell him about the dreams. "Don't pay attention," he said. "They can't hurt you here."

She tried to follow his advice, but it worked less and less well. And slowly, doubt began to seep into the daytime.

*A path led into the forest behind the house, under* those yellow leaves so translucent they might have been made of the thinnest shell. One day Pearlshell thought: the path must lead to the creek that supplied the house with water.

She could picture such a creek, rushing through shade and dappled sunlight. The noise of water over stone would be as lovely as a song, always changing, never ending.

When she asked her husband's oldest sister about it, Gaze-of-Summer said, "You don't want to walk in the forest."

"The trees are sharp," said Noon, the only child of the king whose eyes were black like the queen's. "The leaves will rip your clothes and cut your feet."

Pearlshell was puzzled because they never denied her anything. "Couldn't I go along the beach to the creek?"

"There's no creek," said Noon.

"Oh, Pearlshell," Gaze-of-Summer said, "weren't we going to have a game of throwing sticks? Don't disappoint us!"

Her look of playful entreaty was irresistible, and Pearlshell dropped the subject. But she began to notice how freely *they* came and went from the house. The queen was away often, and the king left nearly every morning, returning only at night. When the king rested, her husband would go instead. Center-of-Heaven would tie on a pair of odd, unadorned shoes and fetch something from his father's apartment that he carried out of the house. Like the king, he returned after dark, weary as if from a day of labor. At the house, no one ever labored.

They did take her when the entire household traveled to a feast. From the king's great canoe, Pearlshell would watch the passing forest, but she never spied the outlet of a creek.

After one of these feasts, she would gaze into the abalone mirror her husband had given her. With her dark eyes, small nose, and copper-brown skin, she did not look like anyone else she had seen. Wherever her people lived, it was so far away that she was the only one here.

*One night, after waking from a dream, she rose on* impulse and crept across the silent hall to the beach. Outside it was bitterly cold. The house shed yellow-copper radiance on the sand; in the sea swam a multitude of stars. Elsewhere profound darkness hid the world. The sand smelled of dew.

When she heard someone else coming through the door, she slipped behind the king's canoe, half-ashamed to be spying.

The king emerged wearing a pair of those plain shoes,

and, on his head, a headdress of the glowing abalone her mirror was carved from. He headed into the forest, crunching in the fallen leaves. After a moment's hesitation Pearlshell followed.

At first the light from the king's headdress and his luminous person guided her. But the leaves were indeed knife-sharp as her attendants had warned, and the king walked so swiftly that he had soon shrunk to a distant speck of light. She stumbled on, shivering. The leaves under her feet gave way to sand, and she stood above starry ocean once more. She had crossed a point.

Then, as she stepped toward the sea, a hole gaped before her. Below it hung a bottomless void of gray mist.

Pearlshell stumbled back, dizziness sweeping over her. The hole wavered out of existence. Then the blinding disk of the sun swelled up into the world, and she stood above a blue sea like the one that lapped every day in front of the king's house. Morning filled the air with warmth.

Shaken, she started back toward the house, mincing over the cruel leaves. Now the daylight showed her something else. Atop a little-used midden, nearly concealed by fallen leaves, sat a pile of soiled, scuffed, reeking leather. Her nose wrinkled, but her curiosity was whetted by its very lack of resemblance to anything in her husband's house.

She did not immediately have a chance to investigate. The air behind her rumbled and a blast of cold wind set the forest chiming. When she whirled to look, a terrifying form stood at the bottom of the beach where the hole had been.

An unfamiliar voice deep inside her said, *A bird.*

But she knew that this was not what a bird should be, this dark creature taller than the trees, with its beak and claws smeared with a sticky red-brown that smelled—

—that smelled of—

Again the unfamiliar voice spoke: *blood.* Eagerness stirred in Pearlshell, shocking her.

When she blinked, only her dour mother-in-law stood

there, pushing a feathered cloak from her shoulders. Pearl-shell fled.

**Relief and reproaches greeted her at the house.** "Your poor feet!" Gaze-of-Summer cried.

Only then did Pearlshell notice that she had tracked blood across the spotless floor of the house. The cuts on her feet did hurt, but less than they seemed to think.

Her attendants told her never to go into the forest again, but she could not forget what she had seen: a hole in the world, a huge and bloody bird, a pile of something ugly and worn in a country where nothing else was. The reek of that pile stuck like a splinter in her thoughts.

By nighttime her feet had nearly healed. After Center-of-Heaven fell asleep, she took her abalone mirror and crept back to the midden. Beyond the glow of her mirror, the forest was black and featureless. An icy wind made the leaves rattle like knives. She jumped when a shriek echoed over the forest.

She squatted beside the pile of leather. The voice named the odors rising up from it: *mold, earth, smoke, brine.*

Another shriek cut through the night. *Something is hunting,* the voice inside told her.

Beneath a robe, a cloak, and other soiled clothing lay a large and heavy bag. As she lifted off the clothing, gingerly shaking away the leaves, two objects rolled loose. One was a little carving, the other a bulging pouch. Both had been strung on braided thongs.

The carving depicted a bird. Its beak was straight like the queen's other shape, but its gaze was rakishly curious rather than ferocious. She sniffed at it. Whatever smell she expected was not there.

But then a rush of memory brought it back to her: sweet-grass and mock-orange. She smelled it on her mother's neck, in her glossy black hair. Thrush held her, saying, "Oh, my baby, oh, my little girl."

Otter had made the carving. He sat on the far side of a campfire, whittling. Her father? She loved him.

How could she have forgotten them? Pearlshell began to cry, hollow with loss, hungry with longing.

Heavy footsteps crunched, close by—

Pearlshell shoved the carving and pouch into the bag, grabbed her mirror, and ran. The footsteps followed, gaining on her, shattering leaves at every step. She ducked into the house and crawled all the way to her bedroom so as not to leave bloodstains on the floor. A ponderous tread circled the house.

She wanted to rouse her sleeping husband and make him chase away her terror. Instead she slipped the bag down behind the stacked chests and crawled into bed. She was still panting and shivering long after the footsteps departed.

**She tried to immerse herself once more in the ocean** of kindness that was her husband's house. But the endless play now seemed irksome, and she could not help but dwell on all that her husband's family must be hiding from her. At night she lay in bed smelling the bag in its hiding place: mold, dirt, leather, cedar bark. Its rich odors were so different from the fleeting perfumes of her husband's country.

Center-of-Heaven did not seem to be able to smell them.

For a long time she did not open the bag, afraid of what might wait inside it. But her doubts began to change her into a mannerless stranger. One day, as her attendants were fitting the dresses they had made to accommodate her increasing plumpness, Pearlshell asked Gaze-of-Summer, "Where does the king go every morning, when he puts on his shoes and headdress?"

Her sister-in-law's smile faded for only an instant. "The king's business takes him from home, sister. Look at this border I embroidered for you; do you like it?" And Gaze-of-Summer held up a new red dress decorated with bands of yellow leaves.

Pearlshell the princess would have understood that the truth about the king's absences mattered less than the love Gaze-of-Summer offered in its place. But the stranger who had taken up residence in Pearlshell smelled evasion. "The queen goes that way, too," said the stranger, using Pearlshell's mouth.

"Perhaps you saw her returning from a visit to her relatives," Gaze-of-Summer said, smoothing the dress against Pearlshell. "I think this will fit you for a while, sister."

The stranger, who had keener senses than Pearlshell, heard the worry in those words; her sister-in-law was afraid she had seen the giant blood-smeared bird, the secret shape of the queen! A long-forgotten emotion reared up in Pearlshell, as frightening as it was compelling. "Why don't you want me to go in that direction?" demanded the stranger.

"We only . . ." Gaze-of-Summer made a visible effort to produce another loving smile. "Pearlshell, don't torment yourself with such questions! What matters is that you're here, and you're happy, and that makes our prince happy!"

Evasion and secrets: the foreign emotion swelled, crested, and roared through her. Pearlshell remembered its name: *anger.* "Why won't you tell me the truth?" she screamed, and she ripped the dress from Gaze-of-Summer's hands and threw it to the ground.

Her attendants stared at her slack-jawed. Then the anger drained away, leaving Pearlshell as surprised and appalled as they were. She began to weep. "I'm sorry, I don't know why—"

They hugged her and stroked her hair. "Hush, little sister," Noon said. "It's all right."

But it was not all right. She was humiliated by her outburst. She longed to remain Pearlshell, the adored, the comforted, the sweet-tempered and loving. Why couldn't she be happy being happy? No one could love this awful stranger.

And yet the doubts kept returning.

One morning, as she played on the beach with the other girls, she found herself gazing again at the forest. She was so tired of brightness, she realized. She was tired of the shining sea, the shadowless sky, the glittering sand, the eternally glowing house. The only darkness that came to this country was at night, outside, and they did not let her out once sunlight had disappeared from the sea.

She longed for shadow and the smells of damp secret places: moss, wet leaves, rotten bark. She longed to walk.

Pearlshell begged out of the next round of their guessing game. And while the other girls laughed and shouted questions, she set off down that path strewn with knife-sharp leaves. Even in the forest, there was no real shadow, only degrees of glare shining through the translucent leaves.

Footsteps were already pounding along the path behind her. Voices called, "Princess! Sister! Lady!"

"You mustn't go this way," Gaze-of-Summer panted as she ran up. She clutched Pearlshell's shoulder.

Noon caught Pearlshell's wrist. "You've cut your feet again."

A girl named Sunbeam gripped her other hand. "Come back with us. The cuts must hurt so. Let us tend them!" Their feet were also bleeding.

"My feet don't hurt," Pearlshell lied. She tried to take another step, only to discover that the three young women held her so firmly she could not move at all. Anger spilled through her like blood from a wound.

"*Let me go!*" she screamed.

They did. She backed away from them. They watched her without moving.

The path led out of the trees to the other beach. Her feet left blood in the sand.

A blue sea lapped at that beach. But as she approached it, the white sand wavered and the water thinned, and suddenly she teetered at the brink of a windy abyss. A black shape swooped toward her, wings thundering, up through turbulent, uprising mountains of gray and white. Pearlshell scrambled backward as the gigantic black bird alit on the precipitous beach and folded its wings. The bird's talons were red with blood.

Terror welled up in Pearlshell as cold as her anger had been hot. She backed slowly toward the forest. The bird fixed one eye on her and stepped after her.

"You! Little mortal!" it screeched.

The black-robed queen, still tall as a tree, stood where the bird had been. She looked fierce enough to kill Pearlshell.

Pearlshell stumbled back. The queen kept stepping after her, huge and inexorable. "Do you have any gratitude for their generosity? Do you think you can dispense with their protection?" She bent to thrust her face at Pearlshell's. *"Do you think you're strong enough for this place?"*

Pearlshell's teeth chattered, but she said, "I just wanted—I just wanted to walk—"

"If you are going to go your own way, little mortal," Stoops-From-Above hissed, "you had better be strong. You had better stick fast to your nature. Are you able? *I doubt it.* Do what you like, but then *don't ask for help.*"

And then, shrinking to human size, the queen stalked up the path in a cloud of black, rain-wet feathers. Her daughters scurried out of her way.

In the direction the queen had come from, the beach had steadied; the cold void was a placid blue sea once more.

"Why are you staring at me?" Pearlshell screamed at her attendants, and she, too, pushed past them. She ran back to the house to hide in her bedroom.

*"What's wrong, darling?"* Center-of-Heaven asked.

Pearlshell knew the queen was right: she wasn't strong. And she knew how they all took care of her. But she needed to know what they were hiding.

"Where does the path through the forest lead?" she said. "Why doesn't anybody want me to go there? Where does your father go every day? What did your mother mean when she called me a *mortal?* Where did I come from?"

"That's a lot of questions," he said gently.

She took that as another evasion. Anger blazed up again.

"I just want you to be happy here, and safe," Center-of-Heaven said. "Everything I do is for that and no other reason."

He began to kiss her, and after a while he succeeded in turning her thoughts to love. But now there was an icy lump in her belly that would not melt. When he had fallen asleep, she puzzled over what the queen meant by being *true to her nature.* What was a mortal? What was a mortal's nature?

Pearlshell knew what *she* was. Ungenerous. Restless. Unhappy. Unwise.

As quietly as she could, Pearlshell crawled out of bed and retrieved the leather satchel. The pouch and carving lay inside it where she had hurriedly thrust them before. She opened the pouch and pulled out the first object her hand touched, a bottle of stone or rock crystal. Had this, too, come from her mother and father?

When she extracted the stopper, out welled light and a rich, sweet smell she had no name for, only a picture: a vast sea of rainbow-shot water.

But close on its heels, another vision wrenched at her. Her husband held the bottle, or one like it, and rainbowed drops spilled from it onto her chest. His face was as she knew it—kind, adoring—but over his head hung racks of split-open corpses whose skull-tops had been emptied. Mouthfuls of teeth grinned at her. Eye sockets stared accusingly, imploringly.

Pearlshell pressed the stopper back into the bottle as far as it would go. But awful images kept spilling out—

A giant bird stalked her through those racks of corpses—

A dirty woman crouched in the smoke beneath them. She offered Pearlshell a crude bowl full of—

—brains, from the dead men—

That woman looked just like the queen, if the queen quit bathing and dressing her hair, and took off her bright clothes and jewelry.

*—Her beloved husband had been there.*

Now a hundred sparks of doubt caught fire. Her husband's family didn't want her to know anything, wouldn't let her out of their sight. What mattered, Gaze-of-Summer had told her, is that their prince stayed happy. Was she just a captive whom he had rescued for his pleasure?

Weeping, she tried to shove the bottle back into the pouch. But it would not go in at first, and when she tried to push aside the obstruction, her careless movement dislodged something sharp—a *harpoon point*—with a bundle of string attached. As the string emerged, rope big as her wrist spilled onto her lap. Huge coils of it knocked her down, and fathom after fathom burgeoned around her and writhed through the bedroom. A coil fell on the sleeping Center-of-Heaven.

Pearlshell frantically tried to push the rope back into the pouch, but even a single handspan of it was too big. Center-of-Heaven stirred and murmured her name. Then it occurred to her to slide the harpoon point into the pouch. In an eyeblink, the rope had turned back into a bit of thin string.

Center-of-Heaven said, "What are you doing, love?"

She hastily stuffed pouch, bottle, and bag under a new dress that no one had yet folded into a chest.

He sat up. "You haven't opened any of the boxes, have you?"

"No," she said.

"You've been crying." Center-of-Heaven came over to her and wrapped his arms around her, wiped tears from her cheek. "More of your nightmares, love? Let me make you happy again."

How dare he pretend love or kindness? She snarled, "You haven't been trying to keep me *safe*. You've been *deceiving* me!"

He blinked. "I only did what you wanted."

"I didn't want to forget my mother and father!"

He said nothing. Her rage mounted until she felt she had claws inside her hands, as if powerful jaws lurked in her skull. "What was that house with all the dead people? Why were you there?"

"It was my aunt's house," he said. "My mother sent me. She worries that her sister is ill."

"Did your aunt kill my parents?"

"No," he said. "No, she did not. But, Pearlshell, my mother's people are very fierce. How could I protect everything they hunt? I did my best for *you.*"

So sincere. But he had always seemed sincere, and look what he had done: stolen all she had known and loved before him.

He kissed her. He whispered endearments and pleaded with her. But for the first time she could not respond at all. She could only sit stonily, wishing for darkness.

"Don't throw my love back at me, Pearlshell," he begged.

She did not reply. Eventually he lay down again. When she was sure he had fallen back to sleep, she pulled out the chest he opened when he went out in his father's place. She would not have thought to do so if he hadn't mentioned it.

The shoes he wore at those times lay atop a robe of spotless white feathers. She tried on the shoes. They were far too large. She considered the robe; the nights outside the house were very cold. But she decided she would rather have her own robe—the one they had discarded on the midden.

She replaced everything and returned the chest to the stack. Then, taking the pouch, bag, and mirror, she crept through the house, too angry to care about the dangers outside.

**At the midden, she shook the leaves from the fur** robe and outer cloak and settled them around her shoulders. Then she rolled up the rest of the clothing, tied it atop the bag, and slung the bag on her back.

Weighed down with her own things, she felt not just warmer but more solid. They gave her hope she could find her way home.

She continued on the path, slicing her feet no matter how carefully she stepped. At the other beach she put away the mirror, lest its glow betray her to the things that hunted at night.

Her husband and his family did not want her to come this

direction, but except for the cold wind and scattered leaves, it seemed just like the beach in front of the house: a strip of sand between forest and star-filled sea. There was a strange red light on the horizon that she hadn't noticed before.

The king had gone this way. How dangerous could it be?

Pearlshell crept forward. Vertigo rolled over her in waves, and the hole at the bottom of the beach flickered in and out of visibility. Tonight the void it opened into was charcoal gray.

On its far side, her dizziness lessened and she set off. She walked until her muscles ached, her feet burned from leaf cuts, and a long-forgotten pain stabbed at her belly: hunger.

The first time she heard wingbeats, she pulled her gut-skin cloak over her head and scrambled under the trees until the noise passed by. The cloak protected her face and arms, but the leaves slashed viciously at her feet.

Another of the great birds winged overhead, and then a flock of smaller birds crying harshly. The moon swam up into the sea. It was long past full, a deflated kelp-bulb of light. The wind grew colder. In the forest, leaves chinked like ice.

The glow spread across the horizon until the ocean glittered red. At last the shore bent away, leaving only a windswept promontory that pointed straight ahead. Pearlshell stopped. She had come this way not at all certain that it would lead her home, but guessing, or hoping, that all the secrets of her husband's house were connected.

As she hesitated, a fallen leaf snapped behind her. A figure strode toward her with a gleam as if from a large eye. She scrambled behind a dune to hide, only to discover, vertigo rushing over her, that below her gaped another of the holes in the world. This one was full of moonlight.

Footsteps rasped above her head. It was the king who walked by; the gleaming abalone disk of his headdress was the eye she had seen. He waded into the ocean where a dark trace of sand led across the stars, skirting the hole. The water did not reach higher than his knees.

Fighting the overwhelming dizziness, Pearlshell waded after him. The king, who moved so much more swiftly, had already rounded the hole and was descending over a near horizon: feet, legs, waist, shoulders dropping out of sight. The submerged sandbar deposited Pearlshell at a sliver of dry beach. No more black sky here, only the brilliant red glow—

—the source lay *below* her, below the horizon—

—It was churning fire at the bottom of an abyssal cliff.

*That* could not be where she had come from.

The fire spread left and right as far as she could see. Its brightness seared her eyes. There was no ladder or stair. No one could descend the precipice—but there was the king, climbing down and down with impossible speed.

The king shrank until she could no longer see him. Did a shape swim toward him through the sea of fire?

She drew back trembling from the brink. Then a bone-jarring screech ripped the night, and black wings thundered out of the hole in the sea behind her. A cold, wet gust flung her cloak across the sand. Trying to brace against the sudden pull, Pearlshell lost her balance and fell.

She managed to keep her arms atop the crumbling bridge of sand, but her body slid off and her heavy bag tugged her down. Red sky and starry sea, moonlit void and fire-lit cliffs swung end over end as if surf tumbled her.

The terror of falling gave her the strength to drag herself back onto the sandbar. Then the sun popped into view. She squeezed her eyes shut. The immense bird thundered away, screaming its displeasure.

The image of the sun kept exploding behind her eyelids: a blazing disk, and inside it a face and fish-like body. Heat and light fell on her like a landslide. She pressed her face on her arms, expecting her hair to burst into flame. After a moment, though, the brutal heat lessened. She slitted her eyes open.

The king had just passed her by. On his forehead where the abalone disk had been, he bore the sun, and the cheerful, affectionate king, who always had a kind word for her, walked stooped and burdened, his face distorted with terrible effort.

The king had not noticed her presence. Perhaps the sun blinded him, too.

Now Pearlshell saw that she lay on, not beach or sea bottom, but a transparent solidity the color of seawater. A void of sunlit mist hung *above* her. She had slipped through the hole, but instead of falling into the void, she had stuck like a limpet on the world's underside. The king walked upside-down on that blue surface, daylight racing ahead of him. Carrying the sun from one end of the world to the other.

Vertigo claimed her again. Billows of shadow and orange light spun through the void.

The queen was right. This was no place for mortals.

Clouds drifted beneath the world. Black specks circled in them. Carefully, afraid she might come loose and plummet into those depths, Pearlshell rose and hurried after the king.

She chased him all day across the barren blue expanse on her bloody and increasingly sore feet. Despite his burden, the king drew rapidly ahead. Meanwhile all sense of dimension and distance faded. She could not look straight at the king because the sun was too bright; if she looked anywhere else—at the featureless blue, at the cloud masses sailing through the void—dizziness overwhelmed her.

Then a break opened in the clouds. Through a deep canyon she saw another country: snow-capped mountains, winding inlets, cloud-shadow chasing sunlight over the water.

She stopped. It was heartbreakingly beautiful. Homesickness pierced her to the bone, even though nothing looked familiar except for the fact of that world, green forest, gray sea. The memory of smells swept over her: wild onion in the summer heat, mint crushed between her fingers, rain on new cedar boards—bits of memory lodged deep in her heart, no piece connected to any other one, but all an inextricable part of who she had been.

The scent of mock-orange and sweetgrass. Warm arms holding her close, hands stroking her hair. Thrush's soft voice. *Home.*

Here was the reason they had tried to keep her from the path into the forest. Once she looked down through the clouds and saw that world, she would never be happy again.

She was lost among the cloud tops. How did she get down—

—from the *sky*?

A new wave of dizziness crashed over her, and she squeezed her eyes shut.

When she opened them, the gap in the clouds had closed. Her longing for the land below was so intense she wanted to leap into them. After a while she remembered the harpoon point. The mere thought of trying to climb down those uncountable fathoms of rope made her sick with terror. What if it wasn't long enough?

But how else would she get home? She was a captive here.

At last she fished the harpoon point out of the pouch. She was careful to leave the bundle of string inside until she had stabbed the point deep into the slick blue surface of the sky.

*It never lets go.* Who had told her that?

A line of dark clouds sailed toward her, so tall that the tops flattened against the sky. She threw the string upward into their depths. It unfolded, swelled into rope thick as her wrist, fell, fell, fell—she turned her gaze away and fixed it on the point. The rope, she now saw, had been braided from several smaller strands. She worked her fingers among the strands, gripped tightly, reached over her head for another handhold—

Thunder boomed, echoed and reechoed, became wing beats. Up through the gloom flew one of the huge black birds, lightning crackling from its head, gale-blasts roaring from its wings. The smooth expanse of the sky offered no place to hide. All she could do was cower, clinging to the rope as the bird stooped straight at her, claws outstretched like an eagle snatching a fish.

The impact struck her like a boulder. The claws slid off the gut-skin cloak, but the force of the blow rolled her across the underside of the sky, ripping her hands from the rope. Thunder rumbled continuously as the great bird flapped after her. She struggled onto hands and knees to face it—

The bird pulled up, screeching in anger, then winged away into the clouds. Thunderclaps rolled into silence.

Panting, she climbed to her feet. But a figure blocked her way. It was Center-of-Heaven. He held the harpoon point, and the rope trailed over his head into the clouds.

"Pearlshell," he said, cold and harsh. "I can't keep you safe if you run away."

He wore the cloak of white feathers, now pushed back from his shoulders. With a chill she realized that he, son of Stoops-From-Above, also possessed a bird-robe.

She had angered the prince of heaven. Thrown his love back at him. What would her punishment be?

Then he said, "Come back with me, darling."

Looking into those blue eyes, color of the sea of heaven, she could not help but long to see them warm toward her again. But her own anger pushed back the tide of longing. "How can I? You deceived me in so many ways. You took away my memories!"

"You can have them back," he said, "if you want them."

"Another *gift*?" she said bitterly.

"I only tried to make you happy. I tried so hard."

*Happy.* Her ache for Otter and Thrush, for the world below, told her that real love didn't leave a bewildered blankness at the center of your being. It was as compelling as the smells of earth and brine, it struck deep into your bones. Real love was sharp as a knife.

*Stick fast to your nature,* the queen had said.

Whatever her nature was.

She wanted to scream at him, but there was still enough

of the princess in her to keep her voice steady, her words measured. "Do you really want to make me happy?"

"Oh yes," he said. "What can I give you, Pearlshell? What will make you happy?"

"I want to go home," she said, and then, on the verge of tears, "I'm sorry. But I want to go back where I belong."

It seemed like a very long time before he replied. "Of course. If that's what you want."

**Center-of-Heaven led her back to the king's house,** where he announced to his family that she wanted to go home. The softening of the queen's expression into approval was so slight that Pearlshell at first thought she had imagined it.

In the morning, though, as she said her final goodbyes, the queen surprised her with a pair of the plain shoes her own size. "They may not be pretty," Stoops-From-Above said, "but they will never wear out." Pearlshell stammered her thanks, even while she privately wondered what kind of hide they had been sewn from.

She and Center-of-Heaven accompanied the king on his eastward journey as far as the hole in the sky. There the two of them stopped. Center-of-Heaven rammed the harpoon point, which he had kept, into one of the trees. With his hand closed over the bundle of string, he payed out enough rope to knot a harness around her.

"I'll let you down," he said. "I know where you want to go." And then, when she hesitated, "I'll make sure you land safely. Otherwise you could come down in the middle of the ocean, or worse places."

PART FOUR

# FIFTEEN

# Return

*The rope lowered her for a long time. Pearlshell* could not see down to the lower world, and impatience squeezed her heart. Surely Center-of-Heaven was sending her home? *I know where you want to go.* He must be sending her back to Thrush and Otter.

If they were still alive.

Dawn, when it came, illuminated only gray mist that pelted her with rain. She tried to remember the life she was returning to. She had borne another name then, she thought. *Pearlshell* now sounded too pretty, too gentle to be hers.

At last, trees jutted out of the mist. A mossy knoll rushed up and took the weight of her feet, and she collapsed onto it.

Wet sphagnum moss. Spruce sap as thick in her nostrils as wood smoke. Brine and the roar of breakers.

Pearlshell tugged off the harness and, when the awful tingling in her legs had subsided, stood up. Dripping forest bordered the knoll on three sides. On the fourth side, a harbor, mossy rooftops—

She *remembered* that harbor—

A noise made her turn. Rope cascaded down, coils and

loops and great snaking lengths rippling like water, rasping like sharkskin, thumping and slithering onto the moss. It fell for a long time. Finally the upper end plopped onto the mountain of rope, and after a bit of settling all movement ceased.

No going back. Pearlshell climbed onto the mound. When she located the harpoon point, she looked up and said, "Thank you." What else could she tell him that would matter now?

She slipped the point into her pouch. The rope shrank to a bit of string, which she coiled and stuck in the pouch as well.

*A trace of a path wound down one side of the knoll.* Pearlshell shouldered her bag and followed it to the beach. When the row of ramshackle houses came into view, she hurried across the gravel, a wave of longing and memory breaking over her. This was Whale Town, where Otter lived—

She stopped.

The beach was empty of people and canoes. Spruces poked up from collapsing rooftops, and brushy alders clogged the alleys. Fire had reduced many of the houses to charred timbers, although Snag House, where Otter had lived, had suffered less than some.

She shoved through the alders to its door. Inside, gray light and a steady drip of rain fell through the roof. The floor was a chaos of splintered boards, alder whippets, and drifted leaves, and in places it sagged under her feet. Beneath the smell of mold and burned cedar lurked a sweetish odor of death.

She soon tracked the smell to a dead raccoon, but after that she returned outside and fought her way from house to house. She climbed over charred, rain-wet planks; she poked and prodded through tangles of trailing blackberry, sniffing all the while for the sweet-rotten stink of death.

But Whale Town was empty.

She sat down on the foreshore. Hunger poked her belly

sharply. After a while she recognized her perch as an abandoned canoe-to-be. Rainwater filled the hollow its maker had burnt in it, and vetch straggled from the cracks.

Pearlshell remembered another ruined town, where someone named Raven Tongue had lived. There, trees a foot thick sprouted from the house floors. Enemy warriors had destroyed that town. Had such men come to Whale Town? And how long ago? The spruces in *these* ruins were no taller than she was.

She remembered: trees in this world grew and died. Everything changed with the passage of one moment into the next: clouds, tides, seasons, years. The world below was full of life and death—but that death was not the deadness of the upper world. It was life in waiting. Food for someone else. Even the monsters of heaven, it seemed, came here to hunt.

She was no hunter. But after another long while memory stirred again, and she ventured down to where oysters grew on the rocks. She smashed one open with a stone and, trying not to think of the sweet food of heaven, gnawed the tough, gritty meat right out of the shell.

When she was done, it was as if she had eaten nothing.

Darkness arrived and still the rain fell. She sat in the door of Snag House and chewed more oysters. Yellow leaves blew across the water. She remembered what they meant: winter was coming.

*I know where you want to go,* Center-of-Heaven had said. Yes, she had longed to go to Otter. But Center-of-Heaven had delivered her to *this* desolation. He had after all inflicted punishment on her, and the one he had chosen was mocking as well as vengeful.

The smells of this world were so rich they dizzied her, so sharp they cut her to the bone: moldering leaves, wet earth, old burned wood, kelp washed up by the tide. But she was going to die in these ruins, she thought. Alone.

**By the light of her mirror, Center-of-Heaven's gift of** love, she cleared debris from a corner of Snag House and lay down. She told herself she could stand to miss a few meals; she had grown so fat that she could hardly bend over.

That night she dreamed of a glade where a huge animal skull sat in a tree. Children wept somewhere out of sight, calling out to her, "Save us, save us!"

She woke after the dream, wracked by hunger and chilled to the bone. And then, as she lay alone in the empty house, the monsters Pearlshell had feared at last broke the surface. Through the smells of decay, through the rattle of cold rain and crash of breakers, came *remembrance*—

*Otter was dead,* killed by mortal men but strung up by the queen's sister in her smokehouse. *She could never go back to Thrush.* She was alone and had no home at all, had survived only with the aid of the orcas, who had then abandoned her to her fate on the island of the bones. Her real father was a bloodthirsty animal, and she carried his inheritance inside her, however much she might long to be only a girl.

Her name had been *Cloud.* Except that it was not her real name at all.

Those monsters pulled her down into their darkness. She was drowning now; they were tearing her to pieces; she was bleeding out her life into those obsidian-sharp depths.

*This* despair was what Center-of-Heaven had taken from her, in exchange for the bright image of Pearlshell in her mirror. *I did what you wanted.*

At that moment, if she could have given Cloud back to him, she would have.

The night stretched on, sleepless. In the morning Cloud-Pearlshell, nameless mortal, sat down again in the door of Snag House. No one would rescue her now. Center-of-Heaven would see to that. It was up to her to survive—if she could manage it.

The first thing she did was remove the shoes Stoops-From-Above had given her, which had become waterlogged and now rubbed painfully. Another thing she had forgotten: in constant rain, even cut and bruised feet were more comfortable bare.

She emptied Winter's bag but found no means of starting a fire. As she unrolled her old clothes, a yellow-copper leaf fell out and embedded itself in the plank beside her. Cloud gingerly wrapped the leaf in cedar bark. Then she used the slate knife from the bag to open the seams of her deerskin dress until she could pull it over Pearlshell's sleeveless red garment.

More oysters; then she tied on her rain hat and searched the ruins again. This time she collected anything of possible use: rope, a net, a bowl, a singed paddle, a berry basket.

Although surviving a winter here did not seem possible, she felt less hopeless walking, moving. So she set out in the rain to explore. Rampant growth clogged most of the paths leading away from town, but the trail along the north shore had been so well trampled that it was still passable. As she picked crabapples on its margins, she encountered much evidence of the people of Whale Town: a collapsing shed, a derelict fish trap, a half-finished plank. The trail split at a stream. One branch veered into the forest, a second forded the stream to keep paralleling the shoreline, and a third dove down to the ocean.

Cloud chose the third branch, thinking that since people did most of their work on the beach, she would be most likely to discover something useful there. And only a few steps beyond the split in the trail, she came upon a little canoe. It had been overturned onto logs to raise it out of the mud, as if merely stored for a season and awaiting its owner's return.

*Once she found the canoe, she knew she would try* to leave the island—though she did not know where to go, and she would have to depart before winter storms trapped her here.

She heaved the canoe onto its keel, no easy task, and pulled it into the stream. When it proved not to leak, she moored it with an anchor stone she hauled from Whale Town.

Then she spent a few days gathering food. She found a grove of hazelnuts, which she stripped, and she picked all the late salal and huckleberries she could find. As she worked, she searched her disused memory for a possible refuge. Other than Sandspit Town, the only place she knew how to reach was the cliff-top fort where she had stopped with Otter. In Waterfall the king had at least tried to help them.

Every night now she dreamed of the skull and the weeping children. In her dreams in heaven she had always been searching; these bones must be what she had been searching for.

*I know where you want to go,* Center-of-Heaven had said. She did not want to go to the bones, but she went nevertheless.

One morning she packed her canoe. Then, although she kept slipping into black hopelessness, she stowed her anchor, climbed in with the burned paddle she had found, and let the current carry her to the sea.

**From the northern tip of the island, she followed Ot-**ter's northeastward route. She had forgotten what hard work paddling was, and out in the strait there were waves to contend with, too. Still, Whale Town's island slowly receded. She passed the next small island and aimed for the one after.

By the time she reached that landfall, fiery agony burned in her muscles. She beached her canoe and headed wearily over a rise toward mud flats where she hoped to find clams.

But at the top of the terraced, mossy outcrop, she smelled odors she did not expect: pitchwood, wet cedar rope, smoked fish, tanned hide. The odors drew her gaze to a salal patch on the far side. Seven midsized canoes and a pair of large painted war canoes had been drawn up into the dense evergreen thicket.

Her first thought was that their owners had failed to realize the extent of the mud flats and now waited for the incoming tide to float their canoes. But she immediately discarded that notion. No one would haul canoes all the way off the beach for such a short time.

As she stood in puzzlement, a man of about Otter's age emerged from the woods beyond the salal thicket. He wore a dagger around his neck and, beneath his rain cloak, a painted hide tunic that looked very much like armor.

After the immortals she had met, he didn't appear particularly dangerous. And he approached in a relaxed and unhurried way. A dozen feet from her he stopped and said, "Hello, miss. What brings you this direction?"

"I'm looking for my aunt," she said, cautiously.

The stranger nodded. "And where does your aunt live?"

"Well . . ." Cloud hesitated. "She used to live in Whale Town, but no one's there now. I've been away a long time. Do you know what happened? I thought she might have gone to Waterfall."

"Waterfall!" The man stroked his chin. "No, no, the survivors built a fort at Whirlpool Channel. But you don't want to go there, miss. It's hard for King Rumble to get in, but it's hard to get out, too, and they're starving—so I hear."

So *Rumble* had burned Whale Town! Guilt pierced Cloud. Were Winter and her children among the survivors? Were they now starving in the fort?

From the direction of her canoe, Cloud heard a faint rasp of footsteps. She glanced back but could not see her landing from this spot. "Where are *you* from, sir?" she asked timidly.

"Oh, us," he said. "We're from Round Bay Town, traveling to a feast. I'm sorry we can't take you along, but if there's any way we can help . . ."

Cloud considered. The people of Round Bay Town were not enemies. They had attended Rumble's big feast and, Cloud recalled, Glory had once lived there. Whirlpool Channel did not sound like a passage to try on her own. That meant many days of paddling to reach Waterfall, and she would greatly have preferred not to go the whole distance by herself. But she supposed it made sense that these people would not want strangers with them. And they might in fact be bound for Sandspit Town—it couldn't be more than a day's journey away. She did not want news of her to reach Rumble sooner than she could help.

The sounds of movement at her canoe continued. "Do you have food to spare, sir?" she said at last. "And something for fire?"

He smiled, nodding, to all appearances a genial stranger. "Food, of course. But no fire, I'm afraid. What did you say your name was? And your house?"

"Pearlshell," she said. "I'm from—Celestial House."

"Celestial—? Is there such a house in Whale Town? Well, I am Osprey."

The footsteps Cloud had been hearing grew louder, and a pair of young men clambered up from the direction of her canoe. They, too, wore long elk-hide tunics, and one carried a spear.

"Stay back, idiots!" Osprey commanded, startling her with his sudden harshness. The young men stopped. "Bring food, at least a two-week supply. And blankets. Go on!"

They ran off into the trees and returned right away with fur blankets and a large basket of food. Osprey pointed. "Put it down there, stupid, and go away!"

The young men did as they were told, gaping at Cloud. Had her mirror lied to her? She no longer looked much like a princess, but she kept her hair combed and her face clean. Had she become weirdly disfigured in the upper world? Or—

Spears, armor: she remembered then how the southern wizard had objected to her presence. Glory had also told her that women could bring bad luck to hunters and warriors.

Of course you would haul those canoes into the brush for only one reason: to conceal them. She had stumbled into a war expedition waiting out the daylight hours. Fear stirred in her at last. "Thank you very much, sir," she said to Osprey.

He bowed his head and withdrew to the trees.

**Daylight was fading. Cloud picked up Osprey's sup**plies and hurried toward her belongings, anxious to see whether the young men had disturbed them. Her bag and clothing, at least, lay as she had left them, tucked under mats beside a grassy rock.

But they had cut loose her canoe.

It drifted on the current, already twenty yards from shore. She nearly plunged into the water before she remembered that she couldn't swim.

Shock and anger roiled through her. Osprey intended to maroon her until his return. A slave again!

After a while, hunger drew her to the basket he had given her. She chewed dried salmon until her jaws hurt, but that did not lessen her anger, or her fear.

Night deepened. When she heard men crashing through the salal, she crept over the point as silently as she could.

Several men had come down from the woods and now stood on the beach above the mud flats. Under the overcast sky, she could barely make out their shapes, but she could hear their voices.

"The tide is up," said Osprey. "He'll be here soon."

There was a silence. Then a man with a deeper voice spoke. "My sister won't be happy when you bring home a pretty slave girl."

Meaning Cloud, of course. Except then Osprey startled her by replying, "Brother-in-law, that young lady is Rumble's daughter, Radiance. She doesn't remember me, but I recognized *her* right off. Her husband is a mean-tempered man; I saw her in River Town last summer with two black eyes. I'm not surprised she's running away. I'm just surprised she got this far." He chuckled mirthlessly. "Looking for her aunt!"

"That would be the Lady Winter?" said the other man.

Osprey grunted in assent. Cloud bitterly castigated herself: she had forgotten that people always recognized her as Thrush's daughter. Thrush was a public figure whom people had been staring at since childhood, and Radiance—how well Cloud remembered that hateful and perfect princess, the very image of Thrush—would have had the same kind of life.

But—Radiance married? Just how many years had passed? And who would dare take Radiance as a slave?

Osprey's brother-in-law said, "So you're going to offer her for ransom?"

"Who will be left to pay it?" Osprey said. "If there is, I'll ask the highest price for her, and if they can't meet it, that will be their eternal shame. King Rumble's lovely daughter a slave for the rest of her life—it won't bring back the dead, but I'll see her emptying my wife's chamberpot and know I did my best to give my murdered brother justice."

Another silence. Cloud tried to assure herself that Osprey was only boasting. No one could inflict upon Sandspit Town a slaughter that would leave Radiance with *no* protectors. Rumble was strong, and he had Bone to help guard the town. Look how masterfully Bone had diverted the southern war party! The other wizards in Sandspit Town would be watching, too. Sandspit Town was safe no matter how many enemies approached. Thrush was safe.

Osprey said, "Look, there he is."

"I'll tell the others," said the brother-in-law, and he thrashed away through the salal.

Cloud looked out from shore, too. Dark canoe-shapes swarmed around a point, numerous as a flock of terns. The paddles were visible as constant motion, like a bee's wings.

A torch flickered to life in the convoy, and a single canoe approached shore until the man holding the torch could jump to the beach. Cloud did not hear what the man said to Osprey, but the light of the torch showed his carved helmet, and she also recognized the strange, smoky, skeletal figure perched on the prow of his canoe. The sights crushed the breath out of her.

The Gull Islands king, who had kept Raven Tongue's finger bone, must have used it to win the dead wizard's allegiance while Cloud had been away from mortal lands. And of course the king would first have asked his new foot-servant why the southern warriors had come to massacre his people.

Right now Raven Tongue's former servants would be hunting down Bone's spirits and blindfolding them; they would blindfold every wizard in Sandspit Town; they would be smoothing the way for this great secret assault. Gull Islanders, men from Round Bay Town—how many towns were seeking blood vengeance right now against Rumble and his warriors? How could even Rumble and Bone fend off so many hundreds of men?

Warriors poured out of the woods, crashing and crunching as they hauled down their canoes. In a few moments all were afloat. The Gull Islands king extinguished his torch, and the great war expedition departed.

Despair clawed at her. Sandspit Town would be destroyed and there was nothing she could do to stop it. By loosing those spirits into the world, she had helped make it possible. Cloud buried her face in her hands, yearning with all her heart toward Thrush. "Mama," she whispered. "Oh, Mama, I'm so sorry."

*She dreamed that she soared to Sandspit Town like* a bird and flew into a room where Thrush lay alone. "Mama, Mama," Cloud wept, "They're coming, warriors are coming, they'll kill all of you." Thrush murmured in her sleep but did not wake.

In the morning, heavy fog wrapped the shore. When Cloud tried to rise, she discovered she had been trussed in a net of what looked like jellyfish tentacles. Above her stooped the drowned woman. Even as Cloud began to struggle, the spirit swam away into the fog.

Voices sounded in the near distance. A man wearing a great shaggy robe leapt down the rocks, battle-axe in hand. The sticky net bound Cloud's arms against her body, so she could do no more than roll away. But Rumble dragged her to her feet and struck her across the face. "So King Osprey tired of you already, did he? Did you enjoy shaming me, little slave-slut?" He struck her again. "What can I do to cleanse this stain from my name?"

Behind him, through involuntary tears of pain, Cloud saw Bone hobbling down the rocks. The drowned woman walked beside him, whispering in his ear.

"Lord," Bone said, "I doubt they've touched her. Osprey is a careful man and will stay celibate and well purified while he is at war. Anyway, this is not your daughter."

"Not my daughter!" said Rumble scornfully. But his mouth twisted. He drew back from Cloud. "Not my daughter."

He ripped at the neck of Cloud's dress, exposing her shoulder and the old scar upon it. "You're dead!" he screamed, and he threw Cloud from him.

"It's the four-legged girl," shouted Rumble to Bone. "You told me she was dead! Look at her! Look at her! What now?"

"You can kill her, Lord," said Bone. "But you will have to purify yourself and your weapons afterward."

"I've already touched her!"

"Yes," said Bone.

The wizard reached Cloud. His gaze poked at her roughly. At the edge of her vision, he wore a dark, wavering halo. "Where were you, little four-legs, when my servants could not find you?"

"Lord," Cloud said. Was that how she should address Rumble? She had never spoken to him. "Lord, there were canoes here from Round Bay Town and from the Gull Islands, too, at least thirty large ones. They're headed for Sandspit Town."

"Don't lie to me!" Rumble shouted, pointing his axe at her. But he glanced at Bone.

Bone shook his head. "My spirits would have told me."

"He has powerful, terrible spirits," said Cloud to Bone. "Don't you remember Raven Tongue? You tried to prevent me from gaining those spirits. Now the Gull Islands king has them."

"What is she talking about? What spirits?" said Rumble. "Who is Raven Tongue?"

"Please believe me," Cloud begged Bone. "I don't want my mother hurt. *Please!*"

Bone frowned at the drowned woman, who said, "I told you what I saw, master."

Said Bone, "Lord, your warriors counted the marks of only nine canoes in the sand. That agrees with what my servants told me. As for the spirits she mentions, I will see what I can discover. But we can't linger if you want to catch Osprey. Kill her if you like, and purify yourself after, but if I leave her bound, she will die anyway."

"That," Rumble said, face still dark with rage, "is what you said before!" But he turned away and leapt up the outcrop.

Bone and the drowned woman followed more slowly, leaving Cloud alone once more. Their footsteps dwindled into the fog.

*Strange, all these strong warriors afraid of a little* female blood. Her bear mask had disappeared when she reached the age of womanhood, but being female hadn't otherwise kept the spirit world from entangling itself in her life, had it? Spirits buzzing around her like wasps. Immortals encountered without their masks. Impossible gifts given for unfathomable reasons.

Perhaps it was as Foam had said: fortune and misfortune often went together.

Cloud twisted and strained, but the drowned woman's net kept tightening. She wormed over the moss to her bag. By poking a thumb and finger through the holes of the net, she could lift the flap of the bag and pull out objects one by one, but it was slow, frustrating work.

Finally she reached her slate knife. She hacked at the net, but no matter how many times she tried to cut them, the tendrils merely stretched and snapped back.

Almost sobbing now with panic, Cloud let the knife fall. She should have guessed an ordinary tool would not sever spirit bonds.

There *had* to be some way to warn Sandspit Town. Was it

possible that Center-of-Heaven had meant only to punish her, not kill her? If he would help now, she would humble herself, no matter what it would cost afterward.

She would, she thought, pray to Center-of-Heaven as a mortal prays to an immortal: "Take pity on me, great one, rescue me from evil, divine one, grant me life."

But as she lay there, another notion occurred to her. She was ashamed to act on it, but if she was going to beg an immortal for aid, better one who had never harmed her.

"Black Fin?" she said, swallowing tears. She forced herself to speak louder. "Black Fin? I know I have no manners and I acted like a child. But I need help now. Please help me one last time. I just need—I need help or my mother will die."

She waited, straining for the sounds of his approach, but heard only the slow gurgle of water in the rocks. She should not expect him to come, not after what she had said and done.

If he did not come, Sandspit Town would be destroyed.

Panic and terror rose so easily out of her belly. Cloud willed them down and tried to think. The First People might never again intervene in her life directly, but she still had their gifts: the fish-skin pouch, the abalone mirror, the shoes.

The pouch was inaccessible right now, the net tightly binding it under her cloak, and she could not think how either mirror or shoes could help her. But the shoes reminded her of the knife-sharp leaves of the upper world, and that in turn reminded her of the leaf she had accidentally brought to mortal lands. That leaf now resided, wrapped in cedar bark, at the very bottom of her bag.

Cloud returned to the laborious task of emptying the bag. Shoes, comb, awls, coils of spruce root: at last she reached the leaf. She rocked its bark wrapping against a stone until all the fibers fell off, then drew the leaf against the net. A tendril parted, and then the next one. She hacked at it until she could put her hand through, and then she was able to slice in earnest. The net attempted to mend itself, tendrils reaching for each other and splicing themselves, but now she could slash it apart faster than it could mend. She discovered that she could use the knife to guide the reknotting tendrils. After she cut away all of the net, she helped it tie itself into a hopeless snarl.

At last she was satisfied it could no longer harm her. She set to bandaging the cuts on her palm. A loud exhalation made her jump, and then Black Fin walked out of the fog, frowning.

*"Can't your husband help you?" he asked sharply,* without even a greeting.

"He's not my husband anymore!" Cloud said. The subject of Center-of-Heaven made her angry and ashamed.

Black Fin's frown only deepened. "Did he treat you badly?"

*It's none of your business,* Cloud wanted to shout. At least Center-of-Heaven had never been quarrelsome. He would have fussed over the wounds in her hand, the bloody lip Rumble had given her, her filthy clothes and disheveled hair. He would worry about how she had been frightened and in pain.

"No!" she said, and then, angry at herself for the tears that again spilled over, "Yes! But, Black Fin—"

He sighed, deeply and impatiently, and nudged the wadded-up, wriggling net with his foot. "What's this?"

"One of Bone's servants trapped me in it. Please, Black Fin—"

"Was that why you called me? You seem to have freed yourself easily enough."

Had he come just to inflict his bad temper on her? "I asked for your help because my mother is going to die if I can't warn Sandspit Town in time! Hundreds of warriors are headed there—"

"You don't need me," said Black Fin.

"I said I was sorry. I really am. I was just scared to go into that forest. I know you have every right to be angry at me, but my mother—"

"Was that why you went with him? Because you were scared?"

She said, "I don't remember why! He took away my memory!" But of course Black Fin was right. Center-of-Heaven had given her what she wanted, and one of the things she had desperately wanted was to escape the horrors of his aunt's house.

Black Fin sighed again, and then he dropped down beside her, folding his long pale legs under him. He rested his arms on his knees. Seawater still dripped from his hair.

"Please help me, Black Fin," she said. "I'm not asking you to stop them! I just need to warn them, and I *can't*. They cut loose my canoe, and I can't paddle there fast enough anyway. They're going to kill my mother or worse, and Aunt Glory, and maybe my other aunt and her children, or they'll be taken away as slaves, and there'll be no one to ransom them. I know there's no reason why you should help me, but *please*—"

"Cloud—"

"Please!"

"Cloud," he said, putting his hand over her mouth. She tried to push it away, but before she could stop him, he caught hold of her own hand.

He reached forward to grab the drowned woman's net and kneaded it into a slab of transparent jellyfish-like substance no larger than his hand. Then he unwrapped her blood-soaked bandage and applied the slab to her palm. It settled onto her skin, immediately stanching the flow of blood. She rubbed the slab. "Black Fin—" she began again.

"You didn't lose my mother's gifts, did you?"

"No," said Cloud, touching the fish-skin pouch through her cloak, "but—"

"Where is the canoe?"

"Canoe?"

He lifted the pouch over her head and pulled out a toy canoe made of burnished copper. Now she remembered seeing it on Foam's palm. "I thought these gifts were for Huntress's house."

"What would you do with a canoe in the middle of the forest? It was a gift, plain and simple. Cloud, I can take you to Sandspit Town. But this canoe will take you faster."

Foam had given her a real canoe after all. "Am I stupid?" Cloud asked. "I didn't know what the gifts would do. I didn't know the rules."

"You're not stupid," he said. "Just unbelievably stubborn."

"Stubborn?" Cloud asked. "I really didn't—"

"You're stubborn! You won't use any of the power in your grasp! Not what you were born with, not those little spirits who wanted to serve you, not my mother's gifts. Why do you avoid it? It's not because you're a coward. Cowards like power. Did you even try to use the gifts in Huntress's house?"

"I was stupid. I didn't realize what she was until it was too late—"

"No," he said. "It's more than that."

He looked toward the sea again. Probably to where he had left his canoe. He was tired, Cloud thought, of her stupidity and stubbornness.

Or maybe he was tired of not hearing real answers. She always found it so difficult to condense feeling into understanding, into words. She had never been able to do it, not with Glory or Thrush, not with Otter, and certainly not with Center-of-Heaven. But she did not want Black Fin to leave as he had the last time. She did not want him to leave at all. In his company, for the first time since her return to the world below, she felt as if she might not drown after all.

She had been wrong about him, she realized. He was not asking the question of his imaginary princess but of *her,* Cloud the bear girl.

Did she even know the answer to his question?

Of course she did. "I just don't want," Cloud said with difficulty, "to be like them."

He looked back at her. "Like who?"

"Like my father, and Rumble, and that dead wizard. That king from the Gull Islands. Raven Tongue serves him now! Like Huntress. I don't want to be that kind of person."

"You didn't know your father," said Black Fin.

"I know what he did," Cloud said. "I don't want to hurt people. You don't know what it's like to be—without power. To be mortal. A slave. A girl no one wants to be alive. Or if anyone does, they can't protect her, they just get hurt, too, or killed. You've always been what you are. You can't know."

He was silent. After a long moment he said, "It's true I've never been a slave. But I know that it's impossible to live without hurting someone, whether it's yourself or other people. And you don't stop anyone from being hurt by refusing all the gifts within your reach. I *know* you're wrong if you think you'll become evil by putting on your fur robe and becoming whole. You aren't evil just because you're big and strong."

"But sometimes I—I *want* to hurt people. I'm afraid I'll . . ." She stopped. She did not want to speak about this to anyone, did not even want to acknowledge to herself the terrible truth. But she wanted to give him a real answer.

"Sometimes I—get hungry," she said. "For human flesh."

Black Fin nodded solemnly. "That happens to me, too." Then he grinned. "But, really, fish tastes better."

Anger spiked up in her, hot and sharp. How could he joke about *such* a subject! How could she have expected an *orca* to understand? But then—

For some reason—perhaps it was the curve of his neck as he hunched there, or the spill of wet black hair across the muscles of his back—Cloud remembered him dancing in the house of the Lords of Summer, fierce and joyous.

"I have to go," she said.

He stood in a single motion. She shoved everything back in Winter's bag and scrambled to her feet much more awkwardly. At the waterside where his own canoe waited, he gave her the pouch and the toy canoe. "Put it in the water, bow outward."

She placed the toy in the water, and—there bobbed a copper canoe as big as her lost wooden one. "It doesn't have paddles."

"You don't need any." He held it steady so she could climb in. "The canoe's name is Copper Orca. Say its name and then, 'Take me to Sandspit Town.'" He stepped back.

"Copper Orca," Cloud said. She felt silly addressing a canoe. "Take me to Sandspit Town!"

Nothing happened. She looked at Black Fin.

"You can call for me anytime, not just when you think you need help," he said.

And then the canoe shot away over the water. "Goodbye," she said, but the fog had already closed around her and she could no longer see the shore.

*Now terror tied her gut in knots.* She had lingered too long with Black Fin. The northerners had left half the night ago, and Sandspit Town could not be far. In the fog, the only indication of her speed was the canoe's foaming wake. She kept seeing the slaughter at the Gull Islands camp, the heaped bodies and pooling blood. "Faster," she urged. "Copper Orca, faster! As fast as you can go!" The canoe responded with only a small jolt.

She opened Foam's pouch. The bottle from King Swimming was presumably not one of the gifts she could use in any way she chose, but Foam had given her three others. *A chest full of wealth. A harpoon that never lets go of its target. My amulet.*

Perhaps the wealth could someday be used as payment for the people Rumble had killed, but it would not stop the warriors today. Cloud poked Foam's amulet into better light. It was an ivory cylinder about the size of her thumb. Each end of the exquisite carving bore a head with a gaping mouth, and in the center was a third face with its mouth firmly closed. All three heads had eyes of inlaid abalone.

She wished she had asked Black Fin what the amulet was for. The two gaping mouths looked eager for food, but maybe that was only because *she* was always hungry. When a pair of eyes blinked at her, Cloud shuddered and closed up the pouch.

Suddenly Copper Orca emerged from the fog. Ahead sat Maple Island and the long arm guarding Sandspit Town's harbor.

To the north, another fog bank rolled across the water, and in the corner of her eye, its belly held a fleet of canoes.

She approached across open water and with no magical fog to hide her. But she was closer and moving faster. She would reach Sandspit Town in time after all. "Copper Orca," she said, "take me to the spit, straight ahead."

The shore approached steadily. Then a slight thump shook the canoe. A shadow blocked her vision. "Bear girl," said Raven Tongue, "you should not have tried to thwart my master."

He lifted a smoky shadow-hand on which one finger remained black and dimensionless. Upon his palm sat a frog.

He tossed it at her belly. She flung up her hands too late; the frog had already sunk into her flesh, a dagger-thrust of searing heat that doubled her over in helpless pain.

She knew what was going to happen. And as Copper Orca closed on the shore, the frog in her stomach multiplied into two frogs, four, eight, an entire hearth-full of white-hot coals jostling, shoving outward. Excruciating cramps wracked her.

But she still had to try to deliver her warning. When her canoe bumped to a stop, she managed to climb over the gunwale. Then a spike of agony toppled her gasping into the surf, and an incoming wave broke over her head.

As she choked on saltwater, some of it slid down into her stomach. It was wonderfully soothing, like ice, like cold fat on burned skin. When another wave poured over her, she swallowed huge gulps. The jostling coals in her stomach lifted and sank.

Then nausea convulsed her. A searing, lumpy flood of

vomit shot out of her mouth, and then a second one. Again and again she spasmed until she thought she must have wrenched out her intestines, and still waves of seawater and white-hot, wriggling lumps spewed from her mouth. A croaking and splashing rose up all around her, along with the stink of mud and bile.

At last the agony in her belly quieted sufficiently for her to crawl through the hundreds of frogs onto the beach. There she crashed face-first on the sand and spun away into darkness.

*Another convulsion brought her to consciousness.* More frogs squirmed out of her mouth. She wiped away mud and climbed to her knees. The number of frogs swimming, or croaking, or crawling ashore, was much less than it had been.

Again nausea rolled through her, but this time only a single frog surged up. Cloud crawled up the beach. Only when she had reached the trail across the spit did she realize that the shrieks in the near distance were not from gulls.

She pulled herself to her feet and stumbled forward. The screaming did not stop. Now she heard men yelling and dogs barking ferociously. When she rounded the corner of Halibut House, it all came into view: enemy canoes choking the harbor, smoke and flames pouring up from the town. In places men battled with spear and club, axe and dagger, but elsewhere a flood of armored warriors coursed unimpeded, clubbing women or dogs, chopping at barricaded doors, setting fires along the house walls. The northern warriors were thickest around Storm House.

"You are strong, bear girl," said Raven Tongue's deep voice, "but you cannot fight all of us." Behind him stood the dwarf, the owl woman, the woodworm, all the rest of his former servants. Raven Tongue lifted his fist again—

This time Cloud pulled Foam's amulet from the pouch and brandished it. "Swallow them!" she panted. "Swallow them, swallow them, swallow them!"

The amulet buzzed like a hummingbird. The spirits bent toward one or the other of its mouths, elongating and attenuating like smoke in an updraft. "Vomit them!" Raven Tongue commanded, but the amulet was pulling him, too. "Swallow them!" Cloud kept yelling. The amulet sucked in their heads. One by one, spirit feet tore from the ground, shot between ivory jaws and vanished.

Raven Tongue was the last to be swallowed. Cloud dropped the amulet back in her pouch and stumbled toward Storm House again, splashing across the creek, struggling once more through soft, churned sand. Once she had been good at running, but now she could barely place one foot in front of the other. So many houses in the town. She passed a dead dog, and then the body of a woman she recognized. A northerner dragged a screaming girl from a canoe where she had tried to hide. Now Cloud was among the swarming warriors. She dodged, caroming from one bloody, shrieking northerner to another. One of them tried to grab her, but at that moment a convulsion pushed another frog out of her mouth, and he dropped her arm in horror.

Near Storm House, she slipped in an old man's guts. Another northern warrior grabbed her arms and she struggled furiously, biting him. They were chopping at the planks on the front of Storm House. "Mama, Mama," she cried, "Mama," but she was too far away and so pathetically feeble, she could not shake her captor loose. The planks shattered. They were dragging out the women and children. A warrior clubbed the old woman, Thrush's attendant, and two other northerners hauled a young girl along who looked like Thrush, who looked like Rumble; the Gull Islands king stabbed her in the neck.

A woman screamed with heartbreak. "Mama, Mama," Cloud wailed. They had Thrush, too. They pulled her along as she sobbed, and they dropped her in front of the Islander king, where she fell weeping on the dead girl's body. The king seized Thrush by the hair, lifted his bloody dagger—

"*Mama!*" Cloud screamed.

The king slammed the dagger into Thrush's chest.

The uproar turned to utter silence. A bolt of red lightning blinded Cloud, a cold icicle speared downward from the base of her skull. A distant voice in her head shouted, *hungry, hungry.*

Scalding, ungovernable rage poured into the wounded space in her belly. The noise of battle burst back into her ears. Exalted, she reared up like a giant. They had killed Thrush.

They had killed Thrush.

They had killed Thrush.

She grabbed the head of the nearest warrior; she sank her teeth into his throat and ripped. Blood gushed into her mouth, sweet and hot, but she threw him aside to fell the next warrior; she knocked down the Gull Islands king and clawed away his face, swallowing gouts of blood; another man poked her with a spear, so she tore off the arm that held the spear. They all ran screaming, and falling before her like grass. She was a giant wading in their blood, and hungry for it, so hungry, but she did not stop, she chased them down. They had killed Thrush.

When there were no more warriors in front of her, the red glare in her vision flickered and went out. Part of her shot into the sky like an arrow. The rest of her, blood in her mouth, blood on her hands, stayed on the beach of Sandspit Town, where men lay strewn like leaves after a storm. Something dripped down her chin and she wiped it off; blood, a man's blood. Her mouth tasted like copper.

She spat. But the blood was in her stomach, too.

Cloud turned. She had rampaged nearly the whole length of the beach. Bodies littered the sand all the way to Storm House.

She began the long trip back, stepping over men from Sandspit Town, from Round Bay Town, from the Gull Islands, men and women dead and dying, a few still strong enough to crawl from her in terror; some northerners were trying to flee in their canoes. Cloud's belly cramped again, but no more frogs came up. People emerged from the houses to extinguish fires and tend to the wounded, to wail over the dead, to gawk. No one spoke to her. Blood soaked the beach and glued sand to her feet. She had done all this, the bear's daughter.

The worst slaughter waited in front of Storm House, where the ones she had killed and the ones the enemy had killed lay heaped together. Thrush curled beside the dead girl, cheek pressed into her hair, bloody lips parted and still moving. Cloud did not know the girl; another half-sister, like Radiance, it seemed, born in the years she had been gone.

The wound in Thrush's chest bubbled and squeaked. Cloud dropped on her knees. "I'm sorry, Mama," she whispered. She wanted to touch Thrush but her hands were sticky with blood. "I tried to get here in time. I'm sorry." She felt hollow as a broken egg. "Mama?" she asked again, because Thrush had stilled, and her wound no longer bubbled.

The world became very small and far away. More canoes landed. Axe in hand, Rumble raced up the beach, his robe flying behind him, the necklace of teeth bouncing on his chest. Behind Rumble hobbled Bone with his four servants.

"Bind her!" Bone shouted, and the servants rushed toward Cloud like blankets flung by a gale.

In the distance, Cloud's hand fumbled for the amulet. Someone—it must have been her—whispered, "Swallow them."

The amulet sucked Bone's servants out of the air.

Bone stopped in his tracks, gray-faced. But Rumble kept coming, as wild as if he wore her father's bulk and rage the way he wore that shaggy robe. She had always been terrified of him. But now—

Even in his rage, what was he compared to Huntress, or Stoops-From-Above? Just another *little mortal*.

She stood and put out her hand as if to stop him. And he did, indeed, pull up, and when her fingers brushed his chest, his necklace fell onto her hand as if the knot had slipped open.

But this time Rumble was not trying to kill her. He did not even glance at her. He was staring at Thrush, his mouth pulled down as if tasting poison. Only his eyelids moved, blinking.

Then tears spilled down his face.

Cloud did not expect the hard, sharp rush of sympathy she felt, the kinship of shared grief. It knocked the world back to its ordinary size. "I can save her," she whispered.

She unstoppered the bottle from beyond the world. With trembling hands, she tipped it first over her mother's chest, and then her sister's. Fish-bright water splashed up, soaked in. When Thrush's chest rose and fell, and her staring eyes blinked, Cloud's own tears at last began to flow.

They dripped onto her mother whom she was unfit to touch. Cloud turned away, because she would not be able to endure the loathing in her mother's face.

And there stood Aunt Snow, with wild hair and a deep gash across her scalp. "Where are the others?" Cloud asked roughly. "Only the worst, the dead ones and the ones who won't live otherwise. I don't have enough for everyone."

Aunt Snow gaped. Then she led Cloud to first one Storm House cousin, then another. Cloud worked as fast as she could, despite the cramps still afflicting her; perhaps the frogs would kill her after all. She made Aunt Snow have the dead and dying of other houses brought to her. Many people had sought refuge in the houses or escaped into the forest, and Rumble had taken many of the men of fighting age with him, so fewer had died than she feared. By using the water sparingly she was able to restore all the dead to life, if not to perfect health.

She shook the last drops over the dead slaves. She had insisted on the slaves, to Aunt Snow's pursed disapproval, and if she had had enough, she would have healed the fallen northerners, too. They were here only because their kin had been killed.

None of this would have happened if she had succeeded

in her task. Foam had said that Rumble's act, binding her father's ghost so he could keep feeding on its power, had ripped a hole in the masked world. The rage would keep on bleeding through that rip, flooding outward, and Rumble would not or could not control it.

It was time to take up her burden and mend the hole before that river of anger and pain engulfed the whole mortal world. It was time to take *all* the wild power away from Sandspit Town, what she carried in herself included.

At last Cloud put away the empty bottle. They watched her, Rumble, Bone, Aunt Snow—and Thrush, too, though Cloud still could not look at her mother, who held that little half-sister in the embrace Cloud would never receive again.

Another excruciating cramp wracked her. When it eased, she fished out the spirit-eater from the pouch. "Raven Tongue!" she shouted into one end of it. "Take away your frogs!"

"Does that mean that you will accept our service now?" Raven Tongue sounded very far away, as if deep underground.

Cloud's gaze traveled to Bone. If she didn't accept these servants, who would command them next? "Yes! Take them away!"

"Let us out," said Raven Tongue.

Cloud said, "You must bind Bone's servants and keep them from following you out."

"We have already bound them," he said.

"Spirit Eater," Cloud commanded the amulet, "Open your mouth!" For a moment nothing happened. Then the center face parted its ivory lips and belched a flood of spirits, blue and feathered and fiery. In another instant Raven Tongue and all his old servants stood in front of her.

"Get your missing finger," she told him.

The dead wizard strode to the body of the Gull Islands king and removed the finger bone from the pouch around its neck. He stuck the bone into the black place on his hand. Bone turned to watch him, but the other people stared at

Cloud. They could not hear Raven Tongue and must wonder whom she was talking to.

"Now," she gasped, as another cramp seared through her belly, "take away the frogs."

"Bear girl, you have already rid yourself of my frogs," said Raven Tongue in his deep, smooth voice.

Before she could rebuke him for not simply *doing* it, Glory walked up. Cloud braced herself for Glory's reaction to the bloody monster she had become. There was a long silence while Glory gazed at her. The cramp slowly relented.

"How long have you been having the pains?" Glory asked. When Cloud just stared at her, Glory sighed and held out her hand. "Come, child, let's get you to Halibut House."

*They had to stop several times because of the* cramps. "Later," Glory said in her most disapproving voice, "we can talk about how you got this way."

Cloud did not know what Glory meant. Glory led her firmly around corpses and pools of blood, supporting her when a cramp made her unable to walk. After one of those cramps, because she felt so lost now and Glory seemed so much her old self, so confidently in charge, she asked, "Aunt Glory, what's happening to me?"

"You don't know? Oh, child." Glory sighed.

When they reached Halibut House, Glory called out orders to the people inside. Then Glory took her to a shed in back where menstruating women often stayed. Women bustled in with shredded bark, mats, fresh water: "Pull up your skirts," Glory said. "I have to feel how far the baby has come along."

"Baby?" said Cloud.

The baby, it seemed, was quite far along, but it took forever coming the rest of the way. The cramps grew worse, and closer together, until Cloud would gladly have traded them for Raven Tongue's frogs.

Then she had to push the baby out. She was as glad to get

rid of it as the frogs, wondered at times if it, too, was trying to tear her open, but then there it was in Glory's arms. "Perfect," said Glory, offering Cloud a bloody, wrinkled thing.

"He's very strange," said Oriole from Cloud's other side.

The baby's eyes were blue. Its yellow-copper skin lit the shed like a lamp. It saw Cloud and squalled.

"Don't you want to hold him, Cloud?" Oriole said.

"No," Cloud said. "Take it away." And she burst into tears.

# SIXTEEN

# The Island of Thorns

*The next morning, Glory and Oriole helped her* bathe, and Glory found a clean dress that fit over her still-swollen belly. The women marveled over Pearlshell's embroidered red dress. "You can have it," Cloud said.

She asked Glory for supplies for her journey. Glory refused and tried again to make her hold the baby. Cloud turned away. "I'll go without them."

In her discarded clothes she found Rumble's necklace. She crawled out of the shed and, stiff and sore, hobbled along the trail that crossed the spit. Copper Orca rocked on the waves exactly where she had left it, gleaming in the fitful autumn sunlight.

Glory hurried after her. "Cloud! Cloud, please!"

Glory looked so old and tired. Remorse and longing tugged at Cloud. She wished she could tell Glory everything that had happened since her first departure, and at the same time she was floundering in dark waters again. She could not possibly talk about any of it.

"I'm a four-legs," Cloud said. "You saw what I'll do if I stay. I *have* to go."

"Don't say such a thing!" Cloud realized with surprise that Glory was crying. "You can always stay with your aunt, always!"

Cloud hugged Glory as hard as she could, feeling her aunt's thin old bones through her clothes.

But then Glory said, "You can't leave your baby, Cloud. He needs you to nurse him."

Another tug of remorse. Cloud did not want any child to suffer, not even Center-of-Heaven's, not even one forced on her when she did not want it.

But that ocean of darkness was crushing her in its depths. She had been pregnant and no one, not Center-of-Heaven and his family, not anyone she had met since, had told her. Maybe Black Fin assumed she knew. But she hadn't. She knew her body had changed in the upper world, but she hadn't known what it meant. She knew babies happened after you married, but Glory had explained such things only in the vaguest terms.

Now she was ashamed of the way Center-of-Heaven had touched her. He had stolen not just her memory but her very flesh. The baby had grown in her like an evil spirit, like Raven Tongue's frogs, and she wanted to expel every trace of it from her insides and from her life.

"Let his father take care of him," she said.

*In the end Glory packed what she asked for. And* without further goodbyes Cloud climbed aboard Copper Orca and departed from Sandspit Town. This time it would be forever.

She did not let herself glance back. Instead, she fixed her eyes on the banks of fog still crawling across the horizon. When Raven Tongue alit on the prow of her canoe, she snarled, "I thought spirits didn't like the smell of female blood."

She still bled copiously from the birthing. Glory had told her this was normal, but it frightened her, as if the baby had wounded her and she could not heal.

"It has power over us, over some more than others," he said. "Without thread, the clothes do not hold together."

Cloud hated his riddling, but she had to try to understand it now. She had to use all the power within her grasp, because her failure to do so before had brought disaster on so many.

Without thread, she thought, clothes fall off. Did he mean that blood stitches together the masked world? Or: female blood can unstitch spirit works, it unmasks what is masked?

"Where are the others, then?" she said.

"They'll come if you call. Let us serve you, Lady. Give us a task."

"All right," said Cloud. "Command your former servants to keep Bone and Rumble, and their warriors, in Sandspit Town. But they must defend the town if anyone attacks. And I want them to protect my mother and Aunt Glory from *anyone* who tries to hurt them. And the baby, protect the baby."

"Which baby?" he asked.

"You know which baby! *My* baby!" She did not even like saying the words. "They are not to hurt anyone if they can stop that person another way. Do you understand me? You'll tell them faithfully? Protect but don't hurt?"

"Yes, Lady," Raven Tongue said. "I will tell them."

"And you . . ." She loathed this dead wizard so indifferent to human suffering. But who was *she* to complain about such company?

"Tell me how to call you when I need you," she said.

He sang a droning, wordless song and made her learn it. "This was my song when I was alive," he said. "Now it is yours." It sounded even worse coming out of her mouth.

She was relieved when she could dismiss him and retreat to her thoughts. Not that she liked her thoughts any better. Her transfiguration on the beach had given her back her true name. *Hungry*. She could not deny that it fit her: how exalted she had felt as she slaughtered those men, how filled

with glory, as if the red dawn-fire blazed out from her own
flesh! In that moment she had not been Cloud. She had been
whole and certain.

She had been her father's daughter.

Black Fin had almost convinced her she would not turn
vicious by putting on her fur robe. But viciousness, it
seemed, was her true nature.

Copper Orca bore her along. Sharp pains like those of
childbirth wracked her from time to time. After a while
Cloud slept. When she woke, the canoe had entered that
dark bay whose name she had never learned. Snow-crowned
mountains towered over her head and hung below her, rippling. At their feet, also casting its wavering reflection,
waited the island of the bones.

*She had left everything else behind, Pearlshell's life*
and now Cloud's, too. Now she had only her task.

Only water or fire from beyond the world, Foam had
said, was strong enough to break the bonds that tied her father and brothers here. If Cloud had not used up Foam's
most precious gift on the people of Sandspit Town, she
could have brought the water to the bones. Now she had to
carry the bones to the fire. Which meant she had not only to
reach what Huntress so jealously guarded, but to steal it
away.

The fire Foam had spoken of must be the blazing abyss
Cloud had spied from the dawn-edge of heaven. She did not
know how to reach it from mortal lands. But—one impossible labor at a time.

She directed Copper Orca to the beach in front of the ruined town. When she had unloaded her boxes of provisions
and dragged the prow of her canoe ashore, it blinked to the
size of a toy again. She slipped it into Foam's pouch.

How many years had passed since her last visit to the island? She hadn't asked Glory.

It had changed further in that time. A haze of acrid smoke
clung to the trees, and even here the air stank of putrefaction,

as if Huntress's house were swelling to engulf the entire island.

But Otter's canoe still lay among the jumbled driftwood.
It was broken now in three pieces. While the ghosts cried in
her ears, Cloud cleared a space beneath the biggest section
and lit a fire with the slow match Glory had provided her.
Just before nightfall, a four-legged footstep caused her to
start up in alarm. But it was just Otter's skinny dog come to
sniff at her food boxes. Somehow it had managed to survive.

"Seal," she called. "Come here, dog."

The dog eyed her warily. Perhaps it had been on this island so long it had begun to forget human beings. Cloud
held out a strip of dried venison. After a moment Seal si-
dled over to snatch it from her. She wiped dog spit on her
dress and then gingerly patted its head. Seal's tail gave a
tentative wag.

She had always hated dogs. But perhaps, in the end, a
dog was no worse than its master. She fed Seal more meat, as
much as she herself would eat, and then tied the food boxes
shut.

The cold, smoky forest loomed over her. When a wolf
howl soared down through the trees, Cloud gave in and sang
Raven Tongue's song. Seal barked when the dead wizard arrived. She, too, found him deeply unsettling, and she wished
she could send him away forever. But she needed his help.

"While I sleep," she said, "keep watch and protect me."

"Yes, Lady." He withdrew to the blackness under the
forest—not liking her smell right now, she supposed.

She curled up beside the fire. Seal lay down next to her,
pushing his back against her leg. She did not shove him
away.

When she slept, Cloud dreamed as always of her brothers' ghosts. But then the dream changed. Thrush was calling the four of them home, calling their names: Claw,
Tongue, Black, and herself, Hungry. She ran with her brothers beneath tall dawn-lit crags, and the odor of pines spilled
over them like cool shadow.

She woke in the dark with Seal's warm head on her stomach. So hard to believe that she, too, had once been as she remembered her brothers: noisy, dirty, laughing, beloved, and beautiful. Maybe her brothers had not shared in their father's inheritance. Or maybe it was growing up that turned bear children bloodthirsty.

What she did know was that, since her brothers' deaths, she had never stopped being lonely.

Feet crunched in gravel. As wolves ghosted out of the darkness, Seal woke, growling. Cloud grabbed his scruff and threw more wood on the fire, but the wolves trotted past her camp to disappear under the forest eaves.

"Raven Tongue!" she yelled.

He half emerged from the shadows. "Yes, Lady."

"I told you to guard me!"

"From the canoe," he said, "the fisherman hailed his brother."

Cloud worked out this riddle, at first shocked and then grimly accepting. She and the wolves were the brothers: Winter People, killers. The wolves recognized her as kin.

*In the morning she asked Raven Tongue, "Can you* watch Huntress? And tell me when she leaves the island, and it's safe for me to enter the forest?"

"My kind cannot enter the houses of the First People," he said. "But I can watch her door, until she learns I am yours."

For the next quarter-turn of the moon, while fear and impatience crawled over her skin like a swarm of ants, Cloud waited at her camp. She tried to prepare. She fashioned her mirror into a necklace by twining a rough net around it, and attaching a cord. She packed her bag with food and tinder, and sticks she had cut for torches. She crudely hafted the leaf-knife with flat stones—the only substance it did not slice through—and stowed it in Foam's pouch in place of the now-empty bottle.

Her bleeding lessened. One morning she woke up with breasts so swollen that she thought she must have an infection, but no fever burned in her, and after a few days the swelling went down. Cloud tried not to think about who might be nursing her baby—if Glory had found anyone at all.

Sometimes she summoned Raven Tongue. At first she thought he could teach her wizardry, but his riddles on the subject too often defeated her. "Why," she demanded, "do you talk in riddles when I could understand plain speech better?"

He said, "The first ancestor to open a shell discovered the oyster inside."

She groped after meanings: riddles reveal what you cannot otherwise see. Or perhaps: by opening up a riddle, by explaining it, you kill its meaning.

She tried again. "What are riddles good for?"

"The splice joins the ropes."

A splice joins two things. Was the riddle the splice, or Raven Tongue's kind of spirit? Both riddle and wizard's servant joined here to there, known to unknown, mortal to spirit world.

"Is a spirit mask a kind of riddle?" she asked.

"The outside and the inside of the box fought a war."

She guessed again: the mask, simple and determinate, was the outside of the box, while the unmasked world, with all its immensity and changeability, was the treasure the box contained. Or perhaps the mask was the closed, limited interior, while the spirit realm was the unbounded world outside. At any rate they were not two things spliced, but two faces of the same thing. If mask and soul fought a war, neither could win.

She did not ask why she dreamed of the glade. Raven Tongue had already said to her, *What did you lose that you think you'll find in this spot?* Her mask had come and gone, but this island stayed with her. In the mortal world, she kept traveling here, and when she had gone outside the world, she still had tried to reach the bones, like a salmon struggling up-river.

**At last, on a rainy day, Raven Tongue came to her** and said, "The fisherwoman has left the streamside."

Cloud fed Seal and herself. She wrapped up and packed a length of smoldering slow match. She hung the mirror and pouch around her neck and put on the shoes from the upper world. She already wore the gut-skin hat and cloak Foam had given her.

"Watch her," she told the wizard. "Warn me when she comes."

She climbed with Seal through the wet, smoky forest. The trees stalked beside her, huge as mountains. "You should not come with me," she told Seal, and then, when he nosed her hand, "I'll take you away from the island this time." She did not really believe that she would live to do so.

The forest grew ever darker and more uncertain in her vision until at last the path descended toward the maple. She crossed the glade slowly. Yellow leaves lay adrift beneath bare salmonberry canes. Her father's massive thigh bones were sunk into the soil now, and a seamless cloak of moss joined his skull to the tree. Overlying the smells of smoke, rotting offal, wet grass, and autumn leaves, was another odor, sour and foul. Huntress's stink.

For all the ghostly cries in Cloud's ears, the glade itself was silent and airless, as if buried deep in the earth. Even the rain seemed to make no noise here.

She glanced back. Seal had stopped at the edge of the glade. "Stay there," she told him, and then wished she had not broken the stillness.

Last time, Cloud had encountered Huntress's house in the forest, but today its smoke rose from that dark hole on the far side of the glade. The house must have slid down into the hole.

Or perhaps the house was still here in the glade, and Cloud just couldn't see all the way into the unmasked world.

No, the masks on this island were ripping away. The glade was foundering into the earth. Huntress's house was swallowing the glade; the two places were merging and multiplying and turning ever more uncertain, a reflection on rippled water.

Cloud made herself step past her father's skull. Over the years the rope and basket that held her brothers' bones in the tree had rotted, spilling them to the ground. She pulled dead grass away from one of the little bear skulls. It was small enough to fit on her palm. Had *she* ever been so tiny?

Her brothers' bones surely ought to have begun to decay by now. They looked only dirty and moss-stained.

She tried to lift the little skull. It would not come loose. She dug with her fingers, tore away mud and roots, excavated with a stone and then her leaf-knife, but she could not shift the skull no matter how hard she pulled. She tugged at other bones, a rib, a shoulder blade. It was as if ropes anchored the bones to the earth now, instead of to the tree.

Then, between one eyeblink and the next, her brother's skull became a human child's. Her heart jumped into her throat.

Things of the unmasked world, she reminded herself, always had more than one form. Cloud stood and once more surveyed the glade. At the edge of her vision, the earth in the surrounding forest drifted in a slow current beneath tree and moss, rocks and grass. But here under the maple, all was still. If she gazed at the glade long enough, if she let herself fall into the dizzying abyss of the unmasked world, she could even glimpse an upside-down reflection, as if another thicket hung beneath the soil, growing downward. Was that an underneath-place like the underside of the sky?

She reluctantly called her brothers' names: "Claw! Tongue! Black!" They did not come to her as they had the first time.

The little human skull stared at her until she thought she would cry. She tried again but could not pry up even the smallest vertebra.

She would have to find what anchored them. Cloud could only think that it lay beneath her feet, at the other end of that passage into the earth. She did not want to go there. The stench wafting out of the hole reminded her all too vividly of the middens of human bone and offal she had fallen into while dying.

A shadow swept over the forest canopy. "She is coming," Raven Tongue said, suddenly beside her.

Cloud ran. Bones tripped her, thorns grabbed her, but she managed to shove free of the thicket. As she labored up the slope in the direction she had come, a wave of bitter cold poured through the forest. Smoke and rain swirled as a feathered shadow flapped down to the glade.

Cloud ducked behind a young hemlock, panting. Rain began to fall harder, the drops sharp and noisy in the trees.

Huntress could surely smell her blood, would know a human female had just walked past her doorway—would know it was *Cloud*. She would hunt Cloud down with that terrible swiftness.

And Huntress did jerk up her head and gaze around wildly. She dropped her human prey, tiny as a doll at this distance, to screech with rage. But she did not seem to be able to locate the direction in which Cloud had fled.

That was hard to believe. Cloud could smell Huntress even upwind—a more potent whiff of the pervasive sour-sharp stink.

If Huntress could not smell keenly, how did she track her prey? In this hilly forest, surely not by sight alone.

Seal padded up, flicking his ears first toward Huntress, then back at Cloud.

Was it possible that Huntress tracked her prey by *hearing*? Cloud tried to still her breath, but the very drumbeat of blood in her ears sounded loud enough for Huntress to hear, if that immortal had not begun to scream and tread in circles, angrily stabbing the ground with her beak.

And then, with a last resounding screech, Huntress burst up from the glade, driving up through the trees. When the thunder of her wings rolled away, Cloud whispered, "Raven Tongue!"

"Lady," he said, beside her.

"Watch her."

*Perhaps Huntress had gone hunting for Cloud.* Perhaps she had flown to the upper world to demand why her nephew had broken his promise to keep Cloud away. No way of knowing how long Huntress would be gone. But reckless impatience prickled on Cloud's skin.

The daylight was fading quickly. She lit one of her torches from the slow match and stored her bag in a nearby tree. "Stay here," she said to Seal, but again he followed her to the glade.

Her torchlight flickered over her father's skull, and then Huntress's abandoned prey, a warrior whom Cloud did not recognize. Huntress had taken the time to crack open his skull and sample her favorite delicacy. Still no sign of the house.

With ice-cold hands she hammered the harpoon point into the old maple. As she payed out string inch by careful inch, it swelled into fathoms of braided rope. She looped the rope between her legs and around her waist as Center-of-Heaven had done, then walked over to crouch near the hole in the earth. Her torch did not illuminate its wavery blackness in the slightest.

So many questions she wished she had asked Raven Tongue. Would the blood smell affect Huntress even if that immortal's sense of smell was weak? Would it enrage her or repel her?

The rope was rough under her sweat-slicked palms. Foam had given her the harpoon point. *It never lets go.* Foam had seemed to believe she could accomplish this task. So, for that matter, had Black Fin. Cloud took a deep breath and crawled forward.

*At first she felt only wet leaves and mud under her* palms. Then the night forest spun around her and she fell.

She dropped into the whirling immensity of the unmasked

world, only this black chasm reeked of smoke and human meat, of putrefaction and sour-sharp sickness, a reek so thick she could hardly draw breath. Cloud fell into cold earth and clay and then stone, and still she dropped away from the world. She was going to fall forever, suffocating, a ghost who could not be reborn.

Then she realized she had squeezed her eyes shut. When she opened them, blackness still seemed to rush past, but she had stopped falling and merely swayed as she dangled head downward, clutching the rope. Her torch burned feebly nearby, where it had come to rest at this lower end of the passageway.

Cloud dug fingers into the mud to haul herself out of the hole. After retrieving the torch, she crawled away until her vertigo lessened enough that she could climb to her feet.

She stood on the shore of a river of black mud whose languid current carried bones, sticks, ash, and cadavers past her, out of the torchlight and into utter darkness. Out on the river, wisps of light glimmered and died, and ghosts whispered more softly than her heartbeat. She could not see the far bank.

Behind her, deep inside wavering shadow, clamored other, louder voices. The smoke billowed up from there.

It was bitterly cold in this underworld, and the foul air clogged her lungs like clay. Cloud blew on her torch until she was dizzy, but it would not burn well, so she pulled the mirror out of her clothes. The combined light of mirror and torch resolved the smoky shadows into a tangle of naked, thorny canes arching over her head. The canes were as thick as her arm.

If this place was in fact a kind of upside-down reflection of the glade, Cloud thought, she should look for what anchored the bones at its center, below the maple. Heart pounding, she payed harpoon line out of the pouch, adjusted the line around her waist, and stepped forward to look for a path through the canes.

She did not find one, though she found much evidence of

Huntress. At the edge of the thicket, canes had been trampled into river mud and layered over with giant feathers and
a few old piles of bird dung, or heaps of crushed bone and
matted hair like huge owl castings. Animal long bones had
been driven through the tangled canes like stakes. These
bones rose above Cloud's waist even though planted deep in
the mud. After a while she saw that the canes of the thicket
had been woven together, like a crude fish trap or a bird's
nest.

As she slogged through the mud, thorns slid scratchily off
her hat, cloak, and shoes, but slashed her bare ankles bloody.
Then she came upon her rope again. Fighting down panic,
she made herself retrace her steps so she did not tangle it.

If this *was* a bird nest, she thought, Huntress would enter the thicket from above. But Cloud had no wings. When
she reached her starting point again, she took out the leaf
and sliced first at the long hooked thorns, then the canes
themselves. But the wall was flimsier than it looked. As she
pulled on a cane, a clump of wall fell loose, making a hole
big enough to duck through.

Inside was Huntress's house as she had found it before: a
chaos of boxes, bales of hides, and racks of corpses obscured
by choking clouds of smoke. Ghost-voices wailed from the
rafters.

Cloud groped her way to the hearth and scattered the
logs. As the smoke dissipated, her mirror glowed brighter.
Its light revealed her father's skull, now black with soot,
cradled in the mud like an egg in a nest. Huntress had built
her fire on it.

Cloud jerked back. But in that moment, the tangled cane
walls had become crude planks, and blocking the hole where
she had entered, pinning down Foam's rope, was the door-
plank that had trapped her before. She yanked at her rope in
vain.

How did a mortal travel this country, where everything
had more than one form and existed in more than one place,
each in some way the same place?

Hugging herself, trying to press down her panic, Cloud stared up at the impenetrable shadows where the ghosts clamored. The ghosts were high overhead now. They had been close by, though, in that other place she had fallen into from Huntress's house, while suffocating in her own blood.

To pass deeper into the unmasked world, surely that was where she had to go. But how could she face the bone middens again?

She could not turn back now.

She tossed aside her useless torch, put away the leaf-knife, stacked boxes against the wall, and with trembling hands payed out more rope. Then she started to climb into the rafters.

But atop the first box, she had to stop to catch her breath. As she leaned against the house's corner post, a tremor rolled through the walls, and the post toppled outward. She fell after it—

—Dead canes snapped under her weight, thorns slashed—

She crashed into stinking, viscous mud. Cold, cold mud slid over her face, over her head. She pulled on Foam's rope, but it sagged loose. Cloud flailed, arms and legs pushing at mud as if she were running. She had been good at running—

Her hand struck something miraculously solid. She hauled herself out of the mud by it, and retching, spitting, she wiped her face until she could gasp at the thick foul air again. Finally she was able to clean off her mirror and aim it around her.

She clung to an animal thigh bone driven into the mud. But the unmasked world had rippled again, and now the latticed structure it staked down resembled a dam with a gigantic cylindrical fish trap. Vagrant glimmers on the river showed her that Huntress had built the trap backward, mouth facing upstream, to catch what drifted down the river rather than what swam up.

What drifted down was the dead. Corpses that slipped around the dam floated onward, but inside the trap, ghosts trailed crying along mountains of bones. She had found Huntress's middens.

Cloud wrapped her muddy cloak around her hand, grabbed a section of lattice, and pulled herself up.

The huge canes snapped. Moving a little quicker, she managed to hook her knee over the tip of the bone-stake, and heave her body atop it before the lattice broke. The stake trembled under her weight but did not pull loose.

Again she took out the leaf-knife and hacked at the canes. It was strange—wherever she touched the canes, they snapped and unraveled. It was as if her very flesh unwove the trap.

A section of lattice fell into the mud with a plop and floated away. A small landslide of bones clattered after it. Cloud pulled her rope out of the mud and, trying not to think or feel anything, crawled up onto the tottery slope.

As if her weight unbalanced it, the entire trap swayed, nearly spilling her back into the river.

She scrambled upward. Mountains of human skulls glowered in the light of her mirror. Ghosts drifted from her, mumbling and wailing. "Tongue!" she gasped. "Black! Claw!" The putrid darkness inside the trap, thick and cold as river mud, swallowed her words.

At the top of the slope, she called again. "Claw! Tongue!"

"Save us!" a child's thin voice pleaded.

Her beloved brothers stood atop another of the mountains. As she climbed toward them, the trap swayed again and a piece of the midden under her feet caved away. Hacked-open skulls, splintered long bones, and liquefying offal tumbled down, throwing her toward the bottom of the trap.

The slide clattered to a halt. When she regained her feet, she saw what had stopped it: a forest of drying frames that stretched along a muddy valley between the middens. Split-open corpses had been strung up all along the frames.

"Save us," the little boys wept. "Help us. Please don't go." They had followed her down but would not approach her.

326        JUDITH BERMAN

Panting, Cloud floundered toward them over the bone-slide. The trap creaked and shuddered and more bones tumbled down. With difficulty she sucked in enough air to speak. "How do I take away your bones? Where is the anchor?"

"Don't go," her brothers said, even as they backed away from her.

"You must go, Cloud," said Otter's voice.

Cloud turned. In the dim, dim light, Otter's ghost could almost have been his living self. The sight stabbed through her like a spear. "Uncle?" she whispered. She stepped toward him but he, too, recoiled. It must be the smell of her blood.

"Leave me, Cloud," he said. "You must go on."

But she had already left him too many times. Weeping now, Cloud slogged from corpse to corpse, shining her mirror on the smoke-blackened faces. Otter had worn his hair long and knotted atop his head—but so had others, and Huntress had cracked off all the skull tops. No mustache or hair on his chin. No gray hair. So hard to tell in the dim light. So many it could be.

As she splashed deeper into the forest, descending to the very bottom, canes sagged and broke under her feet, the trap shuddered, bones rolled down the midden slopes. Ghosts scattered from her like startled birds, fleeing the blood of childbirth that still trickled from her womb.

"Leave me!" Otter said.

"I won't!" she sobbed. And *there,* hardly visible on darkened skin, the tattoo of Otter's little servant—

When she laid hands on Otter, the cords that tied him to the frame fell away. She hoisted his desiccated corpse, light as driftwood, to her shoulder—

Then she saw her father's skull.

Half-submerged, weighting down the trap like a stone, the enormous skull sat in a muddy pool at the center of the forest. Cloud stared at it. She had been wrong; not everything here possessed more than one form. Her father's skull had not changed through all the permutations of Huntress's house.

But *of course*: Huntress had used her father, skull and bones, to build the house.

"You must finish your task, Cloud," said Otter's ghost.

But for a too-long moment, sinking with broken canes into the mud of the river bottom, Cloud did not move. She had to go on, but she could not bear the thought of touching that skull.

In the end, fear of Huntress won out. She set Otter's body aside and plunged her arms into the mud.

But just as with her brothers' much smaller skulls in the forest above, she could not budge it. Leaf-knife in hand, she groped after cords without finding any. Cloud crouched down, scooped away mud to aim her mirror inside the skull—

—teeth snapped down on the mirror. She stumbled back, yanking it free. A lizard swarmed out of an eye socket. It was the size of an ordinary beach lizard but colored a sickly phosphorescent green, and teeth like icicles hung from the roof of its mouth.

The lizard flicked a tongue at her. The barbed tip missed Cloud's hand and instead struck her rain cloak, where it pumped out a glowing green droplet of venom.

"You should not have brought your blood here, little four-legs," said the lizard in Bone's voice.

The shock of that voice pierced Cloud with hot and cold. When the lizard sprang at her, she slashed with the leaf-knife, slicing off its foreleg. The creature cried out and fell into the mud. In the corner of her eye, it was not a living thing at all, but a great whorled knot.

The lizard jumped again. Cloud hacked fiercely, this time cutting it almost in two. As it convulsed, her father's skull rocked and the trap heaved like a log in a storm sea. She slashed again and again. The lizard's jaws were opening and shutting, its tongue flicking. Then something dark dribbled out of its mouth. The lizard unraveled into black slimy ropes like snake tails that thrashed, spasmed, coiled, and at last fell still.

Gasping for breath, Cloud leaned against her father's skull. But it skidded away. The trap itself slewed suddenly. An avalanche of bones roared down, toppling a great swath of corpse-forest.

"You must go, Cloud!" said Otter's ghost.

Now it must all be adrift: fish trap, dam, islet, Huntress's house, the bones in the glade above, Rumble's stolen power—

Cloud shoved the knife into her pouch, lifted Otter's corpse, and turned to follow her rope out of the trap. "Claw! Tongue! Black! Uncle! Follow me!"

"You can't go," boomed a deep voice.

A huge, hairy, naked man stood on the skull in front of her. Severed ropes like snake tails dangled from wounds in his chest. He gazed on Cloud with an intense wounded, rage-filled stare that frightened and repelled her.

She thought she had swallowed so much awfulness that she could not feel any more. She was wrong.

Here, at last, was her father's ghost.

Cloud backed away, panic roaring through her. But she had to return by the route she had come by or she would ir-reparably snarl her rope.

Then she remembered that ghosts fled her blood-smell. She dodged past her father, floundered onto the toppled corpse-trees, and scrambled up the collapsing slope of bones, yanking the harpoon line after her.

Her father waited at the top, once more blocking her path. "You can't go!" he roared. "You are *mine*!"

But the trap shook and then rolled violently, throwing her past her father against the side of the trap. Long thorns raked her, and then a great sheet of latticed canes dropped away and pitched her outward.

She lost her grip on Otter as she fell. Both of them landed atop the broken lattice, but the lattice unraveled where her body touched it, and she began to sink. Bones and offal roared down all around her, driving her under the surface even as she clutched at the tangle of rope and canes bearing Otter. The great wall of the trap rolled inexorably toward her.

But then Foam's rope pulled taut around Otter and the buoyant canes. And now the huge trap was drifting past her, twisting in the current, breaking into pieces. As the ghosts spilled into the river, their wails died to whispers growing ever softer, vanishing into distance and darkness.

Cloud clung to the makeshift raft. She was so tired. She wanted to drift after those ghosts, to sink down into silence and cold forever. But Foam's harpoon line held her back.

And finally she began dragging the raft hand over hand along the rope. She was numb with cold; she had no more breath; dizziness rolled over her in sickening waves. But then other smells wafted through the dark: fir resin, wet grass.

And then, as above and below changed places, her feet touched firmer mud. She climbed, reaching arm over trembling, burning arm, heaving herself and Otter's corpse up and up until she burst into the glory of a gray, dripping winter dusk.

*She had made it back.* Sucking in clean air, she crawled away from the door until the glade stopped spinning. Then she collapsed.

This twilight, so much brighter than the world below, showed her Otter's corpse in pitiless detail: the shrunken, eyeless face, the emptied skull-top, the gutted body with its flesh peeled away from the bones and spread wide—

Cloud pushed herself into a sitting position to haul up the rest of the harpoon line. After slicing the canes from the rope, she crawled to the maple. Her brothers' bones had not disappeared with the destruction of Huntress's fish trap. When she pushed at one of the tiny skulls, it rolled from the spot where it had been resting, but slowly, as if through pitch.

She tried her brothers' other bones. She could lift them, but only with difficulty, as if something still anchored them.

"It worked," she said out loud, unconvinced.

She chopped Foam's harpoon point free with the leaf-knife and slipped the point and then the muddy string into the pouch. She wiped her mirror clean. Then she sat, leaning against the maple.

Given the slip between the masked and unmasked worlds, she had no idea how long she had she been gone. Days? Weeks? She knew she should leave the glade, but she was utterly drained.

The taste of the river filled her mouth, and she hawked and spat. After a while, she heard a four-legged footstep. Seal had come to sniff at Otter's corpse.

A sharp lump swelled in Cloud's throat. She wished she had someone to talk to—not a dog, not a grotesque riddling foot-servant, but a person, Glory, Black Fin, someone to whom she could say: Otter cared for me. I loved him. He was one of the few solid things I had in my life.

If she had not used up the salmon king's gift in Sandspit Town, spending it on people whose names she didn't even know—

Cloud began to cry again. Instead of freeing Otter, she had stupidly brought him to where Huntress could find him again. Better the wolves did eat him and chew his bones. Better she had let him float away in the underworld river. Eventually he would have spilled into the ocean and drifted west into the jumble of the world's debris, until he rode the rapids out of the world into the bright, rainbowed sea beyond. There he would have found his way back to life . . .

A wolf howled nearby. Cloud woke with a start. How stupid to fall asleep! Stupid, stupid, stupid!

Black night had fallen. Almost too cold to move, she struggled to her feet, hefted Otter's body to her shoulder, and by the light of the mirror, set off with Seal through the forest. No matter what Raven Tongue said about her kinship to the wolves, she was not going to face them without fire.

At the tree where she had cached her bag, she dropped Otter to the grass, retrieved tinder and her still-smoldering the fisherman making repairs, or whether this was advice to her. She turned away and, starting to shiver, trudged between the mounds and pools of vomit to where she had left Otter's body.

The corpse was not there.

For a few heartbeats she stood in cold, miserable shock. "Uncle, where are you?" Cloud wailed. There was no answer.

Her fire had been extinguished by the rain. She found no trail of broken twigs or trampled grass leading away through the trees, although right in that spot the muddy ground was well trafficked with dog footprints.

"Are these your tracks?" she asked Seal. "Where did Otter go? Who took his body? The wolves?"

Seal glanced toward the deep forest, then sat and looked at her. Raven Tongue had drifted in her wake from the glade, and Cloud put the same questions to him. He said, "The women left the short clover roots in the soil."

A useless answer: Otter *hadn't* been left.

One of the amulets from the necklace Huntress had been wearing lay among the rain-soaked leaves. Cloud picked it up, too worn out to cry. "Raven Tongue," she said, "help me find the rest of my uncle's amulets."

But he couldn't find them. Nor could he locate the remains of her spirit eater, or Copper Orca or the little box. Huntress had flown away with the harpoon and leaf-knife embedded in her, and evidently the rest of Foam's treasures had vanished with her as well. Cloud retained only her clothes, and one shard of mirror that Huntress had not trampled to dust.

She tried to think through her bruising fatigue. *The women left the short clover roots.* What about the *long* roots? The women dug them, of course, roasted and ate them. So: Otter had been taken away for someone's dinner. Better the wolves than Huntress.

Otter was gone. But her grief and guilt would stay with her forever.

Winter's bag still lay on the grass. Cloud slung it across her shoulders and headed back to her camp on the beach.

*She built up a fire, ate, slept. When she woke, it was* still day, or perhaps it was another day. It was still raining. She scrubbed the filth from her skin, hair, and clothing, scoured and squeezed out all her wounds. Then, wrapped in all her blankets, she curled up to sleep again with Seal.

She dreamed that she slept in a warm heap with her brothers. She dreamed that she fought Claw over a salmon backbone. She wrested it from his hands and ran away.

She dreamed of the glade. Her brothers waited beneath the shattered maple. "Don't leave us," they begged. This time when she woke, she could hear their weeping inside her ears, though the fainter clamor of many voices was gone.

To deliver them to death, to return them to life, she had to take their bones to the dawn fire. But she had lost Copper Orca and could not even depart this island. And since her arrival she had seen neither canoes nor orcas crossing the bay. Still, perhaps a canoe from Waterfall would at last investigate her fire. She had to be ready when it came.

She emptied Winter's bag and set out with Seal for the glade. The smoke had cleared from the forest, but the trees still loomed half-unmasked, treading slowly through the edges of her vision. As Cloud approached the glade, trying not to inhale the awful stink, a vulture flapped away, a raccoon scurried into the brush. Larger scavengers had been busy as well, scattering bones and leaving many doglike tracks: the wolves again.

That gray-brown soup, now diluted by several days of rain, had probably originated as Huntress's favorite meal, human brains. Among the smaller shards of bone lay cracked skull tops like bowls, and still-articulated hands and feet. Something—Cloud supposed it was living atop Bone's binding—had stopped up Huntress for a long time.

Whatever had caused it, Cloud now had to dig through it. Her brothers were weeping again. Cloud walked around the maple. There was nothing to do but wade in. At least she had Raven Tongue to help locate all her brothers' bones, so she did not have to dig in vain. But the work was unspeakably gruesome and foul, and the door into the world below gaped at the edge of her vision, dizzying her. Her brothers sobbed, "Help us, help us!" even while she labored at heaving up fallen limbs or raking aside vomit. If she talked to them, they stayed calmer, but she could not pause or they would start again. "Don't go! Save us!"

For the most part her father watched silently. She hated the feeling of it. When she came near, he would step back from the smell of her but growl, "You can't go. You are mine."

At times her brothers' bones looked human, at times bearlike. Either way they were so pitifully small that all three sets fit into Winter's bag. But they were so heavy that lifting a tiny rib was like raising a stone, and when she was finished and hauled up on the bag, its seams ripped, spilling the contents.

She had destroyed Bone's lizard-binding. Why couldn't she move the bones? "What did I do wrong?" she asked Raven Tongue in despair.

"Chop down the fir and it dies," he said. "Chop down the maple and it sprouts again."

She had to dig up the roots of the maple that bound them. Not, surely, this real maple before her? Rage at his inscrutable riddling swelled so large that for a moment she could not speak.

"Claw!" she snarled. "Why can't I lift your bones?"

"Help us, help us," the child-ghosts wept.

"I'm trying to!" Cloud screamed. They just cried harder.

Her father's ghost glowered from the other side of the maple. Winter had said she might have to ask his advice. But she didn't want to talk to him. She didn't want to look at him. She had lost Otter and was stuck instead with *her father*.

"Stink!" she yelled. "Stink! Talk to me, Lord Stink!"

And he stood before her, huge, hairy, naked, full of rage, his very gaze as threatening as a blow. Even though he was a ghost who could not bend a blade of grass, she stepped back.

"Why," she said, trying to control the quaver in her voice, "can't I move my brothers' bones?"

"They are mine," he said.

"They are *dead*," Cloud said. "Let them go—"

"She is mine," said Stink's ghost.

Fury returned. "No, she is not! Thrush did *not* belong to you!"

"You," Stink said, "are mine, too. My blood. Mine."

There he stood, her mother's kidnapper and slaughterer of her people, the embodiment of her deepest dread, the source of what she most loathed in herself. His blood had *poisoned* hers.

But now that she saw her father, lost memories returned to her. He was the big one, the powerful one, the one who slept with her mother, whose rough smell Thrush wore every day. His was the smell of home.

An immense pang of grief squeezed through her belly. "I am," said Cloud, the fight going out of her. "I *am* your daughter."

Now she understood. She should have understood it a long time ago, but she had not wanted to. Her bound father had in turn bound her. In dreams and in life, she came to this glade to search for him.

But not because *she* belonged to him, as he claimed.

It was the other way around. He belonged to her. He was the warp of her childhood and she had been woven over it. How could she pull him out and have any of herself left?

If not for Rumble, she would never want to free him. But then she would be haunted by this glade for the rest of her life. And was it possible that he, too, longed to escape his dying rage? *She is mine. You are mine.*

Murderous possessiveness filled his face, but his eyes were dark and wounded. Behind him, her brothers wept. She could not free them or herself unless she also freed him.

She walked around to her father's skull and stood on tip-toes. Her skin crawled when she grabbed hold of it. It was heavy, but not out of proportion to its size, and it came out of its resting place with only a shower of sodden leaves. As Cloud lifted it down, something hard rattled, and she turned over the skull. A small cedar box had been placed inside. She did not need Raven Tongue to warn her against opening it.

**She poured all her brothers' bones out of the bag,** laid branches over them to thwart scavengers, and returned to her camp. There she took out the sewing tools that Winter had long ago packed for her. Her lacerated hands were even clumsier than usual, and she stabbed her fingers with the awl as often as she poked it through the right hole, but she managed to resew the seams of the bag. Then, her palms already cramping from the labor, she took up the coils of root fiber that Winter had packed for her and made a big, ugly knot to start a basket.

To carry her father's bones into the mountains, even just to haul them to the beach, she needed a large and sturdy pack, and none of the boxes from Sandspit Town were big enough for the purpose. The pack did not have to be woven more tightly than a clam basket—or a fish trap. That she should be able to manage.

Probably any girl in Sandspit Town could have twined such a basket in a few hours. Cloud worked the rest of that cold, drizzling day, stopping only to eat, flex her cramping fingers, and throw more wood on the fire. By nightfall she had progressed only a handspan above the bottom.

While she worked, Seal slept at her feet. His muzzle was shot with gray now. How many years had passed since she had first fled Sandspit Town? Glory had grown old; lines showed on Thrush's face; Radiance had married. The new half-sister, whose name she didn't know, stood as high as Thrush's chest. Otter's children must have grown up, too, unless they'd starved to death.

And meanwhile only a year or two had passed for Cloud—she did not know how long she had lived with Center-of-Heaven. Did she look as much older to them as they did to her?

If her brothers had grown up in mortal Sandspit Town, they would be young men now. What sort of men would they have grown into? Men like Otter? Or like Rumble, like their father?

If her brothers had lived, would she have grown up with them as she had done without them: lonely, angry, fearful, a stranger to laughter?

She had shed her bear robe, but she had never become either a bear or a human being. She wished, though, that she could shed her childhood in the same way. Instead she kept dreaming of its ghosts, and now she had to haul away its heavy bones. That was her fate, in Foam's words, and she had to shoulder it.

She began another row of twining, trying hard to keep the spacing narrow. Her father had been a child once, she thought. Her father, too, long ago must have run laughing through the pine woods, must have splashed happily in that mountain stream. If her brothers were not evil, then her father could not be either, at least not in origin, not in his totality.

But what turned boys into men whose grief could only be assuaged by hurting others?

Oh, she knew at least part of the answer: having a nature like hers, where emotion always stepped out before reason, where anger flooded and withdrew as uncontrollably as the tides.

And then she thought, clumsily splicing in a new warp: she had never reconciled herself to being a bear, but she had never reconciled to being a girl either. And she wasn't even a girl anymore, but a woman—at least she had been a wife and borne a child, even if she did not want to think about that child.

She did not want to be any of them, not a bear, not a girl, not a wife, not a mother.

She did not want to become her father, but it was also Thrush she did not want to become, brutalized by each of her husbands, her children by one husband murdered by the other. She did not want a woman's fate.

And yet: her woman's body, with its blood that had formed the baby she did not want and still leaked from the wound the baby had made, had to be counted with the gifts that had aided her in the underworld and against Huntress. Its power could birth souls and destroy spirit works, sewing and unsewing the world itself.

And here she was now, able to free her ghosts only by woman's work—she, Cloud, with the bear paws that could not be trained to twine a basket or set a stitch any better than a child's first effort. Now she *had* to do it, no matter how difficult, no matter how unsuited she was to the labor.

*Days passed while she labored over the basket,* crouched in her shelter with Seal, watching the rain-veiled bay for canoes that never came. Huntress did not return. Every night the wolves howled on the island and on the mainland. On the mountains, the line of white crept lower. One day Cloud realized that even if she found a way off the island, she would not be able to travel into the mountains until spring. And if she could not leave—

Finally she dared send Raven Tongue to Waterfall, and he reported back the very news she feared. Waterfall, like Whale Town, had been abandoned. She was afraid Rumble was the cause, but she could not extract the story from her servant's riddles.

The consequence to her was the same.

Snow flurried over the empty bay. That night the wolves fell silent and did not howl again.

The next morning she looked at the huge, misshapen basket, half an armspan deep and nearly as wide, and decided it was big enough to hold the bones. She finished off the rim and headed back to the glade with Seal.

She had not made the long hike while she worked on her pack. The snowfall showed her that the wolves had been recent visitors, feeding along with many smaller scavengers. The mounds were scattered and much reduced.

Cloud followed the wolf tracks through the forest for several miles to see if they might lead her to Otter's remains, but they did not. Whenever Seal put his nose to the ground, she asked him if he had found Otter. But he could not lead her to the body, either.

At last she returned to the glade. Into her pack went her father's huge skull, the pelvis, ribs, long bones, and vertebrae. The mended bag she filled with his small bones and her brothers' remains. Once again Raven Tongue helped her locate them all.

Finally she wedged Winter's bag at the top of the pack, between the protruding long bones, and tied everything down.

Then came the test. Cloud crouched and slid the carrying strap onto her forehead. And then she stood, slowly lifting the pack. It was heavy and badly balanced, like a too-large burden of firewood, but she could move it.

Still, the thought of hauling this load to the edge of the world was daunting, to say the least.

She had to stop and rest several times on the way to the beach. Her brothers followed, pleading, weeping, whining. Her father stalked after, a relentless presence even in his silence.

Back at her camp Cloud burned the ropes that had once tied the bones to the tree, and—using tongs—set the wooden box from her father's skull on the coals. She was not surprised when it failed to ignite. She returned the box to the skull and summoned Raven Tongue. "How do I get off this island?"

"The mallard keeps watch for the weasel," he told her. These days he hardly seemed able to speak without a riddle.

Ducks flew. Ducks swam. Cloud could do neither. But weasels loped on four legs. Perhaps Raven Tongue meant she could walk off the island—ford the channel at low tide, then climb around the bay to Waterfall. She had a better chance of surviving the winter in an abandoned house than crouched under a canoe hull.

She pulled out her sewing kit again, this time to construct a pack for Seal. For the straps she dismembered a pouch from Glory's stores, and she stitched the carrying bags—one for each side and one for the top—from cedar-bark mats. It took several tries to make a harness that did not slip.

While she worked, she had to reassure her brothers' ghosts constantly that she would not abandon them. Her dreams of them now took place on the beach.

She filled Seal's pack with food and tools. When she tried it on him, he put his ears back and gazed at her mournfully. "I'll be carrying a heavier weight than you," she told him.

She stowed Rumble's necklace of teeth in the bag with the small bones, then filled every remaining space with food, even stuffing it among the bones. One fur robe she fastened atop her pack and another around her shoulders. Then she tied down the lids on her storage boxes and carried them up into the woods.

The next morning, she and Seal set out along the beach. The ghosts followed. Seal did not like his pack: whenever Cloud stopped to rest, which was frequently, he chewed at the straps.

By the end of the first day they had covered only half the distance she had hoped for. And her legs trembled, her neck and shoulders had knotted painfully, and fresh bruises covered her back where the bones poked her.

On the second day, the rain turned to sleet, icing the rocks and slowing her progress further. Seal lagged, too. "*Your* pack will get lighter," she said. "We'll eat the food soon enough."

On the third day, they reached the strait separating the island from the mainland, and Cloud saw that she would never walk across it. Sheer cliffs bordered the channel on both sides. As they plodded through the rain along the cliff edge, the passage narrowed until she thought a strong man could shoot an arrow across it. The sea that poured through the cleft was an angry, roaring current like river rapids. While she watched, the tide changed: a moment of slack water, then a terrible grinding and booming as the current poured through in the opposite direction.

Cloud watched enviously as a petrel swooped along the channel. Walk off the island, she thought in disgust. Weasels and mallards. She could not even get down to the water, much less cross it or climb the other side.

They camped under the trees. She lay awake for hours with Seal leaning against her side. It was only deep in the night that she realized what was bothering her: the wolves had been quiet for several days now, on both the mainland and the island.

Perhaps two packs had stopped howling at exactly the same time. But somewhere in the back of her mind, Cloud had always assumed that a single pack came and went from the island. Seal could swim; she had seen him chasing ducks. Surely wolves could swim, too. But not across that channel.

Didn't weasels den *underground*?

*A bear could have followed the wolves by scent.* Cloud had to find their tracks.

She did ask Raven Tongue for guidance, but from his cryptic utterances she extracted only that she should look in the forest, which she already knew.

"Seal," she said, "I have to find the wolves."

He laid his ears against his head and lowered his tail.

"I'm sorry, but I do. I have to find where they went."

After stuffing shredded cedar bark in her moccasins to warm her toes, Cloud headed into the forest. At this end of the island, snow had been piling up for days, but rain and refreezing had hardened it to something like slippery compacted sand. Remembering how a Waterfall slave had hauled wood on the snow, she cut branches and tied them into a little raft. On this she was able to tow their packs. Freed from the weight of the bones, she hardly sank into the snow at all.

Cloud had been prepared to return all the way to the glade to pick up the wolves' trail. The next day Seal found a track in the snow made of many crisscrossing sets of prints. Rain had melted each print into a circular depression the size of her palm, so that it was impossible to be sure what animal they belonged to. She turned to follow the track anyway.

The footprints took them into the island's interior. Later that day, a blizzard closed in. As fresh snow accumulated, she asked Seal if he could follow the tracks by smell. For a while he did, leading her up a forested slope to a barren, snow-blown clearing. There he lost the trail. He cast around without result, then glanced back at her. He looked so miserable hunched beneath his pack, ice matting his hair, that she did not have the heart to make him keep searching.

But now she didn't know how to find the wolves.

Night was falling; she had to stop anyway. Experience was teaching her how to camp in snow. At the edge of the clearing, Cloud found a young fir where snow had weighted down the tips of the lower branches to form a cave. She chopped branches to lie on and to form a base for her fire. Inside the cave it was quiet and almost warm, but high overhead, squalls prowled the forest, roaring past and fading away like swells in a storm sea.

Seal woke her during the night, growling. As she roused, Cloud heard the earth rumbling beneath them as if with a continuous distant peal of thunder.

There was a rhythm to it, like a heartbeat, a drumbeat.

She crawled out of the shelter. The wind had died, and fat snowflakes dropped straight down through the air. The snow was bright enough that she did not need a torch.

A winged shape glinted in the corner of her eye and vanished. The deep booming under her feet went on. "Seal," she whispered, "where's the sound coming from?"

Seal led her back across the clearing to where he had earlier lost the scent. Now he cocked his head and, whining, pawed at a rock as if something lay beneath it.

"Hush," Cloud whispered, putting a hand on his muzzle.

She squatted down. The thunder did boom louder in that spot. When she pushed at the rock, it shifted slightly and warmer air and the smell of smoke wafted up. Now she could hear a high, eerie song accompanying the drumbeats. Cold prickled up and down her spine. People were dancing down under the earth.

Cloud returned to her campsite and picked up a few sticks to use as torches. She lit one. Then, not knowing if she was stupid or wise, she dragged out their packs.

"Seal," she said, "I'm going into that hole. Don't come with me. I think the wolves are down there."

Seal licked her hand. She squatted down and hugged him farewell, burying her face in the shaggy fur of his neck.

And then she climbed into her pack of bones and slung his pack across her front. Thus burdened, she returned to the rock.

Seal followed her. "No!" she whispered, pushing him away. He resisted, ears back, and she realized she would have to tie him up to prevent him from following her. And if she did that and failed to return, he would die.

She pushed the rock away from the hillside. Beyond lay a low tunnel better suited to wolves than human beings. She got down on her knees to look in, saw only dirt and dangling roots. But inside, high clear voices rose above the drumbeats:

> Try to lift it up,
> Try to lift it up,
> Try to lift it up,
> Howling-on-the-Mountaintop.

As she crawled into the tunnel, the blackness inside wavered dizzyingly, and her time in the world below crashed down on her. For a moment she could not go forward.

But then a clean draft spilled past her, making the little flame of her torch leap. Under the earth the voices sang:

> *Set it on his head,*
> *Set it on his head,*
> *Set it on his head,*
> *Gray-Tail-at-the-Headwaters.*

She scurried forward as fast as she could. The air grew warmer, and up ahead firelight flickered on the tunnel walls.

Then, all at once, the music stopped.

**The passage opened into a large cavern walled by** tree roots and compacted earth. The cavern was empty, but someone had recently scattered a fire. As she crossed the floor, her feet stirred eagle down that must have been left by the dancers.

An enormous tree root thrust along one side of the cavern. It had been hollowed into a drum. She tapped softly and heard the deep, resonant response.

The dancers were gone, but other figures glinted, slipped sideways, and disappeared. Wizard's servants? They weren't supposed to be able to enter the houses of the immortals!

But perhaps these spirits had been *invited* in.

Seal trotted out of the tunnel behind her. Together they sniffed at the other two passages leading out of the cavern. A doglike smell was strong and fresh in the first. The draft winding up the other passage made her shudder: a familiar smell of cold stinking decay.

She would follow the dancers, Cloud thought, try again to surprise the wolves as she had the orcas. She would demand not just the way off the island but Otter's corpse. She would—

She would ask for Otter whole and alive. The wolves, who

had brought wizardry into the world, could surely bring
Otter back from the dead. *She could have him back.*

A chasm of desire yawned and she teetered on its brink.
But.

She couldn't afford to get it wrong again.

It wrenched 'at her guts to stop wanting and *think,* but
she had to. Blind emotion always led her to disaster: *wanting*
the southerners dead, *wanting* Raven Tongue to leave her in
peace, *wanting* Center-of-Heaven to keep her safe. Her pointless effort to bring Otter's corpse out of the underworld
would have gotten her killed if Huntress had returned just a
little earlier.

It would be as pointless to run after the wolves. They had
already smelled her human flesh, her female blood. It would
be just one more way of turning aside from her real task.

She had to give up Otter now and forever.

It hurt more than Raven Tongue's frogs, more than having the baby. And she could not push it out and leave it behind. She had to let the pain fill her up until it crushed her,
and then she still had to go on.

**Cloud tied Seal's pack on him again and they took**
the other passage. Seal sniffed the air doubtfully.

This passage led down through earth and clay and folds
in granite bedrock, a long, dizzying descent into blackness.
Water dripped on the floor. The smell of the underworld
grew stronger.

The wolves' doorway into the country below was a black
hole at the bottom of narrow steps cut into bedrock. "When
we go through that hole," she told Seal, "what's down will
become up, but if you keep touching the ground, you won't
fall."

Seal's hackles bristled, his tail curled between his legs,
and he trembled as if with cold. He was terrified, she
thought. "I told you not to follow me," she said roughly.

Cloud took off her pack for better balance and inched
down the last few steps. But crossing the threshold here

proved not very difficult; the steps continued on the opposite side and the wolves had laid down a knotted rope as a
handhold. She helped Seal across, then put on her pack
again.

As before, it was hard to breathe properly. Her torch
smoked and guttered. The stink was not as bad as at
Huntress's fish trap, though: more swamp mud and less putrefying flesh.

The torchlight revealed no more than the black earth
they stood on. She took out the remaining fragment of her
mirror and held it up. Its wan light illuminated naked canes
arching over their heads. The wolves had worn a muddy
trail through the thicket, littered with broken thorns as
long as her hand.

She looked back at Seal. "Watch where you step."

The trail wound into darkness. Thorns ripped at her
pack. The bones weighed more in this world, and she was
soon panting from effort and from the heaviness of the air.
After a while, the trail came out along the whispering river
of the dead. The mud turned softer and more slippery, and
sucked at her ankles.

Her own ghosts followed her. In daylight, they had been
more shadow than substance, but now they were solid enough
to rattle the canes and leave footprints. She did not mind her
brothers so much, though she so fervently wished they would
stop weeping. But she loathed her father's nearness. It was
bad enough that she had to haul his bones through this dead,
cold, lightless country where thorns slashed her legs at every
step and the mud kept trying to swallow her. She should not
also have to look at him and listen to him. "You are mine," he
was muttering again, "my blood."

Cloud walked and walked, with such slow, labored steps
that she thought they would never reach the other end. Her
torch flickered out. Hours stretched onward, became days;
lack of air set her mind adrift. If she stopped to catch her
breath, she sank slowly into the mud. She did not dare take
off the pack to rest for fear the mud would eat it whole.

And it was so cold that despite her exertions she shivered convulsively. You would die regardless if you stayed in this world, she thought. It leached away breath and warmth and strength as swamp water rots a green leaf to brown.

At one point she stumbled and slid into the river, and the bones nearly pulled her under. That was when she dropped the last fragment of mirror. After that the only light came from ghost-flickers over the river, and to follow the trail she had to keep one hand on Seal's pack.

At last a draft of fresher air blew across her face. After a day, or perhaps only a few minutes, they reached another set of steps, another rope. Another dizzying switch when up and down switched places, and then they were climbing up stone and then clay, splashing through water, crawling up and up toward light—

Sunlight blinded her. She stepped out of a cave onto pink-flowering clover. A creek roared from a nearby snow-field. Above them, snow-wrapped crags thrust into a clean blue sky.

She turned to Seal. "We're in the mountains!"

They were in the Mountain Land and it was spring. A season had passed while they were under the earth. Seal trotted to the creek and lapped water.

**They hiked farther down the valley to camp.** Cloud bathed in the milky, shockingly cold water, then curled up to sleep in the afternoon sun. The ghosts filled her dreams, as always.

Frost iced the grass that night, but the sun rose again into a blue sky.

She did not recognize the peaks. Since they were once more in the mortal world where Raven Tongue could guide her, she sang his song. He did not come. She sang it four times, and then another four times. He still did not appear.

Perhaps she was too far away. But it worried her. Without his aid, she was lost before she started.

She did not want to backtrack toward Waterfall. She could

not stand the thought of carrying her burden in the wrong direction, not when the valley stretched east under the sun and she did not even know how far behind her the sea might lie. But she had never intended their supplies to last for the entire long trek to the edge of the world.

Finally Cloud tied on Seal's pack, hoisted her own, and set out in the direction of the sunrise.

They hiked across meadows swampy with runoff, through forests of twittering birds. Bugs flew at them in clouds. The valley bent north, emptying into a wider valley. Cloud recalled from her journey with Winter how the valleys flowed one into another like rivers, but she did not know which route to follow.

That evening she called Raven Tongue, again without success. Afterward she lay on her back looking at the astonishingly bright stars. A bat darted high in the air. If she had been able to travel night after night to the bones, Cloud thought, why couldn't she fly like Winter?

In her dreams that night, her brothers wept as always, but she ignored them and gazed at the stars. For a moment, vertigo overcame her: if she jumped off the earth, she would fall upward until the hard surface of the sky rushed up to smash her—

Then she remembered she was dreaming, that whatever form she was in right now, it was not her body. If she could fly at all, she would not fall. She jumped toward the stars—

She drifted over the orange speck that was her fire. Then, at a thought, she soared up through the night in widening, ever-higher circles, until she rose above the surrounding peaks. To the west, rivers of mist flowed down toward an ocean of cloud. To the east, range after range of mountains marched away under the stars, the maze that had defeated Bone's servants.

Cloud flew east, noting landmarks: a lake, a broad river, a smooth upswept cone. An orange moon lifted out of darkness and for an instant its light shivered along pillars as tall as the sky. As she sped toward the pillars, looking in vain for a gap like the western door, something warm as the sun fell aslant the night air, touched her skin with a wild tingling. Those jagged peaks—how many times had she dreamed of playing at their feet?

But she was not headed to her father's house. Discouraged, she labored home, heavy as stone, to drop into her body again.

**The next morning, they set out for an eastward**-leading pass she had spotted during her flight. And that was how they traveled. Flying wearied her too much to do it often, but on those trips, she would scout a course toward the pillars. And then they would trek on foot around ice-green lakes, across lush, buggy meadows or trackless slopes of scree, covering in long, tiring hours what she could fly over in a single breath.

When she flew, she sometimes sighted the crags of her childhood home, but she never saw the doorway out of the world.

On the ride to the western edge of the world with Black Fin, she had felt exhilaration. On this trip, she woke and slept with loathing, with bone-deep weariness. Day after day, while the moon waxed and waned again, insects bit her until she bled, the sun burnt her skin and dazzled her eyes, her pack strap rubbed first her forehead and then her shoulders to raw flesh that never healed. Her back and neck became knots of shooting pain. She wanted nothing more than to shed her burden and abandon her sullen father and her whiny, weepy brothers.

She was grateful to Seal for his company, but she wished every day that he could take off his mask and talk.

Every day she called for Raven Tongue, but he never came.

The Mountain Land was not empty of human beings. Several times she saw smoke in the distance. One day, after hiding her pack behind a tree, she dared to visit a camp where men, women, and children fished along a river. The people received her kindly, if warily. In return for a fur-seal blanket from Glory, they gave her newly dried chinook salmon, smoked goose, last year's blueberries, a large sack of roots that needed roasting, and a new supply of slow match.

They asked her where she had come from and where she was bound. She said only that she had many dreams that told her to travel to the edge of the world. It was not much of a falsehood. When she asked how to reach it, they could only point eastward. She felt lonelier than ever when she left them.

The moon waxed again. She and Seal passed animals she had seen at Oyster Bay, and animals whose identity she could only surmise: mountain sheep, cougars, elk, foxes. Loons were visiting from the ocean, and she even spied a seagoing petrel.

From time to time she spotted black bears, and also the larger brown grizzlies, some trailed by frolicking cubs. That sight pierced her to the core. Seal always barked when they were near—perhaps to warn Cloud, perhaps to warn off the bears. When she started her monthly bleeding after a time of none, she stayed in the low country, mindful of the warning Glory had long ago given about her father's people.

During thunderstorms she would watch the flashing, rumbling sky with dread. But she never saw Huntress.

The high snowfields retreated, looking ever dirtier. She and Seal grew leaner and stronger, her clothes more filthy and ragged. The bones stayed as heavy as ever.

Sometimes spirits flocked around her: glints of light where there should be shadow, birds or wind-chased leaves that turned to mice and scurried under the trees. She would call to them, thinking they might know how to reach the edge of the world, but they always blew away without answering her.

She began asking the animals they encountered how to find it. None of them lifted their masks to tell her.

Long ago Raven Tongue had warned, *Your shortest journey will be longest and hardest.* This trip was certainly the *longest and hardest* journey she had ever made, but she had yet to discover how it was also the shortest. She began to believe that she would never find her way into the spirit lands.

In rare moments, though, when the ghosts fell silent, she could savor the smells: sweetgrass, fir needles, lichen baking in the sun. When the wind sang in the trees, her whole being would grow quiet and the soaring peaks would carry her heart up to the sky. Sometimes as she flew in the night, she felt light as a leaf, free as a hawk.

Their stores grew thin again. One day, spotting red-flushed sockeye working their way along a creek, she shed her pack, cut a pointed stick for a spear, and spent an afternoon splashing after them. She and Seal gorged that night on fresh salmon.

She considered stopping to build a trap, but her compulsion to keep moving won out. As they set out the next morning, she had reason to be glad of her decision. A grizzly prowled the stream above their camp. Seal barked, and the bear raised its head. Heart pounding, Cloud grabbed Seal's scruff and averted her eyes, groping in vain after the prayer Glory had taught her long ago. "Oh noble one," she improvised, "it is good that we meet today alive. Grant me good luck, walker of the mountains." She added, "I'm taking the bones to where they belong."

The bear did not move. Surely, Cloud thought, it could see and hear the ghosts. She backed slowly away, hauling Seal with her, until the bear turned and splashed downstream.

They trekked across snowfields, forded torrents of snow-melt, inched down sheer rock where a misstep would send them plunging. Still she could not summon Raven Tongue. She wondered if it was possible to lose your foot-servants' allegiance.

But another fear, small at first, grew until it seemed most likely. Breaking Foam's spirit eater had freed Bone's servants. If they had surprised Cloud's own spirits . . . Cloud thought about flying home, but she needed all her strength for this grinding journey, and she was afraid she herself was so deep in the mountains that she could never find her way out—or back again.

They came in sight of the tall, conical mountain that on her first spirit flight had looked close to the pillars of the sky. But when she flew that night, the maze of mountains lying to the east was as vast as ever, the pillars just as distant.

That was when Cloud finally understood that she could travel in the right direction the rest of her life and never reach the edge of the world.

"We're lost," she said to Seal the next morning, as they shared a fresh-caught salmon. "You're an immortal, aren't you? Can you find the way for me?"

But he put his tail down. Seal had been born in mortal lands; perhaps he didn't even know how to take off his mask.

Cloud looked at the ghosts. "You!" she said to her father. "You know how to reach it!"

But her father's ghost, raging, just said what he always said: "You are mine. You are my blood."

"Don't leave us," her brothers wept.

Rage surged through her. "I wish I could!" she screamed.

They fell silent. Then they began to sob again. "Oh, I'm sorry," Cloud whispered, and she was: sorry she could not help her brothers, much sorrier she had to keep trying.

"You are my blood," said her father's ghost. "Mine."

She walked away from them. *I just don't know what to do,* she had told Foam. And Foam had said, *Am I to believe those little servants told you nothing?*

Raven Tongue had riddled, *You will need water that isn't water, fire that isn't fire. Your shortest journey will be longest and hardest.*

What was the shortest journey she could take? Not to move a single step. But it wasn't a journey if she didn't go anywhere.

The only place to go without taking a step was inside, and inside Cloud was emptiness. But it was the place her bear self, the other half of her nature, had once occupied.

*You are my blood.* Her father's blood, inside her. Her father, the warp on which she had so imperfectly been woven.

Had Raven Tongue meant that she must become a bear in order to find the door?

She had lost her servants; she had lost her spirit treasures; she had no one to ask who would answer. She still had her bear nature. The shortest journey, to what lay inside her.

But right now she was worn down and despairing. She had no great blinding rage. Without that, she did not know how to make the transformation.

Nevertheless, as she strapped Seal into his nearly empty pack, she told him, "If I turn into a bear, leave. I don't know what I'll do."

Then she realized she had spoken the word you were not supposed to utter, lest the bears come for you. Although they must all know where she was and what she was trying to do, and had so far ignored her.

She hoisted her pack. As always, the pain made her gasp while she settled it on her bleeding sores. They headed upstream along the river. Raspberries were ripening among the fireweed, and she picked and ate them as they walked.

The raspberries reminded her of the feast in the house of the salmon, where the berries had really been brine-pickled human eyes. And she thought, suddenly: her eyesight had often deceived her where the unmasked world was concerned, but smell had never failed her.

She closed her eyes and sniffed the air.

Crushed raspberries. Sun-warmed dirt and cottonwood bark. Her filthy dress, full of wood smoke and still faintly stinking of Huntress's fish trap. Her hair and skin that smelled all too human right now. A fainter whiff of the bones, dried now by the mountain sun. Seal's doggy odor.

And inside it all—inside the smell of the devil's-club and thimbleberries lurking in the shade, inside the breeze that riffled the water—she caught a scent of tree sap that was not Douglas fir or hemlock or cedar, and something else, warm as sunlight, that tingled over her skin, deep in her belly.

She and Seal followed the smell. For two days it led her up the river and along a brushy creek she would not otherwise have bothered with. The tingling in the pit of her belly grew rougher and stronger. Colors became purer: leaves greener, the sky bluer. Mica-flecked stones in the creek glinted as brightly as a sunlit sea. Even here salmon wriggled, pressing upward.

The first tall pines they encountered—

Heart pounding, Cloud stopped to breathe their heady fragrance. These trees were so different from the ragged little pines on the cliffs near Sandspit Town. This was the forest of her dreams: trunks tall and straight, and at their feet, a carpet of red needles, thickets of pink roses perfuming the afternoon heat. The wind that breathed through their long needles was the lullaby that haunted all her earliest memories—

She and Seal climbed to a higher valley. There the creek bent around a meadow, spreading noisily over rocks. In the meadow stood a rude house. Two women slept on the grass nearby.

# EIGHTEEN

# The Bears' Treasure

*The house, the streamside meadow, the pines, and* the high dawn-lit crags were all as she remembered. But at the edge of her vision, the women floated over the grass like immense shadows; the pines loomed big as mountains. The meadow wavered dizzyingly. The rank smell from those shaggy fur robes beside the women—

Panic swept over her. Those women must be bears: vicious, hungry Winter People like her father.

Seal growled, a low, nearly inaudible whine. The two women stirred sleepily. Cloud gripped Seal and hauled him backward. But well before they reached the concealment of the forest, one of the women jerked upright, sniffing. "What's that?" she said.

Cloud froze, heart pounding.

The bear woman's small, round eyes focused on Cloud, and she prodded the woman beside her. "Nose, can that be a mortal?"

Nose sat up more slowly, scratching her armpit with fingers that bore large, filthy claws instead of nails. "It smells like one, sister," she said with a yawn. "Shall we eat it?"

Seal's growls rumbled louder. Again Cloud tried desperately to think of Glory's prayer for bears, of any prayer at all.

The first woman kept sniffing. "It smells like a mortal, and it doesn't." She frowned. "Its smell is familiar."

"If you say so." Still blinking sleep from her eyes, Nose reached for a half-chewed salmon carcass and bit into it.

The first woman reared suddenly to her feet, provoking Seal to an outburst of savage barking. "You—little female!" she yelled. "Why do I know you?"

Cloud tried to calm Seal, though she herself was trembling like grass. She wanted beg them, *Just let me go on my way.*

But the bear woman's question hung in the air.

In Sandspit Town she had harbored a secret hope that she would someday meet her father's relatives. Now that she stood face to face with them, the thought of them learning her identity filled Cloud with shame. It was odd: with their straggling hair and soiled dresses, with the fish scales clinging to their cheeks, the bears were so unlike anything she wanted to be. Yet she was afraid of what they would think of her, this weak mortal girl who had failed at nearly everything important.

She still couldn't remember Glory's prayer.

"I think, great one," Cloud said, shouting to hear herself over Seal's frenzied barks, "you're my father's relatives."

"You think what?" The bear woman advanced closer. She towered head and shoulders above Cloud.

Cloud took a deep breath. "My father was Lord Stink."

"Who?"

"Lord Stink!" Cloud shouted.

"What'd she say about Brother?" asked Nose through a mouthful of fish.

"She claims he was her father," said the other.

Cloud's heart jolted. These were her father's *sisters?*

"She doesn't look like even half a bear," said Nose.

But Nose's sister exposed teeth in what might have been either a smile or a snarl. "Who was your mother then—*niece?*"

"My mother was a mortal," Cloud said.

"A what?" Nose's sister shouted.

"Be quiet, Seal!" Cloud put her hands over the dog's muzzle in a vain attempt to silence him. "A mortal!" she yelled. "She lived in this house! I was born here!"

Nose dropped the fish to gnaw her arm like a dog with a flea. "What's she saying?" she mumbled. "Born here? A mortal?"

The other woman grimaced, staring at Cloud with distaste. "You remember, sister. There was that prissy little creature, what's-her-name. She caused him a whole lot of trouble. He went off after her and never came back."

"Oh, *her,*" said Nose.

"So which of the cubs are you?" Nose's sister asked.

Anger blazed in Cloud's belly at the callous description of Thrush's torment. She did not want to speak her bear name, did not want to acknowledge it. But at last she said, "I'm Hungry."

"Oh, and you think we'll feed you?"

"That's my name!" Cloud shouted. "My bear name is Hungry!"

"Then what *do* you want?" asked Nose's sister.

*Nothing at all,* Cloud wanted to scream. She could have accepted rage from them, the wild violence that she had seen so often in Rumble's face. But contempt hurt. So she was Thrush's child, a mortal. She was also their niece. And what about her burden? She had arrived carrying their brother's bones, trailed by his ghost: wasn't *that,* at least, of interest to them?

She tried to haul back her anger as she was restraining Seal. "Great ones," she said, "I'm headed to the edge of the world. I have to throw this"—she gestured—"out the door."

"Your slave?" the bear woman said. "You want our help throwing your dog out of the world?"

"Be quiet, Seal! The bones!" Cloud shouted. "My father's and my brothers' bones!"

"Oh!" mumbled Nose, gnawing her arm. "I wondered why she was packing them around."

"We're rather busy right now . . ." said Nose's sister.

*He's your brother!* Cloud wanted to shout in their faces.

". . . but I suppose, since you're hungry, we have to feed you." She sighed, aggrieved. "All right, come inside."

Cloud's anger grew. "I don't know your name."

The bear woman stared until Cloud's face reddened with fury and embarrassment. "Oh, I'm your sweet Auntie Growl," she said, "and this is your other auntie, Nose."

They were indifferent and ungracious, they regarded Cloud and her mother with contempt, her presence here was an imposition—they weren't going to help with *their own brother.*

With enormous difficulty Cloud reached for politeness and forced it on herself, an uncomfortable, badly fitting garment. "Thank you," she shouted, "great—queens of the mountains."

Again the ambiguous snarl-smile spread across Growl's face. "Oh—now we have manners! Did you think that was nice, Nose?"

Nose shrugged, chewing at her flea bite.

**"Leave your noisy slave out here,"** said Growl, "unless we're going to have him for dinner."

"*Don't* eat him!" Cloud said, forgetting politeness all over again.

Growl shrugged. "Oh, if you want to save him for yourself."

"He's not to eat!" Cloud shouted. "He's my friend!"

"Your friend!" said Growl with surprise and distaste.

"Come, now, sister," said Nose. "She's been on her own all this time. She didn't even have a dolly to cry over! Let her keep her slave."

"Oh, all right." Growl made an impatient gesture toward the door of their house. "Go on in, then."

Cloud hesitated. Straight on, the house was a tumbledown

shed, its doorway no more than a hole chopped into a rude plank. She could also see, however, how it teetered on the brink of a dark, spinning vastness.

You had to be polite to the First People, and refusing hospitality, however reluctantly offered, was not polite. The first rule is respect.

But these weren't just any immortals; they were grizzly bears, about whose viciousness and unpredictability Cloud had been warned so many times. She was also afraid on Seal's account: no telling what her aunts might do once Cloud left his side.

Still, wasn't it possible that her aunts *would* help her? Wouldn't they *want* their brother returned to life?

These were her kin. They might not be kind to her, but it was still hard not to be curious about them, not to long to sit down in their house at least once.

Cloud shed her heavy pack and removed Seal's. He kept growling and barking, and his hackles bristled. She stroked his head. "Stay out here," she whispered in his ear, "unless they try to hurt you. Then run as fast as you can. Don't *bother* them, no matter what they do. I'll try to bring you food."

Then she crossed the meadow and crawled through the door.

Inside she found a large dirt-walled cave like the wolves' dance house. But this cave was filthy. Litter covered the floor, and it stank of bear fur, bear urine, bear scat, old fish bones. The smell was so profoundly familiar that she might never have left.

It made sense, she supposed: the dishevelment of her aunts, the dirt and garbage everywhere. This was Cloud without Glory.

Fleas jumped so thickly that black specks already swarmed over her ankles. In the middle of the floor burned a smoky fire. She edged toward it. There were fewer fleas in the smoke.

Belatedly she remembered what else, besides Nose and Growl, that she needed to fear in this house. According to

Bone's servants, her bear mask was here. What should she watch for—a rank fur robe like her aunts'?

She turned, taking in the storage boxes heaped against one wall of the cave, the crumpled and smelly bedding. Other than herself, the cave was empty. The chuckle of the creek outside sounded muted and distant. She could hear her own breath, and from one of the chests, a slow tapping.

Only then did Nose's last words sink in. *On her own—not even a dolly?* Nose surely hadn't been referring to Cloud's time in Sandspit Town. Nose hadn't even been able to remember Thrush!

Growl and Nose loomed suddenly behind Cloud, making her jump. She hadn't noticed them enter.

"Our little niece is half-starved, poor thing," said Growl. "All dirty and scabby. Blood is blood, sister. We have to take care of her."

Even though Cloud knew she ought to regard these words skeptically, they filled her with a rush of gratitude—and eager anticipation. She wouldn't mind if she had to eat the salmon as Nose had been dining, skin, bones, guts and all.

Nose shambled to the wall and rummaged through one of the storage chests. When she returned to the fire, she thrust toward Cloud a bowl heaped with muddy, squirming grubs.

Horrified, Cloud took the bowl. She looked at the grubs sideways, hoping that for once an immortal had served her something *better* than its appearance. But the grubs did not change. They wriggled and squirmed and pulsed gently. Among the grubs were also pellet-like pupae half-metamorphosed into beetles, with wings and carapaces sketched in chitin. Cloud suddenly remembered how they would *crunch between her teeth*—

She shuddered involuntarily. Nose loomed over Cloud. "You don't like our food?"

Cloud closed her eyes. "It's lovely," she said. "Thank you, my father's sisters."

The smell wasn't bad: humus, bark, and rotten wood,

mixed with a little insect muskiness, a little meatiness. Seal, she thought, would eat the grubs without hesitation. So would Otter, had he been offered them, or Glory, for that matter: not because they liked them, but because it was necessary.

"A spoon!" said Growl. "Of course! Our little niece is so refined now that she can't eat without a spoon!"

"Oh," said Cloud weakly, when Nose hastened to offer her one. "Thank you."

She decided the best course was not to look at the grubs, just to dig in her spoon and eat. There were no mats on the floor, so she sat on the dirt. They settled down to watch her. Even sitting, the bear women towered over her.

She tried swallowing grubs one by one, chewing briskly to stop the squirming. Their skin had a tendency to squeak. Legs had already erupted from one pupa and tickled the back of her throat; she gagged and nearly spewed that one out.

She tried shoveling in huge spoonfuls of grubs, in order to empty her bowl as quickly as possible.

She was sure she could feel them wriggling in her belly. When she burped, the acidic aftertaste reminded her all too clearly of the lumpy trip down.

While she struggled with the grubs, she was alarmed to see two large grizzlies lumber through the door. One lay down at Growl's feet. The other sat beside Nose, staring balefully at Cloud. They stank of rotten fish and rank fur.

At first Cloud thought these must be other residents of the house who would soon strip off their masks. But in the corner of her eye the bears had a flat, unchanging quality, like a portrait mask next to the person it represented. In fact, the bear next to Growl had exactly the same broad forehead and tiny eyes as she did, the same brown coarse hair.

These bears *were* masks. They must be the cast-off robes from the streamside. Strange how much a bear face looked like a fat, furry dog's. She hoped the masks had not harmed Seal.

The heap of grubs in her bowl did not shrink no matter

how many she scooped and swallowed. She looked once more at the grubs out of the corner of her eye, and then at the bowl itself. The bowl was a strange, vast thing, big as a lake. A spirit treasure. Her whole life she had wanted a bottomless bowl of food; at last she held one in her hands, and it contained *grubs*.

She set down the bowl. "You are very generous, my father's sisters, great rulers of the forests. Thank you for this meal, which is more bountiful than my mortal stomach can contain."

Nose made an odd sound like a stifled giggle. They were tormenting her on purpose. Why treat her this way? They were her *kin*!

Cloud longed for a drink to rinse away the residue of grubs from her mouth. In other houses she had visited, the host had served it. Here there was no bucket in sight, and Growl and Nose just sat in the dirt beside their bear shapes, watching.

At least they hadn't yet flown into a rage.

Cloud realized then what was so strange about the silence. She could not hear the ghosts at all.

"What happened to the ghosts?" she asked her aunts.

"Why worry now?" said Nose, leaning forward through the gloom. "Didn't you abandon them for years?"

The naked contempt in Nose's voice rekindled her anger. "I didn't abandon—"

Then Cloud stared at Nose. Nose hadn't recognized her, didn't remember Thrush, but knew about Cloud's dead brothers?

What sort of game were her aunts playing with her?

In the corner of her eye, shadows loomed where dirt walls had been. The door had shrunk to a distant speck of light. The bear women flickered darkly, immense as mountains.

"How nice to have a little niece about the place," sighed Growl. "Tell us, what happened to the rest of your litter? Are they all strong, handsome boys—have they all become great hunters like their uncles?"

Hunters? At first Cloud thought Growl was referring to Cloud's bear uncles. But no: she must mean *Thrush's* brothers, the great hunters whom Cloud's father had murdered. Her anger blazed hotter. She opened her mouth to protest.

Only—wait—hadn't Nose just accused her of abandoning her brothers' *ghosts?* What her aunts admitted to knowing about Cloud's life shifted wildly from one moment to the next; they were baiting her, or punishing her, or just being cruel.

"No, no, sister, you remember," said Nose, licking the red splotch where she had earlier chewed on her arm. "Her mother's lover killed them all. That's why she's carrying those little bones around with Brother's."

"I suppose she ran away when her brothers were killed," Growl said. "But I'm sure King Rumble took good care of *her* once he saw what a pretty thing she was! Just like her mother!"

Cloud knew she was snarling. If she had learned one thing, it was *to show respect in the houses of the immortals.* But she could not stop herself.

"No, no," said Nose, "she didn't even have a dolly to cry over. I told you, sister."

Growl feigned astonishment. "You mean her *mother* didn't take care of her, either? She dragged her babies away to be slaughtered, then abandoned her only surviving child to fuck the man who'd murdered the others?"

"That's not what happened!" Cloud shouted. "She didn't—she was forced—my mother *suffered*—"

"*We* fight to protect our children," said Nose grimly.

"And where's *your* baby?" said Growl. "Do you take after your mother *that* way, too?"

Scalding rage burst through Cloud's veins like lightning. Red light blinded her. She swelled in strength—

Cloud fought it down. She tried to breathe. She had to think like a human, not a bear.

"Now look what you've done, sister," said Growl. "Our niece has just arrived and already you've made her angry!"

"Not," said Nose, "as angry as she should be."

A silence followed so complete that Cloud could hear the tapping inside the box again. "No, no," said Growl, "we haven't made her very welcome! You came to ask for help, didn't you, little Hungry?"

No, she had not. But she did need help. Cloud struggled in vain to squeeze her rage down into her belly and tie the lid on it. At last she managed to say, "I need to take the bones to the fire beyond the world."

The ferocity of her anger made speaking feel as unnatural as embroidering with her toes. But she pushed onward:

"Maybe you know that something was done to their bones, and their ghosts—my father's and my brothers'— they were trapped—"

But the sisters had already lost interest. Growl picked up a discarded salmon head and sucked at the scraps of rotten flesh clinging to it. Nose scratched herself with filthy claws.

Foam, Cloud thought, had given her the very gifts she needed for her task. And who was Foam? A stranger encountered by chance. Growl and Nose were *her kin*. Cloud's burden was *their dead brother*.

Again she struggled to swallow her fury. "In the west," Cloud said, "there was a doorway out of the world. Is there a doorway in the east? I've looked and looked but I can't find the edge of the world. Can you tell me how?"

Growl spit out a bone and yawned. "Help yourself to our goods, little niece. This is your father's house. Everything in it is yours."

"If you can take it away with you," said Nose.

*Growl curled up on the refuse-strewn dirt. Her mask* sniffed at her face, then settled into its own doze.

"But—aunt, how do I find the doorway? Is there one?"

"Oh, there's a doorway," said Growl through another massive yawn. "But you might wish you'd stayed away from it."

And Growl fell asleep, or appeared to. Her mask snored.

JUDITH BERMAN

Nose's own bear scratched its ear with a hind leg. Nose began poking through its fur, no doubt chasing a flea. Cloud scratched her own legs. Bites already covered them.

Now the door out to sunlight had vanished altogether, trapping her. How was she going to get out of this house? It was so hard to *think* when her aunts kept making her so angry.

If Nose would only go to sleep, too, she could look for the door. Meanwhile—

Cloud stood, brushing off fish bones, and approached the boxes stacked along the wall. *Everything in them is yours.* She recalled the creatures scuttling in Foam's treasure boxes, the yellow-copper chests in the upper world. She had handled a few treasures of the immortals but was ignorant about the rest.

Around her the cave grew larger, more shadowed. *Everything in the house is yours. If you can take it away with you.*

Foam's harpoon had been a lifeline between worlds; Foam's canoe, a gift of orca speed. Could there possibly be anything in this filthy house that Cloud might want or need? And how, without her aunts' guidance, would she know what it was?

The boxes, like the house itself, kept shifting in her vision, receding, expanding. Most bore carvings or paintings of various forest creatures. One of the boxes opened its eyes to gaze at her. Another bared its teeth in a yawn—or perhaps that was a snarl. The box lids were not tied down.

Whatever she found in those boxes, Cloud thought, would be like the meal Nose had served her: unpleasant, better suited to bears than a mortal. Likely dangerous as well.

She glanced over her shoulder at Nose, who had extracted a flea from her mask and was crushing it between her front teeth. Blood from previous such efforts flecked her lips. Nose seemed engrossed in the task.

Fresh loathing filled Cloud. Why had she ever wished, deep in her heart, that her father's kin would welcome her?

She chose a box with a nicer painting than most, pulled it off the stack, and lifted the lid. In the dim firelight, the contents were nearly invisible. She leaned closer. Atop a heap of objects lay a kelp bottle. Except for its unnatural size—it was as big as two fists—it appeared ordinary enough: an almost spherical bull-kelp float and a short length of adjoining hollow stem. Cords tied both ends shut.

It buzzed when she picked it up. In the corner of her eye it looked much bigger than the space it actually took up, like the bowl of grubs, or the house, or Growl and Nose themselves. A bitter, unkelplike odor clung to it. Cloud gingerly worked the cord loose.

Black wasps poured out. They swarmed onto her face and body, stinging viciously. They crawled under her clothes and onto the bare skin of her breasts and belly and thighs. Crying out, she brushed at them, tried to shake them out, but they clung to her, chewing right into her flesh, burrowing down and down into her bones, setting them afire.

And then, at the height of her agony, a bear paw thrust out of the box. Cloud jerked back, but not before claws raked her cheek.

When the paw slid down into shadow again, the pain of the wasp stings vanished. The red welts on her skin also disappeared. But when she touched her smarting cheek, her hand came away bloody.

The box was not big enough for a bear to hide in. It had no scent of bear—only a musty smell, as if infrequently aired.

She yanked the cord tight, tossed the bottle into the box, and slammed the lid shut. What was wrong with her? She should have known better than to open an unknown spirit treasure, especially one from the bears' house. She *did* know better.

Nose was grinning as if amused by Cloud's mistake. That stirred Cloud to even greater anger. She hauled down another box and threw off the lid. This time she immediately stepped back, but when nothing moved inside the box, she edged closer. Within lay a folded robe, but it was not a bear's shaggy coat. This was sewn from luxurious black pelts glossier than sea-otter fur. The robe reminded her of Center-of-Heaven's beautiful hair. How she had loved to slip her fingers through it. How softly it fell against her cheek when he leaned to kiss her . . .

She reached out a hand to stroke the robe. She did not need another one. The sea-otter robe the orcas had given her had so far been adequate for the mountain nights.

This one was so beautiful, though. The perfume clinging to it was Center-of-Heaven's, the scent of their long nights together. In the corner of her eye its depths were endless. It made her warm as summer just to look at it, warmer still to touch it. How her skin longed for his. Its blackness reminded her of Black Fin as well: of his sleek hair, of his strong hand gripping her shoulder, of his fingertips brushing her neck.

Heat swept in waves across her skin. Cloud tried to pull her hands from the robe, but huge bear paws grabbed her roughly and dragged her toward the box.

She ripped loose, jumped back, and threw the lid on. The paws shoved upward, jostling the lid. To weight it down, she stacked other boxes on top. The paws thumped and scratched but could not push free.

Cloud tried to catch her breath. Her encounter with the robe had left her sweaty. She still wanted to touch it. Her reaction embarrassed and disgusted her.

Nose, biting on a flea, leered; of course she knew what lay in each box! Cloud snarled. But Nose just grinned more broadly.

In a fury Cloud yanked down another box. Her careless movement brought three or four tumbling off the stack at once: as they struck the ground, lids popped loose and the contents scattered across the floor. From one box spilled bear cubs, all furry ears and legs. She thought they were asleep until, her throat tightening, she recognized her dead brothers. And among them sprawled her own luminous baby.

Its tiny limbs were as stiff and motionless as her brothers', its blue eyes wide and unblinking.

Horror pierced her. And then, when one of the dead cubs collapsed like a puffball, and its dust rose up like smoke, she realized that *four* cubs had spilled from the box. That milky dust wrapped around her head to blind her—

—she was crying, running, the dogs and men rolled toward them like an avalanche, and here was one from home, huge and strong, and for a moment she hoped he would save them. But he roared in despairing rage, "She is mine!" and he smashed her with his paw, hurtling her into the air. It was all chaos after that, her brothers screaming, her mother screaming, sky and earth roaring and red with blood—

Cloud brushed and blew frantically at the dust to shake away the vision. But then her gaze was caught by a chest that lay tipped against another, only half-overturned. A mask hung from it. The mask was exquisitely carved, perhaps from maple wood, and painted with the sparest lines of red and black.

Cloud reached for it, working to free its ties from the splintered edge of the box so she could examine it more closely. At first, because of the snout and teeth, the lolling tongue and upright ears, she thought it must depict a wolf.

Then the mask sprouted shaggy fur. Its jaws yawned wide and heavy claws seized her, yanking her into the chest.

Blackness smothered her. She struggled against the grip of those claws, but they were her own hands. She tried to tear loose the shaggy paws and the fur that covered her, but she only slashed herself to the bone.

Other things lurked in the depths of that box. They buffeted her, groped her. Intense odors poured from them: salmon roasting inside her mother's house. Rotting scraps on the midden, the sharp wet stink of the dogs that drove her away. Wet ferns at dawn, rotting bark on a fallen tree, rain splashing on sun-heated rock; always and everywhere the pangs of hunger. Sweetgrass and mock-orange on Thrush's skin, mingled with the smell of Rumble's sweat.

The smell of her own bleeding flesh. The stink of blood and shit and fear on her still, silent brothers, and on Thrush, who cradled them, sobbing as if she would never stop.

The smells were more powerful than thought. They crushed the breath out of her. They *were* her: longing, loneliness, grief, and bitter, roiling rage.

The wasps inside her caught fire again. Red-hot wasps crawled along her bones, searing her flesh. Red flame swept through her, incandescent fire blinded her, she was a giant—

She burst out of darkness in a rain of shards. And there at the dirty hearth sat Nose, grinning as she bit another flea. Cloud leapt toward her with a roar. But Nose swelled, too. She and Nose met like two boulders crashing together in a landslide, jaws biting, claws ripping. Nose lost her balance and crashed onto the sleeping Growl, who rose up in a fury and slammed Cloud to the ground with a single paw—

Chest heaving, Cloud struggled, still too wild with rage to be frightened. Growl, sitting on her haunches like a dog, released Cloud to pull off her bear's head. It flopped down her back like a poorly secured hat.

"Well!" Growl said with that terrible grin like a snarl. "I see you found your mask, little niece."

**Cloud discovered she still held the wooden mask.** She sat up and threw it as far as she could. But as soon as it came to rest, it grew fur, sprouted legs, and trotted toward her.

Nose said, "We almost gave it away. You didn't seem to have any use for it."

"It kept setting out to search for you," Growl said. "But it couldn't find its way, not when you wouldn't call it. We've had to bring it back I don't know how many times."

"It's got your smell now," said Nose. "It won't lose you again."

"I hope you appreciate the trouble you've made for your aunties," said Growl.

Cloud buried her face in her hands. Her cheeks were wet

with tears she did not remember shedding. She couldn't look at anything, not her spirit mask, not her cruel, cruel aunts, and especially not the dead children scattered across the floor.

But she couldn't shut out the smells. Her brothers' blood. Her mother's sweet and milky breasts. Rumble's sweat.

The anger roared through Cloud again. Wasps burned in her bones. When her bear mask nosed at her, she moved to shove it away but instead found herself gripping the shaggy fur of its neck the way she sometimes held Seal.

"My *aunts,*" she spit out. "What trouble? You've done *nothing* for me! You let my brothers be killed. You would have let my own father kill me! And when my brothers were dead, and their ghosts bound, and I was alone in Sandspit Town, you still did nothing! You knew everything and you *abandoned* me!"

"Oh!" said Nose. "How could we know how much of our blood flows in your veins? Your mother was such a prissy little thing. I never understood what Brother saw in her."

"She was the wrong sort for a bear," said Growl. "We warned him from the start. She's the kind of woman who doesn't know her own belly, much less where her food goes after that."

"We're shy," said Nose. "Sweet-tempered, really—"

"No, not *sweet,*" Growl said.

"Speak for yourself, sister. What I'm trying to say is, we don't hurt anyone. Not unless you make us angry. Not unless you try to hurt our babies."

"You kill people!" Cloud said. "You eat them!"

"Oh, well," said Nose impatiently, "sometimes."

"My father kidnapped my mother!"

"She was very rude to him," Growl said. "I can't remember what she said now. It made him angry, and he brought her here to teach her a lesson."

"Oh, you remember," Nose said. "She complained about his shit. She stepped in it and said it was nasty."

"That's right," said Growl. "What a little prig!"

"His—she stepped in—?" Cloud didn't know whether to believe them. No one had ever told her what Thrush's misdeed had been. "You inflicted such a terrible punishment for—for *that?*"

"We're sweet-tempered," said Nose, "but we're sensitive. You have to treat us with respect."

"It's ridiculous!" Cloud shouted.

Said Growl, "*I* thought he should just kill her if he was so upset. But he was stupid enough to fall in love with her. He didn't treat her badly."

"He forced her to be his wife—"

"She didn't tell him no," said Growl.

"She didn't have a choice!"

"He was a bear," Nose said. "What do you expect?"

"If she had any belly," said Growl, "she didn't know where it was. She certainly didn't have the strength to leave this house on her own. The only way she got out was trickery. Brother thought she had eaten his food, but she never did."

"She'd have had more taste for him if she had," said Nose.

Cloud, remembering Center-of-Heaven and his sweet, sweet food, swelled in a fury of hatred—for them and for her own weak self. "She was just a mortal!" she yelled. "My mother couldn't have stood up to him! It's cruel and *ridiculous* to say she *brought it on herself* by complaining about some droppings. It's a despicable lie saying she wasn't treated badly, she would have liked it if she'd eaten his food, that she caused the death of her children because she tried to escape!"

"But that's all true," said Nose.

*"But it's not right!"*

"Well," said Growl, "if it's fairness you're looking for, you've come to the wrong house."

"You," Cloud said, "caused my brothers' deaths more than she did—by not stopping my father. By not stopping Rumble! My mother is mortal, but *you* have power. You could have helped *anytime!*"

"Did anyone ask us to?" said Growl. "Did you?"

That stopped Cloud. She never had. Had Thrush?

"If it's rescues you're looking for," said Nose, "don't expect much from bears."

A lump swelled in Cloud's throat. "Do you practice being unkind?" she asked. "Have you been trying, since I got here, to be as cruel as possible? You have, haven't you? Do you get pleasure from it?"

Nose whooped with laughter. "Poor thing, did you expect *bears* to coddle you? You'll have to go somewhere else for that."

"Sister, she did!" said Growl. "That lovely young man took her up to heaven."

"Oh, that's right," said Nose. "She liked *him,* didn't she?"

Growl sniggered. Cloud closed her eyes, ashamed of her tears. She shouldn't *want* her aunts to love her, should she?

If she wept, it would only cause them to ridicule her even more mercilessly.

And then she thought: since entering this house, she had hardly been able to think. Storms of emotion had tossed her this way and that—if not of rage, then of longing or self-pity.

Perhaps it was the house. Perhaps it was them. Perhaps it was the nearness of her bear mask. They had tried very hard, had they not, to push her toward it?

"He gave me what I wanted," said Cloud, opening her eyes, unable to stop her tears. "What I thought I wanted."

"Do you *know* what you want?" Nose asked.

What she wanted was for them to stop giving her more reasons to be angry.

But beyond anger and hurt, a thought was stirring. *Not strong enough to leave on her own.*

Had Thrush been imprisoned here by something like the longings that had trapped Cloud in the upper world?

Maybe the country of the immortals was like tree sap for ants, a sticky place where your feet got tangled in your own passions, your own weaknesses. If you got stuck, the immortals would use you as their natures dictated.

Or maybe the unmasked world was just a hard thing to look at. You made a mask to cover it out of what was in your own mind. Or maybe the mask was for your own face. It was the kind without holes for eyes, where the wearer has to dance blind.

What had Winter told her, long ago? *What Thrush saw of your father might have been more her own thoughts than his true face.*

*She was a captive!* Cloud had yelled at Winter. And Winter had answered, *A captive of what? In the end she just walked away while your father was sleeping.*

Cloud had been trapped in Huntress's house and by Center-of-Heaven; she had barely escaped the underworld and perhaps the wolves' dance house as well. She had been blinded by her fear of strength, by terror of her father, by longing for Otter, by her desperate wish to crawl into some other girl's flesh, some other story. Among the orcas, though, her feet had become tangled but not stuck, and she had mastered her weaknesses just enough. *The first rule is respect.*

*Anything in this house is yours, if you can take it away with you.*

Until she stopped being angry long enough to think, she was as trapped as Thrush had been.

Growl and Nose watched her expectantly. They had as much as admitted they were testing her. What were they, really, beyond the mask of her fear and longing? Rough, powerful, merciless—yes. Vicious? Unkind?

Cloud sighed and rubbed the tears from her face. "I suppose I've done this all badly," she said. "I'm not very good at thinking. At thinking first, anyway."

Nose scratched herself. Neither of them spoke.

"Maybe I got that from my father. Or Thrush. I suppose it doesn't matter. I know it's late, but there's something I should have said first thing." And with Glory's prayer at last clear and whole in her mind, Cloud said to them: "Oh noble ones, divine ones, I am glad that we met today. Grant me good luck, remove all evil from my path, great queens of the mountains."

Growl stirred. "That was nice, don't you think, Nose?"

"She said it by rote," said Nose. "It wasn't heartfelt."

Cloud took another deep breath. "It's true I thought you could have made my life more fair. You could have changed the bad things. You have so much power. When my mother ran away—"

She had to walk so carefully through the forest of her emotions. Anger and regret lay everywhere in ambush. She had to think, think—

"It was winter," said Growl, "if you really want to know. We're very sleepy in wintertime. And we had a slave who helped her. I knew she didn't have the strength to escape on her own, so I was careless—"

"Don't help her!" Nose said, indignant.

"Well, never mind that," said Cloud, though it was in fact exceedingly hard to let the subject alone. "It's the bones I wanted to talk about. My father's power has caused so much evil in the mortal world. I partly understand why it's up to me to stop it—even if someone else *could* take the bones, it wouldn't free *me* of them. I just don't understand why—so you don't care about mortals, you don't care about me, but don't you care about my father? He's your brother. Your king."

Cloud had to stop herself; she was becoming impassioned again, forgetting where she needed to go.

"We couldn't get to the island," said Growl. "Not with Huntress watching. We couldn't swim *that* channel anyway. And we're not wolves. You have to be a wizard to go through the underworld and come out alive. And how were we supposed to—"

"Growl!" Nose complained again. Growl closed her mouth.

Cloud pondered Growl's speech. "But since I got to the mainland, you've been no help either. So should I believe you? Or—are you angry at *him* for being so stupid? Is that it?"

This time, they both stared at her in silence.

"It's true I didn't ask for help before," said Cloud, rubbing her face again. This was enormously hard work. "And I shouldn't expect you to be kind just for the sake of it. You're Winter People. I'll take the bones the rest of the way. If that's my burden, then I'll do it, whether it's fair or not. But now that I am here—regardless of what you did or didn't do in the past, and why, I just want to ask for your help in one thing. If you could just tell me the way? Please."

They looked at each other. "Was that good enough?" Growl asked Nose.

"It was adequate," said Nose.

Growl dropped the rancid fish head she had been holding, slid all the way out of her bear skin, and stood up, a wavering, terrifying immensity. The walls spun away into limitless space.

"See, little niece," she said, "it wouldn't have done any good for us to be kind or generous before, and it doesn't now. If you had what it took to return here, you'd come back. If you have what it takes to leave the house, you'll go."

Nose's form also shivered and loomed huge. "As far as what happened in the past goes," Nose said, and her rough voice had turned somber, "we *would* have stopped it if we could. But all those things did happen, and once the darkness gets into your flesh, no one can rescue you from it. The best your blue-eyed lover could do was make you forget. Maybe the salmon can go on overflowing with love and kindness, but we're not like that, we bears. It's in our bones forever.

"But there's one thing you should understand, little Hungry. No, Brother's power doesn't belong in King Rumble's belly. But don't turn up your nose at your inheritance. Without our power, *all* you would have is the darkness in your bones. Our power is to change that darkness into something else: say, loss into grief, or wishing into passion, or fear into courage, or pain into rage. You may not like what you are, but the world needs our power as much as it needs love."

There was another long silence. They were falling, falling,

through slow, spinning, shadowy vastness without ever coming to rest.

Then the bear women seemed to become smaller and more ordinary. Growl said, "We really *can't* do anything for you beyond giving your mask back. You just have to finish the trip."

Cloud realized she was clutching her bear mask by its fur and let go. "But which way? Where?"

"Where do the salmon go?" said Growl.

"Upstream," said Cloud. "To the Headwaters Women." And then, sighing, "Is it a long trip?"

"What's long?" said Growl.

**Cloud looked around the house.** All that remained of the mess she had made were a few overturned and empty boxes. She felt obliged to restack them. When she was done, she turned toward the shadows where the door of the cave had been before.

She glanced back: Growl and Nose watched her.

Her bear mask lifted its nose and sniffed. Cloud sniffed, too, and found, beneath the smells of dirt, smoke, bear scat, and rotting fish, the scent of pines baking in the sun. She closed her eyes and followed it, got down on her hands and knees when the cave roof lowered. And then she was crawling through grass into the long golden rays of afternoon.

Growl and Nose followed Cloud out of the house. There waited the ghosts. "She is mine," Cloud's father raged.

"Brother, you are so tiresome," said Growl to him. Cloud had to agree; it was tiresome being angry all the time. "You stay here. And you, little ones," Growl said to the weeping children, "we'll take away your loneliness soon."

To Cloud she said, "We'll walk with you up the valley and find some dinner. Go on, get your pack and your slave."

"He's not my slave," said Cloud, but she said it mildly. She knew Growl was baiting her.

She hoisted her pack and tied on Seal's again, and then sent Seal ahead because the proximity of the bears upset him so. They walked upstream through the pines where Cloud had played with her brothers, past shallow pools where dying salmon floated. Eventually they came to a steep meadow carpeted with blueberries. There she and her aunts ate in the warm, declining sun: lean salmon carcasses, sweet blueberries, crunchy roots. Growl showed Cloud how to sniff out and dig for lily, sweetvetch, and fireweed. "What did you think your claws were for?" she asked Cloud. Nose, with a sly smile, offered Cloud a handful of grubs. To be polite she ate another handful.

The sun went down. Owls hooted in the pine forest. The crags above them still glowed with the rosy light of dawn. The answer, Cloud realized, had been in her memory all this time.

They slept under the stars and the reflected rosy light. In the morning, the ghosts had returned and her aunts had gone, leaving only bear tracks on the stream bank. Cloud's own mask slumbered beside her.

"Well," she said to Seal, "let's go."

# NINETEEN

# The Last Mountain

*She and Seal walked all that day through the forest,* following the creek, following the salmon. The living salmon were few and far between now, and their skin was dull and peeling. Stinking carcasses littered the shallows.

The long-needled pines gave way to Douglas firs and then scrawnier firs and pines. Above them hung the summits of the last mountains, ice and sheer rock reddened by endless dawn. The masks of the world were very loose here: faces peered out of stone, trees stalked beside her. Wild spirits glinted over the water. The smell of the edge of the world, a warm tingling that slid through the air like sunlight, floated everywhere.

Her bear mask accompanied her, splashing through the creek, nosing at salmon carcasses. Seal soon grew less wary, until he trotted in front of it or behind it as if it were just another Cloud, and in the soft mud of the bank their three sets of footprints twined around each other like strands of a rope.

Cloud tried to maintain her distance for longer. But the bear kept nosing her hand or leg, or when they stopped, it

would lean against her body, unbalancing her. And echoes of
its senses kept spilling into hers: the smell of wet gravel, or
wild roses, or pinecone fragments where a chipmunk had
gathered seeds. She resisted those echoes, but it was difficult
not to be seduced by its nose, so much more sensitive than
her own. And as the day progressed, the echoes strengthened until they became a tributary of her own senses.

And then the bear thrust its nose deep among mock-
orange flowers, and Cloud was pierced with unbearably sharp
longing for Thrush, whom she would never see again. The
nose *became* her own. She stood on four clawed feet. A flea was
biting her shoulder. The pack of bones slid from her back.

Terror and panic surged in her. She, Cloud, was smother-
ing inside the bear skin, trapped in crushing darkness.

But she knew what the darkness was now: her bear's
heart. *The inside and the outside of the box fought a war,* Raven
Tongue had riddled, a war neither could win. She did not
want to touch her bear self—but it was the other side of her
human skin, and she could not rid herself of it.

And, as if she had always known how to do it, she folded
her bear self inside her, turning herself inside out like a
dress, and she stood again on two legs, once more lifting her
pack onto her scabbed shoulders. A fur robe fell to the
ground and climbed to its feet, a bear.

That night, by the light of their small campfire, she studied her bear mask. It was smaller than Growl's or Nose's. Its
fur was darker, finer, more like Cloud's own hair, or
Thrush's. She was beginning to feel its flea bites in addition
to her own. She wondered whether she could remove the
fleas with aged urine, the way you washed blankets.

No: she was thinking like someone who lived in a mortal
town, where such cleanliness was possible. She could never
return to a place like that. Bears and humans did not mix.

The night smelled of dew and firs. Crickets sang beside
the rushing creek, their noise almost loud enough to drown
out the ghosts. This would not be a bad place to live, she
thought, except for the intolerable loneliness.

They had finally climbed above the last salmon. Over the course of the next day the creek became ever more steep and rocky. The valley narrowed until its walls met in front of them. Then they had to scale that wall, crawling up sheer water-slicked expanses of stone to a saddle between the peaks. The wavering distortions in her vision made footing even more uncertain. But Seal bounded upward, and the bear followed, as agile as a mountain goat. Cloud knew she would do better wearing her mask, but the bear could not carry the pack.

As they ascended ever higher, the air thinned until she was panting and dizzy. The sky over their heads deepened to the rich blue of a mussel shell.

They crossed a steep meadow. The creek, spilling through grass and blue lupines, had shrunk to a rivulet a few feet wide and only ankle-deep. She and Seal drank from it. The water was cold enough to hurt her skull.

She caught sight of her reflection: a strange wild creature wearing a filthy dress and a pack of bones. The ghosts peered over her shoulders.

Perhaps her aunts had lied. She would climb higher and higher on this mountain until she could touch the slick underside of the sky, and still she would not reach the door.

She splashed water on her face. Then the bear's more sensitive nose caught a new scent. Cloud glanced up. A girl just a little older than she stood on a boulder in the creek.

The girl wore a beautiful doeskin dress embroidered with dyed quills. Her glossy black hair fell to her waist. Seal had climbed up beside her, and she stroked his head.

"Did you come to see me, too?" the girl asked.

Cloud forced her weary body to stand. She could not think of anything polite to say to this girl, who was obviously an immortal. She was jealous of the way Seal licked the girl's slender hand. Finally she said, "Thank you for letting me walk through your country, Lady. I'm searching for the door of the world. I have to put these bones into the fire beyond, but I don't know where to find it." She remembered to add, "My name is Cloud. Or Hungry."

The girl nodded. "My house is nearby. I can show you after we eat."

Cloud had met enough immortals to be wary of their hospitality. Still, she turned her sore feet to follow the girl. Perhaps it was because of how sweetly this girl smelled: of lupines and warm grass, of cold water in the shadow of snow.

The immortal led her through a stand of dwarfed firs, and up a last slope of wildflowers. There, beside a snowfield, sat a small wooden hut. Cloud stepped over the threshold of the hut, shed her pack, and sat down, bone-weary, on the stone beside the girl's simple hearth. The bear settled beside her.

**"My name is Lupines-by-the-Snow," the girl said,** "and these are my sisters."

A handful—a dozen?—other girls sat around in the house, embroidering little girls' dresses. They were all very like Lupines-by-the-Snow in appearance, although Cloud's bear's nose told her that each had her own smell: this one of fir needles and moss, this one of lichen-covered granite, this one of warm, slushy snow turned pink with sun-bloom.

"There are too many of them to name." Lupine laughed. "You couldn't remember." Lupine's sisters smiled at Cloud, who wished she had combed her hair and cleaned her face that morning.

The sisters put down their embroidery and brought Cloud fresh blueberries, barbecued salmon, and sweet, slow-roasted lupine roots. Thanking them as best she knew how, Cloud inspected the meal, then swiftly consumed it. Her bear sniffed some of the little dresses. They smelled not of deerskin or quills but of water: water on stone, water in darkness, water seeping through sedge. Like the sisters, each had its own scent.

Cloud belatedly realized that Seal had not followed her inside. She went to the door. When she looked out, she did not see the mountainside and the grove of little firs, but rather a rocky pool in an alder wood. Seal was nowhere in evidence.

Cloud glanced behind her. The house was now much larger and finer than had been her impression when she entered, and a door opened in each wall. Thinking that perhaps she had picked the wrong side of the house, she crossed to another door. But through that opening she found a long, narrow lake, with snow-topped mountains reflecting on its surface.

Outside another door, a thin stream of water plummeted from the threshold, splashing on rocks far below.

She had thought the house was square, but in fact it had many sides, more than she could count. Cloud moved from door to door. Each showed a different view and none showed her Seal, or the way she had entered. In the corner of her eye, doorways overlapped in layers; they separated and wavered and shifted like the leaves of a tree stirred by wind.

"Lady," she said to Lupine, then realized that she was speaking instead to one of the sisters. Surely there were a hundred of them now, and among them twice as many girl children of every age. They looked so much alike she could not find her original host. The house had grown bigger than King Swimming's.

But her bear nose easily sniffed out the girl who smelled like cold clay and warm lupines. The bear shambled over to her, and she scratched behind its ears, smiling. Cloud felt the immortal girl's fingers on her own head.

"Lady," Cloud said to Lupine, "I came with a friend, but I don't see him here."

"Oh, I thought he should stay outside," said Lupine. "We fed him out there."

Cloud could only hope they wouldn't hurt Seal.

The noisy ghosts *had* followed her into the house and clustered near the pack of bones. When she turned toward them, the house had changed again: a red fire still burned on the hearth, but instead of ashes, water gathered beneath the slow-burning fir branches. It spilled across the floor, trickled across the stone threshold, flowed out of the house—

—spilled in all directions toward each of those doors, flowing outward into pools and lakes and swamps.

"Lady," Cloud said to Lupine, blinking, as the house shimmered and wavered and doors multiplied, "where am I? I mean, what is this house?" She hoped this wasn't a rude question.

But Lupine smiled at Cloud. "We're the guardians of the headwaters. Isn't this where you asked to go?"

*These* were the Headwaters Women, daughters of Wily One and his mysterious wife? Cloud shivered. "Is this where the eastern door is?" she asked. "The door into the, the fire?"

Lupine nodded slowly, still smiling that warm smile. "Would you like more to eat first?" she asked.

Cloud thanked her again and sat down at the hearth while Lupine refilled her bowl. She wished as always that the ghosts would take their noise elsewhere. She needed to think. She wanted to distrust Lupine and her sisters, but it was so much easier to love them. She could see why the salmon came here.

She longed to bask in their kindness. They had taken her in as if there were nothing more welcome in their house than a dirty, flea-bitten, half-starved mortal girl.

But hard as it was to find the houses of the immortals, it was almost always harder to leave. While Lupine's sisters stacked wood on the fire, Cloud examined the house.

That was difficult. It wavered and shimmered. Doors and walls multiplied like leaves, like salmon entering a river. The one still point, the hearth, was as immense as the world.

One hearth, many doors, many houses. The salmon climbed the rivers to visit the Headwaters Women. One house for every river and creek, one sister for every house. Ten times ten thousand creeks, ten times ten thousand doors. And here, the center of each house, the one spring that fed them all.

Cloud knew where the water in the spring *went*: down

through the Mountain Land to the sea, and eventually out the western door of the world. But where did it come from?

If the house was like her mask, the fire inside it, at the center, might also lie on the outside—outside the world entirely. This very hearth, where fire became water, would then be the eastern doorway she had been searching for.

With that realization, Cloud felt such lightness in her body that she seemed to float. In Sandspit Town, you could burn salmon bones in the fire; here, at the headwaters of the world, she could set her burden on the hearth, and all the bones and knots and ghosts and grief would be immolated together. She would at last be free.

"Lady," Cloud said to Lupine, who set down her embroidery. "Is this the door here? Is this where I should put the bones?"

"It's the doorway, friend Cloud," said Lupine.

Cloud waited for Lupine to say more, but the girl merely looked at her, as if waiting. So Cloud, near-delirious with relief, lifted her pack, and stepped up to the fire.

"Will the ghosts follow?" she asked Lupine. "Or do I have to send them through somehow?"

"The ghosts will follow the bones," Lupine said.

Cloud dropped the pack of bones on the fire. Wood and embers scattered. A tongue or two of flame licked at the pack but the basket fibers did not catch. The fire flickered and died back, and the water trickling from it stopped.

With an exclamation, another of the sisters rushed over. "Take them off, please!" she said. She and several other girls began gathering up the scattered, half-burned branches.

"But . . ." Embarrassed, Cloud lifted her pack. "What—"

"It's the doorway," said Lupine. "But you have to take them *through*."

The house changed again. The trickle from the hearth had become a clear, cold stream and Cloud stood shin-deep in it. Around her swam salmon, gray and scabrous, or mere skeletons with clinging bits of skin. The bones of the dead salmon scraped her ankles as they rushed by.

They swam toward one of the doorways of the house and into a rosy light so bright that Cloud had to slit her eyes. Holding her pack awkwardly, she waded to that threshold and peered out.

She stood atop a precipice that sank dizzyingly to a sea of turbulent red light. The fire spread out forever with no horizon; it bent away upward or poured away downward, or both at once. More cliffs rose above her, sheer red-lit crags touching the sky. At Cloud's feet, the creek with the dead and dying salmon poured over the brink, vanishing into a cloud of spray. The salmon would swim through that fire, Cloud knew, and into the rainbowed sea at the opposite end of the world.

The warm tingling smell of it soothed her, but its brightness scalded her eyes. She turned her face away as she inched forward. Extending her arms, leaning out cautiously from the precipice, she released the bones.

They stuck to her hands. They pulled her forward like a sack of stones. With all her strength she threw herself back from the edge, onto the threshold, and then, scrambling, dragged the pack into the house.

There she crouched, shaking. The ghosts milled, weeping or silent. Cloud's bear mask stood by the door as if it had been ready to jump over the precipice after her. She hugged the bear as if it were the only solid ground in the house and she were still tipping into that abyss of fire.

The headwaters girls regarded Cloud serenely. For all their kindness, they weren't going to help her. They would just watch her make mistakes. Anger kindled in her.

"How do I drop it?" she asked Lupine.

Lupine shook her head. "If they weren't bound, they could take themselves."

"Bound—you mean the box in my father's skull."

"No," said Lupine, "that's only part of the knot that ties them here, inside the world."

And then she said something that Cloud did not expect:

"You are part of the knot, too. But you know that, friend Cloud, or you could not have come this far."

Cloud gripped the bear as panic rose up in her. "Putting them into the fire was supposed to destroy the knot."

"Oh, it will, my friend. I'm sure of it."

"Nobody," Cloud said furiously, "told me I would have to jump into the fire with them! Because that means I have to die, doesn't it? That means I have to jump over your cliff and *die*!"

Her anger blazed up, red and scorching. And she was a giant with fire in her bones. Hungry roared, scattering them, as she galloped toward another doorway—

And pulled up at the brink of a fiery abyss.

Jumped backward: another doorway—

Red brilliance speared her eyes. The fire spread out forever. Hungry roared again.

Every doorway blazed with the fire. The house itself burned light. Hungry circled and circled through the brightness. The house was vast as the world, every door different, every door overlooking the sea of dawn.

"There are many ways here from the world," said Lupine, red fire shining in her hair, "but there's only one door out."

Raging, Hungry reared up to seize the girl, to savage her. But that smell—

Cold clay in the shadow of snow. Lupines in the grass. Water trickling over stone.

—filled Cloud with sadness. When she died, she would lose the smell forever. She had left behind everything else she loved, and now she would lose this last thing, the meadow on the mountainside.

"No one told me I would have to die," Cloud whispered, tears sliding down her face. She hugged her bear mask as if it were the only thing keeping her alive.

Though it was not quite true no one had told her. Growl had said, *You might wish you'd stayed away from that doorway.*

This house was where the salmon came to die. Lupine had asked her, "Did you come to see me, too?"—like the salmon, except that Cloud was a mortal and did not know how to swim through the fire to the sea of life in the west.

The red light filled the house. The dead salmon swam to the brink and slid over. Her brothers wept and her father raged.

"Why do I have to die for *them*?" she whispered. None of the sisters answered. Perhaps there was pity on their beautiful, implacable faces.

**The house changed again, as when a fire that has** flared shrinks down. The light that had blazed through myriad doors burned on a simple hearth once more. Through those doors Cloud could once more see forests and lakes, cliffs and streams, but she did not doubt that the house would turn inside out again if she tried to cross any of the thresholds.

She sat down by the hearth. The bear lay down next to her and rested its head on her lap. She wanted to push it away, but it, too, was part of the world she must leave. She smoothed its dark fur.

The sisters picked up their sewing again. "Lady," she said to Lupine, "when—when my father returns to life, will he be released from his anger? Will he come after my mother again?"

Lupine smiled her warm smile. "He'll be born as a baby. After that—who can know?"

"And my brothers? Will they be reborn as bears or humans?"

"I don't know," Lupine said.

Cloud sat there for a long time after that, eyes closed, hugging her bear mask and smelling through its nose: the bones in her pack, still faintly musty and mossy even after months away from the glade. Traces of salmon and blueberries in the bowl she had eaten from. Bear fur and her own not-so-clean human body. The headwaters girls, who had all the smells of forest and mountain: fir and skunk cabbage, horsetail and sedge, cottonwood and yarrow, water and mud and stone.

She felt dry and light. She felt infinitely heavy, weighted

with hot and bitter grief. She did not know how she could possibly swallow this fate; her anger was so immense that she would never reach the end of it. And yet there was no place to go but onward. She could not change the tragedies and violence that had made her, and had knotted her fate together with these hated bones. She could not change the fact that even though Thrush should be here in her place, saving her dead children, her mother had abandoned her, and them, long ago. She could not change the fact that she had done no better with her own child. *Once the darkness gets into your flesh, you can never get it out. That's what we bears are made of.* The only way to rid herself of bones and ghosts was to burn up with them.

With his last breath Otter had tried to say, *You must go on.*

Cloud remembered those moments in the Land of Wealth when she had imagined herself a girl from a story, a mortal who through whatever turn of fortune had won the grace and the gifts of the First People.

This moment wasn't part of any story she had ever heard. In the stories, you returned home triumphant from your harrowing in the lands of the immortals, and you displayed the tokens of your suffering and your victory: spirit treasures, new powers, new names, a new self. You were received with joy and awe.

In her own case, whatever she had been given she had lost. None of her names fit her, and the only one that was comfortable was the one she had started with—though she was not, now, Glory's Cloud, incandescent summer white; nor the Cloud she had lived with for so long, insubstantial mist; but a solid and real Cloud of darkness, rain, and winter cold, her bear's heart filling the hollow she had begun with.

Her story would not end with her return home. She would never return home, not as herself, anyway. Whomever she became in rebirth would not know the smell of Lupines-by-the-Snow. Would not possess Cloud's longing to see Thrush again, the mother who had abandoned her to fighting over garbage with dogs. That reborn girl would have some other mother, who would love her or not. She would live in some other town that would honor her or not. She would have some other name. It would be some other life. Not her own.

She couldn't even say goodbye to Seal. She could not have a last moment of silence free of the ghosts.

Cloud knew now that the First People suffered, but they would never suffer as much as mortals, who had to feel all the pain and say goodbye to the pain and the goodness as well, goodbye forever. Goodbye to sun-sweetened blueberries, goodbye to fresh-cut fir branches. Goodbye to the person who had to say these goodbyes.

Cloud curled up, face buried in bear fur, and awoke sometime later with a flea biting her cheek. The house was dark and still and cold. It had turned back into that first small weathered hut she had seen. The house seemed empty now, except for Cloud's own things, the ghosts, and the fire on the hearth. Lupine was nowhere in sight, but her smell filled the hut.

Cloud washed her face and hands in the stream flowing across the stone floor. She combed her hair. She examined the pack and the bag inside it to make sure no holes had opened and bones escaped, and that Bone's cedar box still sat inside her father's skull. There was nothing to do after that. She wouldn't have minded another meal—her stomach was complaining again—but she didn't want to wait until Lupine returned.

So, alone, she hauled the pack to the hut's single doorway and looked out from the high shoulder of the last mountain. Overhead, the sky glowed a deep translucent indigo. A few stars glittered in its depths. To the northwest and southwest, other mountains lay in shadow.

But the crags above her glowed in eternal dawn, and at her feet, at the bottom of a thousand-foot precipice, burned the vast and restless sea of light.

Cloud could never be like the salmon, walking joyous

and proud to the sacrifice. She could only be true to her rough, awkward nature, to the darkness inside her flesh. She did what she did reluctantly, angrily, because there was no other choice.

"Save us," said her child-brothers, and to them she said, "Yes, we'll go now." "You are mine forever," said her father, and to him she said, "Now we'll both be free."

She dragged the pack over the threshold, pulled out one of her father's shoulder bones, and tried to throw it into the gulf. It stuck to her hand as if pitch glued it there. She tried a pair of rib bones, then one of her brothers' skulls. None would leave her hand. She had not expected otherwise.

Cloud glanced behind her: the house itself had disappeared, leaving only the foothold she stood on, a narrow ledge on a sheer rock face. The cliff reached as far as she could see, from north to south, descending from sky to the sea of fire. She was outside the world with no way back in.

It wasn't fair that she had to do this. But what about her life had been fair?

Her life-to-be was unknown and beyond her control. All she could do was fall into the light.

So, before she could hesitate any longer, she lifted the pack and jumped.

She fell.

Past dark cliffs, into unendurable brightness. The bones caught fire and evanesced like smoke. Her arms that held them melted to bright rosy translucence—

—and still she fell.

Light crashed over her like a storm sea, shattered her into ten thousand roiling, dancing, incandescent motes. And then, still tumbling and toppling through the endless abyss, each of those motes exploded like lightning.

"You will never be free of me," he said, and for an instant he stood before her, a shadow in brightness, the terrible king of rage and passion.

And then brightness tore him apart, too.

\* \* \*

*After the brightness came warm, still night.* It rocked slowly, like the sea. Then she was pushed through a tight place into a different, gentler light. Faces sang to her. Arms held her. Warm milk trickled into her mouth.

Cold water washed her. Now she stood on two feet, or sometimes four. They were always kind, those faces, and she loved to burrow into their warmth.

She played with other children, running, laughing. More cold water. Now she knew words, names, the taste of blueberries and lupine roots. The smell of frozen fir branches melting by the fire. The women wiped her nose and combed her hair.

Another bath in that cold water that poured out of the hearth. Now she was as tall as they were.

With the fourth bath, she remembered her names. Hungry. Pearlshell. Cloud. She remembered where she was and how she had come there.

*"You let me pass through unchanged,"* Cloud said.

Lupine smiled. "Are you unchanged?"

Cloud said somberly to the immortal who had nursed her, washed her, and combed her hair, "I don't know."

"It's only the salmon who come here to die," Lupine said. "Everyone else comes *into* the world through our house. In the ordinary course of things you would have died and gone west before you came here, but that's not what happened, is it?"

"You could have told me," said Cloud. The old anger stirred.

Lupine shook her head. "You're only half a mortal. We couldn't know how you would return to us. Don't think we own or understand the sea the world swims in. I am glad, though, to have birthed you back into the world. I've always been fond of your kind, you know, your father's kind. They come to my meadow in spring. Now I've had a bear child of my own."

Lupine hugged and released her. "Thank you," said Cloud,

a lump swelling in her throat. "For—I don't have the words—"

"Goodbye," said Lupine, wiping tears from Cloud's cheek. "You may always use my name, if you like, to remember me by."

Cloud did not want to leave, but she could not stay in that house, either, as shifting and multifarious as it was. She picked up her bear robe and other possessions and, with a backward glance at Lupine, walked out the door.

Outside, snow lay deep on the mountainside. Cloud followed trodden snow through the grove of firs. On the far side waited—

"Seal!" Relief flooding through her, Cloud ran to him. For the first time since Otter's death, he looked clean and well fed. "They took good care of you, then."

He wagged his tail, smiling a dog's smile. It made her wonder—

"Seal," she said, "you're the best friend I've ever had—"

He wagged his tail and licked her hand.

"—but I want you to be happy. You don't have to come with me. You're not my slave."

He glanced back through the trees and then trotted ahead.

She followed him, heading down the mountain.

*Cloud's slow match had burned out. She had no* food. She did not know where to go, except down from these cold heights. After a while, she put on her bear robe, now clean of fleas. She and Seal traveled quicker on four feet.

That night they slept in the snow, cold and hungry. The next day Seal found a stillborn elk calf and they exhausted themselves gnawing at the frozen meat. With her adze, Cloud hacked off the legs and strapped them to Seal's pack.

Again she traveled on four feet. They stopped outside the bear house. The meadow lay under a trackless blanket of snow. She did not want to disturb her sleeping aunts, had nothing to say to them, nor did she want anything inside. And Seal couldn't stay there. It wasn't her home any more than Lupine's house. Perhaps she would visit again—someday.

They continued down the creek, down the small river it emptied into. The snow was melting at lower elevations. In a soggy meadow, Cloud dug sweetvetch roots with her bear claws, offering some to Seal. He chewed one halfheartedly.

They had traveled east across valleys and over mountain passes; now they followed the watercourses. The water took them down. As the days passed, the river joined a bigger river filled with jostling ice. The mountains rose ever higher over their heads. The forest grew wetter and mossier, and the weather turned rainy. One day Cloud smelled salt, and a wave of homesickness coursed through her. Soon they reached the ocean. Beside a row of collapsing, long-abandoned smokehouses, Cloud dug clams for the two of them.

She hadn't intended to return to mortal lands, but she hadn't yet found a place to stay.

The coastline was unfamiliar. That night she sent out her spirit and found they were only a few miles north of the narrow fiord where Waterfall had been built. Cloud resolved to travel there, thinking that she might live for a while in one of the empty houses, or at least scavenge something useful from them. The next day they set out over the cliffs.

Then, among the driftwood piled up at the head of the fiord, she found a battered little canoe.

She hauled it to the water. It leaked. As the hull soaked up water, though, the cracks swelled shut and it leaked less. Nearby she found a weathered but usable paddle. She fashioned a bailer from a scrap of bark, and the next morning she and Seal climbed aboard the canoe and headed down the inlet to Waterfall.

At the fort's landing, the ropes had been cut and the log stairs thrown down. She and Seal struggled up the cliff to the palisade, disturbing a family of nesting eagles. A petrel watched her from a rooftop. She poked through the houses, but they had been more thoroughly cleaned out than at Whale Town.

The abandoned town filled her with sadness. She returned to her canoe and headed south along the steep-sided bay, aimless and hungry. She clung to the shore, in part because she had no confidence in the canoe, in part because if any warriors still patrolled the bay, they would spot her more easily on open water.

That evening Cloud sat on the rocks with Seal, staring out at the empty bay, longing for fire and the sight of a human face. For the first time since her rebirth, she sang the song Raven Tongue had taught her. He did not come. That night, she couldn't help herself: she flew to Sandspit Town.

At least this town had not been burned or abandoned. Smoke clung gently to rooftops. Firelight shone through smoke vents, and canoes lay drawn up like so many giant wooden fish. Cloud yearned to sit at one of the hearths and listen to people talk. Thinking of Thrush, she drifted toward Storm House, but a white-haired dog sat in its doorway.

A spirit servant. Bone's dog had returned to him. She fled into the darkness, hoping the dog hadn't seen her.

The next morning, as weary as if stones weighted her down, she again tried to call Raven Tongue, again without success.

She kept heading south, in the direction of Sandspit Town. She knew she should resist the temptation. She was a bear and should avoid humans, and she certainly could not fight Bone without spirits of her own.

Her shore-hugging route necessarily took the canoe past Huntress's island. "I am so glad," she said to Seal, "that we don't ever have to go there again." She resolved to paddle along its beaches without even looking at it.

But no sooner had she made that resolution than she spotted smoke rising from the tip of the island. She stayed on course, uncertain. Could a human being have set that fire? If so, from what town—Waterfall, the Gull Islands, Round Bay or Sandspit Town, some town unknown to her? If she tried to round the point in daylight, they could not fail to see her.

The fire drew her. She might, she thought, be able to steal a coal or two, at night while they slept.

She landed the canoe behind a headland. After asking Seal to stay behind, she set out along the beach—on two feet, thinking hunters might shoot if they saw a bear.

When she had nearly reached the source of the smoke, Cloud got down and crawled until she could peer over a last hump of rock. On the beach, a man was burning a log. The boxes from Glory lay open nearby, and to add to her shock, Seal had sneaked past her to sniff at the stranger. He turned to look at Seal—

"Otter!" Cloud cried out, and she was running across the beach. His mouth opened in surprise. She flung her arms around him. "Uncle, how did you *get* here?"

# TWENTY

# Hungry

*"Cloud?" Otter said. "What are you doing here?"*

"I stopped to see who it was."

He gripped her shoulders and pulled back to look at her. His body bore no scars from his sojourn in Huntress's house. There was no sign that a giant bird had split open the top of his skull and scooped out the contents. Cloud wiped away her tears and looked carefully to make sure he was not some awful spirit-thing. But he remained Otter in all parts of her vision. He even wore his string of amulets—except for the one she had found and kept. He really seemed to have returned from the dead.

He hadn't returned unchanged, though. Lines scored the corners of his mouth, and gray threads glinted in his hair. In his face she saw the quiet steadiness that she had loved, the reserve that kept her at a distance, and something else: cold that had not thawed, darkness not yet dispelled. He, too, had been harrowed in the world below.

There was also a deepness to him that grabbed at her belly, a dark-bright halo like the heat over a flame.

"Last I saw you," said Otter, "a southern warrior was drag-ging you through the forest."

"I last saw you . . ." Cloud swallowed. "You don't re-member?"

Otter regarded her grimly. "Remember what?"

"We met in the world below. In Huntress's fish trap."

"Who is Huntress?"

"The immortal wh—who killed the southerners. Re-member? And took you to the underworld."

"The southerners killed me, Cloud."

"Yes, but she took you . . ." Cloud had always needed courage to speak in the face of Otter's reserve, and this new grimness made it even more difficult. "Uncle, I don't want to—to pry if you don't want to talk about it, but you were *dead*! For years! Mortals don't return to life, to their old lives, except as a gift from the immortals—isn't that right? So how—"

He looked away. After a while, he said, "The wolves took pity on me. I woke in their dance house."

"Was that when . . ." Cloud began, thinking of the elu-sive dancers under the earth.

But Otter spoke at the same time and did not hear her. "What about this Huntress?"

She told him in as few words as possible and then said, "I had your corpse, but the wolves stole it."

Silence poured from Otter like smoke. Cloud wanted to ask what was wrong, but her months in the wilderness hadn't made her better at talking to people. At last he said, "How many years was I dead? It must have been years, but—"

"I'm not sure. Seven, eight, maybe. I've been—away."

He turned back and regarded her again. "In the under-world."

"And other places," she said uncomfortably.

"And you, too, received gifts from the First People."

"Yes, but I lost them all, except . . ." She was going to say, except for her bear skin, but then she thought that Otter's return was a gift better than all the others put together, even if she had not been the one the wolves intended to favor by it.

"And your brothers? Your father?"

"They—I took them—I took the bones to the end of the world. That's all over, Uncle."

"So it's all finished? What we came here for?"

She nodded. He sighed deeply and glanced at the drift log he had been hollowing with fire. "Now we just have to get home."

*Home.* A familiar pang coursed through Cloud. She had no home; she did not belong in the immortal world and could not stay in the mortal one.

Then she wondered what Otter meant by *home.* "Uncle, Rumble destroyed Whale Town. Winter escaped, but—"

He nodded as if he had guessed as much. Then she realized that Otter had said *we.* Whatever cold darkness he dwelt in, he thought his home was hers, and they should go to it together.

She couldn't go home, but she could help him do so. Not that anything could repay the debt she owed him.

"Uncle," she said, "I have a canoe. It's leaky, but it looks better than yours."

For the first time, a shadow of a smile touched Otter's face. "Let's go see," he said.

*Otter pronounced her canoe usable, with repair and* caulking. He took her adze and they walked into the forest to collect cedar twigs and rotting pitchwood. She could not help but glance over her shoulder, but with Huntress gone and the knot binding her father destroyed, the strangeness had entirely vanished from the island.

Then Otter produced fish hooks he had made, the wooden barbs tied on with the last root fiber from Cloud's cache. They spent the next few days fishing from the point near Raven Tongue's old grave house, catching rockfish, perch, and tomcod.

Cloud wore her bear mask as a robe, and if her uncle noticed it, he made no remark. He insisted on hearing her story, though, in detail, from the moment of his death. He listened without comment, asking questions only if she stopped or skipped ahead too fast. Cloud wasn't sure she liked talking so much, even to Otter. By the end of the first day she had only reached the feast in the salmon house, and she was sure she had spoken more words than in her entire previous life. What she had said and done in her travels sounded even stupider and more cowardly now than it had seemed at the time.

But more than that, she burned to hear how Otter had returned to life. The story seemed to have sunk to the bottom of the deep lake of his reserve. When Cloud handed him the single amulet she had kept, he thanked her but restrung it without a word. The wolves must have given him back the other amulets, she supposed, as well as the fine clothes he now wore—a deerskin tunic and a robe of undyed mountain-goat wool.

Occasionally a small piece of his story would surface. One day, as he was cutting up a rockfish for bait, Cloud asked, "Uncle, did the wolves give you that knife?"

His hands stilled. "I found this with some bones and—other things—in the forest. I . . . needed the knife."

"That must be where Huntress vomited." Cloud was surprised that Otter would feel bad about taking the knife. Perhaps she had spent so much time with the dead that using their possessions did not seem remarkable.

Otter speared a chunk of bait with one of the wooden barbs. "It looked as if all the bones were human."

"I think she only hunted one kind of food." He did not reply. Then it occurred to Cloud that Otter had been searching for *tools*. "I have some elk bone with me," she told him, "if that would work better than wood for the fish hooks."

He looked at her, and his expression softened. "Yes, Cloud, it would."

She gathered, eventually, that he had left the wolves at

the end of winter, with only the clothes they had given him. In the weeks since, with the forest animals still too lean to provide nourishment, he had had to work hard to survive.

"Are you the only one the wolves brought back?" she asked, thinking of his men.

The grimness descended again. He said, "You don't ask the immortals for favors. They grant you their grace or they do not. I can't tell you why they chose me and no one else."

But Cloud said, suddenly remembering, " 'The women left the short clover roots in the soil.' "

Otter looked at her questioningly.

"It was Raven Tongue's riddle about the wolves taking your body," she said. "I thought—well, it doesn't matter. Maybe it means they left the others in the underworld to grow another season? Maybe they took you because you're a wizard, like them?"

The suggestion didn't seem to improve his mood. She guessed that guilt weighed him down. Guilt she understood.

She didn't know if she would ever learn what had happened in the wolves' house, but she could imagine how it might be to emerge into the snow, cold and alone, finding nothing but heaps of human bone, and the evidence of lost years piled up like fallen leaves.

*Because Otter insisted that she narrate everything in* order, it was not until the first night, while they ate fresh-roasted perch at his fire, that she reached the events of a year and a half earlier, and she could tell him about the siege of Winter's fort and Raven Tongue's disappearance.

"I trapped Bone's servants," she said, "but when Huntress destroyed the amulet, they escaped—"

"I suppose that's why my own servant hasn't come back." Otter said.

"Your servant found you again?" Cloud said. No answer. "Uncle, I could look for Winter."

That made Otter glance up from his meal. "How?"

She told him. He shook his head. "I sent out my servant and he hasn't returned. Your servants have disappeared as well. It's too dangerous."

"But if I—"

"No," Otter said.

**She had difficulty telling many parts of her story** even in barest outline—especially about her first visit to Huntress's house, her rampage in Sandspit Town, and the baby. But he never chided her. When she reached the end, he said nothing for a long time. His hands were busy twisting cedar twigs from which he had stripped the bark.

"You were right," he said at last, "to come straight here when you left Sandspit Town, and not to go to Winter."

"But—"

"It's what Winter would have wanted."

And so Cloud understood that, whatever he might say, a part of him wished she *had* gone to Winter.

She helped Otter sew the crack in the canoe with the cedar withes. Together they caulked it by pounding in the rotten pitchwood they had gathered, and then painting on a mixture of powdered charcoal and fish oil. Cloud could not help but remember the orcas mending their canoes. "We should coat the whole canoe," Otter said, but he was clearly impatient to leave.

Otter ballasted the canoe with beach stones. Cloud packed the fish she had been drying, and they loaded the boxes. Otter produced another weather-beaten paddle, broken and spliced, that he had scavenged from beach drift. Then they departed. Otter steered south from the island.

"Where are we going?" she asked.

"Sandspit Town," he said, as if surprised she should ask.

**Cloud wanted to stop him. How could he survive a** confrontation with Bone and Rumble on their own ground, without even his servant to aid him? It was too much to presume that Otter, even with the favor of the wolves, could simply arrive at Sandspit Town and dictate how things were going to be.

"We should find Winter," she said.

"Yes," Otter said, "I want to find her, and our children. But they wouldn't be in trouble if it weren't for Rumble."

In the canoe, smelling sea air and pitchwood through her bear's nose, further misgivings rushed upon Cloud: Otter should not take *her* to Sandspit Town, she shouldn't go to any towns, she shouldn't even be with him.

Although against Bone and Rumble, he might need a bear. Cloud wondered what had happened to Rumble after her father's power had left him.

They paddled through showers and weak sunshine, along a route familiar to Cloud from her long-ago flight with Winter. During the day, Otter paddled, deep in his silence. In the evenings, when he lay down and closed his eyes, something heavy would tug at Cloud's belly, and the bright-dark halo pushed out from him like a flame. She longed to know what he was doing. She knew that wizardry was not a subject you talked about lightly, and his reticence was, as always, a tricky channel to navigate. She, too, had been scarred by the otherness of the unmasked world, but *she* felt lighter and more hopeful when he talked to her, more attached to her own humanity.

One day she overcame her shyness to ask about it. Otter raised his eyebrows as if taken aback. But he answered, "I am trying to make us invisible to wizards and their servants. Even a big log can drift unnoticed among the waves."

"You sound like a foot-servant," Cloud said, before she considered that it might seem disrespectful.

But Otter actually laughed. "You're right," he said.

Another time she asked him, "Uncle, what do you plan to *do* in Sandspit Town?"

"I'm going to talk to Rumble," he said. "I'll ask indemnity for my murder. I'll tell him that yes, my son belongs to his mother's house, but some other clansman, not my

murderer, will have charge of his education. I'll tell him
that Winter is my wife until *she* says otherwise."

"But Bone—" Cloud said.

"Yes," Otter said, "Bone is a problem."

A bit more than a *problem*. She wondered whether Otter's
calmness was born from confidence, from the recklessness of
rage, or from simple grim determination.

And then she heard his words again. *My wife, until she
says otherwise.* Otter must be wondering whether Winter had
remarried.

Lost in thought, Cloud did not notice the swimmers until they were nearly upon the canoe. Huge black-and-white
bodies, black dorsal fins as tall as a man—she stood up so
fast that the canoe heeled. Otter yelped a protest.

"Welcome, great ones," she said under her breath. "I am
glad that we meet today. Protect us that no evil befalls us,
great swimmers, guard us from evil, great spirit powers."

They were so beautiful. As the orcas disappeared into the
rain, an ache swelled in her throat, and she considered what
she might also have said—

"Is it anyone you know?" Otter asked.

She turned. He wasn't ridiculing her. "I don't know."

She was the one who was silent the rest of that day.

**After the first few days, they began seeing large ca-**
noes on the horizon and switched to traveling at night. Now
Otter would, from time to time, ask Cloud to steer while he
lay down. On one such night, as she pushed the canoe
slowly across a moonlit channel, she spotted a bird overhead. At first she could make out no more than a small,
roundish shape, not sufficiently erratic in flight for a night-
hawk or bat.

Then the bird circled lower, and moonlight showed her
the distinctive pale rump and notched tail of a petrel. Most
petrels she had seen flitted just above the waves. But this
one sailed like a seagull on the wind, and there was no wind
tonight.

A shiver crawled down her spine. Hadn't she seen a petrel at Waterfall, watching her? And—she had seen petrels, or the same petrel, while traveling in the mountains.

Cloud looked at it sidewise: a dark and wavering halo, a shape almost human.

The petrel circled the channel, light as a hawk. She wanted to rouse Otter, but did not dare interrupt the wizardry that kept them concealed.

Then the moon slipped behind a sheet of cloud. Across that muted brightness flew a shadow trailing many arms.

Seal pricked his ears. Cloud leaned forward to shake Otter awake. But the shadow-octopus arrowed instead toward the petrel, which swooped away. Both vanished into the night.

Heart drumming, Cloud pulled her hand from Otter and once again took up her paddle. But now she kept her gaze on the sky. Seal sat wakeful as well.

The moon sank toward the west; the east brightened. At last the canoe reached the far side of the channel. Otter roused, and she began to tell him what she had seen.

Just then a hard weight rammed their keel, and the hull split with a loud *crack.* Suckered arms flung themselves over the side. Before Cloud could react, Otter cast a harpoon of light. The octopus vanished in a bright spray.

But the canoe broke in two, spilling her into the water. Cloud's bear robe slipped off her shoulders. When she grabbed after it in a panic, she lost her grip on the canoe and flailed wildly.

Her bear flailed, too, but as its powerful legs pushed the water, it moved toward shore.

Cloud kicked as the bear had kicked, pawed as it had pawed. "Cloud?" Otter sputtered, shoving boxes aside.

"I'm here," she said, pushing in the wake of her bear.

Otter helped her to the beach. Ahead of them, the bear climbed out and shook water from its fur. Seal, who had already reached shallow water, licked the bear's nose and then Cloud.

\* \* \*

*Otter made several trips into the water to bring* ashore all the boxes, paddles, mats, and pieces of canoe.

"Can you repair it?" Cloud asked.

"Maybe," he said. "With better tools, a box of caulk, and a half-turn of the moon. By that time the spirit will have freed itself and returned to Bone, and he'll know we're coming—if it didn't tell him before attacking us."

"How far are we from Sandspit Town?"

He sighed. "Hardly two days."

"Do you know any wizardry that would fix the canoe?"

"And keep it seaworthy that long?" He sounded impatient, weary, discouraged.

Cloud began carrying the boxes up from the water's edge. Then she noticed Otter staring at her bear mask, no longer a lifeless robe. It was nosing at a dead crab.

"Oh," said Cloud, acutely embarrassed. "I forgot—"

He looked at her. "It's all right," he said.

*Otter lay down in his wizard's trance. Cloud ate and* fed Seal, then, fatigued from paddling most of the night, spread out her bear robe and lay down as well.

She slept until dusk. By that time Otter was truly asleep and snoring gently. Cloud wondered if Bone knew yet where they were. She considered and discarded the notion of calling Black Fin; he wouldn't carry Otter and Seal as well as her.

Eventually she lay down again and pushed out the top of her head. She spiraled up until she could see both the dark mountains in the east and the fading sunset in the west, and the islands in shadow below her, laid out on the sea like shells.

No spirits or strange birds moved in sea or sky. She flew toward Sandspit Town. The stars came out, hard and brilliant. When the dark silhouette of Maple Island swelled on the water, she swung south in order to approach the town from the forest.

She dropped down and flew through the trees until she reached the cleared area behind the town, then dropped still farther to drift slowly through the grass. The buildings hulked black against the glimmering harbor, except where a thin fog of blue sparks wreathed Storm House. Cloud sank into the grass and like a mouse, like a beetle, crept between the wall boards of Storm House, across a storeroom, and into Rumble's great hall.

A bright fire burned in the hearth. Cloud searched the faces gathered around it but saw only Rumble's warriors and their wives and children.

She crawled to the back of the house, behind the massive thunderbird posts. There she slipped through the boards into the apartment of the king and his wife, her mother, where she had never been in the flesh. Rumble lay beneath luxurious blankets of sea otter and marten, and above him danced Bone, a huge and wavering shadow. To one side, by the flickering lamp, knelt Aunt Snow and Thrush with two children. That gangling boy had to be Cloud's half-brother Great Mountain, and the young girl was the half-sister whose name she did not know. Thrush's head was bowed.

Cloud crept into the next room. She found Winter in bed, eyes closed, beside a girl of ten or twelve years, who watched the blue sparks winking by the door. Cloud slid under the floorboards to the corner, drifted upward. On the platform atop Winter's room, an older boy sat cross-legged, gazing down at the warriors by the hearth. A few ice girls flickered here, too, so Cloud drifted into the smoky gloom of the rafters.

Then she saw a small shape crouched on the frame of the smoke vent, just under the roof boards. Cloud floated closer, slower than a leaf on a still pond. A petrel stared through the opening. Outside, a white dog stood guard upon the roof ridge.

The petrel looked at her, eyes glinting in stray gleams of firelight. Cloud understood, at last, who the petrel was, and why it had been watching her. She burst out the smoke vent and struck the dog hard in the chest, bowling it off the roof, and then she soared up toward the stars. The petrel swooped after her. The dog barked savagely, and blue lights swarmed upward, but she and the petrel had already left Storm House far behind.

The petrel chased her over islands and through winding channels. When Cloud was sure they had not been followed, she returned to the passage where she and Otter camped, spiraling down to land on her own body. The petrel dropped lower, too, circling, finally coming to rest on the gunwale of the wrecked canoe. And there Winter sat, gazing at her sleeping husband.

She was gone when Cloud woke, a few hours before sunrise.

*At first light, Otter took the adze and set out along* the beach. Cloud began checking the boxes to see if water had leaked into them, a task she should have undertaken the previous day.

One box, in which she had packed the clothes she was not wearing, had leaked; another, with their food, was dry. In a third box, Otter had stored tools and odds and ends which, Cloud guessed, he had dug from Huntress's castings: a thong, a blunt arrowhead for shooting birds, a loop of corroded copper wire—

—Foam's fish-skin pouch.

Cloud lifted it out. Otter had folded the pouch over the tear and wrapped it with twine. She felt through the fish skin. A small wooden box. A tiny canoe.

She unwrapped the pouch and drew out the canoe. Copper Orca shone a burnished salmon-orange in the morning light, intact.

Cloud closed her fingers around it and ran along the shore after Otter. "Uncle?" she called. "We can leave now."

When she held out the tiny canoe, Otter's eyebrows drew together. "Cloud, that's a spirit thing. You shouldn't—"

slow match, and with fingers made clumsy by the cold and
many painful gashes, ignited one shred of wood after another until she had a fire hot enough to burn wet twigs.

Another wolf sang, close, close, and then a third, with
high descending wails that raised the hair on her neck. Seal
began to bark. "Stay here, Seal!" she said sharply.

*Blood has power over us.* Cloud pulled off the bloody cedar
bark she still wore, as caked with mud as the rest of her, and
knelt to tie it onto a torch.

"Lady!" bellowed Raven Tongue, diving out of the sky.

Thunder rolled. A shadow stooped shrieking through
the trees. With a deafening *crack!* like a tree toppling, it extended wings that blotted out the sky. Cloud dove to the
ground, but claws whistled past, knocking the torch from
her hand.

Huntress's wings boomed upward again. Cloud frantically cast around after her torch. It had fallen into the fire,
and a stream of acrid smoke now rose from it. As Cloud
lifted the torch, Huntress screeched—

—and fell out of the air, crashing through the canopy
with a great rattling of feathers and snapping of branches—

—and Huntress lay in woman's form, pale and bleeding.
The necklace she had stolen from Otter had snagged on a
branch, and his amulets rained to the ground one by one.

Seal barked furiously at the fallen immortal. Astonishment and terror warred within Cloud. In the corner of her
eye, Huntress's human-looking body was a shadow pooling
in the earth, immense and dizzying—

Huntress climbed to her feet, coughing out waves of that
sharp, sour reek. The grotesque swelling that hung from her
throat was huge now, protruding through her torn clothing
like a gravid belly. She yanked her hair from a currant bush.
"Burn your blood all you like, thief!" she screamed. "It
won't protect you long!" And she limped away with extraordinary speed, a shadow vanishing into darkness.

"Raven Tongue!" Cloud panted. "Watch her!"

She turned to flee. But she had taken only a few steps when

lightning forked in the treetops, thunder shattered the air, and rain roared down on the forest. Her torch went out.

Trying and failing to think how Raven Tongue could aid her now, Cloud groped for her leaf-knife and sank to all fours. At first she could hear only the rattling downpour. Then Huntress's rancid stink wafted past. A branch snapped. The mirror's gleam showed rain, darkness—

—a sharp yellow beak the length of a man. Cloud waved her extinguished torch. The beak snapped the torch in two and tossed away the pieces. Then it speared down. Cloud struck hard with the knife. As the leaf-blade sank deep, Huntress screeched and jerked upward, tearing the knife from Cloud's hand.

Huntress clawed furiously at the leaf-knife with a giant talon, trying without success to dislodge the knife. She screamed again in a blast of rancid breath, and then, in a terrible quick movement, stabbed Cloud in the chest.

The force of the blow flung Cloud into the air and slammed her against a tree trunk. Fragments of shattered mirror rained down, followed by the spirit eater in two jagged pieces. One piece spewed a glowing pellet that unfolded and unfurled into Bone's dog, octopus, drowned woman, ice girls. Hovering in the air, the spirits glanced at Cloud, at the giant talons stepping through the downpour— and they fled.

But Cloud, half-stunned, could only crawl away, clutching Foam's torn pouch to prevent more of her treasures from spilling out. The last feeble gleam of the broken mirror, before Huntress planted a foot upon the shards and dowsed them, showed Cloud a yawning yellow beak.

Rancid air wafted over Cloud, but again she could not dodge fast enough. A weight crashed on her back, a huge fleshy muscle pressed upward; she was tossed into the air. Then—

Beak and tongue closed over her, swallowing. Cloud tried to force her way up and out against that powerful tongue, but its sharp spikes slammed her ever deeper into a hot constricting passageway coated in mucus. There was no air, just a horrible fetid sourness, a hot stink of rotten meat and rancid fat so intense she nearly lost consciousness. Cloud slid helplessly down into a lake of sludge as soft and thick as fish grease.

Only then did she realize that one hand still clutched Foam's ripped pouch.

She fumbled for the harpoon point and stabbed with it. Rope burgeoned around Cloud, splashing, coiling, looping. She held tight to the point to keep the weight of the rope from smashing her down into that hot foul swamp, but more rope kept pressing on her, and Huntress herself was now pitching and yawing. Muscles heaved all around Cloud. Great mounds of rope pushed up and fell back. At first the spasms threatened to force Cloud's head under the surface. But convulsions kept wracking Huntress's throat, pushing up the rope, pushing up everything the rope had tangled with. Hard-packed waves of cracked bone and hair tore past Cloud on their way upward. Floods of the meaty sludge washed over her. And finally Cloud came shooting up with the rope, tumbling over that spiked tongue, plummeting—

She splattered onto a mound of crushed bone and rolled. Rope snaked around her ankle, yanked upward. Cloud tore it free. Nearby, more landslides thundered onto the forest. Wings boomed in the air. Huntress's shriek split the blackness. Cloud heard the rope slither up through the trees, snapping branches. Another, fainter shriek, and Huntress flew into the sky, rope trailing endlessly from her wounded gullet.

# SEVENTEEN

# The Maze of Ten Thousand Mountains

*She must have slept. Eventually she became aware* of Seal nosing her. She grabbed his scruff to pull herself upright.

Morning had come and it was still raining. Huntress's convulsions, or her anger, had shattered the crown of the maple, and the contents of her crop and stomach had flooded the glade: a sea of gray-brown sludge, castings of bone and hair bigger than Cloud. But her father's skull still sat in the crotch of the tree. And now his ghost glowered beside its trunk. And her brothers—

"She's here!" Claw cried to the other little boys. They smiled through their tears.

Raven Tongue waited quietly beside her, rain beading his translucent shadow-flesh. Cloud had to hawk and spit before she could speak. "Why aren't you watching Huntress?"

"After the storm," he said, "the fisherman patched his canoe."

Cloud was too exhausted to decide whether Huntress was

The amulet resembled a translucent version of Foam's spirit eater. Behind the central face, colors swirled. She pushed her claws toward it with all her strength—

Bone shoved her upward. As she flew into the air, her claw snagged the amulet, tearing it. Colors sheeted around her, a tangle of heads, wings, claws, and legs writhing, separating. She crashed hard into the sand; above her, above Bone, spirits hovered like a rockslide about to drop and crush them both—

But Bone cast a net over the spirits, snaring them tight. And then, wheezing, his face purple with fury, blood pouring from his wounds, he climbed to his feet and hobbled toward her.

"I should have let the king kill you long ago," he said. He opened his fist to reveal a knot, and then he threw it at her.

*The power is in my hands,*

sang a soft voice from the ocean. And somehow Bone had slowed down. The arm tossing the knot at Cloud was still rising into the air, and the knot hadn't yet left Bone's palm.

*The power is in my hands,*
*The power is in my hands,*
*Dancers at the center of the world.*

Otter emerged from the ocean so slowly that Cloud felt birds would fall out of the sky, water would cease flowing downhill, and her own breath would stop before he reached dry land. But Bone was already drawing back his arm to throw the knot again. Otter cast his harpoon—

—not at Bone, but at the netted spirits in the air—

The net fell apart in flames. The spirits plunged downward through Bone's body, a swirl of blue worm, brown fur, owl wings, shark smile, shadowy hand, all sinking into Bone's flesh and then bursting outward again, vanishing.

Bone lay still upon the sand. A frog climbed out of his mouth and hopped away.

The cold that had paralyzed Cloud melted, and her heart started to beat properly again. A furry creature, half mink and half marmot, jumped to Otter's shoulder, hair standing on end.

Cloud pushed herself onto two feet. Otter blinked and swayed; for a moment she thought he would collapse from exhaustion, but he recovered sufficiently to climb past Bone's body toward the line of warriors in front of Storm House. They shifted nervously at his approach. Winter now stood beyond them. Winter and Otter looked at each other but neither said anything.

"Go," Otter said to the warriors again, and he seemed to be regaining his strength. "Bring out your master to me."

Otter waited before the stairs of the house, motionless as a stalking heron. When Rumble came out, leaning on Thrush, Cloud hardly recognized him: he was thin, pale, and frightened.

**There they all were on the beach together: Rumble** and Thrush, Winter and Otter. And Cloud. Once she would have felt uniquely alone and apart, the outcast who could never belong. Now she saw that they were all strangers to each other, and that none of them knew what to say.

Pushing her bear robe over her shoulders, Cloud stepped back as unobtrusively as she could and walked away from Storm House. The onlookers parted to let her through.

It was over at last. Everything Rumble had tried to prevent had happened, and he could no longer hurt anyone.

Strange how it had ended, though. As in the stories, the hero had returned victorious, cloaked in spiritual power. But this triumph, this story, had turned out to be Otter's, not hers. He had not even needed her help. It was what she would have most wanted for him, and she had not expected a triumphant homecoming for herself—*her* story had surely ended in Lupine's house—but it left her adrift. There was no reason for her to be here. She could not, after all, stay in a human town.

Without her intending it, her feet took her toward the summer side of town, where people were still emerging to buzz over the excitements at Storm House. Halibut House, she saw, was more dilapidated than ever: roof boards had fallen, cracks gaped in the wall boards, the spruce seedling on the ridge beam had grown as tall as a man. Cloud approached slowly. It was better if she didn't go inside to speak to anyone. Easier to leave again.

Except that she had to find out—

She glanced through the door with trepidation. Everything looked so worn out. Glory tonged cooking stones onto the fire while Oriole swept the floor and fended off shrieking children. At least the house smelled the same: smoke, fish, cedar, fresh-cut spruce branches. A child's diaper needed changing.

She ducked through the doorway. Still no slaves. Rumble had killed them all, and now Glory, looking so old and tired, Glory the old king's sister, stooped over the hearth. Not that cooking was a bad thing. But Glory should not have to do it.

"Aunt?" she said, stepping down to the hearth well.

Glory straightened. Her face lit up. "Cloud?"

Cloud enveloped her in a fierce hug.

**Glory wiped tears from her eyes. "You are disgrace-**fully filthy," she said, as Cloud knew she would.

For a moment Cloud smiled. Then, guts knotting, she asked the question whose answer she had dreaded for so long. "Aunt Glory, what happened to my baby?"

Glory raised her eyebrows. "Oriole," she called, "bring the child here."

Oriole sighed, put down her broom, and waded among the screeching children. A filthy little creature dodged away from her, laughing, until Oriole seized his arm.

He was still laughing when she set him before Cloud, though when he caught sight of her, the stranger, his blue eyes widened. His face was so dirty that the luminous skin hardly showed. "You would not believe it," said Oriole, "but he had a bath this morning." She sounded half affectionate, half fed up.

"Oriole," Glory said, "weaned her own baby to nurse him."

"Thank you," said Cloud in a whisper. She could not believe this child had come out of her belly.

Except for the color of his skin and eyes, he did not in the slightest resemble his father, the beautiful, soft-spoken, ever-immaculate Center-of-Heaven. An ache swelled in her throat. What her son most reminded her of was her lost brothers, sticky and muddy, running forever for the sheer joy of it.

"I suppose you know where that comes from," Glory said, nodding at the corner. There sat a chest that shed a sunny glow into the gloom of the hall. "No one can open it."

"I expect . . . he'll be able to open it when the time comes," Cloud said. "Does he have a name?"

"He told us his father had named him Walking-Above-the-Mountains." Glory seemed to disapprove of such precocity.

The boy was staring at Cloud. "I'm your mother," she told him. Even to her ears that sounded improbable. And then, utterly at a loss, "Would you like some berry cake?"

He grabbed the piece she held out and raced away. "He never stops eating," said Oriole.

Cloud laughed through tears. "He really *is* my child."

**Somehow, Glory talked her into bathing and eating.** Then Otter and Winter arrived, and the house turned out to welcome them. Glory led Otter to the seat of honor, shooing children from it. "Our king has returned!" she scolded them.

Otter's hands fidgeted until he pressed them against his thighs, but he thanked Glory, ate the roasted halibut she served him, greeted cousins, asked the names of children, and glanced, without comment, at the missing roof boards.

Thrush had come, too, seeming oddly forlorn and out of place. When the formalities concluded, she edged toward Cloud. Cloud did not know what to say to her mother any more than to her child, but at least her son was not afraid of her; he had already returned twice to beg for more berry cake.

When she went to Thrush, her mother burst into tears and embraced her. "Oh, look at you, baby, all scratched and skinny. Look at this hair! Are you going to stay now? Are you going to live here? Oh, darling—"

Cloud hugged Thrush in return, burying her face in her mother's fragrance. "I took care of their bones, Mama," she whispered. "They're at peace now."

The breath caught in Thrush's throat. But her scarred hands plucked at Cloud's dress. "We'll have to get you nice clothes. Something pretty—"

So that was all Thrush had to say about her dead sons, Cloud's lost brothers? And why insult the plain but clean garment that Glory had given her? Or was it Cloud's bear robe—and surely Thrush, of all people, recognized what Cloud wore over her shoulder—that she wanted Cloud to change?

Anger crested inside Cloud, then washed away. If her mother were stronger or more courageous, everything would have been different. But Thrush was not. There was nothing to do about it.

Besides, Cloud hadn't shown she could do any better by her own child.

But as Cloud pulled away, Thrush clung to her hand. "Thank you," she whispered, tears spilling down. "Oh, thank you. I never forgot them. Or you, Cloud."

*Cloud tried to slip out the back door. But somehow* Winter stood in her path. "Hello, Aunt," she said.

"What's wrong?" said Winter.

"I just want some air," said Cloud.

"No," said Winter, "you've been skulking in the corners of the house, looking distressed, especially when you see me."

Cloud could not meet Winter's gaze. "He died trying to help me," she said finally. "I'm sorry—I don't know how to say how sorry I am."

"He died because of Bone and Rumble," Winter said. "*I* should thank you for all you tried to do. For bringing him home. Is that all that's bothering you?"

Cloud wanted to say, *That's all, I'm fine,* but under Winter's narrow-eyed gaze her tongue faltered. Once again she wished Winter were gentler, but she knew that was just her own cowardice speaking.

"I'm a bear, Aunt," Cloud said. "I want to stay here, but almost everyone's afraid of me, even Thrush. When I was last here, I killed people. I don't know who I hurt. I don't— what if it happens again?"

"This morning," said Winter, "I saw a girl trying to help her uncle. As for that last incident . . . I heard that you saved the town and hurt no one except the enemy. You showed mercy on my undeserving brother and even on his wizard, whose passing today I do not mourn at all. And you surely saved the town, again, when you released Rumble from the burden of your father's power. Who has the right to live here if you don't?"

Cloud looked at her feet. "Even if that's all true, it doesn't mean people want me here."

Winter snorted derisively, and Cloud glanced up. "You have to make your own place," Winter said, "four-legged or not. Everyone does."

"But what if I hurt someone?"

"Is there anyone you *want* to hurt?"

Cloud thought about it. "Aunt Snow."

"Oho," said Winter. "My favorite aunt, too."

Cloud surprised herself by laughing. The beginnings of a smile appeared on Winter's face as well. "Do you want to go away again?"

"No," said Cloud.

"Then you'll just have to learn to control your temper."

*But she needed a respite from the crowded house;* the noise and commotion were overwhelming after so many months in the mountains. Cloud finally managed to slip out the door with Seal. For a while she was happy just to walk through the sun-dappled alder woods behind the town. One thing she needed to mention right away to Otter: how Rumble had married Radiance, the princess of Halibut House, to a man who beat her.

Something tugged at her belly, and Seal barked once. Cloud looked up to see Raven Tongue, and behind him the dwarf, the owl woman, all Cloud's servants—

"Let us serve you, Lady," said Raven Tongue. "Give us a task."

It wasn't difficult to think of one. Rumble had made enemies in who knew how many towns. With Bone dead and Rumble ill, and Otter having no reputation as a warrior, Sandspit Town was more in danger than it had ever been.

"Guard this town as I asked you to before," she told them. "And this time, if you're attacked, one of you come *tell* me before you all rush to help your fellows."

She sent them on their way and walked on. The trail, the one Rumble had chased her down so long ago, led her through sunlight and shade to the beach. Something was splashing out in the channel. Likely it was just a seal thwacking its tail, but she spoke her first hopeful thought out loud. "Black Fin?"

Likely he had forgotten about her by now. And did she even know, anyway, what she wanted to say to him? But still—

She and Seal walked along the water's edge. To the east, the layers of islands grew ever bluer until they merged with the mainland, which in turn receded and faded, range after range, mountains becoming indistinguishable from sky.

She was content to look at her birthplace from here. Here, among the islands at the center of the world, sunlight danced on the ocean. A breeze carried the perfume of moss on stone, of sun on cedar driftwood, of drying seaweed and salt.

She was home. She thought she had lost the end of her story, but after all it was the beginning she hadn't been able to find.

Seal stopped and sniffed. Cloud stopped, too.

A hundred yards ahead, where the shore bent outward into the afternoon sun, a long canoe had been drawn up. Beside it waited a tall young man, pale-skinned, black-haired.

Water fell glittering from his sleeked-back hair. A sweet briny smell wafted toward her. As she came up to him, he reached into his canoe and lifted out a fish.

Black Fin offered the salmon to her without speaking, but he gazed up at her through his lashes, a smile gathering at the corners of his mouth. Lightness filled Cloud's chest and fluttered up like a bird. She *was* hungry. She was going to feast on his gift, on him, and on the whole world, and never be sated.

"Share it with me," she said, and she stepped forward to kiss him on the mouth.